William Chambers

Memoir of Robert Chambers

With Autobiographic Reminiscences

William Chambers

Memoir of Robert Chambers
With Autobiographic Reminiscences

ISBN/EAN: 9783337029012

Printed in Europe, USA, Canada, Australia, Japan

Cover: Foto ©Raphael Reischuk / pixelio.de

More available books at **www.hansebooks.com**

PREFATORY NOTE.

On the death of my brother, DR. ROBERT CHAMBERS, numerous Biographic sketches of him appeared, both in Great Britain and the United States, all of them kind and complimentary, but in many cases imperfect or erroneous as regards certain leading details. It seemed to me that, while still spared life and opportunity, I might try to do justice to the memory of the deceased, by giving a correct history of his life and principal writings.

The attempt, however, involved a difficulty. Having been intimately associated with my brother, not only in early life, but in literary enterprises, it was scarcely possible to relate the story of one without frequent reference to the other. I have so far yielded to this necessity, as to offer some Autobiographic Reminiscences, in subordination to the principal object in view. To this extent only is the Memoir that of two individuals.

I need hardly say that the retrospect of some early events, which could not well be omitted, has not been unaccompanied with poignant recollections ; but if a perusal of the narrative serves in any degree to inspire youth with notions of self-reliance, along with a hopeful dependence on Providence when pressed by adverse circumstances, I shall be more than recompensed.   W. C.

January, 1872.

CONTENTS.

CONTENTS.

MEMOIR.

CHAPTER I.

EARLY YEARS — 1800 TO 1813.

MY brother and I were born and spent our early years in a small country town in the south of Scotland, situated amidst beautiful scenery, and had therefore the advantage — as advantage it might be called — of being acquainted from infancy with some of the noble works of nature, along with rural objects and circumstances. The place of our birth was Peebles, an ancient royal burgh on the upper part of the Tweed, where our ancestors had dwelt from time immemorial — the tradition among them being, that they were descended from a personage inscribed as " William de la Chaumbre, Bailif e Burgois de Pebles," in the list of those who signed bonds of allegiance to Edward I., 1296. However that might be, I was born in this little old burgh, 16th April, 1800; and Robert, coming next in order in the family, was born 10th July, 1802.

For the place of birth and early associations almost every one has a peculiar affection; and among the Scotch, as is well known, this feeling is a marked national characteristic. It will not seem surprising, therefore, that through life Robert cherished kindly remembrances of the scenes of his infancy. A few years previous to his decease, he began notes of what may have been intended as a memoir of himself, but which were not carried farther than reminiscences from the dawn of intelligence to about his tenth year. Fragmentary as are these memoranda, they abound in the geniality of sentiment for which the writer was remarkable, and serve to illustrate the state of things in certain by-corners of Scotland sixty to seventy years since. The following portions may accordingly be acceptable, supplemented here and there by such particulars from my own remembrance as may help to complete the picture : —

"In the early years of this century," he proceeds, "Peebles was little advanced from the condition in which it had mainly rested for several hundred years previously. It was eminently a quiet place — 'As quiet as the grave or as Peebles,' is a phrase used by Cockburn. It was said to be a finished town, for no new houses (exceptions to be of course allowed for) were ever built in it. Situated, however, among beautiful pastoral hills, with a singularly pure atmosphere, and with the pellucid Tweed running over its pebbly bed close beside the streets, the town was acknowledged to be, in the fond language of its inhabitants, a bonny place. An honest old burgher was enabled by some strange chance to visit Paris, and was eagerly questioned, when he came back, as to the character of that capital of capitals ; to which, it is said, he answered that ' Paris, a'thing considered, was a wonderful place — but still, Peebles for pleesure ! ' and this has often been cited as a ludicrous example of rustic prejudice and narrowness of judgment. But, on a fair interpretation of the old gentleman's words, he was not quite so benighted as at first appears. The 'pleesures' of Peebles were the beauties of the situation and the oppor-

tunities of healthful recreation it afforded, and these were
certainly considerable.

"There was an old and a new town in Peebles — each
of them a single street, or little more ; and as even the
new town had an antique look, it may be inferred that the
old looked old indeed. It was indeed chiefly composed
of thatched cottages, occupied by weavers and laboring
people — a primitive race of homely aspect, in many instances eking out a scanty subsistence by having a cow
on the town common, or cultivating a *rig* of potatoes in
the fields close to the town. Rows of porridge *luggies*
(small wooden vessels) were to be seen cooling on win-
dow-soles ; a smell of peat smoke pervaded the place ;
the click of the shuttle was everywhere heard during the
day ; and in the evening, the gray old men came out in
their Kilmarnock night-caps, and talked of Bonaparte, on
the stone seats beside their doors. The platters used in
these humble dwellings were all of wood, and the spoons
of horn ; knives and forks rather rare articles. The
house was generally divided into two apartments by a
couple of *box-beds*, placed end to end — a bad style of
bed prevalent in cottages all over Scotland ; they were so
close as almost to stifle the inmates. Among these humble people, all costumes, customs, and ways of living
smacked of old times. You would see a venerable patri-
arch making his way to church on Sunday, with a long-
backed, swing-tailed, light-blue coat of the style of
George II., which was probably his marriage coat, and
half a century old. His head-gear was a broad-brimmed
blue bonnet. The old women came out on the same occasions in red scarfs, called cardinals, and white *mutches*
(caps), bound by a black ribbon, with the gray hair folded
back on the forehead. There was a great deal of drug-
get, and huckaback, and serge in that old world, and very

little cotton. One almost might think he saw the humbler Scotch people of the seventeenth century before his eyes.

"Apropos of the box-beds, there was a carrier named Davie Loch, who was reputed to be rather light of wits, but at the same time not without a sense of his worldly interests. His mother, finding her end approaching, addressed her son, in the presence of a number of the neighbors : —

"'The house will be Davie's, of course, and the furniture too.'

"'Eh, hear her!' quoth Davie ; 'sensible to the last, sensible to the last.'

"'The lyin' siller'—

"'Eh, yes ; how clear she is about everything !'

"'The lyin' siller is to be divided between my two daughters'—

"'Steek the bed-doors, steek the bed-doors,' interposed Davie ; 'she's raving now!' And the old dying woman was shut up accordingly.

"In this old-town population, there survived two or three aged persons who professed an adherence to the Covenant and covenanted work of Reformation. One of these, designated Laird Baird, remains clearly daguerreotyped on my memory, — a tall, bony, grim old man, with blue *rig-and-fur* stockings rolled half-way up his thighs, and a very umbrageous blue bonnet. His secular business consisted in thatching houses ; his inner life was a constant brooding over the sins of a perjured and sinful nation, and the various turns of public affairs, in which he traced the punishments inflicted upon us by an outraged Deity, for our laying aside the Solemn League and Covenant. He came up to my mother one summer evening, as she was standing at her door with her first-born in her

arms. ' Ye're mickle pleased wi' that bairn, woman,'
said the laird gruffly. ' If the French come, what will
ye do wi' him? I trow ye'll be fleeing wi' him to the tap
o' the Pentland Hills. But ye should rather pray that
they *may* come. Ye should pray for judgments, woman,
— judgments on a sinfu' land. Pray that the Lord may
pour out the vials of his wrath upon us, — it would be for
our guid.' And then he went on his way, leaving the
pretty young mother heart-chilled by his terrible words.
Having known something of old-town worthies of this
kind, there was no novelty or surprise to me, a few years
thereafter, when I read of Habakkuk Mucklewrath in
Scott's ' Old Mortality.'

" I had reason to know the old town in my earliest
years, for our family then dwelt in it, though in a modern-
slated house, which my father had had built for him by
his father when about to be married. Our ancestors had
been woolen manufacturers, substantial and respectable
people, although living in a very plain style. My father
growing up at the time when the cotton manufacture was
introduced into Glasgow, had there studied it, and now
conducted it on a pretty extensive scale at Peebles, having sometimes as many as a hundred looms in his employment. My earliest recollections bring before me a
neat, small mansion, fronting to the Eddleston Water ; a
tastefully furnished sitting-room, containing a concealed
bed, one or two other little rooms, and a kitchen ; a
ground-floor full of looms, and a garret full of webs and
weft. Games at marbles played with my elder brother on
the figures of the parlor carpet, when recovering from an
illness, come back upon me as among the pleasantest
things I have experienced in life ; or wandering into the
workshop below, it was a great entertainment to sit beside
one of the weavers, and watch the movements of the hed-

dles and treadles, and hear the songs and the gossip of the
man. Weavers were topping operatives in those days,
for they could realize two pounds a week, sometimes even
more, and many young men of good connections had
joined the trade. My father, as agent for Mr. Henry
Monteith, for Mr. M'Ilroy, and others, in Glasgow, realized a good income, which enabled him to live on an
equality with the best families of the place.

" To a child, of course, all things are new, and the first
occurrence of anything to his awakened senses, never
fails to make a deep impression. I think I yet remember
the first time I observingly saw the swelling green hills
around our little town. I am sure I could point to within
ten yards of the spot where I saw the first gowan and the
first buttercup ; first heard the hum of the mountain bee ;
first looked with wonder into a hedge-sparrow's nest,
with its curious treasure of blue eggs. A radius of half
a mile would have described the entire world of my infancy : of that world every minute feature remains deeply
stamped within me, and will while life and consciousness
endure. There is a great deal of studious observation in
a child. Casual, trivial, and thoughtless words spoken by
his seniors in his presence go into him, to be afterwards
estimated and judged of ; so it is a great mistake to speak
indecorously before children.

" At the time when I was coming upon the stage of the
world, a number of old things were going out of it. The
Rev. Dr. Dalgliesh, the minister of the parish, still wore
a cocked hat. He died in 1808 ; and I can just remember seeing him one Sunday, as he walked home from
church, with that head-gear crowning his tall and dignified figure. There were still a few men with pigtails
whisking constantly over the collars of their coats. Spen-
cers still lingered in use. Boots, formerly used only in

riding and travelling, were also in vogue with men who desired to be smartly dressed. One could either have *top-boots*, that is, boots with a movable cincture of pale leather at top, or *tassel-boots*, by which was meant what were afterwards called Hessians, terminating in a wavy line under the knee, with a tassel hanging out over the middle in front. A buckish weaver, called Willie Paterson, had got a pair of tassel boots, on which he could fasten tops, and thus enjoy tops or tassels at his pleasure. People meeting him when he went to church would say : 'Willie, I see this is top-day with you.' Top-day or tassel-day for Willie Paterson's boots was a favorite joke. As an alternative for boots were gaiters to the knee, originally tight, but latterly lax, with vertical foldings.

> " ' Lax in their gaiters, laxer in their gait,'

is a line in the ' Rejected Addresses,' which strongly recalls to me the year 1812.

" The new town was a smarter place than the old ; yet it contained many homely old thatched houses, and few of any elegance. The shops were for the most part confined and choky places, with what were called half-doors, a bell being generally rung by customers to summon the worthy trader. The shop of the candle-maker was provided with a bell-pull consisting of an old key dangling at the end of a cord, which was put in requisition to summon ' Candle Nell,' as the female in charge of the establishment was familiarly called. No attempt was made to keep up an appearance of business. All was quiet and sombre by day, and in the evenings a dim candle on the counter made the only difference. A favorite position of the shop-keeper was to lean on his arms over the half-door, gazing abroad into the vacant street, or chatting with a casual bystander. I do not think there were more than three traders in the town who had any apprentice or hired assistant. If the husband was out for a forenoon's fishing in the Tweed, his wife was his sufficient lieutenant. It seems to me remarkable that, small as the concerns generally were, the family life of these people was of a somewhat refined character. The tone of the females was far from being vulgar. Accomplishments, such as are now so common, were unknown; but all had a good education in English, and their conversation was not deficient in intelligence."

Considering how little business was done, and also the easy way in which things were conducted, one would scarcely be prepared for the genteel interior of many of the dwellings, or for the tasteful dresses and courteous manners of the wives of the tradesmen. Though a trifle too obese, Candle Nell herself, when the shop was shut, could receive company in style, and, addressed in her proper name, do the honors of her brother's household. A considerable number of persons, as has been said, kept a cow. The going forth of the town cows to their pasturage on a neighboring hill, and their return, constituted leading events of the day. Early in the summer mornings the inhabitants were roused by inharmonious sounds blown from an ox-horn by the town-herd, who leisurely perambulated the streets with a gray plaid twisted around his shoulders. Then came forth the cows, deliberately, one by one, from their respective quarters, and took their way instinctively by the bridge across the Tweed, their keeper coming up behind to urge forward the loiterers. Before taking the ascent to the hill, the cows, in picturesque groups, might have been seen standing within the margin of the Minister's Pool, a smooth part of the river, which reflected on its glistening surface the figures of the animals in various attitudes, along with the surrounding scenery ; the whole — river, cows, and trees — forming a tableau such as would have been a study for Berghem or Wouvermans.

There was much pleasant intercourse among families at a small cost. Scarcely any gave ceremonious dinners. Invitations to tea at six o'clock were common. After tea there were songs, with perhaps a round of Scottish proverbs — a class of sayings which, from their agreeable tartness, found scope for exercise in ordinary transactions, and were more especially useful in snubbing children, and keeping them in remembrance of their duty. The Peebles people were not behind their neighbors in the art of applying these maxims. As, for example, if a fastidious youth presumed to complain that his porridge was not altogether to his mind, he would have for reply, — "Lay your wame to your winnin' ; " that is, " Suit your stomach to your earnings," — a staple observation in all such cases. Or, if one of unsettled habits got into a scrape, such as " slumping" in the ice, and coming home half-drowned, instead of being commiserated, he would be coolly reminded that " An unhappy fish gets an unhappy bait." Or, if one hinted that he was hungry, and would not be the worse of something to eat, he would, if the application was inopportune, be favored with the advice in dietetics : " You'll be the better o' findin' the grunds o' your stamick." Or, if he, on the other hand, asked for a drink of water shortly after dinner, he would be told that " Mickle meat taks mickle weet ; " by which wholesome rebuke he was instructed in the ex cellent virtue of moderation in eating. Or, if one, when put to some kind of difficult task, said he wanted assistance, he would get the proverb pitched at him : " Help yoursel', and your friends will like you the better."

Or, when a family of children quarreled among themselves, and appealed to their mother for an edict of pacification, she would console them with the remark, "You'll all agree better when ye gang in at different kirk doors." A capital thing were these proverbs and sayings for stamping out what were called notions of "uppishness" in children, or hopes of having everything their own way.

It must not, however, be inferred, from a proficiency in hurling these repressive maxims, that there was any actual deficiency in the affections. Along with a singular absence of demonstrativeness, there was often a spirit of true kindness. At that period, and till comparatively recent times, there was no demoralizing poor-law, such as now exists, to steel the hearts of the people, and create paupers by wholesale. Those in easy circumstances helped, and gave some little personal attention to, their poorer neighbors ; and I can remember that, on the occasion of a sudden death by a distressing accident in the family of a laboring man, the feelings of the whole community were munificently stirred up in compassion.

The country was still haunted by mendicants of various orders, including old decrepit women, who were carried about on hand-barrows from door to door, begging meal or half-pence. The town, also, was never without two or three natural idiots, generally harmless in character. The most interesting and amusing of these was Daft Jock Grey, — or, to give him his proper title, "Daft Jock Grey of Gilmanscleugh," — a wanderer through Roxburgh, Selkirk, and Peebles shires, who was known to Sir Walter Scott, and possessed qualities not unlike those assigned to the character of Davie Gellatley. Jock was a kind of genius, had a great command of songs, and composed a ballad, which, commencing with an allusion to his own infirmity, recited, in jingling rhymes, the names and qualities of a number of persons whose houses he frequented in his extensive rambles. It may be amusing to read this curious jingle of names and places, which, as far as I remember, ran as follows, though it is proper to mention that Jock seldom sang it twice the same way — sometimes throwing in a new verse, or leaving out an old one : —

DAFT JOCK GREY'S SONG.

" There's Daft Jock Grey o' Gilmanscleugh,
    And Davie o' the Inch,
And when ye come to Singley,
    They'll help ye in a pinch.
        And the laddie he's but young,
        And the laddie he's but young,
        And Robbie Scott ca's up the rear,
        And Caleb beats the drum.[1]

" There are the Taits o' Caberston,
    The Taits o' Holylee,
The ladies o' the Juniper Bank,[2]
    They carry a' the gree.
        And the laddie he's but young, etc.

' There's Lockie o' the Skirty Knows,
    There's Nicol o' Dick-neuk,
And Bryson o' the Priestrig,
    And Hall into the Heap.
        And the laddie he's but young, etc.

" The three Scotts o' Commonside,
    The Tamsons o' the Mill,
There's Ogilvy o' Branxholm,
    And Scoon o' Todgiehill.
        And the laddie he's but young, etc.

" The braw lads o' Fawdonside,
    The lasses o' the Peel,

[1] Caleb Rutherford, town-drummer of Hawick.
[2] The Misses Thorburn. Mr. Thorburn, farmer at Juniper Bank, is reputed to have had some characteristics of Dandie Dinmont.

2

"And when ye gang to Fairnielee,
    Ye'll ca' at Ashestiel.[1]
   .   And the laddie he's but young, etc.

" There is Lord Napier o' the Lodge,
    And Gawin in the Hall,
And Mr. Charters o' Wilton Manse,
    Preaches lectures to us all.
              And the laddie he's but young, etc.

" There are three wives in Hassendean,
    And ane in Braddie-Yards,
And they're away to Gittenscleugh,
    And left their wheel and cards.[2]
              And the laddie he's but young, etc.

" There's Bailie Nixon, merchant,[3]
    The Miss Moncrieffs and a',
And if ye gang some farther east,
    Ye'll come to Willie Ha'.
        And the laddie he's but young,
        And the laddie he's but young,
        And Robbie Scott ca's up the rear,
        And Caleb beats the drum."

Jock was also a mimic, and as such gave acceptable imi-
tations of the style of preaching of all the ministers in his
rounds.   Before commencing an imitation, he required to
have an apron thrown over his head, and thus he stood,
like a veiled prophet, for a few moments, as if recalling
the appropriate inspiration.   Attempts had been made to
get him to attend to regular labor, but without effect. The
minister of Selkirk on one occasion addressed him some-

---

[1] At Ashestiel, Ettrick Forest, Sir Walter Scott resided with his
family for several years prior to 1810 ; from this place he dates some
of his beautiful introductions to the different cantos of *Marmion.*
[2] Hand-cards for carding wool.
[3] In Hawick.

what pompously : "John, you are an idle fellow ; why don't
you work ? You could at least herd a few cows."
"Me herd !" replied Jock ; "I dinna ken corn frae
gerss." That answer settled the minister.

Hogmanay, the last day of the year,[1] was the grand festival of all varieties of mendicants, daft folk, and children
generally ; for there was a universal distribution of oat-
cakes, cheese, short-bread, and buns at the doors of the inhabitants. Among those who secured a respectable dole
on such occasions was the town-piper, dressed in a red
uniform and cocked hat, as befitted a civic official. Piper
Ritchie, for such was his name, enjoyed a munificent salary
of a pound a year from the corporation, along with a pair
of shoes ; and it was understood that, besides his dole at
Hogmanay, he was entitled to receive at least a groat annu-
ally from all well-disposed householders. His emoluments
were completed by certain small fees for playing at wed-
dings. In escorting a marriage-party, he marched with
becoming importance in front, playing with might and
main a tune called "Welcome Hame, my Dearie,"— which
air I would be glad to recover.

On Hogmanay Day, tradesmen called personally with
their yearly accounts, of which they received payment
along with some appropriate refreshment. There was *first-
footing* on New-year's morning. And Handsel Monday
— the first Monday in the year — was marked by tossing
a profusion of ballads and penny chap-books from windows among a crowd of clamorous youngsters. New Year
was also signalized by various domestic festivities. The

---

[1] The origin of the word Hogmanay has been very puzzling. None
of the ordinary explanations is worth anything. I venture to suggest
that it is a familiar corruption from an old cry in French : *Aux gueux
mener* (Bring to the beggars). The calling out of the word at doors
by children and mendicants is in this view quite appropriate.

severity of manners of a hundred years earlier had worn off. There was unrebuked joviality at births and marriages, and even in a solemn way at deaths. In the house of the deceased, on the morning before the funeral, there was a Lyke-wake, consisting of a succession of services of refreshments, presided over by an undertaker, one of whose professional recommendations consisted in saying a fresh grace to each batch of mourners. Laird Grieve, an aged and facetious carpenter, carried off the chief business in coffin-making, in consequence of being able to say seven graces of considerable length without repetition. The consumption of whiskey at these lugubrious entertainments was incredible, and sometimes encroached seriously on the means of families. After the funeral, there was an entertainment called the Dredgy, which was a degree more cheerful than the preceding potations.

Although the belief in witchcraft had died out generally, it was still entertained in a limited way by the less enlightened classes. I have a recollection of a poor old woman being reputed as a witch, and that it was not safe to pass her cottage, without placing the thumb across the fourth finger, so as to form the figure of the cross. This species of exorcism I practiced under instructions from boys older than myself. I likewise remember seeing salt thrown on the fire, as a guard against the evil eye, when aged women, suspected of not being quite *canny*, happened to call at a neighbor's dwelling. The aged postman, as was confidently reported, never went on his rounds with the letters without a sprig of rowan-tree (mountain ash) in his pocket, as a preservative against malevolent influences. There was no police. Offenders against the law were usually captured by a town-officer, at the verbal command of the provost, who administered justice in an off-hand way behind his counter, amidst miscellaneous dealings with customers, and

ordered off alleged delinquents to prison without keeping
any record of the transaction. Dismission from confinement took place in the like abrupt and arbitrary manner.
  As will be observed, there was still much of an old-world
air about Peebles. The transit to and from it was tedious
and expensive. In winter, there was a dearth of fuel,
causing the poorer classes to rely for warmth on that species of deposit from cows, mixed with coal-culm and baked
in the sun, which we learn from the Malmesbury Papers
was used as fuel in Cambridgeshire after the middle of last
century. Although the town had existed for a thousand
years or more, it possessed no printing-press. Only two or
three newspapers came to it in the course of a week, and
these were handed about till they were in tatters. Advertisements were made by tuck of drum ; the official employed for the purpose being an old soldier, a tough little
man with a queue, known as " Drummer Will." It was
told of him that he had gallantly beat a drum at the battle
of Quebec until the whole regiment had perished, he alone
being the survivor, and still vigorously beating his drum
like a hero amidst fire and shot. Now settled down as an
officer of the civic corporation, Drummer Will usefully performed the triple duty of acting as jailer, constable, and
agent for advertisements, which after collecting an audience, he read by means of a pair of Dutch spectacles,
and always pronounced *adverteesements*.
  Robert describes the way that the more affluent burghers often spent their evenings.

  " The absence of excitement in the ordinary life of a
small town, made it next to impossible for a man of social
spirit to avoid convivial evening meetings, and these were
frequent. The favorite *howff* was an old-fashioned inn
kept by a certain Miss Ritchie, a clever, sprightly woman

of irreproachable character, who, so far from the obse-
quiousness of her profession, required to be treated by her
guests with no small amount of deference, and, in especial,
would never allow them to have liquor after a decent hour.
When that hour arrived — I think it was the Forbes-Mac-
kenzie hour of eleven — it was vain for them to ask a
fresh supply. 'Na, na ; gang hame to your wives and
bairns,' was her dictum, and it was impossible for them to
sit much longer. 'Meg Dods' in 'St. Ronan's Well' is
what I would call a rough and strong portraiture of Miss
Ritchie, a Miss Ritchie of a lower sphere of life ; and if
I may judge from a conversation I once had with Sir Walter Scott regarding the supposed prototype, I think he
knew little about her. The *tout-ensemble* of the actual inn,
— a laird's town-house of the seventeenth century, with a
grande cour in front, accessible by an arched gate surmounted by a dial, — with the little low-ceiled rooms
and Miss Ritchie herself ruling house, and servants, and
guests with her clear head and ready tongue, jocosely
sharp with everybody, forms a picture in my mind to which
I should now vainly seek to find a parallel.

"Into one of Miss Ritchie's parlors, or some similar
place, would little groups of the burghers converge every
evening after the shutting up of their shops, there to talk
over the last public news, or any petty occurrence that might
have taken place nearer home. There was hardly any
declared liberalism among them, for the exigencies of the
country, under the great struggle with Bonaparte, had extinguished nearly all differences of opinion. Dear to man
is the face of his brother man ; pleasant it is everywhere
to hear this brother man's voice, and have an interchange
of ideas with him. In that lifeless little town, to have
denied the inhabitants these social meetings would have
been to practice the greatest cruelty; and on a liberal

view, admitting that the means of a more legitimate excitement were not to be had, the jug of whiskey-toddy at
Miss Ritchie's in the evening puts on a defensible aspect.
Toddy might there be regarded as the very cement of
society, an attraction of cohesion, without which a small
country town would have been pulverized and dispersed
into space. I suppose the same end was served in former
times by two-penny ale, a liquor of which only the fame
remained in my youthful days ; but since the middle of
the eighteenth century, usquebaugh had been coming into
general use, and a hot solution of it with sugar, under a
name introduced (strange to say) from the East Indies,
namely, toddy, was already universal. The decoction was
made in stone-ware quart jugs, and poured into the glasses
of the company, again and again, in successive rounds, as
soon as each person had drained off what was before him ;
those who lagged in their potations being always duly
prompted and pushed on by their neighbors. They always
met under the belief that they were going to have just one
jug ; but somehow, when that was ended, there was always a painful feeling of surprise, and to have a second
seemed only a doing of justice to themselves, under an
unaccountable wrong continually inflicted upon them by
the nature of things. Matters being so far righted, they
might have been expected to see the propriety of going
home to their beds ; but here came in a local circumstance
which interested them to an opposite conclusion. The
burgh happened to have a most bibulous coat-armorial,
consisting of three fishes (by the way, I suspect that fishes
drink no more than land animals do, though the contrary
is always supposed) ; and so, when the second jug was
emptied, some one was sure to mention ' Peebles Arms,'
thereby hinting the duty they were under, in loyalty to the
town, to have a third jug. Such an argument in such cir-

cumstances was irresistible ; and thus it came about that
the one virtuous jug of the intention always proved to be
three in the guilty event.

" Our neighbor, Laird Grieve, the aged joiner and
undertaker, had a son ' Tam,' who succeeded to his business. Tam was a blithe, hearty man, with an old-fashioned
gentility in his aspect, and was a general favorite in the
town, which he served for many years in the capacity of a
bailie. He had a small carpenter's shop, and a saw-pit,
and an appearance of uncut logs about his premises ; but
I never could connect the idea of either work or business
with Bailie Grieve. He continued, however, all through
life to have a kind of eminence as a maker of fishing-rods.
He was also an excellent angler, in which capacity he was
well known to the late Professor Wilson.

" It used to be very pleasant, in returning to Peebles as
a visitor, to call upon Tam at his neat, small, white house,
near the bottom of the old town, where, in a miniature
terraced garden with a neat white railing, I saw tulips for
the first time, and thought them the prettiest objects in
creation. Being a widower and without children, the
bailie had an old woman, Bet, for a general servant and
housekeeper ; and her reception of us, as she opened the
door, and showed us into her master's little, low-ceiled
parlor, was always of an enthusiastic character. Presently
there would be a gust of kindly and somewhat vociferous
talk, Bet standing within the door (but holding it by the
handle) all the time, and lending in her word whenever
she had occasion. Dear traits of the old simple world,
how delightful to recall you in these scenes of comparative
refinement and comparative stiffness and frigidity ! "

Among that considerable part of the population who
lived down closes and in old thatched cottages, news cir-

culated at third or fourth hand, or was merged in conversation on religious or other topics. My brother and I
derived much enjoyment, not to say instruction, from the
singing of old ballads, and the telling of legendary stories,
by a kind old female relative, the wife of a decayed tradesman, who dwelt in one of the ancient closes. At her
humble fireside, under the canopy of a huge chimney,
where her half-blind and superannuated husband sat doz-
ing in a chair, the battle of Corunna and other prevailing
news was strangely mingled with disquisitions on the Jewish wars. The source of this interesting conversation was
a well-worn copy of L'Estrange's translation of " Josephus,"
a small folio of date 1720. The envied possessor of the
work was Tam Fleck, " a flichty chield," as he was considered, who, not particularly steady at his legitimate employment, struck out a sort of profession by going about
in the evenings with his " Josephus," which he read as the
current news ; the only light he had for doing so being
usually that imparted by the flickering blaze of a piece
of parrot coal. It was his practice not to read more than
from two to three pages at a time, interlarded with sagacious remarks of his own by way of foot-notes, and in this
way he sustained an extraordinary interest in the narrative.
Retailing the matter with great equability in different
households, Tam kept all at the same point of information,
and wound them up with a corresponding anxiety as to the
issue of some moving event in Hebrew annals. Although
in this way he went through a course of " Josephus " yearly,
the novelty somehow never seemed to wear off.

"Weel, Tam, what's the news the nicht?" would old
Geordie Murray say, as Tam entered with his " Josephus "
under his arm, and seated himself at the family fireside.

"Bad news, bad news," replied Tam. " Titus has begun to besiege Jerusalem ; it's gaun to be a terrible busi-

ness ; " and then he opened his budget of intelligence, to which all paid the most reverential attention. The protracted and severe famine which was endured by the besieged Jews was a theme which kept several families in a state of agony for a week ; and when Tam in his readings came to the final conflict and destruction of the city by the Roman general, there was a perfect paroxysm of horror. At such *séances* my brother and I were delighted listeners. All honor to the memory of Tam Fleck.

In the old-town community, where he often figured, our more immediate paternal ancestors, as enjoying the fruits of uninterrupted frugality and industry for centuries, had attained to a somewhat enviable position. My grandfather, William Chambers, continuing the occupation of his predecessors, carried on the manufacture of woolen and linen cloths, on what would now be called an antiquated and meagre scale, in a long thatched building at the corner of a quadrangle which in old times had formed the market-place of the town. One end of this homely structure was his dwelling, consisting of two apartments ; and in the other were several hand-looms and warping machines. All the family labored according to their ability, and the whole arrangements were of a thrifty kind, not absolutely enjoined by the pressure of daily wants, but conformable to the ordinary usages of the period.

The whole establishment might be taken as a type of a state of society once common in the smaller provincial towns of Scotland ; and contrasting it with the present state of things, we may observe the remarkable advances which have been made in the country since the latter part of the eighteenth century. Here was a man of some consideration, — an independent manufacturer, so to speak,— and in no respect penurious, living in a style inferior to that of any mechanic in the present day with a wage of only twenty shillings a week. No elegances, nor what we now deem indispensable comforts. When people are inclined to grumble with their accommodations, and to speak of the dearth of luxuries, would it not be well for them, in however small a degree, to compare their condition with that of their grandfathers three-quarters of a century ago?

Upright, pious, and benevolent, my grandfather very acceptably held the office of an elder of the church for the last thirty years of his existence. To the poor and wretched he was an ever ready friend, adviser, and consoler. I have heard it related that on Sunday evenings he would return exhausted with his religious peregrinations and exercises, having, in the course of a few hours, visited perhaps as many as a dozen sick or dying persons, and offered up an extempore and suitable prayer with each. At his death, in 1799, this worthy man left his widow and second son, William, to carry on the business, my father James, the elder son, having about the same period begun his cotton manufacturing concern.

Of this widow, my grandmother, I retain some recollections. According to an old custom in Scotland, she was, though married, known only by her maiden name, which was Margaret Kerr. Margaret was a little woman, of plain appearance, a great stickler on points of controversial divinity, a rigorous critic of sermons, and a severe censor of what she considered degenerating manners. She possessed a good deal of "character," and might almost be taken for the original of Mause Headrigg. As the wife of a ruling elder, she possibly imagined that she was entitled to exercise a certain authority in ecclesiastical matters. An anecdote is told of her having once taken the venerable Dr. Dalgliesh, the parish minister, through hands. In presence of a number of neighbors, she thought fit to lecture him on that particularly delicate subject, his wife's dress : " It was a sin and a shame to see sae mickle finery."

The minister did not deny the charge, but dexterously encountered her with the Socratic method of argument : " So, Margaret, you think that ornament is useless and sinful in a lady's dress ? "

" Certainly I do."

" Then, may I ask why you wear that ribbon around your cap? A piece of cord would surely do quite as well."

Disconcerted with this unforeseen turn of affairs, Margaret determinedly rejoined in an undertone : "Ye'll no hae lang to speer sic a like question."

Next day her cap was bound with a piece of white tape ; and never afterwards, till the day of her death, did she wear a ribbon, or any morsel of ornament. I am doubtful if we could match this out of Scotland. For a novelist to depict characters of this kind, he would require to see them in real life ; no imagination could reach them. Sir Walter Scott both saw and talked with them, for they were not extinct in his day.

The mortifying rebuff about the ribbon perhaps had some influence in making my ancestress a Seceder. As she lived near the manse, I am afraid she must have been a good deal of a thorn in the side of the parish minister, notwithstanding all the palliatives of her good-natured husband, the elder. At length an incident occurred, which sent her abruptly off to a recently erected meeting-house, to which a promising young preacher, Mr. Leckie, had been appointed.

It was a bright summer morning about five o'clock, when Margaret left her husband's side as usual, and went

out to see her cow attended to. Before three minutes
had elapsed, her husband was aroused by her coming in
with dismal cries: " Eh, sirs ! eh, sirs ! did I ever think
to live to see the day ?   O man, O man, O William ; this
is a terrible thing indeed.   Could I ever have thought to
see't ? "

"Gracious, woman !" exclaimed the worthy elder, by
this time fully awake, "what is't ?   Is the coo deid?" for
it seemed to him that no greater calamity could have been
expected to produce such doleful exclamations.

" The coo deid !" responded Margaret: "waur, waur,
ten times waur.   There's Dr. Dalgliesh only now gaun
hame at five o'clock in the morning.   It's awfu', it's awfu' !   What will things come to ? "

The elder, though a pattern of propriety himself, is not
recorded as having taken any but a mild view of the minister's conduct, more particularly as he knew that the
patron of the parish was at Miss Ritchie's inn, and that
the reverend divine might have been detained rather late
with him against his will.   The strenuous Margaret drew
no such charitable conclusions.   She joined the Secession
congregation next day, and never again attended the parish church.

CHAPTER II

B EFORE introducing my mother to the modest mansion, the first home of her married life, situated on the north bank of the Eddleston Water, a small tributary of the Tweed, something characteristic of old Scotland may be said of her parentage : and here we return to Robert's manuscript.

"In the middle of the last century, the farm of Jedderfield, situated on the hill-face above Neidpath Castle, a mile from Peebles, the property of the Earl of March, was occupied, at the rent of eighteen pounds, by an honest man named David Grieve. While the noble proprietor was pursuing his career of sport and debauchery in London — the course which was consummated by him many years after, under the title which he finally acquired of Duke of Queensberry (familiarly *Old Q.*), — the tenant, David Grieve, reared on that small bit of his lordship's domains a family of fourteen children, most of whom floated on by their own merits to much superior positions in life : one to be a merchant in Manchester, two to similar positions in Edinburgh, one to be a surgeon in the East India Company's service, and so forth. This family afforded an example of the virtuous, frugal life of the rural people of Scotland previous to that extension of industry which brought wealth and many comforts into our country. The breakfast was oatmeal porridge ; the supper, a thinner

NEWBY. 31

farinaceous composition named sowens; for the dinner,
there was seldom butcher-meat: the ordinary mess was a
thin broth called *Lenten kail*, composed of a ball of oatmeal kneaded up with butter, boiled in an infusion of
cabbage, and eaten with barley or pease-meal bannocks.
Strange as it may seem, a people of many fine qualities
were reared in this plain style, a people of bone and mus-
cle, mentally as well as physically — 'buirdly chiels and
clever hizzies,' as Burns says. There was not a particle
of luxury in that Sabine life; hardly a single article of
the kinds sold in shops was used. The food was all obtained from the farm, and the clothing was wholly of
homespun. I cannot be under any mistake about it, for I
have often heard the household and its ways described by
my maternal grandmother, who was David Grieve's eldest
daughter. Even the education of the children was conducted at home, the mother giving them lessons while
seated at her spinning-wheel.

"Janet, the eldest girl, was wedded at eighteen by a
middle-aged farmer, named William Gibson, who rented a
large tract of pasturage belonging to Dr. Hay of Haystoun. This farm, called Newby, was not less than seven
miles long; it commenced near Haystoun, about two miles
from Peebles, and at the other extremity bordered on
Blackhouse, in Selkirkshire, where the Ettrick Shepherd
spent his youthful days. The Gibsons were a numerous
clan in Tweeddale, and some of them, including the
tenant of Newby, were comparatively wealthy. William
Gibson had never less than a hundred score of sheep on
his farm, and such was the abundance of ewe-milk, that,
for a part of the year, his wife made a cheese of that
material every day." The ewes were milked early in the
morning by lasses, who for this purpose trooped off with
bowies, or pails, on their heads from the homestead to

sheep-pens among the hills, — a fashion of rural life commemorated in the songs of Ramsay and other Scottish
poets : —

> " I've heard the liltin' at the ewe milkin',
> Lasses a-liltin' before dawn of day ;
> Now there's a moanin' on ilka green loanin' —
> The Flowers of the Forest are a' wede away."

In marrying William Gibson, the reputedly rich farmer
of Newby, Janet Grieve was thought to make an enviable
match, and of this there was some outward tokens. The
marriage took place in 1768. On the day preceding the
event, Janet's " providing," which was sumptuous, was
despatched in a cart from Jedderfield to what was to be
her new home ; the load of various articles being con-
spicuously surmounted by a spinning-wheel, decorated
with ribbons of different colors. The marriage was signalized by more than the customary festivities, in the
midst of which the young and blooming bride was placed
behind her husband on horseback ; and thus, after pacing
grandly through Peebles with a following of rustic cava-
liers, the wedded pair arrived at Newby. In the present
day, we should in vain look for this old farm-establish-
ment, for every vestige of it is gone ; and we only discover
the spot, which is the edge of a gowany bank overhanging
Haystoun Burn, by a decayed tree that flourished in the
corner of the small garden.

" There was a much less frugal style of life at Newby
than at Jedderfield. Although the homestead consisted
of only a cottage, containing *a but and a ben*, that is, a
kitchen and parlor, with the usual appendages of a barn,
etc., it gave shelter every night to groups of the vagrant
people, the multitude of whom was a matter of remark and
lamentation a few years before to Fletcher of Salton and
other patriots. On a Saturday night there would be as

many as twenty of these poor creatures received by the
farmer for food and lodging till Monday morning. Some
of them, who had established a good character, were entertained in the farmer's *ha'*, where himself, his wife, and
servants ordinarily sat, as was the fashion of that time.
The family rather relished this society, for from hardly any
other source did they ever obtain any of the news of the
country. One well-remembered guest of this order was a
robust old man named Andrew Gemmells, who had been
a dragoon in his youth, but had long assumed the blue
gown and badge of a *king's bedesman*, or licensed beggar,
together with the meal-pocks and long staff. A rough and
ready tongue, and a picturesque if not venerable aspect,
had recommended Andrew in many households superior
to my grandfather's.

" Sir Walter Scott, who commemorates him under the
name of Edie Ochiltree, tells how a laird was found one
day playing at draughts with Gemmells, the only mark of
distinction of rank presented in the case being that the
laird sat in his parlor, and the *blue-gown* in the court
outside, the board being placed on the sill of the open
window between. I can corroborate the view which we
thus acquire of the old beggar's position, by stating that
the guidwife of Newby learned the game of draughts —
commonly called in Scotland the *dam-brod* — from Andrew Gemmells, and often played with him at her hall
fireside. Somewhat to his disgust, the pupil became in
time the equal of the master, and a visitor one day backed
her against him for a guinea, which the old man did not
scruple to stake, and which he could easily have paid if
unsuccessful, as he carried a good deal of money about
his person. When it appeared, however, that she was
about to gain the game, Andrew lost his temper, or
affected to do so, and, hastily snatching up the board,

3

threw the 'men' into the ash-pit. Andrew circulated all through the counties of Peebles, Selkirk, and Roxburgh, going from house to house, and getting an *awmos* (alms), with lodging if necessary, at each, appreciated as an original wherever he came — everywhere civilly and even kindly treated. It must have been, on the whole, a pleasant life for the old man, but one that could only be so while the primitive simple style of farm-life subsisted, that is, while the farmer, his wife, and children, still herded in the same room with their servants, and were not above holding converse with the remembered beggar. Perhaps poor Andrew found at last that things were taking an unfavorable turn for him, for he died in an *outhouse* at a farm in the parish of Roxburgh, in the month of February too (1794).

"My grandmother was wedded, and went home to her husband's house at Newby, in 1768. She was a remarkably good looking, portly woman, bearing a considerable resemblance to a profile portrait of Madame Roland, the famous heroine of the French Revolution. The 'leddies' of Haystoun, sisters and daughters of the landlord, Dr. Hay, felt an interest in the pretty young wife, and put themselves on familiar terms with her. They would send a message to her on Saturday, asking if she designed to go to church at Peebles next day, and if so, making an appointment with her to join their party. The five or six 'leddies,' and the young guidwife of Newby, might have been seen next morning picking their steps along the road to Peebles, each wearing her pretty checked plaid or mantilla over her head, such being the old Scottish succedaneum for a bonnet. A most interesting group it must have been, for the Hays were all handsome people, and the young guidwife was reckoned the bonniest woman in Peeblesshire in her day. A lively gossiping conversation was kept up. The 'leddies' would be telling their young rustic friend of the assemblies they had been attending in Edinburgh, where Miss Nicky Murray (sister of the Chief-justice Earl of Mansfield) was in the height of her authority ; the guidwife probably telling them in turn of the results of the lambing season, or some bit of country news.

"In the second year of my grandmother's married life, one of her Haystoun friends, the daughter of Dr. Hay, was married, and taken to a permanent residence in Edinburgh by Sir William Forbes, the banker, a man who enjoyed as much of the public esteem in Scotland as any man living during his time, whose memory has been embalmed in the verse of Scott, and whose autobiography I had much pleasure in editing a few years ago, through the impression made upon me regarding him by my grandmother's recollections. Two unmarried Misses Hay, who survived to an extreme old age, always kept up their intimacy with my grandmother, and I remember 'Miss Ailie' calling upon her in Edinburgh about 1815. Miss Ailie was understood to be above ninety at that time, but she never seemed to admit or acknowledge the progress of time, and time really seemed to have very little to do with her. A question about somebody's age arose, and I recollect the old lady saying, rather snappishly, and with the air of one whose words admitted of no reply : 'As to age, it's a subject that was never mentioned in my father's family.' Misses Ailie and Betty Hay spent their latter days in a *flat* in West Nicolson Street, Edinburgh, and only once during a great number of years revisited the ancient paternal mansion in Peeblesshire. I was at Newby not long after, and heard from the farmer how the old ladies came and wandered about the place, lingering fondly in every romantic nook

which they had known in former years, and declaring
that they thought they could have recognized the place by
the smell of the flowers.

" I feel impelled here to remark the pleasant old fashion of calling ladies by some familiar form of their Christian name. The world was full of Miss Betties, Miss
Peggies, and Miss Beenies long ago ; nay, the daughters
of dukes and earls were Lady Madies, Lady Lizzies, and
Lady Kates. There was something very endearing in
the custom. It brought high and low together on the
common ground of family fireside life. Your Miss Eliza-
beths and Lady Catherines seem a people in a different
sphere, beyond the range of our sympathies. I have
heard a gentleman say that, in the family of which he was
one, all went well while they continued to call each other
by the pet names of their nursery days ; and that, on a
resolution being formed to exchange these for the formal
Christian names, there ensued a marked diminution of
their mutual affection, and they never afterwards were
the same thing to each other that they had been. This
fact seems to me one well worth bearing in mind.

" My grandmother and her maids were generally up at
an early hour in the morning to attend to the ewes, and
their time for going to rest must have consequently been
an early one. There was always, however, a period, called
' between gloaming and supper-time,' during which another
industry was practiced. Then it was that the wheels were
brought out for the spinning of the yarn which was to constitute the clothing of the family. And I often think that
it must have been a pleasing sight in that humble hall —
the handsome young mistress amidst her troop of maidens,
all busy with foot and finger, while the shepherds and their
master, and one or two favored gaberlunzies, would be
telling stories or cracking jokes for the general entertain-

ment, or some one with a good voice would be singing the songs of Ramsay and Hamilton. At a certain time of the year, the guidwife had to lay aside the ordinary little wheel, by which lint was spun, and take to the 'muckle wheel,' which was required for the production of woolen thread, the material of the goodman's clothes, or else the 'reel,' on which she reduced the product of the little wheel to hanks for the weaver. Even the Misses Hay were great lint spinners, and I suspect that their familiar acquaintance with the guidwife of Newby depended somewhat on their common devotion to the wheel.

" It was on this farm of Newby, while in the possession of Mr. Gibson, in the year 1772, that there occurred a case of the sagacity of the shepherd's dog, which has often been adverted to in books, but seldom with correctness as to the details. A store-farmer, in another part of the county, had commenced a system of sheep-stealing, which he was believed to have practiced without detection for several years. At length, a ewe which had been taken amongst other sheep from Newby, reappeared on the farm, bearing a *birn* (Anglicè, brand) on her face in addition to that of her true owner. The animal was believed to have been attracted to her former home by the instinct of affection towards the lamb from whom she had been separated, and her return was the more remarkable as it involved the necessity of her crossing the river Tweed. The shepherd, James Hislop, did not fail to report the reappearance of the ewe to his master, and it was not long before they ascertained whose brand it was which had been impressed over Mr. Gibson's. As many sheep had been for some time missed out of the stock, it was thought proper that Hislop should pay a visit to Mr. Murdison's farm, where he quickly discovered a considerable number of sheep bearing Mr. Gibson's brand O, all having Mr. Murdison's, the

letter T, superimposed.   In short, Murdison and his shepherd Miller were apprehended, tried, convicted, and duly
hanged in the Grassmarket — a startling exhibition, considering the position of the sufferers in life, and made the
more so by the humbler man choosing to come upon the
scaffold in his 'dead-clothes.'   The long-continued success of the crime of these wretched men was found to have
depended on the wonderful human-like sense of Miller's
dog 'Yarrow.' Accompanied by 'Yarrow,' the man would
take an opportunity of visiting a neighboring farm and
looking through the flocks. He had there only to point
out certain sheep to his sagacious companion, who would
come that night, select each animal so pointed out, bring
them together, and drive them across country, and, moreover, across the Tweed, to his master's farm, never once
undergoing detection. The story ran that the dog was
hanged soon after his master, as being thought a dangerous creature in a country full of flocks ; but I would hope
that this was a false rumor, and my grandmother, who
might have known all the circumstances connected with
the case, never affirmed its truth."

About 1780, Mr. Gibson retired with a moderate com-
petency to Peebles, where he concluded his days.   Here
were born to him a girl and boy, who at his death were
left in charge of their mother and several appointed guardians.   Unfortunately, as regards these children, their
mother made a second marriage with a teacher, Mr. Robert Noble, and in the short space of two to three years
she was again left a widow, with an addition of two boys,
Robert and David, without any provision whatever from
this new connection.   To the two young Gibsons, Jean
and her brother William, this affair led to much domestic
unhappiness, along with a desire to escape from it in the

best way possible. Jean grew up an uncommonly beautiful
girl, and being in some small degree an heiress, had a
number of admirers, one of them being my father, to
whom she was married ; and the young pair began housekeeping in the neat mansion already described.

This marriage took place in May, 1799. I was born in
less than a year afterwards, and, as has been said, Robert
was born in 1802. My furthest stretch of memory pictures
my mother as a gentle, lady like person, slender in frame,
punctiliously tasteful in dress, and beautiful in features,
but with an expression of blended pensiveness and cheerfulness indicative of the position into which she had been
brought. Even as a child I could see she had sorrows —
perhaps regrets. It might have been safe to say that her
union had been " ill fated."

It is not, however, to be assumed from this circumstance that my father was undeserving of regard. He
possessed numerous estimable qualities, but, in association with these, a pliancy of disposition which, according
to the language of the world, renders a man " his own
worst enemy." In my experience in private life, I have
never known any one more keenly conscientious in matters concerning others, and less so in things concerning
himself. Accurate, upright, aspiring in his tastes and
notions, with a fund of humor, and an immense love for
music, he may be said to have taken a lead in the town
for his general knowledge. He made some progress in
scientific attainments. Affected, like others at the time,
with the fascinating works of James Ferguson on astronomy, he had a kind of rage for that branch of study,
which he pursued, by means of a tolerably good telescope,
in company with Mungo Park, the African traveller, who
had settled as a surgeon in Peebles, and one or two other
acquaintances.

He often lamented that his parents had not followed
out a design of bestowing on him a liberal education.
Supposing him to have been under some delusion in this
respect, it could, I think, have been nothing but a sincere love of literature that induced him to acquire a copy
of the " Encyclopædia Britannica," at a time when works
of this expensive nature were purchased only by the
learned and affluent. The possession of this voluminous
mass of knowledge in no small degree helped to create a
taste for reading in my own, and more particularly my
brother's mind; at all events a familiarity with the volumes of this great work is among the oldest of my recollections. Nor can I omit to mention other agreeable
reminiscences of these early days. My father, as an
amateur, was an excellent and untiring performer on the
German flute, an instrument which shared his affections
with his telescope. Seated at the open window of his
little parlor in calm summer gloamings, he would play an
endless series of Scottish airs, which might be heard along
the Eddleston Water; then, as the clear silvery moon and
planets arose to illumine the growing darkness, out would
be brought his telescope, which being planted carefully on
its stand on my mother's tea-table, there ensued a critical
inspection of the firmament and its starry host. From
circumstances of this kind, discussions about the satellites
of Jupiter and the belts of Saturn are embedded in reminiscences of my early years.

Once or twice a year my father had occasion to go to
Glasgow in connection with business arrangements. The
journey, upwards of forty miles, was performed on foot, in
company with Jamie Hall, a stocking manufacturer, who
was something of an oddity. They were usually two days
on the road. Hall made a point of paying his way in
pairs of stockings, of which he carried a choice stock on

his back, calculated to settle all the reckonings till he
arrived at the Spoutmouth in the Gallowgate. In one
of these visits to Glasgow, my father, through his love of
music, purchased a spinet, which, arriving on the top of
the carrier's cart, created some perturbation in the household. It was a heedless acquisition, for there was no
place to put it except in the garret, among heaps of warps
and bundles of weft. There, accordingly, where there
was barely standing-room, the unfortunate spinet was deposited, and became an object of musical indulgence,
sometimes for hours, in which enjoyment all sublunary
cares were forgot.

With these tastes and accomplishments, it was, as just
stated, my father's misfortune to have a remarkable facility of disposition. With a power of penetrating character,
and a correct knowledge of physiognomy, he was disqualified to battle with the realities of life through his guileless·
ness and goodness of heart. Notwithstanding all his
boasted shrewdness, he was constantly exposed to imposi-
tion, being cheated, as it were, with his eyes open. Desirous to please, he could not resist importunities to lend
money or give credit, though conscious that by doing so
he would almost inevitably incur a loss. Yet, with this
pliancy, he could fire up on occasions, particularly when
his word was doubted, or his principles attacked. Careless of consequences, he avowed his hatred of political
subserviency at a time when independent principle, as far
as Scotland was concerned, was very nearly trampled
out of existence. Henry Cockburn, in his " Memorials,"
speaks of the deplorable state of things in Edinburgh.
In country towns, matters were fully worse. My father's
views of public policy were not calculated to make friends
in an age of political sycophancy. In 1807, on the occasion of a contested election for a member of parliament

for the group of burghs of which Peebles was a member, he was threatened with oppressive measures for simply refusing to advise his brother to vote in a particular manner.

The circumstances of the case were these : My uncle, as a member of the town-council, having at the election stuck to the liberal side along with nine other members, — constituting, as they were called, the steady ten, — my father was earnestly solicited to remonstrate with his brother, and, if possible, induce him to vote for the opposite party. Money had been tendered, a place had been offered, but all would not do. Every overture was rejected. To employ a new kind of persuasive, my father was visited by Mr. C——, of K——, a land proprietor in the neighborhood, who spoke rather freely. My father was unyielding, would have nothing to do with the affair ; besides, he thought his brother was in the right. " Well, then," concluded his visitor, " if you are resolved on being obstinate, we know what to do. I think I possess some influence among the manufacturers of Glasgow with whom you are connected, and will get them to remove their commissions ; in short, either help us, or lay your account with being ruined." This, of course, was too much for my father's equanimity. Bursting with rage, he ordered the political emissary out of the house, telling him, at the same time, that he alike despised and defied him. The menace had been idly made ; at least, it came to nothing. I have just a bare recollection of this strange scene, which was called to mind some years ago, when I saw my father's old oppressor walking about Edinburgh, a decayed gentleman, in somewhat melancholy mood, having, from reverses of fortune, been obliged to sell his estate and retire into obscurity. He was undoubtedly a man of amiable character, who, from a too eager spirit of partisanship, had been led to commit a mean and disreputable act, as his threatened attempt to crush my father must be considered to have been. Such is now the improved tone of society and manners, that, in mentioning the above incident, one feels as if digging fossils from the submerged strata of an antediluvian world.

His musical accomplishments rendered my father's society peculiarly attractive. He had a good voice, and sung the Scottish songs with considerable effect ; consequently he was much in request at convivialities, to which, from a fondness for lively conversation, he had no particular objection. There, indeed, lay my father's weakness, — too slight a regard for personal responsibilities. His indifference in this respect could not fail to throw additional obligations on my mother, whose destiny it was to confront and overcome innumerable embarrassments. Acquainted with only the elementary branches of education, and unskilled in any fashionable accomplishments, she nevertheless possessed a strong understanding. I might truly say that, both in appearance and manners, she was by nature a lady, and circumstances made her a heroine. Delicate in frame, and with generally poor health, she was ill adapted for the fatigues and anxieties which she had to encounter ; but such was her tact and dexterity, as well as her determined resolution, that she bore and overcame trials which I feel assured would have sunk many in like circumstances to the depths of despair. What she did may afterwards appear. Meanwhile, a number of young children demanded her care.

Robert and I had a strange congenital malformation. We were sent into the world with six fingers on each hand, and six toes on each foot. By the neighbors, as I understand, this was thought particularly lucky ; but it proved anything but lucky for one of us. In my own case, the redundant members were easily removed, leaving scarcely a trace of their presence ; but in the case of Robert, the result was very different. The supernumerary toes on the outside of the foot were attached to, or formed part of, the metatarsal bones, and were so badly amputated as to leave delicate protuberances, calculated to be a torment for life. This unfortunate circumstance, by producing a certain degree of lameness and difficulty in walking, no doubt exerted a permanent influence over my brother's habits and feelings. Indisposed to indulge in the boisterous exercise of other boys, — studious, docile in temperament, and excelling in mental qualifications, — he shot ahead of me in all matters of education. Though dissimilar in various ways, we, however, associated together from our earliest years. It almost seemed as if a difference of tastes and aptitudes produced a degree of mutual reliance and coöperation. With a more practical and exigent tone of mind than Robert, I might possibly have made a decent progress at school, had my teachers at all sympathized with me. As it happened, I look back upon my school experiences with anything but satisfaction. A very few particulars will suffice.

My first school was one kept by a poor old widow, Kirsty Cranston, who, according to her own account, was qualified to carry forward her pupils as far as reading the Bible ; but to this proficiency there was the reasonable exception of leaving out difficult words, such as Maher-shalal-hash-baz. These, she told the children, might be made " a pass-over," and accordingly, it was the rule of the establishment to let them alone. From this humble seminary I was in time transferred to the burgh school, then under the charge of Mr. James Gray, author of a popular treatise on arithmetic. The fee, here, was two shillings and twopence per quarter for reading and writing, and sixpence additional for arithmetic. The pupils were the children of nearly all classes in the town and rural districts around. They numbered about a hundred and fifty boys and girls. Probably a third of them in summer were barefooted, but this was less a necessity than a choice ; at any rate, it well suited the locality. In front of the school-house lay the town green, and beside it was the Tweed, in which the school-boys were constantly paddling.

Gray was a man of mild temperament, and a good teacher, but his pupils entertained little respect for his abilities. Yielding, like too many others at the time, to over-indulgence, he sometimes went off on a carouse, and entered the school considerably inebriated, which was deemed vastly amusing. Nor did this sort of conduct incur any public censure. The magistrates and council, whose duty it was to call him to account, were associates in his revels, and appreciated him as a boon-companion. When elevated to a certain pitch, he sung a good song about Nelson and his brave British tars ; and this in itself, in the heat of the French War, extenuated many shortcomings. At this school, too, as is usual with such seminaries in Scotland, the Bible was read as a class-book, but with no kind of reverence, or even decorum. The verses were bawled out at the pitch of the voice, without the slightest regard to intonation or elocutionary effect. When the teacher was temporarily absent, there took place a battle of the books — one side of the school against the other. On such occasions the girls, not choosing to be belligerents, discreetly retired under the tables, leaving the boys to carry on the war, in which dog-eared Bibles without boards, resembling bunches of leaves, handily flew about as missiles. To have to look back on this as a place of youthful instruction !

There was another stage in my educational career. I was advanced to the grammar-school, as it is called, a superior burgh establishment, of which Mr. James Sloan was head-master. Here I ,was introduced to Latin, for which the fee was five shillings a quarter. My progress was very indifferent. Of course it was very stupid of me not intuitively appreciating this branch of learning, and likewise in feeling that its acquisition was a cheerless drudgery. Like others, perhaps, in like circumstances, I have lived to regret my inattention, or call it incapacity ; for even the small knowledge of Latin which I did acquire during two years of painful study, has not failed to be of considerable service in various respects.

Mr. Sloan was held in general esteem, and justly reputed as an excellent teacher. He grounded well, and apt scholars got on famously with him. My brother, who, like myself, was advanced from the burgh to the grammar-school, became a proficient and favorite pupil ; his mind, as it were, taking naturally to instruction in the classics. The healthy locality of the school was much in its favor, and attracted boarders from Edinburgh, the colonies, and elsewhere. The association of town scholars with boys from a distance was a pleasing feature in the establishment, and proved mutually advantageous. I could have nothing to say derogatory of the method of culture but for the severity of discipline which was heedlessly pursued, according to what, unfortunately, was too common at the period.

The truth is, violence held rule almost everywhere ; the desperate warlike struggle in which the country was engaged, apparently postponing all pacific and humane notions. Boys — the boy-nature being neither studied nor understood — were flogged and buffeted unmercifully, both at home and at school ; and they in turn beat and domineered over each other according to their capacity, harried birds' nests, pelted cats, and exercised every other species of cruelty within their power. A coarse, bustling carter in Peebles, known by the facetious nickname of " Puddle Mighty," used to leave his old, worn-out, and much-abused horses to die on the public green, and there, without incurring reprobation, the boys amused themselves by, day after day, battering the poor prostrate animals with showers of stones till life was extinct. In the business of elementary instruction, the law of kindness was as yet scarcely thought of. Orders were sometimes given to teachers not by any means to spare the rod. " I've brought you our Jock ; mind ye lick him weel l " would a mother of Spartan temperament say to Mr. Gray, at the same time dragging forward a struggling young savage to be entered as a pupil ; and so Jock was formally resigned to the dominion of the tawse.

I can never forget a scene which took place in Mr. Sloan's seminary one summer afternoon. In the morning of that day a sensation had been created by the intelligence that two of the boarders, gentlemen's sons from Edinburgh, had absconded, and that two town-constables — one of them Drummer Will — had been dispatched in search of them. The youths were caught, brought back in disgrace, and were now to suffer a punishment suitable to the gravity of the offense. Sullen and terrified, the two culprits stood before the assembled school ; the two town-officers in their scarlet coats sitting as a guard within the doorway. The usual hum ceased. There was a deathlike stillness. First reproaching the offenders with their highly improper conduct, the teacher ordered them instantly to strip for flogging. The boys resisted, and were seized by an assistant and the two officers. With clothes in disorder, they were laid across a long, desk-like table, the

rise of which in the middle offered that degree of convex-
ity which was favorable to the application of the tawse.
Kicking and screaming, they suffered the humiliating in-
fliction, and the school was forthwith dismissed for the
day.   Such things at the period were matters of course,
even of approbation, and therefore it would be wrong to
condemn teachers who fell in with the general fashion.
Teaching, it was imagined, could not be conducted otherwise ; school, like army flogging was an authorized national institution.

Laying aside any consideration of the elementary
branches and the classics, the amount of instruction at
these schools was exceedingly slender.   At not one of
them was there taught any history, geography, or physical
science.   There was not in my time a map in any of the
schools, in which respect the place had fallen off; for at
the sale of the effects of Mr. Oman, a previous teacher,
my father bought a pair of old globes, and it was chiefly
from these that my brother and I obtained a competent
knowledge of the terrestrial and celestial spheres.   Possibly I have said more than enough of my school remembrances ; and I finish with stating that my entire education, which terminated when I was thirteen years of age,
cost, books included, somewhere about six pounds.   So
little was taught in the way of general knowledge, that
my education, properly speaking, began only when I was
left to pick it up as opportunities offered in after life.

There are a few circumstances of a pleasing nature
mixed up with these dismal recollections.   I refer to rural
rambles and books.   I spent many hours on the picturesque banks of the Tweed, and in angling excursions
to Manor Water.   Half-holiday visits to Neidpath Castle,
a deserted residence of the Dukes of Queensberry, were a
frequent amusement.   The castle was appropriated as a

dépôt for the clothing and accoutrements of the local militia, placed under charge of a worthy old soldier, Sergeant
Veitch ; and through my acquaintance with one of his
sons, I had the *entrée* to the fortalice. The sergeant was
generally looked up to. In virtue of his military knowledge, he was appointed drill-master to the awkward squad,
and for the same reason was intrusted with the custody of
the local militia arms. Bred a weaver, he worked at a
loom which was placed in a deep window recess, in what
was usually styled the Duke's Drawing-room. At times,
he condescended to speak to me, and to mention incidents
in his career, while a sergeant in a foot regiment, at Bun-
ker's Hill and other places of note during the great American war, all which contributed to my small stock of
knowledge.

Two annual fairs, with their concourse of travelling merchants, shows, gingerbread, and wheel-of-fortune men, made
a pleasing break in the monotony of the place. For many
years these fairs were frequented by a personage known
as " Beni Minori," who carried about a singularly attractive raree show. The real name of this humble show-
man was Robert Brown ; that of Beni Minori having
been assumed for professional reasons. Brown was born
in London in 1737, and reared under the charge of his
grandparents near Carlisle, where he remembered the
passing of Prince Charles Stuart on his way into and out
of England, the subsequent surrender of the Highland
garrison to the Duke of Cumberland, and the still later
and more agitating sight of the bloody heads over the
gates of the city. The early years of Brown's life were
spent as a post-boy. He then went to sea in 1759, was
captured by the French, and remained a prisoner till the
end of the " Seven Years' War." Next he went to the
West Indies, and had a perfect recollection of the famous

4

victory achieved by Rodney, April 12, 1782. Returning to England, he purchased the show-box of an old and dying Italian, named Beni Minori, and assuming his name, he was, from some resemblance to the deceased, universally recognized as the same personage. Now began the wanderings of Beni, otherwise Brown, through the north of England and southern counties of Scotland, everywhere carrying his show-box on his back, and resorting to all the fairs within his rounds. Our first interview with Beni was in Peebles about 1805, and the last time we saw him was in 1839, in the Edinburgh Charity Workhouse, where this aged and industrious man had at length found a sheltering roof under which to die. Here were learned the leading particulars of Beni's variegated life. He mentioned that his mother had been dead a hundred and two years; for, in giving him birth, she survived only a quarter of an hour. He had long ceased to have a single relation in the world. Twelve years ago, he had lost his wife, to whom he had been united sixty-four years. There was no living being to whom he could look with the eyes of affection. The only thing he cared for was his show-box, which he daily cleaned and arranged; every picture, ring, and cord being to him like the face of an old friend. Though thus cast a living wreck on the shores of time, Beni always retained the liveliness which had procured for him the attachment of the boys of Peebles. His appearance was still that of a weather-beaten foreigner. He wore ear-rings, chewed tobacco, and joked till the last. With some little assuagement of his condition, provided by the kindness of a few acquaintances, Beni survived till June, 1840, when he died at the age of 103 years.

Among the musical geniuses, vocal and instrumental, who enlivened, or perhaps troubled the fairs, there was a

venerable violinist, John Jameson by name, a kind of type
of " Wandering Willie." Aged and blind, John wandered
through the county, playing at kirns, penny-weddings,
and fairs ; all his journeys being on foot, and performed
with the assistance of two faithful companions, his wife
Jenny, and an old white horse, probably worth ten shillings. The manner in which this humble trio went about
from place to place, generally getting lodgings at farm-
steadings for nothing, or at most for a tune on the violin,
was so remarkable as to deserve commemoration. First
came the wife, limping, with one hand pressed on that
unfortunately rheumatic side, the other leading the old
horse by a halter. Second, the horse, which never
seemed very willing to get along, and needed to be pulled
with all the vigor which Jenny's spare hand could impart.
Across its back, pannier fashion, hung on one side John's
weather-worn fiddle-case, while on the other was a bag of
apples, an article in which the wife dealt in a small way.
Last of all, came John, led by the tail of the reluctant
quadruped ; so that the whole cavalcade moved in a
piece, — Jenny pulling at the horse, and the horse pulling
at John ; and in this way the party managed to make out
their journeys through Peeblesshire.

Though not disposed to be so sedentary as my brother,
I had scarcely a less ardent attachment to books. These,
however, I possessed no means of purchasing.˙ To procure
the objects of my desire, I executed with a knife various
little toys, which I exchanged for juvenile books with my
better provided companions. The room occupied by my
brother and myself was more like a workshop than a
sleeping apartment, on account of the disorder which was
caused by these mechanical operations.

Let us again return to Robert's account of these early
school-days.

" My first two years of schooling were spent amidst the crowd of children attending Mr. Gray's seminary. On the easy terms of two shillings and twopence per quarter I was well grounded by the master and his helper in English. The entire expense must have been only about eighteen shillings, a fact sufficient to explain how Scotch people of the middle class appear to be so well educated in comparison with their southern compatriots. It was prior to the time when the intellectual system was introduced. We were taught to read the Bible and Barrie's ' Collection,' and to spell words. No attempt was made to enlighten us as to the meaning of any of the lessons. The most distressing part of our school exercises consisted in learning by heart the Catechism of the Westminster Assembly of Divines, a document which it was impossible for any person under maturity to understand, or to view in any other light than as a torture. It was a strange, rough, noisy, crowded scene, this burgh school. No refinement of any kind appeared in it. Nothing kept the boys in any sort of order but flagellation with the tawse. Many people thought the master did not punish enough. This idea, in fact, was the cause of an act of wild justice, which I saw executed one day in the school.

" The reader must imagine the school-hum going on in a dull monotone, when suddenly the door burst open, and in walked a middle-aged woman of the humbler class, carrying something in her right hand under her apron. The school sunk into silence in an instant. With flashing eyes and excited vision, she called out, ' Where is Jock Forsyth ? ' Jock had maltreated a son of hers on the green, and she had come to inflict vengeance upon him before the whole school. Jock's conscious soul trembled at the sight, and she had no difficulty in detecting him. Ere the master had recovered from the astonishment which her intrusion had created, the fell virago had pounced upon the culprit, had dragged him into the middle of the floor, and there began to belabor him with the domestic tawse, which she had brought for the purpose. The screams of the boy, the anxious entreaties of the master, with his constant 'Wifie, wifie, be quiet, be quiet,' and the agitated feeling which began to pervade the school, formed a scene which defies words to paint it. Nor did Meg desist till she had given Master Forsyth reason to remember her to the latest day of his existence. She then took her departure, only remarking to Mr. Gray, as she prepared to close the door, ' Jock Forsyth will no' meddle with my Jamie again in a hurry.'

" Boys for whom a superior education was desired were usually passed on at the beginning of their third year to the grammar-school, the school in which the classics were taught, but which also had one or two advanced classes for English and writing. This was an example of an institution which has affected the fortunes of Scotsmen not much less than the parish schools. Every burgh has one, partly supported out of public funds. For a small fee (in the Peebles grammar-school it was only five shillings a quarter), a youth of the middle classes gets a good grounding in Latin and Greek, fitting him for the university ; and it is mainly, I believe, through this superior education, so easily attained, that so many of the youth of our northern region are inspired with the ambition which leads them upwards to professional life in their own country, or else sends them abroad in quest of the fortune hard to find at home. I observe, while writing these pages, the advertisement of an academy in England, where, besides sixty pounds by way of board, the fees for tuition amount to twenty-five. For this twenty-five pounds, a Scottish burgher of my young days could have

.

five sons carried through a complete classical course. The difference is overwhelmingly in favor of the Scotch grammar-school, as far as the money matter is concerned. And thus it will appear that the good education which has enabled me to address so much literature, of whatever value, to the public during the last forty-five years, never cost my parents so much as ten pounds.

"There was a bookseller in Peebles, a great fact. There had not always been one ; but some years before my entrance upon existence, a decent man named Alexander Elder had come to the town, and established himself as a dealer in intellectual wares. He was a very careful and sober man, and in the end, as was fitting, became rich in comparison with many of his neighbors. It seems a curious reminiscence of my first bookseller's shop, that, on entering it, one always got a peep of a cow, which quietly chewed her cud close behind the bookshelves, such being one of Sandy's means of providing for his family. Sandy was great in Shorter Catechisms, and what he called *spells*, and school Bibles and Testaments, and in James Lumsden's (of Glasgow) halfpenny colored pictures of the ' World Turned Upside Down,' the 'Battle of Trafalgar,' etc., and in penny chap-books of an extraordinary coarseness of language. He had stores, too, of school slates and *skeely*, of paper for copies, and of pens, or rather quills, for 'made' pens were never sold then, one of which he would hand us across his counter with a civil glance over the top of his spectacles, as if saying, 'Now, laddie, see and mak' a guid use o't.' But Sandy was enterprising and enlightened beyond the common range of booksellers in small country towns, and had added a circulating library to his ordinary business. My father, led by his strong intellectual tastes, had early become a supporter of this institution, and thus it came

about that by the time we were nine or ten years of age,
my brother and I had read a considerable number of the
classics of English literature, or heard our father read
them ; were familiar with the comicalities of 'Gulliver,'
' Don Quixote,' and ' Peregrine Pickle ; ' had dipped into
the poetry of Pope and Goldsmith, and indulged our romantic tendencies in books of travel and adventure, which
were to us scarcely less attractive than the works of pure
imagination. When lately attending the Wells of Hom-
burg, I had but one English book to amuse me, Pope's
translation of the ' Iliad,' and I felt it as towards myself an
affecting reminiscence, that exactly fifty years had elapsed
since I perused the copy from Elder's library, in a little
room looking out upon the High Street of Peebles, where
an English regiment was parading recruits raised for Wel-
lington's Peninsular campaign.

"There was certainly something considerably superior
to the common book-trader in my friend Alexander Elder,
for his catalogue included several books striking far above
the common taste, and somewhat costly withal. There
was, for example, a copy of a strange and curious book of
which Sir Walter Scott speaks on several occasions with
great interest, a metrical history of the clan Scott, written
about the time of the Revolution by one Walter Scott,
a retired old soldier of the Scottish legions of Gustavus
Adolphus, who describes himself unnecessarily as ' no
scholar,' for in its rhyme, metre, and entire frame of language it is truly wretched, while yet interesting on account
of the quaintness of its ideas and the information it con-
veys. Another of Sandy's book treasures — and the
money value of them makes the term appropriate — was
the ' Æneidos of Virgil,' translated into Scottish verse by
Gavin Douglas, Bishop of Dunkeld, well known as a most
interesting product of the literary mind of Scotland at the

beginning of the sixteenth century, and gratifying to our national vanity as prior to any translations of Virgil into English.

"In a fit of extraordinary enterprise, Sandy had taken into his library the successive volumes of the fourth edition of the 'Encyclopædia Britannica,' and had found nobody but my father in the slightest degree interested in them. My father made a stretch with his moderate means, and took the book off Sandy's hands. It was a cumbrous article in a small house ; so, after the first interest in its contents had subsided, it had been put into a chest (which it filled), and laid up in an attic beside the cotton wefts and the meal ark. Roaming about there one day, in that morning of intellectual curiosity, I lighted upon the stored book, and from that time for weeks all my spare time was spent beside the chest. It was a new world to me. I felt a profound thankfulness that such a convenient collection of human knowledge existed, and that here it was spread out like a well-plenished table before me. What the gift of a whole toy-shop would have been to most children, this book was to me. I plunged into it. I roamed through it like a bee. I hardly could be patient enough to read any one article, while so many others remained to be looked into. In that on Astronomy, the constitution of the material universe was all at once revealed to me. Henceforth I knew — what no other boy in the town then dreamed of — that there were infinite numbers of worlds besides our own, which was by comparison a very insignificant one. From the zoölogical articles, I gathered that the animals, familiar and otherwise, were all classified into a system through which some faint traces of a plan were discernible. Geography, of which not the slightest elements were then imparted at school, here came before me in numberless articles and maps, expanding my narrow village world to one embracing the uttermost ends of the earth. I pitied my companions who remained ignorant of what became to me familiar knowledge. Some articles were splendidly attractive to the imagination ; for example, that entitled Aerostation, which illustrated all that had been done in the way of aerial travelling from Mont-golfier downwards. Another paper interested me much, — that descriptive of the inquiries of Dr. Saussure regarding the constitution and movement of glaciers. The bio-graphical articles, introducing to me the great men who had laid up these stores of knowledge, or otherwise affected the destinies of their species, were devoured in rapid succession. What a year that was to me, not merely in intellectual enjoyment, but in mental formation! I believe it was my eleventh, for before I was twelve, misfortune had taken the book from us to help in satisfying creditors. It appears to me somewhat strange that, in a place so remote, so primitive, and containing so little wealth, at a time when the movement for the spread of knowledge had not yet been thought of, such an opportunity for the gratification of an inquiring young mind should have been presented. It was all primarily owing to the liberal spirit of enterprise which animated this cow-keeping country bookseller.

"The themes first presented to the young mind certainly sink into it the deepest. The sciences of which I obtained the first tracings through the " Encyclopædia," have all through life been endeared to me above the rest. The books of imagination which I first read from Elder's library have ever borne a preference in my heart, whatever may be the judgment of modern taste regarding them. It pains me to this day to hear severe remarks made upon Fielding and Sterne. I should feel myself to be a base ingrate if I could join in condemning

men who first gave me views of social life beyond my
natal village sphere, and who, by their powers of entertainment, lent such a charm to years during which material enjoyments were few.   These intellectual 'loves
of life's young day' sometimes led literary men in the
choice of themes for their own pens.   It was from such
a feeling regarding Smollett, that I was induced to make
an effort to set his life in a more respectful light before
the world than it had previously enjoyed, while assuredly
invited to other tasks in several respects more promising.
It strikes me that gratitude to an author, also to a
teacher, to any one who has benefited us intellectually,
is as desirable a form of the feeling as any.   I raise
statues in my heart to the fictionists above named, and
to many others who nowhere have statues of bronze or
marble, and I likewise deem it not unfitting that there
should be flower-crowned miniatures in my bosom of
James Sloan and Sandy Elder."

I can unite in these commendations.   With Elder's
field of literature laid open to us, Robert and I read at
a great rate, going right through the catalogue of books
without much regard to methodized study.   In fact, we
had to take what we could get and be thankful.   Permitted to have only one volume at a time, we made up
for short allowance by reading as quickly as possible, and,
to save time, often read together from the same book,
one having the privilege of turning over the leaves.   Desultory as was this course of reading, it undoubtedly wid-
ened the sphere of our ideas ; and it would be ungrateful
not to acknowledge that some of my own success, and
not a few of the higher pleasures experienced in life, are
primarily due to that library in the little old burgh.
   Enough — perhaps more than enough — has been given

of these reminiscences of boyish days, and something may now be said of the circumstances which, in a strangely unexpected manner, sent my brother and myself adrift into the world that lay beyond our hitherto limited horizon.

The calm tenor of my father's affairs was at length abruptly ruffled. The introduction of the power-loom and other mechanical appliances had already begun to revolutionize the cotton trade. Down and down sank hand-loom weaving, till it was threatened with extinction, and ultimately the trade was followed only as a desperate necessity. Happy were those who gave it up in time, and betook themselves to something else. Moved by the declining aspect of his commission business, my father bethought himself of commencing as a draper. For this purpose, he alienated the small property in which my brother and I were born, and removed to a central part of the town. Here he began his new line of business, for which, excepting his obliging manners, he had no particular qualification. As, however, there was then little of that eager striving which is now conspicuous everywhere, matters would have gone on pretty well, but for one untoward circumstance.

As an out-of-the-way country town, Peebles had been selected by government as a place suitable for the residence of prisoners of war on parole, shortly after the recommencement of hostilities in 1803. Not more, however, than twenty or thirty of these exiles arrived at this early period. They were mostly Dutch and Walloons, with afterwards a few Danes — unfortunate mariners seized on the coast of the Netherlands, and sent to spend their lives in an inland Scottish town. These men did not repine. They nearly all betook themselves to learn some handicraft, to eke out their scanty allowance. At leisure hours they might be seen fishing, in long leather boots, as if glad to procure a few trouts and eels, and at the same time satisfy the desire to dabble in the water. In 1810, a large accession was made to this body of prisoners of war, by the arrival of upwards of a hundred officers of an entirely different quality. They consisted of French, Poles, and Italians, in a variety of strange, tarnished uniforms, fresh from the seat of war in the Peninsula. These unfortunate gentlemen, a few of them very young, were accommodated with lodgings in the town, and being scarcely under any sort of restriction, they gradually became domesticated in several families. For their own amusement, as well as to repay acts of hospitality, — perhaps, also, to make friends among the tradespeople, — they set up a private theatre in an old ballroom, in which they enlivened the town by performing gratuitously some of the plays of Corneille and Molière. To these performances I was freely admitted, on my father's account; and so reaped the double advantage of having my ear accustomed to the French language, and of being made acquainted with some of the French dramatists. Nor did I dislike the French on other accounts. The kitchen of their mess offered a market for my rabbits, which I bred as an article of commerce to aid in purchasing books.

My mother, even while lending her dresses and caps to enable performers to represent female characters, never liked the intimacy which had been formed between the French officers and my father. Against his giving them credit, she constantly remonstrated in vain. It was a tempting but perilous trade. For a time they paid wonderfully well. A number of them, when captured in Spain, had secreted sums of money about their persons, and gold ducats and sequins, as I remember, were for a

period as common as guineas in Peebles; though that,
perhaps, is not saying very much. These exiles likewise
occasionally received remittances from France; for although the war was going on very hotly, there was still,
as a matter of public convenience, some kind of postal intercourse maintained with the French coast. With such
allurements, my father confidingly gave extensive credit
to these strangers, men who, by their position, were not
amenable to the civil law, and whose obligations, accordingly, were altogether debts of honor. The consequence
was what might have been anticipated. An order suddenly arrived from the government, commanding the
whole of the prisoners to quit Peebles, and march chiefly
to Sanquhar in Dumfriesshire, the cause of the movement being the prospective arrival of a militia regiment.
The intelligence came one Sunday afternoon. What a
gloom prevailed at several firesides that fatal evening !

On their departure, the French prisoners made many
fervid promises that, should they ever return to their own
country, they would have pleasure in discharging their
debts. They all got home at the peace in 1814, but not
one of them ever paid a farthing. A list of their names,
debts, and official position in the army of Napoleon, remains as a curiosity in my possession. It is not unlikely
that a number of these returned exiles found a grave on
the field of Waterloo. Whatever became of them, there
was soon a crisis in my father's affairs. The pressure
might have been got over, for with patience there were
means to satisfy all demands ; but the possibility of recti-
fying affairs was defeated by weakly taking the advice of
an interested party, a relative of my mother, who recommended a sequestration. The result was that the sage
adviser, as trustee, managed everything so adroitly for
his own benefit, that the creditors received but a small

dividend, and the family lost almost everything. It is hateful to refer to this piece of folly and villainy, because it reminds me of poignant distresses ; but it is necessary to give it some degree of prominence, for it forms the pivot on which the present narrative turns.

By various shifts, the family continued to struggle on for a year or two in Peebles after this catastrophe. The penury which was endured was less painful than the acute sense of social degradation. My mother looked for some sympathy and assistance from her brother, and also from other relatives at a distance, but without avail. Feeling, with a too keen susceptibility, that he had lost caste, my father never quite held up his head after this event ; yet, deplored at the time, it really proved a fortunate circumstance. Like a wholesome though unpleasant storm in a stagnating atmosphere, it cleared the way for a new and better order of things. A seemingly great misfortune ultimately proved to be no misfortune at all, in fact, a blessing, for which my brother and I, as well as other members of the family, could not be sufficiently thankful.

The wise resolution was adopted of quitting Peebles. My mother, animated by keen anxiety and foresight, was particularly solicitous to remove, with a view to procure means of advancement for her sons. Accordingly, impelled alike by necessity and inclination, the family removed to Edinburgh, Robert being alone left to pursue his education for a short time longer. Crowded into the *Fly*, then the only engine of public conveyance to the Scottish capital, we crossed the Kingside-Edge, as a high ridge of land is called, on a bleak day in December, 1813, my mother with an infant daughter on her knee, and a heart full of mingled hopes and fears of the future. It was a five hours' journey, of which one entire hour was spent at Venturefair to rest the horses. Here the party were hospitably entertained with warm kail by Jenny Wilson, who kept the small inn along with her brother William. So reinvigorated, we drove on in somewhat better spirits, entering Edinburgh by the Causewayside ; my mother with but a few shillings in her pocket — there was not a halfpenny in mine.

CHAPTER III.

FAMILIES falling by misfortune into straitened circumstances, of course lose many old friends and acquaintances, at least as far as familiar personal intercourse is concerned. This loss, though often the subject of sorrowful and angry remark, is not an unmitigated evil. Sympathy is doubtless due throughout all perplexing social distinctions ; gracious are the acts of a true friend ; kindness to the unfortunate will ever command approbation ; but let us not forget that it is better for personal intimacies to suffer some modification, than for the impoverished to lose self-respect and become dependent on a system of habitual condescension. It seems hard to take this view of the matter, but I fear that on no other basis can the indigent aspire to be the associates of the affluent. Could matters be seen rightly, they would appear to be as well ordered in this as in other things which concern our welfare.

Happily, the defection, real or apparent, of old friends is not uncompensated. Sinking into a lower sphere, a new and hitherto undiscovered region is disclosed. A higher class, as we are apt to feel, has cruelly turned its back on us ; but we are received with open arms by a very good and agreeable sort of people, in whose moderate incomes, and, it may be, misfortunes and struggles, we feel the pleasures of fellowship. The Vicar of Wakefield, it will be recollected, did not find the jail such a bad thing after all.

My parents, on settling in Edinburgh, may be presumed to have found consolations of this nature. According to immemorial usage, families with limited means from the southern counties of Scotland, who seek a home in the capital, sagaciously pitch on one of the second-rate streets in the southern suburbs. There, sprinkled about in common stairs, they form a kind of colony, possessing a community of south-country recollections and gossip.

Following the established rule, our first home was a floor entering from a common stair in West Nicolson Street. Beneath us, level with the ground, resided a poor widow, who drew a scanty living from a small hucksery concern. Immediately above us dwelt the widow of a Roxburghshire clergyman, a motherly person, with two grown-up daughters. Over this respectable family, and highest of all, was a tailor, who, working in the window-sole of his apartment, had the reputation of doing things cheaply. On a level with us, next tenement, but entering by a different stair, was a family of some distinction, consisting of the two ladies, Miss Betty and Miss Ailie Hay, already spoken of by my brother. The kitchen fire-places of both dwellings being back to back, with a thin and imperfect wall between, the servant-girls of the two families, both exiles from Tweedside, were able to carry on comforting conversations by removing a brick at pleasure in the chimney; through which irregular channel much varied intelligence from Peeblesshire was interchanged between the two families. Here we lived till Whitsunday, 1814, when we removed to a floor of a like quality in Hamilton's Entry, Bristo Street, the back windows of the house overlooking the small court in which is situated a

5

little old building, with a tiled roof, that had been Walter Scott's first school in Edinburgh.

If anything, the families hereabout were more hard-up, and, to be plain, we were more hard-up too. Our dwelling was on the second floor of the stair, and on the flat immediately beneath resided Ebenezer Picken, a scholarly gentleman in reduced circumstances, who, after trying various shifts to secure a living for himself and family, now professed to teach languages, and endeavored to sell by subscription one or two volumes of poems, which, I fear, did not do much for him. He died in 1816. His son, Andrew, who was also a poetic genius, and about my own age, became affected with the mania concerning Poyais, and emigrated with a number of others to that pestilential marsh, where most of the settlers died shortly after landing, Andrew kindly acting as chaplain, with a shirt for surplice, and reading the funeral service. From a fellow-feeling in circumstances, we formed an intimacy with our neighbors the Pickens, while residing in the same tenement, and the friendship was extended over a series of years, until the remaining members of the family went to America.

As regards ways and means. On coming to Edinburgh, my father had resumed his commission business from Glasgow cotton-manufacturers, but this trade had long been declining, and was but a meagre dependence. To aggravate his difficulties, he was not qualified by knowledge of the world to deal with the class of workmen to whom he furnished employment. Some of them were decent enough old sinewy men, sufficiently trustworthy; but others, accustomed to go on the tramp, used artifices that baffled his ingenuity. Carrying on their handicraft in obscure recesses in Fountainbridge, St. Ann's Yards, the Back of the Canongate, or Abbey Hill, it was some-

times as difficult to trace them out as to get any right clew
to their manœuvres. It was by no means unusual to find
that the materials intrusted to them were dishonestly
pawned, and that sums of money advanced for half-done
work on piteous appeals of distress were irrecoverable.
In short, my father was much too soft for this kind of
business ; and the result was what might have been expected. With resources on the verge of exhaustion, there
ensued privations against which it required no small degree of composure to bear up. The old German flute,
preserved as a precious relic throughout all the vicissi-
tudes of the family, was sometimes resorted to as a solace,
although the favorite airs, such as " Corn Rigs," did not
sound half so sweetly, it was thought, in the dingy atmosphere of Hamilton's Entry, as they had done along the
Eddleston Water.

The Dark Ages, as we have since jestingly called them,
had begun, and for a number of successive years an acquaintance was contracted with families and individuals,
who, if not experiencing a similar depression, occupied an
unpretending position in society. I can recollect some of
them, and also the shifty scenes to which they were less
or more impelled, by the necessities of their situation.
Widows of decayed tradesmen, who were moving heaven
and earth to get their sons into hospitals, and their daughters taught to be governesses. Teachers in the decline
of life, like poor Picken, endeavoring to draw a subsistence from the fees of most-difficult-to-be-procured pupils.
Licensed preachers to whom fate had not assigned a kirk,
and who, after years of pining, now made a livelihood by
preparing young men for university degrees. Genteel unmarried women, left destitute by improvident fathers, who
contrived to maintain themselves by coloring maps, or by
sewing fine needle-work for the Repository, — a benevolent

and useful institution, to which be all praise. Why continue the catalogue ?

There was some use in knowing, and being known to,
these kinds of people. I speak not of the value to myself,
as having an opportunity of studying some of the humbler
and more characteristic phases of society. To my father
and mother, these persons, with their varied experience,
could furnish hints as to how petty difficulties incidental
to their condition might be overcome. One or two things
they seem to have made their special study. They knew
the proper methods of applying for situations in public
offices, and what expedients could be attempted to elude
the payment of rates and taxes. For the most part, they
entertained a high respect for, and duly stood in awe of,
magistrates, ministers, and great men generally ; for it
was only through such distinguished authorities that certificates of character and help in various ways could be
obtained in cases of emergency. Far be it from me to
impute dishonesty to these ingeniously struggling and
scheming classes. On the whole, in the darkest of their
days, so far as I knew, they maintained a wonderful de-
termination to keep square with the world. It must be
admitted, however, that the classes to which I allude too
frequently participated in loose notions concerning taxes.
Demands of this nature seemed to be little better than
asking money for nothing. Rates and taxes might be
right in the abstract ; that they did not question. But the
collector who came periodically to your door with a portentous pocket-book, and made point-blank demands for
sums of money, — such as fifteen shillings and ninepence
halfpenny, or one pound eleven and threepence, — which
it was exceedingly inconvenient to pay, was clearly a nui-
sance ; and with no stretch of conscience, he might be
coaxed, wheedled, put off, and told to call again as long as
it was safe to do so.

In the midst of the straits to which these remarks refer, my father, through congeniality of taste, made the acquaintance of several persons possessed of musical and poetical acquirements. One of these was Mr. John Hamilton, author of the song, " Up in the Morning Early," who, drawing to the conclusion of his days, lived in a stair at the south end of Lothian Street, and in good weather might be seen creeping feebly along the walks in the Meadows, deriving pleasure from the sunshine, to which he was soon to bid adieu. Another was Mr. Samuel Clarke, noted for his musical genius, who acted as organist of the Episcopal Chapel in the Cowgate, the services of which place of public worship were at that time conducted by the Rev. Archibald Alison, author of the " Essay on Taste," and " Sermons on the Seasons," and whose son was the late Sir Archibald Alison, author of the " History of Europe." As music was my father's overwhelming passion, his introduction to the church organ under the auspices of Clarke was a matter of extreme exultation. Entranced with the performances of the organ and choir, he became a frequent attender on the ministrations of Mr. Alison, whose persuasive piety, refined sentiments, and elegant diction, possessed, as is well known, an indescribable charm.

Charged more especially with family cares, my mother had other considerations than church music. What was to be done with me, was a primary concern. I was in my fourteenth year. Further schooling was out of the question. Robert might go on with his education as long as seemed expedient, but it was time I should get to work. What would I be? My tastes lay in the direction of books ; any department would do. A friend, put on the scent, reported that on inquiry of a leading member of the profession, bookselling was a poor business ; at best, it was very precarious, and could not be recommended. Not discouraged, I still thought my vocation lay towards literature in some shape or other.

Since our arrival in town, I had read all that could be read for nothing at the booksellers' windows, and at the stalls which were stuck about the College and High School Wynds. I had also become a great frequenter of the evening book-auctions. The principal were Carfrae's in Drummond Street, and that of Peter Cairns in the Agency Office, opposite the University. At present, book-auctions are only during the day ; then, they took place in the evening, and were a favorite resort. The sales were indicated by a lantern, with panes of white calico, at the door, on which was inscribed " Auction of Books." My attendance, punctual on the hanging out of the lantern, was a new and delightful recreation. The facetiæ of the auctioneers, their observations on books and authors, and the competitions in the biddings, were all interesting to a lad fresh from the country. Carfrae's was the more genteel and dignified. Cairns' was the more amusing of these lounges, wherefore it suited best for those who went for fun, and not for buying, on which account it chiefly secured my patronage.

Peter was a dry humorist, somewhat saturnine from business misadventures. Professedly, he was a bookseller in South College Street, and exhibited over his door a huge sham copy of Virgil by way of sign. His chief trade, however, was the auctioning of books and stationery at the Agency Office, a place with a strong smell of new furniture, amidst which it was necessary to pass before arriving at the saloon in the rear where the auctions were habitually held. Warm, well lighted, and comfortably fitted up with seats within a railed inclosure environing the books to be disposed of, this place of evening resort was as good as a reading-room ; indeed, rather better,

for there was a constant fund of amusement in Peter's
caustic jocularities, as when he begged to remind his audience that this was a place for selling, not for reading
books, sarcasms which always provoked a round of ironical applause. His favorite author was Goldsmith, an
edition of whose works he had published, which pretty
frequently figured in his catalogue. On coming to these
works, he always referred to them with profound respect ;
as, for example, "The next in the catalogue, gentlemen,
is the works of Oliver *Gooldsmith,* the greatest writer
that ever lived, except Shakespeare ; what do you say for
it ? I 'll put it up at ten shillings." Some one would
perhaps audaciously bid twopence, which threw him into
a rage, and he would indignantly call out, "Tippence,
man ; keep that for the *brode,*" meaning the plate at the
church-door. If the same person dared to repeat the in-
sult with regard to some other work, Peter would say,
"Dear me, has that poor man not yet got rid of his tippence ?" which turned the laugh, and effectually silenced
him all the rest of the evening. Peter's temper was apt
to get ruffled when biddings temporarily ceased. He
then declared that he might as well try to auction books
in the poor-house. On such occasions, driven to despera-
tion, he would try the audience with a bunch of quills, a
dozen black-lead pencils, or a "quare " of Bath-post, venge-
fully knocking which down at the price bidden for them,
he would shout to "Wully," the clerk, to look after the
money. Never minding Peter's querulous observations
further than to join in the general laugh, I, like a number
of other penniless youths, got some good snatches of reading at the auctions in the Agency Office. I there saw and
handled books which I had never before heard of, and in
this manner obtained a kind of notion of bibliography.
My brother, who, like myself, became a frequenter of the

Agency Office, relished Peter highly, and has touched him off in one of his essays.

Inquiries for the situation of apprentice in a bookseller's shop not proving successful, and time wearing on, I relinquished my preconceived fancies, and stated that I should be glad to be put to any line of business whatever. No sooner had this been concluded on than an opening seemed to cast up in a grocer's shop situated in the Tolbooth Wynd, Leith. Unfortunately, Leith was two miles distant, but it was announced that the grocer munificently imparted board and lodging to his apprentices, and that, in present circumstances, was of some importance. It was resolved I should look after the place. Accordingly, I one day went off to Leith, trudging down from Edinburgh towards the Tolbooth Wynd, not greatly elated with the prospect before me, but determined not to be nice in accepting terms. A friend of the family resident in Leith, was to introduce me.

On reaching the spot with him, nearly opposite the public fountain, I paused a moment outside to reconnoitre the grocer's premises, before proceeding. The windows exhibited quantities of raw sugar in different varieties of brownness, hovering over which were swarms of flies in a state of frantic enjoyment. Sticks of black liquorice leaned coaxingly on the second row of panes, flanked by tall glass jars of sweeties and peppermint drops ; behind these outward attractions, there were observable yellow-painted barrels of whiskey, rows of bottles of porter, piles of cheeses of varied complexions, firkins of salt butter, and boxes of soap. At the counter were a number of women and children buying articles, such as quarter-ounces of tea and ounces of sugar ; and the floor was battered with dirt and *débris*.

I was not much pleased with the look of the place, but

I had no choice. Entering, somewhat timidly, with my conductor, I was described as the boy who had been recommended as an apprentice, and was ushered into the back room to be examined as to my capabilities. It was immediately seen that I was physically incompetent to fill the situation. The chief qualification in demand was muscular vigor. The boy wanted would have to draw a truck loaded with several hundredweights of goods, to be delivered to customers, it might be miles distant. Instead of an apprentice, it was in reality a horse that might have been advertised for, or at the least an able-bodied porter. I was at once pronounced to be unfit for this enviable post ; a much too delicately made youth, a day's work with the barrow or the bottle-basket would finish me. I had better abandon the idea of being a grocer. With these remarks pronounced for doom, I retired, not a little downcast at the unfortunate issue of the expedition, and sorrowfully returned up the Walk to Edinburgh.

CHAPTER IV.

HOW little are we able to penetrate the future! The journey to Leith was not thrown away. In returning homewards, I had occasion to pass the shop of Mr. John Sutherland, bookseller, Calton Street, an establishment opposite the Black Bull Hotel, the starting-place of the mail-coaches for London. In the window was the announcement, "An Apprentice Wanted." Here was the right thing at last. I did not lose time in communicating this piece of intelligence.

Having in the first place narrated the failure of the Leith affair, I proceeded to describe the discovery I had made in Calton Street. There was forthwith a family cogitation on the subject, and it was resolved that next day I should accompany my mother on a tour of investigation into the nature of the place. Next morning, accordingly, after being brushed up for the occasion, I set out for Sutherland's. Our reception was gratifyingly polite. The bookseller expressed himself satisfied with my appearance and the extent of my education. He said that in all respects I should be perfectly qualified for the situation. My principal duties for one or two years would be very easy. I would only have to light the fire, take off and put on the shutters, clean and prepare the oil lamps, sweep and dust the shop, and go all the errands. When I had nothing else to do, I was to stand behind the counter, and help in any way that was wanted; and talking of that, it would be quite contrary to rule for me ever to sit down, or to put off time reading.

In laying down the law, Sutherland admitted that at first the duties, though no way burdensome, might not perhaps be very pleasant, but the routine was sanctioned by immemorial usage. Constable and all the other great booksellers had begun in this way. Every one who aspired to take a front rank in the profession must begin by being a junior apprentice. The period of service was five years at four shillings a week; not high pay, to be sure, but it was according to universal rule, from which he could see no departure.

My mother, who conducted the negotiation, found no fault with the proposed duties and terms; still she had her misgivings, and ventured to remark that her son was surely wrong in wishing to follow the business. " We may manage," she said, " to get him through his apprenticeship, but I have serious fears of what is to follow. We cannot set him up in business, and how " (looking around) " can he ever be able to get a stock of books like that ? "

The bookseller endeavored to allay her apprehensions, and his remarks are worth repeating : " There is no fear of any one getting forward in the world, if he be only steady, obliging, attentive to his duties, and exercise a reasonable degree of patience. I can assure you, when I was the age of your son, I had as poor prospects as any one ; yet I have so far got on tolerably well. In the outset of life it is needless to look too far in advance. We must just do the best we can in the mean time, and hope that all will turn out rightly in the end." These sensible observations left nothing further to be said. The bargain was struck. I was to come next Monday morning to be initiated by an elder apprentice. And so, on the 8th of May, 1814, I was launched into the business world.

About a year and a half after this event, the family quitted Edinburgh. My father was appointed commercial manager of a salt manufactory, called Joppa Pans, a smoky, odorous place, consisting of a group of sooty buildings, situated on the sea-shore half-way between Portobello and Musselburgh ; and thither, to a small dwelling amidst the steaming salt-pans, they all removed except myself. Robert, who had now come from Peebles, and been some time at an academy in Edinburgh, accompanied them, the arrangement being that he should walk to and from town daily. I was left to pursue my business, being for this purpose consigned to a lodging that may merit some notice.

Until this disruption, I had no occasion to rely on myself. Now matters were changed. I was to have an opportunity of learning practically how far my weekly earnings would go in defraying the cost of board and lodging. In short, at little above fourteen years of age, I was thrown on my own resources. From necessity, not less than from choice, I resolved at all hazards to make the weekly four shillings serve for everything. I cannot remember entertaining the slightest despondency on the subject. As with other lads of my age, I had something to interest me in the circumstances attending the close of the war, and the excitement which followed on various matters of public concern.

As favorable for carrying out my aims at an independent style of living, I had the good fortune to be installed in the dwelling of a remarkably precise and honest widow, a Peebles woman, who, with two grown-up sons, occupied the top story of a building in the West Port. My landlady had the reputation of being excessively parsimonious, but as her honesty was of importance to one in my position, and as she consented to let me have a bed, cook for me, and allow me to sit by her fireside, — the fire, by the way, not being much to speak of, — for the reasonable charge of eighteen pence a week, I was thought to be lucky in finding her disposed to receive me within her establishment. To her dwelling, therefore, I repaired with my all, consisting of a few articles of clothing and two or three books, including a pocket Bible, — the whole contained in a small blue-painted box, which I carried on my shoulder along the Grassmarket.

This abode, the uppermost floor in Boak's Land, was more elevated than airy. The back of the tall edifice overhung a tannery and a wild confusion of mean inclosures, with an outlook beyond to the castle, perched on its dark, precipitous rock. The thoroughfare in front was then, as it is still, one of the most crowded and wretched in the city. The apartment assigned to me was a bed-closet, with a narrow window fronting the street. Yet this den was not all my own. For a time, it was shared with a student of divinity, a youth of my own age from the hills of Tweeddale ; and afterwards with my brother Robert, when it was found inexpedient for him to live in the country, and go to and from town daily.

Being all of us from Peeblesshire, there was much to speak of in common, though with no great cordiality of intercourse. In the evenings, when mason and carpenter lads dropped in, the conversation turned chiefly on sermons. Each visitor brought with him experiences as to how texts had been handled on the preceding Sunday ; on which there ensued discussions singularly characteristic of a well-known phase in the Scotch mind.

" Weel, Tammie," inquired the widow one evening of

Tammie Tod, a journeyman mason lately arrived from the country, " what was the doctor on last Sabbath afternoon ? "

" He was on the Song," — meaning the Song of Solomon.

" Ah, the Song ! that would be grand. He's a wonderfu' man the doctor ; and what was his text ? "

" It was a real fine text," said Tammie, " the deepest ever I heard : ' For my head is filled with dew, and my locks with the drops of the night ; ' fifth chapter, second verse, the second clause of the verse."

" I ken that text weel," responded the widow. " I heard a capital discourse on it thirty years syne ; but how did the doctor lay it out ? "

" He divided it into five heads, ending with an application, which it would be weel for us a' to tak' to heart."

And so Tammie, who had a proficiency in dissecting and criticising sermons, proceeded to describe with logical precision the manner in which his minister had handled the very intricate subject ; his definitions being listened to and commented on with extraordinary relish.

Let no one hastily conclude that there was anything to ridicule in these searching, though perhaps too speculative and familiar disquisitions ; for apart from any religious consideration, they bore evidence of that spirit of inquiry and love of reasoning on momentous topics which may be said to have made Scotland what it is. I may not have been the better, but was by no means the worse, for hearing Tammie Tod's sermon experiences in that little upper floor in the West Port, and have often compared what there came under my observation with the unideaed sotting and want of all mental culture which unhappily mark certain departments of the population in different parts of the United Kingdom.

On market-days, my landlady was usually visited about dinner-time by some horny-fisted old acquaintance from about Leithen or Gala Water, with a shepherd's plaid around his shoulders ; and who, after being treated to a share of the bannocks and kail, would finish off with a blast on the widow's tobacco-pipe ; for, with all her saving habits, our worthy hostess indulged — moderately, I must say — in this luxury. The conversation of these worthies ran still on controversial divinity. They talked of the " Hind Let Loose," Boston's " Marrow," the " Crook in the Lot," and the " Fourfold State," — standard topics among the class to which they belonged ; and if I did not quite apprehend or was not improved by the discussions, they at least afforded an amusing study of character.

The charge made for my accommodation in these quarters left some scope for financiering as regards the remaining part of my wages. It was a keen struggle, but, like Franklin, whose autobiography I had read with avidity, I faced it with all proper resolution. My contrivances to make both ends meet were not without a degree of drollery. As a final achievement in the art of cheap living, I was able to make an outlay of a shilling and ninepence suffice for the week. Below that I could not well go. Reaching this point, I had ninepence over for miscellaneous demands, chiefly in the department of shoes, which constituted an awkwardly heavy item. On no occasion did I look to parents for the slightest pecuniary subsidy.

Was there none, all this time, to lend a helping-hand to the struggling bookseller's apprentice ? I did not put any one to the test. My mother had some relations in town moving in respectable circles ; but they were connected with the worthless personage whose conduct had insured my father's ruin ; and, passing over any unpleas-

ant recollections on this score, I felt disinclined to court
their intimacy. Admitting that I may in this respect have
acted with unreasonable shyness, I am inclined to think
that the policy of keeping aloof was the most advantageous in the end. Isolation was equivalent to independence of thought and action. Contact with the relatives I
speak of would have been subjection.

High principle, however, hardly entered into my calculations. Pursuing my course from a resolute feeling of
self-reliance, I just went on without troubling myself about
anybody, trusting that things somehow would come right
in the long-run. I should say from my own observation
that young persons often chafe unnecessarily at being
neglected by those whom they imagine should take notice
of them. On the contrary, as a general rule, they ought
to be thankful for being let alone, with a clear stage
whereon they can act their part, alike unencumbered with
advice or disheartened by adverse criticism. To be always pining to be noticed, brought forward, taken by the
hand, and done for, is anything but wise or manly. There
are, doubtless, instances where the deserving are entitled
to such assistance as can be safely or conveniently extended towards them. But in too many cases the visionary expectation of aid paralyzes exertion, and consumes
valuable time that might very properly be devoted to individual effort. At any rate, I do not doubt that I should
have suffered injury at this critical period, by getting entangled with fine people, invited to fine houses, and led to
mix in fine evening parties. Proceedings of that seductive kind would have been distinctly at variance with
my condition. What was I but one of a thousand name-
less lads, whom in passing no one knew or cared for?
Shrouded by insignificance, I could fortunately, like others in a similar situation, work my way on in silence and

obscurity, without any provocation to false shame, which almost more than anything else is the stumbling-block of youth. The very circumstance of my having come from the country, and of being little known to young men of my own standing, was a point in my favor.

It nevertheless, I own, required some fortitude to bear up against the hardships incidental to my situation as a junior apprentice, literally the slave of the lamp, and the drudge of the establishment. Though not beaten and dragooned as I had been at school, it was my destiny to experience no very gentle treatment. My employer, a stern disciplinarian, took the work out of his apprentices. He seemed to have no regard for the number of miles he caused them to walk in a day in the way of business. In addition to his trade as a bookseller, he kept a circulating library, and also acted as an agent for the State Lottery. Independently, therefore, of a multitude of errands with parcels of books and stationery, I was charged with the delivery of vast quantities of circular letters eulogizing the successive lotteries, which, in reason, ought to have been despatched through the post-office. Frequently I was sent on my travels with as many as three hundred letters, sorted and tied in bundles in the manner of a postman ; and as my circuit took me up dozens of long stairs over miles of thoroughfares, I had an opportunity of acquiring a knowledge of the town and the names of its inhabitants.

In all this I was mercilessly overtasked, and can never cease to think so. But there was something likewise to be thankful for. Sutherland enforced habits of punctuality and order, which happily stuck to me through life, along with a due appreciation of such morsels of time as can be spared from ordinary pursuits. My apprenticeship, like that of many others, was my drill, harsh, no doubt, but it is difficult to see how, without some kind of vigorous

6

training, youth is to grow into manhood with a proper conception of a number of commonplace but important obligations.   Certainly, old injunctions say as much.

My heaviest grievance was the delivery of those odious
piles of lottery circulars, a species of labor that in no shape
advanced my professional knowledge.   To what hand,
however, could I turn to rid myself of this slavery?   The
choice lay between suffering and ruin.   It was my safest
course to submit.   Over the doorway of an old house in
the West Bow, which I passed several times daily, was
the inscription carved in stone —

" HE THAT THOLES OVERCOMES."

I made up my mind to *thole*, — a pithy old Scottish word
signifying to bear with patience ; the whole inscription
reminding us of a sentiment in Virgil : "Whatever may
happen, every kind of fortune is to be overcome by bearing it."[1]

After all, the drudgery I had in connection with the
lotteries is not utterly to be condemned.   It afforded an
amusing insight into the weakness of human nature.   I
could scarcely have learned what I did by sitting with
composure in the lap of ease and luxury.   As regards the
state lottery, it is interesting for me to remember that I
was once a humble minister in that gigantic national concern.   And what a queer, struggling, whimsical set of
people came under notice !   Some would buy only odd
numbers of five figures, such as 17,359 ; some eagerly
sought for numbers which they had dreamt of being prizes,
and would have no other ; some brought children to select
a number from the quantity offered, — a degree of weakness which was outdone by those who superstitiously
brought the seventh son of a seventh son to make the

[1] " Quidquid erit, superanda omnis fortuna ferendo est."— *Æneid*, v.

selection for them ; some, more whimsical still, would only
purchase at the last moment what everybody else had rejected.   Few were so extravagant as to buy whole tickets,
or even halves, quarters, or eighths.   The great majority '
contented themselves with a sixteenth, the price of which
was usually about a guinea and a half; and as the for-'
tunate holder of the sixteenth of a twenty-thousand-pound
prize would realize above twelve hundred pounds, the
temptation to this species of gambling was enormous.

It would be an error to imagine that the dispersion of
those myriads of lottery circulars in the obscurest quarters
had no practical efficacy.   The chief buyers of sixteenths
were persons connected with the markets, hackney-coach-
men, waiters at hotels, female housekeepers, small tradesmen, and those of limited means generally, who hoped to
become rich by a happy turn of the wheel.   Inmates of
the Sanctuary of Holyrood and the debtors' prisons were
numbered among the steady customers of the state lottery.
Both, therefore, as a messenger with lottery intelligence,
and as an errand-boy with parcels of books, I had frequent
occasion to visit and become less or more acquainted with
these places.

The Sanctuary, which embraced a cluster of decayed
buildings in front and on both sides of Holyrood Palace,
was at that time more resorted to by refugee debtors than
it is in this improved age.   It was seldom without distinguished characters from England ; some of them gaunt,
oldish gentlemen, seemingly broken-down men of fashion,
wearing big gold spectacles, who now drew out existence
here in defiance of creditors.   To this august class of persons, who stood in need of supplies of books from the
circulating library, I paid frequent visits ; and conscious,
perhaps, that they gave me some extra trouble, they were
so considerate as to present me with an occasional sixpence, which I could not politely refuse.

Customers in the Canongate jail, and in the Old Tolbooth, renowned as the "Heart of Mid-Lothian," were less munificent, but considerably more hearty in their intercourse. The greater number of them were third-rate shopkeepers, who, after struggling for years against debts, rents, and taxes, had finally succumbed to the sheriff-officer, and been drifted to a safe anchorage, which they did not seem to think particularly unpleasant. The law had done its worst upon them, and for a time they were at rest.

The chief of these prisons, the Old Tolbooth, was a tall black building in the High Street, noted in the national annals : That tolbooth on the lofty pinnacle of which was ignominiously stuck the head of the gallant Marquis of Montrose, in 1650, and whence, after bleaching for ten years, it was taken down and replaced by the head of the Marquis of Argyll : that Tolbooth which Byron has referred to with unjustifiable bitterness in his "English Bards and Scotch Reviewers," —

> " Arthur's steep summit nodded to its base,
> The surly Tolbooth scarcely kept her place.
> The Tolbooth felt — for marble sometimes can,
> On such occasions, feel as much as man —
> The Tolbooth felt defrauded of her charms,
> If Jeffrey died except within her arms."

After undergoing various mutations, this gloomy structure now served the double purpose of a jail for debtors and criminals. The two departments were quite distinct, the apartments for criminals being in the east end, and those for debtors being in the west. But all entered by the same door, that portal where the rioters of the Porteous Mob thundered in 1736. This doorway, situated at the foot of the southeastern turret, was opened by a turnkey who was seated outside, or in a small adjoining vault on the ground-floor of the building. Level with it, facing the north, and occupying the remainder of the street-floor, was the office of the Town-guard, who were ready at hand in case of any emergency. Having gained an access by the outer portal of the Tolbooth, you ascended a flight of about twenty steps to an inner door, which was opened on the ringing of a bell by the outer turnkey. You were now in the Hall, a spacious apartment, with a sanded stone floor, and seats along the sides. It was well lighted by a large stanchioned window facing the south. Fixed on the wall nearly opposite the doorway, there was a black board, on which was painted the following admonitory inscription, that is said to have been originally and specially designed for the King's Bench Prison: —

> " A prison is a house of care,
>   A place where none can thrive ;
>   A touchstone true to try a friend,
>   A grave for men alive : —
>   Sometimes a house of right,
>   Sometimes a house of wrong,
>   Sometimes a place for jades and thieves,
>   And honest men among."

The Hall was a common vestibule, whence an entrance was gained to the two departments. While the criminals were confined to their rooms in the East End, the prisoners under civil process, who were lodged in the West End, moved about at pleasure during the day from the Hall to the several apartments on two upper stories ; and accordingly, for them there was almost the freedom of a lodging-house. The place of public execution was the flat roof of a low building attached to the western gable, and, to reach it, convicts were conducted across the Hall.

My knowledge of this strange old jail needs a word of explanation. Among the debtors whom I visited in the

way of business, there was one, a young man, who had
been previously known to our family. Having failed in
business under circumstances which led to an unusually
long imprisonment, I frequently saw him, and was able to
learn numerous particulars concerning the West-Enders
and their ways of living, which would otherwise have been
beyond my reach. As the Tolbooth was removed in 1817,
it was my fortune to be its visitor during the last three
years of its existence, and to become familiarized with a
condition of things of which there is now no parallel. My
experiences of Tolbooth life were in the days of free-and-
easy prison arrangements. As yet, neither county prison
boards nor prison inspectors had been heard of. The
magistrates and council undertook the responsibility of
cost and management, also appointed the officials, the
chief of whom, honored with the designation of captain,
was ordinarily some old citizen who stood well with the
corporation. There was a simplicity about the whole system which is now difficult to be realized by any description. So far as the debtors were concerned, the prison
was little else than a union of lodging-house and tavern,
under lock and key. Acquaintances might call as often
and stay as long as they pleased. The inmates and their
visitors, if they felt inclined, could treat themselves to
refreshments in a cozy little apartment, half-tavern, half-
kitchen, superintended by a portly female, styled Lucky
Laing, whence issued pretty frequently the pleasant sounds
of broiling beefsteaks, and the drawings of corks from bottles of ale and porter.

Much of the cordiality that prevailed was due to the
governor, Captain Sibbald, a benevolently disposed little
man, with a merry twinkle in his eyes, dressed in a sober
pepper-and-salt colored suit. I heard no end of his acts
of kindness to debtors as well as criminals, or of putting

poor youths in the way of well-doing who had passed through his hands. Although his salary was no more than a hundred and fifty pounds a year, he was known to take on himself the obligation of guaranteeing the payment of a debt, rather than retain in custody a poor man with a large family, brought to him for imprisonment. In the East End, he had almost constantly a male or female convict under sentence of death ; and though not able to mitigate their unhappy doom, he always endeavored to assuage their present sufferings. Until his time, they had been literally fed on bread and water, during the six weeks that elapsed between sentence and execution. He generously broke through this harsh rule, not a little to the dissatisfaction of the Lord Advocate of the day ; but in the contest his humanity prevailed, and the rule was ever after practically relaxed. I heard it approvingly said of him, that at his own expense he procured a dentist to draw a tooth which so tortured a convict that he could not sleep ; it was further reported that he always saw that the men were comfortably shaved on the morning of the day they were to be hanged, and that he uniformly pressed a glass of wine on the women on their being conducted through the Hall to execution. Such was the gossip of the prison.

One of the strange things told of the Tolbooth is, that on various occasions it gave a secure retreat to persons who fled from justice. A gentleman alleged to have been concerned in the Rye-House Plot, in the reign of Charles II., and of whom the civil authorities were in search, received protection from a friend in the Tolbooth, where no one thought of looking for him ; and whence he eventually escaped to the continent. In 1746, there was a similar case of protection to a gentleman who was sought after ineffectually, for his concern in the Rebellion.

I can realize the truth of these traditions, by having found a voluntary resident in the Tolbooth, who was not recognized as a prisoner, or as being there at all. This was a gifted but erratic genius, known by his familiar Christian name, Davie, who, after suffering a variety of disasters, received sympathy and succor among his friends in the West End. Of course, for this indulgence, he was indebted to the good-hearted governor, who, like his predecessors, did not find it to be consistent with his duty to be too particular. In making his last round at night, and ascending the spiral staircase, which was provided with a rope that performed the part of a hand-rail, he would considerately, as if by accident, jingle the bunch of well-worn keys, by way of announcing his approach. In casting a look around the apartment to see that all strangers were gone, and saying, " Good-night, gentlemen," he might have known, had he cared to know, that one of the inmates shared his bed with Davie, who was at that very moment — thanks to the jingle of the keys — ensconced upright in a tight-fitting wall-press at the corner of the apartment.

I had often occasion to meet and interchange courtesies with Davie, who was an essential adjunct of the prison fraternity. Having lost means, character, and friends, in the outer world, he was duly qualified by his obliging manners, his accomplishments, and his poverty, to be an acceptable guest of the West-Enders. The Tolbooth was his home by choice. He lived in it for years, seeing out successive groups of debtors, but always as much esteemed by the new-comers as by the older residents. How they could have done without him, it is painful to consider. He was a general factotum, went out and made purchases for them, carried messages to law-agents, posted letters, and, on great occasions, ordered in dinners

from Mrs. Ferguson's, a noted tavern in the neighborhood. His jocularities, his singing, and his ability to
take a hand at whist, were of course recommendations of
a high order. There were other reasons for thinking well
of Davie. He was modest as regards his own wants.
Debtors of the better class, on quitting the prison, would
make him a present of a few articles of dress, and perhaps
kindly leave half-a-crown in one of the pockets. Davie
could not be said to have any regular meals. He lived
principally on odd crusts of bread, pieces of biscuits,
drams, and drops of ale or porter. Talking of drams, it
was against rule to introduce spirits into the prison, but,
through the agency of Davie, there never was any particular scarcity of the article. As a scout serviceable in
this as in other things, he stood well with Peter, the
keeper of the door in the Hall, rather a good-humored
Cerberus. Peter was blind of an eye, which some might
think an advantage ; he wore a woolen cap on his bald
head, and always walked softly about the sanded stone
floor in carpet-shoes.

The West End was two rooms in breadth, one entering
from the other. The windows in these apartments looked
only south and north, but the inmates had a device for
extending the prospect in other directions. They had
only to hold out a mirror beyond the stanchions to catch
a glimpse of who was at the portal near the northwest
corner of St. Giles, or of what was going on in the street.
By means of this kind, they were able to see the remnant
of the 42d Regiment as it marched towards the castle on
its return from Waterloo. The method of looking directly
westwards up the Lawnmarket was still more ingenious.
In the gable of the building there was a hole or slit into
which the beam of the gallows was inserted for public executions. So intruded, the beam projected about two feet

into one of the debtors' apartments, where it made its appearance near the foot of the bed in which Davie participated. I remember paying a visit to the prison on the day after an execution, while it was still a subject of conversation. Confined to their rooms during the tragical ceremony, one of the debtors, along with Davie, I was told, had jocularly seated themselves on the inner end of the beam at the time the miserable culprit was in the course of being suspended from the other. The hole in the gable was already closed, but as executions, according to the heartless policy of the period, were then frequent, the building was performed in a superficial way. In the centre of the masonry, a cork was introduced by particular request, and this being pulled out at pleasure, a view was obtained in the required direction, a convenience this of no small consequence to the West-Enders, which the obliging governor of the establishment did not notice or call in question.

Besides Davie, who became a naturalized inhabitant of the Tolbooth, there were other hangers-on in whose society the inmates found a degree of solace. For the greater part, the debtors were attempting to carry through the legal process of liberation known as the *cessio*, and accordingly required the assistance of law-practitioners. Professional aid in these and other matters was usually rendered by a class of persons who it would be hazardous to say were on the roll of authorized attorneys. A kind of supernumeraries in the profession, and with a knowledge of forms, they hung about the prisons for jobs ; modestly, as it were, keeping on the outskirts of society, in order to gather up the defiled crumbs which the notabilities of the law disdained to recognize. For the services which they rendered to the poorer order of clients, it is not clear that payment was made in coin. Seemingly, they had the run of the prison. When half-a-mutchkin was smuggled in through Davie's valuable assistance, they came in for a tasting, and at various hours of the day, not being particular as to time of luncheon, they held deeply interesting conferences in Lucky Laing's tavern over smoking dishes of steaks and creaming tumblers of porter. Talking plentifully between mouthfuls, and winking knowingly with one eye, they held out such sanguine hopes of getting things carried through cheaply — no expense to speak of but the office fees — as could not fail to raise the drooping spirits of the poor wives who came to hold council with their imprisoned husbands.

The law agents of this stamp who frequented the West End had for coadjutor a medical practitioner, not less necessary than themselves in carrying on operations. I am not aware that in the present day the doctor who haunted the Tolbooth has any distinct representative. He had at one time occupied a respectable position as a medical practitioner, but now, broken down by intemperance, he confined his professional services to the inmates of the West End, to whom he made himself presentable by blacking the white edges of his button-moulds with ink, and keeping a band of faded crape on his hat, as if always in deep mourning. It was fortunate for the doctor that the law had considerately instituted the *cessio*. He lived upon it. Without it. there was no visible refuge but the work-house. His function consisted in granting sick certificates ; fee, five shillings, with a dram as a matter of course, and a biscuit to give the refection an air of respectability. In virtue of a certificate of this nature, fortified by a warrant from the court, the ailing debtor was allowed to go home to his sorrowing family, and his prescribed thirty days' imprisonment became a sort of legal fiction. At all events, the law was satisfied, which was what the West-Enders

alone cared for. I lost sight of the doctor after the Tolbooth was pulled down in 1817. He then disappeared
from the visible creation, as a result of one of the many
statutory enactments that have latterly rubbed out our
social eccentricities.

As an eddy corner of the world's tumultuous current,
into which light floating wreck was naturally swept, the
Old Tolbooth, with its scenes of grief and drollery, might
not be supposed to be quite an appropriate resort for a lad
who had to make his way in the sober track of life. · All
I can summon to remembrance in the matter is, that I
here incidentally saw down into the depths of society, to
which the affluent classes have little opportunity of penetrating. My experiences among the shifty sub-middle
classes, here as elsewhere, proved by no means the least
valuable part of my training for the career into which I
was ultimately drifted. Nor has the recollection of the
Old Tolbooth and its inmates ever ceased to afford a fund
of entertainment. In the Memoirs of a celebrated duchess,
we are favored with the contrast which Her Grace draws
between her present grand dull routine of existence, and
the times long past, when, skirmishing with pecuniary
difficulties, she pursued the life of an actress — her preference being decidedly given for "lang syne," with its spark-
ling wit, glee, and poverty, unburdened with the vapid
solemnities of etiquette. The duchess, however, had no
wish to return to these delightful early pursuits.

I made such attempts as were at all practicable, while
an apprentice, to remedy the defects of my education at
school. Nothing in that way could be done in the shop,
for there reading was proscribed. But allowed to take
home a book for study, I gladly availed myself of the
privilege. The mornings in summer, when light cost
nothing, were my chief reliance. Fatigued with trudging

about, I was not naturally inclined to rise, but on this and
some other points I overruled the will, and forced myself
to get up at five o'clock, and have a spell at reading until
it was time to think of moving off; my brother, when he
was with me, doing the same. In this way I made some
progress in French, with the pronunciation of which I was
already familiar from the speech of the French prisoners
of war at Peebles. I likewise dipped into several books
of solid worth, such as Smith's "Wealth of Nations,"
Locke's "Human Understanding," Paley's "Moral Philosophy," and Blair's "Belles-Lettres," — fixing the leading facts and theories in my memory by a note-book for
the purpose. In another book, I kept for years an accurate account of my expenses, not allowing a single halfpenny to escape record.

In the winter of 1815–16, when the cold and cost of
candle-light would have detained me in bed, I was so fortunate as to discover an agreeable means of spending my
mornings. The sale of lottery tickets, I have said, formed
a branch of my employer's business. Besides distributing
the lottery circulars, it fell to my lot to paste all the large
show-boards with posters of glaring colors, bearing the
words "Lucky Office," "Twenty Thousand Pounds still
in the Wheel," and such-like seductive announcements.
The board-carriers — shilling-a-day men — were usually a
broken-down set of characters ; as, for example, old waiters and footmen, with pale, flabby faces and purple noses ;
discharged soldiers, who had returned in a shattered condition from the wars ; and tattered operatives of middle
age, ruined by dram-drinking.

Among the last-named class of board-carriers, there
was a journeyman baker who had an eye irretrievably
damaged by some rough, but possibly not unprovoked,
usage in a king's birthday riot. What from the bad eye,

and what from whiskey, this unfortunate being had fallen out of regular employment. Now and then when there was a push in the trade, as at the New Year, he got a day's work from his old employer, a baker in Canal Street. He was not at all nice as to occupation : he would deliver handbills, perambulate the streets with a lottery-board at the top of a pole over his shoulder, or anything else that cast up, only he needed a little watching, for, when out on a job with the relics of the previous day's shilling in his pocket, he was prone to thirstiness in passing a dram-shop, into which he would dive, board and all, regardless of consequences.

From this hopeful personage, whom it was my duty to look after, I one day had a proposition, which he had been charged to communicate. If I pleased, he would introduce me to his occasional employer, the baker in Canal Street, who, he said, was passionately fond of reading, but without leisure for its gratification. If I would go early, very early, say five o'clock in the morning, and read aloud to him and his two sons, while they were preparing their batch, I should be regularly rewarded for my trouble with a penny roll newly drawn from the oven. Hot rolls, as I have since learned, are not to be recommended for the stomach, but I could not in these times afford to be punctilious. The proposal was too captivating to be resisted.

Behold me, then, quitting my lodgings in the West Port, before five o'clock in the winter mornings, and pursuing my way across the town to the cluster of sunk streets below the North Bridge, of which Canal Street was the principal. The scene of operations was a cellar of confined dimensions, reached by a flight of steps descending from the street, and possessing a small back window immediately beyond the baker's kneading-board.

Seated on a folded-up sack in the sole of the window, with a book in one hand and a penny candle stuck in a bottle near the other, I went to work for the amusement of the company. The baker was not particular as to subject. All he stipulated for was something droll and laughable. Aware of his tastes, I tried him first with the jocularities of " Roderick Random," which was a great success, and produced shouts of laughter. I followed this up with other works of Smollett, also with the novels of Fielding, and with " Gil Blas ; " the tricks and grotesque rogueries in this last-mentioned work of fiction giving the baker and his two sons unqualified satisfaction. My services as a reader for two and a half hours every morning were unfailingly recompensed by a donation of the anticipated roll, with which, after getting myself brushed of the flour, I went on my way to shop-opening, lamp-cleaning, and all the rest of it, at Calton Street. It would be vain in the present day to try to discover the baker's workshop, where these morning performances took place, for the whole of the buildings in this quarter have been removed to make way for the North British Railway station.

Such, with minor variations, was my mode of life for several years, — an almost ceaseless drudgery. At that period, there were no public institutions of a popular kind to stimulate and regulate plans of self-culture. The School of Arts, the precursor of mechanics' institutions, was not set on foot until 1821. Young persons in humble circumstances were still left to grope their way. They might spend their spare hours in study, if they had a mind ; nobody cared anything at all about it. Neither were young men, by the usages of business, allowed any time to carry out fancies as to mental improvement. Shop-hours extended from half-past seven o'clock in the

morning till nine at night, with no abatement on Satur-
days. Notions of mere amusement I did not dare to entertain. The Theatre Royal had its attractions, but expense, if nothing else, stood in the way. I had as yet
been only once in the theatre. A friend of our family
had treated me to the shilling-gallery, shortly after coming to Edinburgh; it was to see John Kemble, who played
Rollo, a subject of absorbing interest, and not for a
number of years afterwards could I venture on any species of theatrical indulgence. In gracefully submitting to
this self-denial, perhaps I had no great merit. So far as
spare time was concerned, my mind had become occupied
not only in the morning readings and study, but in sundry scientific experiments, to which I was led by James
King, who was an apprentice to a seedsman next door.

King was two to three years my senior, and I looked
up to him on that account as well as for his general ability.
He came from Fife, which is noted for the saliency and
genius of its people. Our proximity to each other, and
similarity of tastes, brought us into acquaintance. He
had a younger brother, George, an apprentice to Mr.
Crombie, a well known dyer, with whom I also became
acquainted ; and when my brother Robert came to town
to lodge with me, he was introduced to the circle. We
formed, so to speak, a club of four lads, devoted to some
species of scientific inquiry and recreation. The Kings
were great upon chemistry. Their talk was of retorts,
alkalies, acids, combustion, and oxygen gas, all which
gave me a favorable opinion of their learning. They likewise spoke so familiarly of electricity, Leyden jars, and
the galvanic pile, as to excite in me a desire to know something of these marvels. Chemistry and electricity became
accordingly the subject of discussion and experiment ; but
the difficulty was to know where experiments could be

conducted. My lodgings were out of the question. So were those of the Kings. They lived in a garret, situated immediately behind the well on the south side of the Grassmarket, which it was inexpedient to constitute a hall of science, and the notion of resorting to it was given up. In this dilemma, a friendly and every way suitable retreat, which remains vividly in my recollections, presented itself, and was gratefully accepted.

As you go up a narrow and steep road to the Calton Hill, at the foot of Leith Street, a covered passage descends and strikes off to the left, and conducts you to a confined court, wherein stood, and perhaps still stands, a small cottage with a tiled roof, that had to all appearance existed long before the streets with which it was environed. The back window in Calton Street, where I used to clean the lamps, looked into the court, and I could notice that the little old-fashioned cottage was occupied by a thin and aged personage with a bright brown scratch wig, who, in fine weather, made his appearance on the pavement as a common street porter. The name by which he was known in the neighborhood was Jamie Alexander. As voucher for his respectability, he wore on the left breast of his coat a pewter badge, marked No. 3, indicative of the early period at which he had been enrolled by the magistrates in the fraternity of porters ; and of this antiquity of his emblem of office he felt naturally proud ; all other porters, however old, being boys in comparison, and not possessing that distinction of rank which he did.

Jamie was a Highlander by birth, and in his youth, long ago, had been a servant to a Mr. Tytler, a gentleman of literary and scientific attainments, with whom he had travelled and seen the world, and in whose company he had picked up a smattering of learned ideas and words. With this grounding, and naturally handy, Jamie was a

7

kind of Jack-of-all-trades. It was in his capacity of porter that King and I had become acquainted with him, but
at his advanced age he relied more distinctly on less toilsome pursuits. The versatility of his talents rendered
him peculiarly acceptable as an acquaintance, and his
house was well adapted for our meetings. This ancient
mansion consisted of only a single apartment; it was
kitchen, parlor, bedroom, and workshop all in one, a
queer and incongruous jumble, like the mind of the occu-
pant.

Usually, at night, we found Jamie seated at one side
of his fire, and his wife Janet, a more commonplace character, at the other. Behind the old man was his work-
bench, loaded with a variety of tools and odds and ends
adapted to a leading branch of employment, which consisted in clasping broken china and crystal for the stone-
ware shops This operation he performed with a neatness that surprised most persons, who knew that he had
lost the sight of one of his eyes. It did not seem to be
generally understood that Jamie had a contrivance satisfactory to himself for remedying this ocular deficiency.
In his old pair of spectacles he fixed two glasses for the
seeing eye, and he maintained that by this arrangement
of a double lens, his single eye was as good to him as
two, a point we did not think fit to contest.

To vary the routine of employment, and at the same
time enjoy a little out-door recreation, Jamie at times
took a job from the undertakers. Dressed in a thread-
bare black suit, he walked as a *saulie* before the higher
class of funerals, with his hat under his arm, and the
black velvet cap of a running footman covering his brown
wig. In connection with his profession of *saulie*, he related numerous traditionary anecdotes illustrative of the
festivities of deceased *saulie* and *gumfter* men in the ser-

vants' hall of great houses,[1] while waiting in lugubrious habiliments to head the funeral solemnity, his stories reminding one of the interspersal of scenes of drollery throughout the tragedies of Shakespeare, and I doubt not, true to nature. Besides these diverting reminiscences of grand funerals, he gave his experiences of grave-digging in the Calton burying-ground, where he often assisted. He confidently stated that the digging of graves was a wonderfully exhilarating and healthful occupation, if executed with proper skill and leisure. Nothing, in his opinion, was so efficacious in assuaging a rheumatism in the back, or securing long life ; and to hear him on this subject, you would have thought it would be a good thing in the way of health and amusement to take to regular exercise in grave-digging. It appeared that independently of payment for this kind of labor according to tariff, Jamie seldom left the ground without a few bits of old coffin in good condition, which had been thrown to the surface in the course of excavation. Such pieces of wood, improved by seasoning in the earth, he said, excelled for some purposes of art. From them he made a common kind of fiddles, and also cheap wooden clocks.

With much oddity of character, there was a fine spirit of industry, cheerfulness, and contentment in the old man. As a Highlander, he spoke Gaelic, and from him I learned to be tolerably proficient in pronouncing that test in the language, *laogh*, the word for *calf*. With a love of the ancient music of the hills, he played the bagpipe, but this instrument, from deficiency of breath, he had latterly laid aside, and taken to the Irish pipes, which are played by means of bellows under the arm. His

---

[1] Mutes bearing tall poles shrouded in black drapery are called in Scotland *gumfler* men ; such being a corruption of *gonfalonier*, the bearer of a *gonfalon*, or standard, in old ceremonial processions.

pipes lay conveniently on a shelf over his work-bench, and taking them down, he, at our request, would favor us with a pibroch. Having finished the tune, he ordinarily delivered some oracular remarks on pipe-music in general, and of the operatic character of the pibroch in particular, the only time, by the way, I ever heard the thing explained.

Janet, the mistress of the mansion, did not greatly encourage our visits. Her chief concern in life seemed to consist in nursing a small and ingeniously made-up fire, which was apt to be seriously deranged by King's chemical experiments, such as the production of coal-gas in a blacking-bottle, used by way of retort, — the proposal of lighting the city with gas having suggested this novel experiment. For a special reason, this old woman was not more favorable to electric science. Under King's advice and directions, my brother and I contrived, out of very poor resources, to procure a cylindrical electrifying-machine, with some apparatus to correspond. Having one night given Janet an electric *shock*, slyly conveyed to her through a piece of damp tobacco, she ever after viewed the machine with the darkest suspicions. In these apprehensions her gray cat had some reason to join ; when the Leyden jars were placed on the table, she fled to the roof of the bed, and there kept eying us during our mysterious incantations.

Sunday, with its blessed exemption from a dull round of duties, came weekly with its soothing influences ; and this leads to a little explanation. If any one is so complimentary as to think that I had some merit in devising how to live on so low a figure as a shilling and ninepence a week, he may be disposed to modify his surprise on my stating that the expenditure did not include Sunday, so that, after all, the one-and-ninepence weekly inferred as much as threepence-halfpenny a day. For several years, I walked home to the country every Saturday night. Between nine and ten o'clock, in all states of the weather, summer and winter, I might have been found making the best of my way down the North Back of the Canongate, past Holyrood, across the King's Park by Muschet's Cairn, and so on through Portobello. It was necessary not to loiter by the way, for, with a somewhat limited wardrobe, a few things which I carried with me had to be washed and otherwise prepared before midnight. In these night-travels, my brother Robert, while he remained in town, accompanied me.

The Sundays spent on the shore of the Firth of Forth formed a refreshing change on the ordinary course of life. The salt-pans had ceased to send up their nauseous vapors and clouds of smoke. A pleasant and not uninstructive calm was experienced amidst the shell and tangle covered rocks, against which the pellucid waves of the sea dashed in unremitting murmurs. Usually, I went to Inveresk Church with other members of the family, and so became acquainted with Musselburg and its environs. Sometimes I walked by a footpath across the fields by Brunstain and Millerhill to Dalkeith, to visit my grandmother, Mrs. Noble, and her younger son David, who had recently been settled there (Robert, the elder son, having gone to Nova Scotia), and enjoyed the variety of accompanying them to the antique parish church of that pretty country town.

There was an immense charm in these occasional Sabbath-day walks to Dalkeith, in which I usually carried a French New Testament in my pocket for lingual exercise. The sunshine, the calm that prevailed, the fresh air, the singing of birds, the green leafy trees, and the blossoming wild-flowers by the way-side, all filled my heart with glad-

ness, for they renewed my recollections of the country.
The fields, stuck about with coal-pits, at which the gin-
horses had intermitted their accustomed toil, were not
such pretty fields as I had seen on Tweedside ; still they
were environed with hedgerows, and formed a pleasing
contrast to the huge rows of dingy buildings among
which I pursued my ordinary employment. As a boy, I
had passionately cultivated flowers in a little garden assigned to me, and now rejoiced to see a few growing by
the side of the pathway. The Mid-Lothian primroses, I
imagined — considering the neighborhood of the coal-pits
— had not the freshness and bloom of the primroses
which I had gathered in the woods and dells at Neidpath ;
but still they were primroses, and, as the best within
reach, I plucked and carried home a handful as a gift to
my mother in her dreary residence at the Pans, and was
pleased to see her put them in a glass with a little water,
to preserve as a souvenir of my weekly visit.

The small smoked-dried community at these salt-pans
was socially interesting. Along with the colliers in the
neighboring tiled hamlets, the salt-makers — at least the
elderly among them — had at one time been serfs, and in
that condition they had been legally sold along with the
property on which they dwelt. I conversed with some of
them on the subject. They and their children had been
heritable fixtures to the spot. They could neither leave
at will nor change their profession. In short, they were
in a sense slaves. I feel it to be curious that I should
have seen and spoken to persons in this country who remembered being legally in a state of serfdom ; and such
they were until the year 1799, when an act of parliament
abolished this last remnant of slavery in the British
Islands. Appreciating the event, they set aside one day
in the year as a festival commemorative of their libera-

tion. Perhaps the custom of celebrating the day still exists.

After these Sunday communings with the family, I was on Monday morning off again for Edinburgh to have a fresh tug at the shop-shutters, carrying away with me, I need hardly say, all kinds of admonitory hints from my mother, the burden of her recommendations being to avoid low companions, to mind whom I was come of, and " aye to haud forrit." What was to become of me was, as she said, a perfect mystery; still there was nothing like securing a good character in the mean while — that was clear, at all events.

My mother, however, had more cause for uneasiness on her own than my account. The aspect of family affairs was acquiring additional gloom. My father was not the man for the situation he filled. In fact, he detested situations of all kinds. His rough and irritable spirit of independence gave him a dislike to be ordered by anybody. His feelings at this period were in a morbid condition, the result of circumstances already adverted to, and therefore not to be judged severely. Having unfortunately failed in the means of acting an independent part, he was perhaps on that account the more anxious that his sons should be successful in making the attempt. At any rate, he endeavored to impress on me the vast necessity and advantage of, in all things, thinking for myself, and taking, as far as possible, an independent course. He objected to my ever entertaining the notion of continuing to serve any one after my apprenticeship had expired. No amount of salary was to tempt me ; no prospect of ease to seduce me. I should strike out for myself, if it were only to sell books in a basket from door to door. There might be suffering and humiliation in the mean time ; but I would be daily gaining experience, and, with prudence, accumulating means. If I behaved myself properly, a few years would set all to rights.

These disquisitions amused and probably had some effect in inspiring me. My father had strong convictions as to the propriety of allowing children to think and struggle for themselves; such, in his opinion, being true kindness, and anything else little better than cruelty. Seated in his arm-chair at the Pans, with two or three of us about him, he would discourse in this pleasant way, interlarding anecdote with philosophy.

"You think it a hard business, I dare say," — addressing me, — " to live in your present pinching way, scheming as to buying meal and milk, and all that ; but it is doing you an immense deal of good. It is strengthening your mind, and teaching you the art of thinking, that is the great point. You should be thankful for my not doing anything for you. Perhaps you would like to have everything held up to you, — lodgings, tailors' bills, boots, and what not, all paid for the asking. What would be the upshot ? You would never know the value of money. You would grow up as ignorant and dependent as a child, and never be able to take a front rank in the world. It is melancholy to see so many fathers spoiling their children from mistaken notions of kindness. Young men treated in that foolish way can do nothing for themselves, but must have somebody always behind them to shove them into situations, where their minds lose all power of thinking and planning correctly. No doubt, they can plan what they would like to have for dinner ; few folk are ill at that, or about going to the theatre, or what should be the color of their gloves. But that is not what I mean. What I am speaking of is the faculty of thinking and acting for yourself in all kinds of unexpected difficulty. I could tell you plenty of stories about inability to think or act independently. You remember the excise-officer at Peebles, who for a number of years looked after Kerfield Brewery, a most excellent person, but not qualified to think for himself. His mind had been stunted for want of exercise. Stirred up by his wife, an ambitious little woman, with whom he had received some money, he inconsiderately threw up his situation, and purchased the effects of a deceased brewer at Galashiels, his object being to go into business for himself. When he came to look into matters, he was utterly at a loss. It was all simple enough, but the man had no power of planning. Besides putting things in repair, he had to buy grain and hops, order new barrels, purchase horses, and hire servants. For one thing, he had to open and read a hundred and thirty-nine letters applying for the situation of clerk. All this, along with other perplexities, drove him clean wild. He felt that he had got into an affair he could not go through with, and then, when he reflected upon the loss of his comfortable situation, and still worse the loss of his money, he became seriously ill, and took to his bed. In these circumstances, his wife, greatly at a loss what to do, sent for our old friend Smibert, who was once Provost of Peebles, a man of extraordinary shrewdness. From his cleverness, we used to call him Talleyrand. When the poor sick man saw the old Provost make his appearance, he felt a wonderful degree of relief. The wife, sitting by the side of the bed, explained the scrape they had got into, and asked what should be done.

" ' Done,' answered their visitor, leaning on his crooked-headed stick to save his lame leg ; ' what's to be done but to sell off the whole concern, and try to get reinstated in the Excise ? '

" ' Very good,' said the wife ; ' but how is the sale to be effected ? — it's easy speaking.'

"'Leave it all to me,' replied Smibert, briskly; 'I know how to manage : I'll advertise and take in offers.' "The words had not been well spoken, when the sick man declared he found himself getting well, and that they might take the blister from the back of his neck. In a day or two he was quite recovered. Talleyrand arranged matters beautifully. He sold off the concern, though at a sacrifice to the owner, who, after some trouble, got himself reinstated in the Excise ; but he had to begin over again, and lost ten years on the books by his ridiculous attempt at independent exertion."

Such was the run of my father's disquisitions. Unfortunately, his extreme views of independence did not comport with his functions as manager of the salt-works, where he suffered a species of ignominious banishment. Among the near neighbors were a few excise-officers set to watch over the works and give permits to purchasers. One of these officials was a Mr. Stobie, in whom there was a degree of interest ; for, while in the position of an expectant of Excise, he had done duty for Robert Burns in his last illness, April, 1796, when, as the poet says in a letter to Thomson : "Ever since I wrote you last, I have only known existence by the pressure of the heavy hand of sickness, and have counted time by the repercussions of pain." It redounded to the honor of Stobie that he acted gratuitously for Burns at this melancholy crisis, and it was pleasing for our family to make his acquaintance, and hear some particulars of the greatest among Scottish poets.

Beyond such acquaintanceships, there was little to compensate for the smoke, dirt, and misery that were endured at the Pans. The business in itself violated all my father's notions of propriety. It consisted almost wholly in supplying material for a contraband trade across the

Border to England, the high duties on salt in the latter country rendering this a profitable traffic. Purchased in large quantities at Joppa and other salt-works, the bags were transferred in carts to Newcastleton in Liddesdale, where the article was stored by a dealer, and sold by him to be smuggled across the fells during the night. For years this was a great trade. Perhaps it did not pertain to the Scotch salt-makers to urge the extinction of so flourishing a traffic, but neither could any one of susceptible feelings look on it with perfect complacency.

Whatever were the precise causes of discord, a disruption was precipitated by my father having the misfortune to be waylaid and robbed of some money which he had collected in the way of business in Edinburgh. Knocked down and grievously bruised about the head, he was found late at night lying helpless on the road, and brought home by some good Samaritan. The painful circumstances connected with this untoward affair led to his being discharged from his office. In his now hapless state, greatly disabled by the injuries which he had received, and without means, the consideration of everything fell on my mother. Her mind rose to the occasion. Removing from the sooty precinct to one of a row of houses near Magdalene Bridge, on the road to Musselburgh, she prepared to set on foot a small business, and was not without hope of meeting with general sympathy and support, for by her agreeable manners and exemplary conduct under various difficulties, she had made some good friends of different classes in the neighborhood.

With something like dismay, I heard of this fresh disaster, the climax, it was to be hoped, of a series of agonizing misfortunes. The house at the Pans had been about the most revolting of human habitations, but it at least gave shelter, and bore with it some means of livelihood. Now, all that was at an end. The future was to be a matter of new contrivance. Of course, I hastened from town to condole over present distresses, and share in the family counsels. On my unexpected arrival near midnight, cold, wet, and wayworn, all was silent in that poor home. In darkness by my mother's bedside, I talked with her of the scheme she had projected. It was little I could do. Some insignificant savings were at her disposal, and so was a windfall over which I had cause for rejoicing. By a singular piece of good fortune, I had the previous day been presented with half a guinea by a good-hearted tradesman, on being sent to him with the agreeable intelligence that he had got the sixteenth of a twenty thousand pound prize in the state lottery. The little bit of gold was put into my mother's hand. With emotion too great for words, my own hand was pressed gratefully in return. The loving pressure of that unseen hand in the midnight gloom, has it not proved more than the ordinary blessing of a mother on her son?

> "All this, still legible in memory's page,
> And still to be so to my latest age,
> Adds joy to duty, makes me glad to pay
> Such honors to thee as my numbers may;
> Perhaps a frail memorial, but sincere —
> Not scorned in heaven, though little noticed here."
>
> COWPER.

Early in the following morning, I was back to business in Calton Street. My mother's ingenious efforts, con-ducted with consummate tact, and wholly regardless of toil, were successful. Her only embarrassment was my father, prematurely broken down in body and mind. It is not the purpose, however, of the present memoir to pursue the family history. Let us revert to the leading object in hand.

CHAPTER V.

IT will be necessary to go back a little, in order to trace the difficulties that were encountered by Robert in the early part of his career, while I was still following out the duties of an apprentice.

The family depression during this gloomy period was felt more acutely by my brother than by myself, for, besides being more susceptible in feelings, he was, from his gentle and retiring habits, less able to face the stern realities with which we were unitedly environed. Left, as has been said, for a time in Peebles to pursue his studies at the grammar-school, he was finally brought to Edinburgh, and placed at a noted classical academy, — that of Mr. Benjamin Mackay, in West Register Street, — preparatory to being (if possible) sent to the university. There was an understanding in the family that, as the most suitable professional pursuit, he was to be prepared for the church. The expenses attending on this course of education were considerably beyond present capabilities, but all was to be smoothed over by a bursary, of which a distant relative held out some vague expectations.

When the family quitted Edinburgh, Robert accompanied them, but shortly afterwards, with a considerable strain on finances, he was associated with me in my West Port lodgings. Here, from the uncongenial habits with which he was brought in contact, he felt considerably out of

place. I was fortunately absent during the greater part
of the day in my accustomed duties ; but he, after school
hours, had to rely on such refuge as could be found at the
unattractive fireside of our landlady, who, though disposed
to be kind in her way, was so chilled by habits of penury
as to give little consideration for the feelings of the poor
scholar. He spoke to me of his sufferings and the efforts
he made to assuage them. The want of warmth was his
principal discomfort. Sometimes, benumbed with cold, he
was glad to adjourn to that ever hospitable retreat, the
Old Tolbooth, where, like myself, he was received as a
welcome visitor by the West-Enders ; and it is not unworthy of being mentioned, that the oddities of character
among these unfortunate, though on the whole joyous,
prisoners, and their professional associates, — not forgetting Davie, — formed a fund of recollection on which he
afterwards drew for literary purposes. That strange old
prison, with its homely arrangements, was therefore to
him, as to me, identified with early associations, — a thing
the remembrance of which became to both a subject of
life-long amusement. There was also some exhilaration
for him in occasionally attending the nightly book-auctions, where, favored with light and warmth, seated in a
by-corner, he could study his lessons, as well as derive a
degree of entertainment from the scene which was presented. A further source of evening recreation, but not
till past nine o'clock, and then only for an hour, was found
in those meetings with the brothers King and myself for
mutual scientific instruction.

Viewed apart from these solacements, his life was dreary
in the extreme. Half-starved, unsympathized with, and
looking for no comfort at home, he probably would
have lost heart but for the daily exercises at school, where
he stood as rival and class-fellow of Mackay's best pupils.

A good Latinist considering his years, and appreciative of wit and humor, he had an immense love of the odes and satires of Horace, nor was he scarcely a less admirer of the classic myths of Virgil, for they touched on that chord of romance and legendary lore which vibrated in his own mental constitution.

Ever since his arrival in Edinburgh, and without suggestion from any one, he had taken delight in exploring, at fitting times, what was ancient and historically interesting in the Old Town, which, for tastes of this kind, presents a peculiarly comprehensive field of inquiry. Once crowded within defensive walls, the older part of the city remained a dense cluster of tall dark buildings, lining the central street and diverging lanes, or *closes*, with comparatively little change in exterior aspect. However altered as regards the quality of the dwellers on the different floors, the tenements still exhibited innumerable artistic and heraldic tokens of the past ; nor were the environs of the town less illustrative of moving incidents of the olden time. To this huge antiquarian preserve, as it might be called, with its varied legends, my brother immediately attached himself with the fervor of a first love, for so enduring was it as materially to tinge the rest of his existence.

Patiently ranging up one close and down another, ascending stairs, and poking into obscure courts, he took note of carvings over doorways, pondered on the structure of old gables and windows, examined *risps*, — the antique mechanism which had answered the purpose of door-knockers, — and extending the scope of his researches, scarcely a bit of Arthur's Seat or the Braid Hills was left unexplored. The Borough-moor, where James IV. marshaled his army before marching to the fatal field of Flodden ; the " bore-stone," in which, on that occasion, was planted the royal standard, —

" The staff, a pine-tree, strong and straight,
Pitched deeply in a massive stone,
Which still in memory is shown,
   Yet bent beneath the standard's weight
   Whene'er the western wind unrolled,
   With toil, the huge and cumbrous fold,
And gave to view the dazzling field,
Where in proud Scotland's royal shield,
   The ruddy lion ramped in gold." — *Marmion.*

Royston, where the Earl of Hertford landed with an English army, and proceeded to set fire to and destroy Edinburgh ; the spot at the Kirk of Field, where Darnley was blown up ; the tomb of the Earl of Murray ; the grassy mounds in Bruntsfield Links, which formed the relics of Cromwell's batteries when besieging the castle after the victory of Dunbar ; the grave-stone in the Greyfriars Churchyard, on which, in 1638, was signed the National Covenant ; the adjoining inclosure, in which, for a time, were pent up, like cattle, the crowd of prisoners taken at the battle of Bothwell Bridge ; the closed-up postern of the castle surmounting the precipitous rocks up which Claverhouse, Viscount Dundee, clambered to confer with the governor (and how he got either up or down no one can tell), when setting out for his last field, Killiecrankie ; these, and such like historical memorials, became all familiar to my brother by making good use of intervals that could be spared from his daily attendance at the academy.

Though only twelve months had elapsed since he came from the country, and not yet fourteen years of age, he already possessed a knowledge of things concerning the old city and its romantic history which many, it may be supposed, do not acquire in the course of a lifetime. While most other youths, his school-mates, gave themselves up to amusements not unbecoming for their age, his recreations had all in them something of the nature of instruction. And such were his extraordinary powers of memory, that whatever he saw or learned, he never forgot ; everything which could interest the mind being treasured up as a fund of delightful recollections, ready to be of service when wanted.

At the academy were a few boys, the sons of citizens, . who indulged in fancies not unlike his own, and with whom he formed a lasting friendship. They could tell legendary stories of marvelous events in the city annals, connected with reputed wizards, noted eccentric characters, and remarkable criminals, to which he listened with avidity ; as, for example, the story of Major Weir, who, for the commission of a series of atrocities, was condemned and executed in 1670, and whose house in the West Bow enjoyed the reputation of being so much under the dominion of evil spirits, that no person would live in it for more than a hundred years afterwards ; for when any family made the attempt, they were subject to such an extraordinary illusion of the senses, that in going up the stair they felt as if they were going down, and when going down, that they were going up. Or the story of Deacon Brodie, a man moving in a good position, who, having long secretly carried on a system of depredations, was ultimately condemned and executed for committing a burglary on the Excise Office, 1788. Or the still more curious story of a lad who, while under sentence of death in the Old Tolbooth, escaped by a clever device of his father, and lay for weeks concealed in the mausoleum of the " Bluidy Mackenyie," where he was secretly supplied with food by the boys of Heriot's Hospital, till he escaped from the country. Or what remained still a matter of public horror and wonderment, the assassination and robbery of Begbie, a bank porter, in 1806, the perpetrator of which double crime had

never been discovered, notwithstanding all the efforts of
the authorities.

By these varied means in his early youth, in the midst
of difficulties, Robert laid the foundation of much that
afterwards assumed shape in literature, although at the
time he was only satisfying a natural craving for what was
traditionally curious. Looking back to the days when we
lived together in the West Port, I cannot recollect that he
ever spent a moment in what was purely amusing, or of
no practical avail. Nor was this a sacrifice. The acquisition of knowledge was with him the highest of earthly
enjoyments. It was well for him that he had these soothing resources. What his trials were at this time may be
learned from the following passages in a letter written by
him, in 1829, to the young lady to whom he was shortly
afterwards married : —

"My brother William and I lived in lodgings together.
Our room and bed cost three shillings a week. It was in
the West Port, near Burke's place. I cannot understand
how I should ever have lived in it. The woman who kept
the lodgings was a Peebles woman, who knew and wished
to be kind to us. She was, however, of a very narrow disposition, partly the result of poverty. I used to be in
great distress for want of fire. I could not afford either
that or candle myself. So I have often sat beside her
kitchen fire, if fire it could be called, which was only a
little heap of embers, reading Horace and conning my
dictionary by a light which required me to hold the books
almost close to the grate. What a miserable winter that
was ! Yet I cannot help feeling proud of my trials at that
time. My brother and I — he then between fifteen and sixteen, I between thirteen and fourteen — had made a resolution together that we would exercise the last degree of
self-denial. My brother actually saved money off his in-

come. I remember seeing him take five and-twenty shillings out of a closed box which he kept to receive his savings ; and that was the spare money of only a twelvemonth. I dare say the Potterrow itself never sheltered two divinity students of such abstinent habits as ours. My father's prospects blackened towards the end of the winter ; and even the small cost of my board and lodging at length became too much for him. I then for some time spent the night at Joppa Pans, and regularly every morning walked, lame as I was, to Edinburgh to attend school. Through all these distresses, I preserved the best of health, though perhaps my long fasts at so critical a period of life repressed my growth. A darker period than even this ensued ; my father lost his situation, and I was withdrawn from a course of learning which it was seen I should never be able to complete."

Such is a fair account of the termination of Robert's educational career. Of course there was mourning over the ruin of long-cherished hopes, and yet the circumstance ought in reality to have been a cause for rejoicing. I greatly doubt if my brother would, according to ordinary expectations, ever have excelled as a clergyman. He was deficient in oratorical qualities, nor did he possess to a sufficient degree that self-possession which is indispensable to a successful public speaker. Nature had destined him to wield the pen, not to live by exercise of the tongue. In the mean while, he was greatly downcast. Returning home, his privations were now greater than my own, for they were aggravated by the spectacle of domestic troubles, from which, except at weekly intervals, I was happily exempt.

Depressed, and it might be said friendless, with only his Horace and a few other Latin books, over which he would pore lovingly for hours, he was at this painful junc-

ture not unconscious that he should make some sort of
effort at self-reliance. He could arrive at no other conviction. In the picturesque language of the Psalmist, his
" kinsmen stood afar off," a circumstance which unhappily
roused feelings much more bitter than any experienced in
my own less delicately framed mental system.

For a brief space, he procured a little private teaching
at Portobello. Afterwards, a place was procured for him
in the counting-house of a merchant, who resided in Pilrig
Street, situated between Edinburgh and Leith ; but this
involved a journey on foot to and fro daily of altogether
ten miles, with the poorest possible requital. At the end
of six months this employment came to an end, and for a
few weeks he filled a similar situation in Mitchell Street,
Leith. " From that place," he says in the letter above
referred to, " I was discharged, for no other reason that I
can think of but that my employer thought me too stupid
to be likely ever to do him any good. I was now in the
miserable situation of a youth betwixt fifteen and sixteen,
who, having passed the proper period without acquiring
the groundwork of a profession, is totally *hors de combat*,
and has the prospect of evermore continuing so. I was
now, however, at the bottom of the wheel. Now came
the time to rise. You have already some notion of my
self-denial and fortitude of mind. Now came the time to
exert all my faculties." He then alludes to circumstances
of which I am able to give a more explicit detail.

At this dismal period, when, as he says, he was " at the
bottom of the wheel," I saw him only on Sundays, and it
was on such occasions alone that we had an opportunity
for private consultation. On one of these Sabbath evenings, we sat down together in deep cogitation, on a grassy
knoll overlooking the Firth and the distant shores of Fife.
The scene, placid and beautiful, befitting the calm which

seemed appropriate to the day of rest, assorted ill with the pressure of those personal necessities that demanded immediate and far from pleasant consideration. Jeremy Taylor has consolingly remarked, that "there is no man but hath blessings enough in present possession to out-weigh the evils of a great affliction." It may be so. I have no doubt it is so. How the blessings are to be recognized and brought into practical application, is sometimes the difficulty. In Robert's case, the blessings might have been stated as consisting of youth, health, a fair education, moral and intellectual culture, and aspira-tions which embraced an earnest resolution to outweigh, by honest industry, the misfortunes into which he had been plunged by no fault of his own. Evidently, all de-pended on his being put on the right path. The great question for solution was what he should do, not only for his own subsistence, but to disembarrass the family, in which he acutely felt himself to be in the light of an incumbrance.

This was the critical moment that determined my brother's career. I had for some days been pondering on a scheme which might possibly help him out of his difficulties, provided he laid aside all ideas of false shame, and unhesitatingly followed my directions. The project was desperate, but nothing short of desperate measures was available. My suggestion was, that, abandoning all notions of securing employment as a clerk, teacher, or anything else, and stifling every emotion which had hith-erto buoyed him up, he should, in the humblest possible style, begin the business of a bookseller. The idea of such an enterprise had passed through his own mind, but had been laid aside as wild and ridiculous, for he pos-sessed neither stock nor capital, nor could he have re-course to any one to lend him assistance. "I have thought of all that," I said, " and will show you how the thing is to be done." I now explained that in the family household there were still a number of old books, which had been dragged about from place to place, and were next to useless. The whole, if ranged on a shelf, would occupy about twelve feet, with perhaps a foot additional by including Horace and other school-books. They were certainly not much worth, but, if offered for sale, they might, as I imagined, form the foundation on which a business could be constructed. I added that there was at the time an opening for the sale of cheap pocket Bibles, respecting which I could aid by my knowledge of the trade, and even go the length of starting him with one or two copies out of my slender savings.

The project being turned over and over and canvassed, proved acceptable. My father, so far from having any objections, assented to the scheme. The old books, Horace and all, were collected and carried off, the only one left being an old tattered black-letter Bible, of the date 1606, that had been in the family for two hundred years, and which, with scribblings on the blank pages, formed a kind of register of births, deaths, and marriages during that lengthened period. Too sacred to be ruthlessly made an article of commerce, it was fortunately reserved, and in due time became my only patrimony.

With the few old books so collected, Robert began business in 1818, when only sixteen years of age, from which time he became self-supporting, as I had been several years earlier. I should have hesitated to mention these particulars of my brother's early career, but for the fact of his having, in a letter to his friend Hugh Miller, dated March 1, 1854, and published in the " Life and Letters " of that person (1871), given an account, which, as a candid revelation of his own feelings, is fully more painful.

Writing to Miller, he says : "Your autobiography has set me a-thinking of my own youthful days, which were like yours in point of hardship and humiliation, though different in many important circumstances. My being of the same age with you, to exactly a quarter of a year, brings the idea of a certain parity more forcibly upon me. The differences are as curious to me as the resemblances. Notwithstanding your wonderful success as a writer, I think my literary tendency must have been a deeper and more absorbing peculiarity than yours, seeing that I took to Latin and to books both keenly and exclusively, while you broke down in your classical course, and had fully as great a passion for rough sport and enterprise as for reading, that being again a passion of which I never had one particle. This has, however, resulted in making you what I never was inclined to be, a close observer of external nature, an immense advantage in your case. Still I think I could present against your hardy field observations by firth and fell, and cave and cliff, some striking analogies in the finding out and devouring of books, making my way, for instance, through a whole chestful of the ' Encyclopædia Britannica,' which I found in a lumber garret. I must also say, that an unfortunate tenderness of feet, scarcely yet got over, had much to do in making me mainly a fireside student. As to domestic connections and conditions, mine, being of the middle classes, were superior to yours for the first twelve years. After that, my father being unfortunate in business, we were reduced to poverty, and came down to even humbler things than you experienced. I passed through some years of the direst hardship, not the least evil being a state of feeling quite unnatural in youth — a stern and burning defiance of a social world in which we were harshly and coldly treated by former friends, differing only in external respects from

ourselves. In your life there is one crisis where I think
your experiences must have been somewhat like mine: it
is the brief period at Inverness. Some of your expres-
sions there bring all my own early feelings again to life.
A disparity between the internal consciousness of powers
and accomplishments and the external ostensible aspect,
led in me to the very same wrong methods of setting myself forward as in you. There, of course, I meet you in
warm sympathy. I have sometimes thought of describing
my bitter, painful youth to the world, as something in
which it might read a lesson; but the retrospect is still
too distressing. I screen it from the mental eye. The
one grand fact it has impressed is the very small amount
of brotherly assistance there is for the unfortunate in this
world. . . . . Till I proved that I could help myself, no
friend came to me. Uncles, cousins, etc., in good positions in life, some of them stoops of kirks, by-the-by,
not one offered, or seemed inclined to give, the smallest
assistance. The consequent defying, self-relying spirit in
which, at sixteen, I set out as a bookseller, with only my
own small collection of books as a stock, not worth more
than two pounds, I believe, led to my being quickly independent of all aid; but it has not been all a gain, for I
am now sensible that my spirit of self-reliance too often
manifested itself in an unsocial, unamiable light, while
my recollections of 'honest poverty' may have made me
too eager to attain and secure worldly prosperity."

The place at which Robert attempted the adventurous
project of selling the wreck of the family library, along
with his own small parcel of school-books, was Leith Walk,
where a shop of a particularly humble kind, at a yearly rent
of six pounds, with space for a stall in front, was procured
for the purpose. The situation of this unpretending place
of business was opposite Pilrig avenue. Here he may be

said to have set up house, for, provided with a few articles of furniture, and exercising a rigorous frugality, he lived in his very limited establishment. To keep him company, and aid by my professional advice, as well as to lessen his expenses, I went to reside with him, quitting, with my blue-painted box, my quarters in the West Port, to which I had no reason to feel special attachment. The time was near at hand when I would myself have to appear in a new character.

CHAPTER VI.

L ATE on a Saturday evening in May, 1819, my apprenticeship came to a close, and I walked away
with five shillings in my pocket, — to which sum my
weekly wages had been latterly and considerately advanced. My employer, to do him every justice, offered
to retain me as assistant at a reasonable salary; but I
liked as little to remain as to try my luck elsewhere as
a subordinate. Whether influenced by my father's ha-
rangues about independence, or by my own natural in-
stincts, I had formed the resolution to be my own master,
and concluded that the sooner I was so the better. And
so, at nineteen years of age, I was left to my shifts.

The exploit was somewhat hazardous, and unless on
special grounds, I would not recommend it to be followed.
Society is composed of employers and employed. All
cannot be masters. The employed may happen to be the
best off of the two ; at all events, they are burdened with
less responsibility. My resolution, therefore, to fight my
way, inch by inch, entirely on my own account, was, I acknowledge, an eccentricity. Yet, who can lay down any
precise rule on this point? Looking at all available circumstances, every one must think for himself, and take
the consequences. In the ordinary view of affairs, my
prospects were not particularly cheering. Exclusive of
the five shillings in my pocket, I was without any pecun-

iary reliance whatsoever. There were, however, some
things in my favor. As in my brother's case, I had youth,
health, hope, resolution, and was as free from expensive
habits and tastes as from any species of embarrassing obligation. There was nothing to keep me back, unless it
might be the comparatively narrow scope for individual
exertion in our northern capital. At that time, however,
I knew nothing personally of London and its illimitable
field of operation. The best had to be made of what was
within reach. Fortunately, I continued still to have no
acquaintances whom it was necessary to consult; had no
giddy companions, who would have been ready enough to
jeer me out of schemes of humble self-reliance. I had
no dread of losing caste, because I had no artificial position to lose ; and as for losing self-respect, that entirely
depends on conduct and the motives by which it is influenced. It will be seen that I was not without the kind
of ambition which is indispensable to success. On that
very account, I treated all immediate difficulties, or hu-
miliations, as of no moment.

Circumstances concurred to get me over the first step,
which is always the most difficult. The success of my
brother in his enterprise pointed out a line of business
that might with advantage be followed. As Leith Walk
happens to be identified in an amusing way with his as
well as my own early career, I may say a few words respecting it, although at the risk of telling what may be
generally known.

Leith Walk is to Edinburgh what the City Road is to
London, a broad kind of Boulevard stretching a mile in
length to the seaport, and constantly used as a thoroughfare by merchants, clerks, strangers, and seafaring people
In the early years of the present century, it was the daily
resort of a multiplicity of odd-looking dependents on pub-

lic charity — such as old blind fiddlers, seated by the
wayside ; sailors deficient in a leg or an arm, with long
queues hanging down their backs, who were always singing ballads about sea-fights ; and cripples of various sorts,
who contrived to move along in wooden bowls, or in low-
wheeled vehicles drawn by dogs ; all which personages
reckoned on reaping a harvest of coppers in the week of
Leith races, that great annual festival of the gamins of
Edinburgh, which has been commemorated in the humorous verses of Robert Fergusson. Besides its hosts of
mendicants, the Walk was garnished with small shops for
the sale of shells, corals, and other foreign curiosities. It
was also provided with a number of petty public-houses ;
but its greatest attraction was a show of wax-work, at the
entrance of which sat the figure of an old gentleman in a
court-dress, intently reading a newspaper, which, without
turning over the leaves, had occupied him for the last ten
years.

The oddest thing about the Walk, however, was an air
of pretension singularly inconsistent with the reality. The
sign-boards offered a study of the definite article — *The*
Comb Manufactory, *The* Chair Manufactory, *The* Marble
Work, and so forth, appearing on the fronts of buildings
of the most trumpery character. At the time I became
acquainted with the Walk, it owned few edifices that were
much worth. Here and there, with intervening patches
of nursery-grounds and gardens, there was a detached
villa or a row of houses with flower-pots in front, in one
of which rows, called Springfield, in the house of his
friend Mr. M'Culloch of Ardwell, the English humorist,
Samuel Foote, used to dine on his visits to Edinburgh.[1]

[1] The intimacy of Foote and a land-proprietor in the stewartry of
Kirkcudbright will seem a little unaccountable. The friendship accidentally began by both being detained as travellers during a protracted

But the majority of the buildings were of a slight fabric of brick and plaster, with tiled roofs, as if the whole were removable at a day's notice. There being no edifices, however mean and inconvenient, which do not find inhabitants, these frail tenements were in demand by a needy order of occupants, whose ultimate limit in the article of rent was ten to twelve pounds a year, — fifteen a little beyond the thing, twenty not to be thought of.

It was one of these temporary and unattractive buildings, situated, as has been said, opposite Pilrig avenue, that had been rented by my brother, and it was there I joined him in housekeeping, with nothing to keep but the disconsolate walls and about ten shillings worth of furniture, along with a bed of very insignificant value. In 1819, Robert had to quit, in consequence of the proprietor making repairs on the row of buildings, and he removed about a hundred yards farther down the Walk. The alterations on Giles's Buildings, as they were called, had just been made when I stood in need of a place of business, and I rented one pretty nearly on the spot which my brother had vacated. The changes that had been made partook of the usual character of the neighborhood, — shabby pretension. The proprietor, a builder in Edinburgh, had accumulated a number of old shop doors and windows, which, dismissed as unfashionable, gave a genteel finish to the new fronts that were stuck up along the row of mean brick edifices. Here I procured a place of moderate dimensions, for which I was to pay an annual rent of ten pounds.

Without stock, capital, or shop furniture, my attempt at

snow-storm, first in an inn at Moffat, and afterwards at the Crook, in the winter of 1744-45. They were detained no less than twenty days altogether in effecting a journey from Moffat to Edinburgh, which may now be performed in about two hours. A daughter of M'Culloch was married to Thomas Scott, brother of Sir Walter.

beginning business would almost seem like trying to make
something out of nothing.   I admit, the problem was difficult of solution.   In one respect, it was fortunate in the
way of example that Robert had begun first, but in another it was a disadvantage.   In setting up he had cleared
my father's house of all its old books, which, though not
many in number, or of great value, still bore bulk so far,
and giving a face to things, served for a not positively bad
beginning.   Coming later into the field nothing was left
for me to lay hands on in the like predatory fashion.   I
should doubtless, as a last resource, have procured a portion of Robert's stock of books, which, in the course of a
year, had increased by his industry to be worth about twelve
pounds, but, by a remarkably happy turn of events, I did
not need to encroach on his painfully accumulated property.
    During the first week of my freedom, there arrived in
Edinburgh a travelling agent for an enterprising publisher
in London.   He had come to exhibit to the Scottish booksellers specimens of cheap editions of standard and popular works.   Until within a short time previously, editions
of the works of Johnson, Gibbon, Robertson, Blair, Hume
and Smollett, Burns, and other standard writers, had been
a monopoly of certain publishers, who united to publish
them, and gave them the imposing name of " Trade Editions."   Long out of copyright, these works were public
property, and could legally be printed and issued by any
one, but not until now had any one had the audacity and
enterprise to disregard the assumed etiquette of the profession, and print and sell editions on his own account.
In daring to break down this monopoly, the publisher I
refer to encountered some abuse, which, however, did not
deter him in his operations.   His editions, as a rule, were
not so highly finished as those issued under the auspices
of the trade ; but as they were sold at about half the price,

they were correspondingly appreciated by that portion of the book-buying world who are not scrupulously nice as to typographical elegance.

This active personage, well known in Cheapside, had another and quite as successful a branch of business. It consisted in purchasing, wholesale, the remainders of editions which hung on the hands of publishers, and of issuing copies at a cheap price under new attractions, such as a portrait frontispiece and a flashy exterior, by which means two important ends were served : the shelves of the publishers were relieved of much dead stock, and the public were satisfied.

It was the agent of this enterprising tradesman who, by a singular accident, fell in my way. In concluding his business tour, he had arrived in Edinburgh to hold a trade-sale previous to proceeding to London. A trade-sale, as it may be known, comprehends a dinner at some noted tavern. A large number of booksellers are invited to attend, and immediately after the cloth is withdrawn, and the wine decanters put in circulation, the sale begins. All the guests are provided with catalogues of the books for disposal, and as each work is offered in turn at a specified price, copies are handed about as specimens. The inducement to make purchases is a certain reduction on the ordinary allowance, and, in addition, thirteen copies are usually given for the price' of twelve. At the period to which I am referring, trade-sales of this festive description were more common than they are in these sober-minded days, and at them such large quantities of books were ordinarily disposed of, that the seller, who acted as host, and sat at the top of the table, did not find occasion to grudge the expense of the entertainment. The business was conducted with a blending of fun and conviviality. There was occasionally a toast, with the honors, as an interlude, and it was not unusual for one or two of the guests to be called on for a song.

The sale on the present occasion took place in the Lord Nelson Hotel, Adam Square. The agent in charge requiring some one acquainted with the handling and arranging of books, previous to the dinner, heard of me from a bookseller as being unemployed and likely to suit his purpose. I agreed to assist him as far as was in my power, and did so without any notion of requital.

The trade-sale was well attended, and went off with uncommon *éclat.* Mr. Robert Miller, of Manners and Miller, told his drollest anecdotes, whistled tunes with the delicacy of a flageolet, and sung his best songs as few men can sing them. There was a large sale effected ; for it was the first time that a variety of standard works had been offered at considerably reduced prices. On the day succeeding this bibliopolic festival, I attended to assist in packing up, in the course of which I was questioned regarding my plans. I stated to the friendly inquirer that I was about to begin business, but that I had no money ; if I had, I should take the opportunity of buying a few of his specimens, for I thought I could sell them to advantage. " Well," he replied, " I like that frankness ; you seem an honest lad, and have been useful to me ; so do not let the want of money trouble you : select, if you please, ten pounds' worth of my samples, and I will let you have the usual credit."

That was a turning-point in my life. In a strange and unforeseen manner, I was to be put in possession of a small collection of salable books, sufficient to establish me in business. Gladly embracing the offer, I selected a parcel of books great and small, to the value of ten pounds, which I proceeded to pack into an empty tea-chest, and carry off without incurring the aid or expense of a porter. Borrowing the hotel truck, I wheeled the chest to my shop in Leith Walk, elated, it may be supposed, in no ordinary degree at this fortunate incident, and not the least afraid of turning the penny long before the day of payment came round.

Though furnished in this extraordinary manner with a stock, I was still unprovided with any kind of fixtures, such as counter or shelving. But this deficiency gave me little concern. It was not my design to sell books inside a shop. That, I knew, would never do. My plan, like that of my brother, and also many illustrious predecessors, was to expose my wares on a stall outside the door. I had years previously read the "Autobiography of James Lackington," who mentions that he began business as a bookseller in 1774, the whole of his stock of old books, laid out on a stall, not amounting to five pounds in value ; that in 1792, when he retired into private life, the profits of his business amounted to £5,000 a year ; and that he had realized all he was possessed of, by "*small* profits, bound by *industry*, and clasped by *economy*." I could not possibly expect to reach anything like this marvelous success of Lackington, but at any rate there was an example offered in his small beginning, which it was my resolution to follow.

I spent little time in preliminary arrangements. With the five shillings which I had received as my last week's wages, I purchased a few deals from a neighboring woodyard, and from these, with a saw, hammer, and nails, I soon constructed all the shop furniture which I required ; the most essential articles being a pair of stout trestles, on which was laid a board, whereupon to exhibit my wares to the public. With these simple appliances, I am to be supposed as beginning business one day in June, when, the weather happening to be fine, I had the satisfaction of

9

making several sales. Daily, the contents of my small
establishment disappeared, and I was able to introduce
variety by buying lots of second-hand books at the nightly
auctions, which I regularly attended with my brother. As
regards the account I had incurred, I discharged it in the
due course of business, and for some time continued to
order and pay for regular supplies. Within six months,
the first and most critical part of my struggle was over.
In a small way, I may be considered as having been fairly
established.

By studying to sell cheaply, my profits in the aggregate
were not great; but along with Robert, I lived frugally,
incurred no unnecessary expenses, and all that was over I
laid out in adding to my stock. As my sales were to a
large extent new books in boards, I felt that the charge
made for the boarding of them was an item that pressed
rather heavily upon me. Why, thought I, should I not
buy the books in sheets, and put them in boards myself?
It is true, I had not been taught the art of bookbinding,
but I had seen it executed in my frequent visits to a book-
binder's workshop, and was confident that if I had the
proper apparatus I could at least put books in boards;
for that was but a rudimentary department of the craft.
The articles available for the purpose at length fell in my
way. After this, I procured my books in sheets, which I
forthwith folded, sewed, and otherwise prepared to my
satisfaction, thereby saving on an average threepence to
fourpence a volume, my only outlay being on the material
employed; for my labor was reckoned as nothing.

In this droll scheming way, I tried to make the best of
my lot. The condition of the weather was an important
element of consideration. In fine days, the Walk was
thronged with foot-passengers, a number of whom found
some recreation in lounging for a few minutes over my

stall. If there was a prospect of rain, they hurried on ; and when it became determinedly wet, business was over for the day. I might as well bring in my books at once, and try to find something to do in-doors. When the stall was not in operation, sales were almost at a stand-still. Hundreds, I found, as Lackington had done before me, would buy books from a stall, who would not purchase them equally cheap in a shop. The advantageous pecul- iarity of the stall is, that it secures those who have formed no deliberate intention to buy. Lying invitingly with their backs upward, the books on a stall solicit just as much attention as you are pleased to give them. You may look at them, or let them alone. You may, as if by chance, take up and set down volume after volume without getting compromised. The bookseller, however, is perfectly aware of what is likely to ensue. When he observes that the lounger over his stall is not satisfied with a casual glance, but goes on examining book after book, he is pretty cer- tain there is to be a purchase. Continued inspection ex- cites an interest in the mind. There is perhaps no inten- tion at first to buy, but gradually the feelings are warmed up, and it is then scarcely possible to resist asking the price of some book which more particularly strikes the fancy. Asking the price is equivalent to passing the Rubicon. After that, the desire for purchasing becomes nearly irresistible. Going into shops to buy books in cold blood is quite a different thing. Before entering, there must in general be a distinct intention to purchase.

Stall-keepers of all varieties know the value of the ob- trusive principle ; and it may be doubted if the modern shop system is in most cases an improvement on the old practice of exposing wares in open booths along the sides of the thoroughfare. The original *Stationarii*, who ex- posed their books at the gateways of universities, immedi-

ately after the invention of printing, what were they but
stall-keepers?   Did not also many booksellers of good repute last century set up stalls for the sale of their wares
on market-days?   One does not read without interest the
anecdote of Michael Johnson, bookseller at Lichfield,
who, being unable from illness to set up his stall as usual
at Uttoxeter, requested his son Samuel to do so in his
stead, which request was refused, from a feeling of false
pride ; and how this act of filial disobedience, having
preyed in after-life on the morbidly susceptible mind of
the great lexicographer, he, by way of expiation, went to
Uttoxeter on a market-day, and stood in a drenching rain
on the site of his father's stall, amidst the jeering remarks
of the bystanders.   There is something, therefore, like a
classic authority for book-stalls.   They remind us of the
infancy of printed literature and the usages of an olden
time.

The Walk offered uncommon facilities for the traffic in
which I was engaged.   Long stretches of the footway,
from thirty to forty feet wide, admitted of stalls being set
outside the doors without obstructing the thoroughfare.
Some might think that they were an attraction to what
was otherwise a pleasant promenade.   The book-stalls
were four in number — those belonging to my brother and
myself, and two others.   They were all situated on the
shady side of the road, forming at proper distances from
each other a series of literary lures, likely to be visited
en suite.   Interesting from the diversity of their wares,
they to a certain extent were mutually helpful.   There
was nothing like a feeling of rivalry among us.   Accustomed to discuss professional matters, we were able to
cultivate a few jocularities as a seasoning to a too frequent
dullness.   We learned how to distinguish habitual nib-
blers, who never bought, but only gave trouble, from those

on whom we could reasonably reckon for a purchase, and knew how to act accordingly. The stall offered a study of character. There was not a little perversity or stupidity to be amused with. Some stall frequenters would buy nothing but books which had been used. Defective in judgment, they could not imagine the possibility of getting a new book as cheaply as an old one. The stall-keepers on the Walk found it necessary to humor purchasers of this sort. It was not difficult to do so ; they had only to cut up the leaves, and soil the outside of a book, in order to make it thoroughly acceptable.

With all the diligence that could be exercised, there was little scope for expansion in my small trade. With every effort, time hung heavy on my hands. I fretted at inaction. To relieve the monotony of the long, dull hours during bad weather, I took to copying poems and various prose trifles in a fine species of penmanship, in the hope of selling them for albums. It was assuredly a weak resource, but what could I do ? If I spent days over the manufacture of a few verses, which sold for only a single shilling, it was employment, better than sitting vaguely idle.

The notion of attempting to write in a style closely resembling the delicate print-like lettering on copperplate engravings, occurred to me two or three years previously. A retired naval officer in poor circumstances had written an account of his captivity in France during the war, and raffled it for five pounds. The penmanship was exceedingly elegant, and I felt desirous to attempt something that might prove equally tasteful. From time to time, I made attempts at imitation, but never came up to the original. I had, however, acquired a facility in the art. The work was executed with a finely pointed crow-pen on smooth paper, ruled with lines for the purpose, and cost prodigious care and patience, because any blunder would have been fatal. Occupying any spare hours when the stall could not be put out, and poring over a desk, I was able to realize a few shillings by these laborious transcriptions. . What was of much greater value, these little pieces of penmanship helped to bring me more into notice, and to procure me the friendship of some estimable persons.

A gentleman who happened to see one of my specimens of calligraphy, was pleased to think better of it than it deserved, and without solicitation patronized my humble business establishment. He was about to be married, and wished to procure a quantity of books of a superior kind, in the finest bindings, for his library. One day, he called to inquire as to the practicability of my supplying his wants. Satisfied with the information, he gave an order of such magnitude as astonished me, and raised serious doubts as to how, with my miserable resources, it was to be executed. Apprehending some difficulty on this score, he relieved all anxieties by stating that I should bring the books in parcels from time to time, and that each parcel would be paid for on delivery.

This fortunate transaction gave me a lift onward, and stimulated to new efforts. The fact that I had unexpectedly benefited in a large degree by a gentleman seeing one of my small pieces of penmanship, suggests the reflection, that in business, as in human affairs generally, incidents which are seemingly insignificant often lead to important results. Young men are apt to treat what appears a small matter with indifference, if not disdain, without being conscious that in commerce nothing is small or to be passed over as of no moment. I once heard a merchant who had risen to great wealth say, that civility in serving a woman in humble circumstances with a pennyworth of tape, had led, by a remarkable chain of circumstances, to dealings to the extent of hundreds of pounds. In my own case, as just stated, a small piece of transcription with a crow-pen had, by an unforeseen current of events, terminated in a manner much more advantageous than I had any reason to expect.

The progress I had made during the first year rendered it expedient to procure an enlargement of my premises. This being effected, I was able to appropriate a small back-room as a dwelling, so as to be near my work ; the furniture as meagre as might be, for I could not indulge in the luxury of a carpet, and was fain to inclose my bed with a drapery of brown paper in place of curtains. I was also enabled in various ways to extend my business operations, and accommodate those who did me the honor to call. Among these visitors were several literary aspirants who hung about the outskirts of society. Few are aware of the great number of poets in Scotland. Those whose names become generally known are insignificant in number to the host who are never heard of beyond the limited locality in which they move. My brother's and my own literary tastes, to say nothing of our connection with books, made us acquainted with several poets of this order. Among these, the oddest was an aged shoemaker, who, deserting his last, had taken to the writing of poems and dramas. His standard production was " The Battle of Luncarty," which his admirers thought " almost " as good as Shakespeare. William Knox, the author of " The Lonely Hearth and other Poems," was a gentle enthusiast of a different stamp, but succumbed at an early age to what were mildly termed his " genial propensities."

We were more happy in knowing intimately Robert Gilfillan, still a young man, writer of some pleasing and popular Scottish songs, who had been bred in Leith as an apprentice to a grocer, and had therefore undergone that routine of duties which I had narrowly escaped. He was a person of amiable temperament, simple in his habits, with whom it was a pleasure to interchange courtesies. I may say the same of Henry Scott Riddell, who was numbered among our early friends, and has left some singularly touching lyrics and other pieces.

There was still another of these geniuses, John C. Denovan, an excitable being, who lived in a world of romance strangely at variance with his actual circumstances. I first knew Denovan when he was a porter to a tea-dealer at the foot of Leith Street Terrace, directly opposite the spot where I had been an apprentice. He was the child of misfortune. His father had procured for him the position of midshipman, in which capacity he made a single voyage and acquired notions of life at sea. Then he was somehow deserted, and left to his shifts with his mother, a poor abject being, to whom he stuck to the last. In his reduced condition, he acquitted himself honestly, but his wayward fancies did not square with the difficulties with which he had to struggle. He was always overflowing with allusions to Wordsworth, Byron, Keats, and Leigh Hunt. A little crazy on poetical subjects, he, by an easy transition, become half mad on politics, and edited a weekly periodical called "The Patriot," which was desperately radical in character. One of its leading articles, I remember, began with the portentous words : "Day follows day, and chain follows chain." Yet Denovan was a harmless creature. His poetical pieces were noticed with some approbation by Sir Walter Scott, who, while visiting Ballantyne's printing-office at Paul's Work, now and then, in a kindly way, looked in upon him at his den in Leith Wynd, where he latterly made a livelihood by coffee-roasting, and where he died in 1827. There was a little exhilaration in having an occasional conversation on literary topics with these writers. To a higher region we did not yet aspire.

I still at odd times continued my labors with the crow-pen, but at best this was a trivial art, and I had secret yearnings to procure a press and types, in order to unite printing with my other branches of business. I partly formed this desire by having employed a printer to ex-ecute a small volume, purporting to be an account of David Ritchie, the original of the Black Dwarf, whom I had seen when a boy in Peeblesshire. The success of · this enterprise, commercially, led to the conclusion that if I could print as well as write my poor productions, I might add to my available means. It would be enough if I could procure an apparatus sufficient for executing small pamphlets, and the humbler varieties of job-print-ing.

For some time my inquiries failed to discover what would be within the compass of my means, until at length a person who had begun business in a way not unlike my own, and constructed a press for his own use, intimated his desire of selling off, in order to remove to a distant part of the country. The whole apparatus, including some types, was to be disposed of cheaply by private bar-gain. The price sought could not be considered exces-sive. It was only three pounds. To set up as a printer on a less capital than this was surely impossible. I paid the money, and became the happy possessor. From that time I troubled myself no more with imitative print-writ-ing. That branch of art was taken up and followed for a time by my brother, who so greatly excelled in it as to leave my efforts far behind.

I hesitate to think that I acted properly in directing my mind towards letterpress printing, while deficient in capital to pursue the profession with any solid advantage. My best excuse was the wish to occupy idle time. In the mornings when the sun was up, I endeavored to make use

of the daylight by reading and study, as I had done formerly. Perusing the " Spectator," I carefully scrutinized
the papers of Addison and other writers, sentence by sentence, in order to familiarize myself with their method of
construction and treatment. But beyond this I had little
patience. I felt that the time had come for action, and
that every hour spent in doing nothing was little better
than wasted. Yet, with every excuse, I have never ceased
to be amazed at my presumption in trying, without any
knowledge of the typographic art, to set up with such
miserable mechanical appliances. The press, which was
constructed to stand on a table, was an imperfect little
machine, with a printing surface of no more than eighteen
inches by twelve, and when wrought, a jangling and creaking noise was produced that might be heard as far as two
houses off.

As regards my font of types, it consisted of about
thirty pounds' weight of brevier, dreadfully old and worn,
having been employed for years in the printing of a newspaper, and, in point of fact, only worth its value as metal.
Along with the fount, I had a pair of cases, in which the
letters were assorted. My bargain did not embrace a
frame or stand for the cases. That I supplied by the ordinary resource of wood bought from a timber-yard, and
the application of my carpenter's tools. For a small additional outlay, I procured a brass composing-stick, some
quoins and other pieces of furniture, an iron chase, and a
roller, along with a pound-weight of printing-ink. I was
now complete.

As soon as I had arranged all parts of my apparatus, I
looked abroad over the field of literature to see which
work should first engage my attention. My best plan, as
I thought, would be to begin by printing a small volume
on speculation ; sell the copies, and with the proceeds

buy a variety of types for executing casual jobs which might drop in. A small volume I must print, and finish in a marketable style, that is clear, in order to raise funds. Fixed in this notion, I selected for my first venture a pocket edition of the songs of Robert Burns.

I had never been taught the art of the compositor, but just as I had casually gleaned some knowledge of book-binding, so I had picked up the method of setting types. When an apprentice, I had been frequently sent errands to the printing-office of Mr. Ruthven, in Merchant's Court, the premises which, two centuries previously, had formed the town mansion of Thomas Hamilton, first Earl of Haddington, jocosely styled by James VI., "Tam o' the Cowgate." In the fine old dining-hall where "Tam" had entertained royalty, I was, while waiting for proofs, favored with an opportunity of seeing the compositors pursue their ingenious art, and learning how types were arranged in lines and pages. Recollections of what I had thus seen of compositorship were now revived, and I began to set up my song-book without receiving any special instruc-tion ; my composing-frame being placed in such a situa-tion that I was ready to attend to other matters of busi-ness. While so occupied, I was visited by my old friend, James King, whom I had for some time lost sight of. His taste for chemistry had brought him into the employment of a glass manufacturer ; and now, in connection with that line of business, he was about to sail for Australia, where a useful career was before him. He was amused with, and, I think, compassionated my feeble efforts We parted, not to meet until both were in different circumstances, many years afterwards.

My progress in compositorship was at first slow. I had to feel my way. A defective adjustment of the lines to a uniform degree of tightness was my greatest trouble, but

this was got over. The art of working my press had next
to be acquired, and in this there was no difficulty. After
an interval of fifty years, I recollect the delight I experienced in working off my first impression ; the pleasure
since of seeing hundreds of thousands of sheets pouring
from machines in which I claim an interest being nothing
to it ! If the young and thoughtless could only be made
to know this, — the happiness, the dignity of honest labor
conducted in a spirit of self-reliance ; the insignificance
and probably temporary character of untoward circumstances while there is youth, along with a willing heart ;
the proud satisfaction of acquiring by persevering industry instead of by compassionate donation, — how differ-
ently would they act !

I think there was a degree of infatuation in my attachment to that jangling, creaking, wheezing little press.
Placed at the only window in my apartment, within a few
feet of my bed, I could see its outlines in the silvery moonlight when I awoke ; and there, at the glowing dawn, did
its figure assume distinct proportions. When daylight
came fully in, it was impossible to resist the desire to
rise and have an hour or two of exercise at the little
machine.

With an imperfect apparatus, the execution of my song-
book was far from good. Still, it was legible in the old
ballad and chap-book style, and I was obliged to be content. Little by little, I got through the small volume. It
was a tedious drudgery. With my limited font, I could
set up no more than eight small pages, forming the eighth
part of a sheet. After printing the first eight, I had to
distribute the letter and set up the second eight, and so on
throughout a hundred pages. Months were consumed in
the operation. The number of copies printed was seven
hundred and fifty, to effect which I had to pull the press

twenty thousand times. But labor, as already hinted, cost nothing. I set the types in the intervals of business, particularly during wet weather, when the stall could not be put out, and the press-work was executed late at night or . early in the morning. The only outlay worth speaking of for the little volume was that incurred for paper, which I was unable to purchase in greater quantities than a few quires at a time, and therefore at a considerable disadvantage in price, but this was only another exemplification of the old and too well-known truth, that "the destruction of the poor is their poverty," about which it was useless to repine.

When completed, the volume needed some species of embellishment, and fortune helped me at this conjuncture. There dwelt in the neighborhood a poor but ingenious man, advanced in life, named Peter Fyfe, with whom I had already had some dealings. Peter, a short man, in a second-hand suit of black clothes, and wearing a white neckcloth, which he arranged in loose folds so as effectually to cover the breast of his shirt, was from the west country. He had been a weaver's reed-maker in Paisley, but having been unfortunate in business, he had migrated to Edinburgh, in the hope of procuring some kind of employment. Necessitous and clever, with an inexhaustible fund of drollery, he was ready for anything artistic that might come in his way. Peter did not want confidence. I am not aware of any department in the fine or useful arts of which he would have confessed himself ignorant. At this period, when few knew anything of lithography, and he knew nothing at all, he courageously undertook, in answer to an advertisement, to organize and manage a concern of that kind, and by tact and intuition gave unqualified satisfaction. Peter was just the man I wanted. Although altogether unacquainted with copperplate engraving, he ex-

ecuted, from the descriptions I gave him, a portrait of the
Black Dwarf, for my account of that singular personage ;
which sketch has ever since been accepted as an authority.

I now applied to this genius for a wood-engraving for
my song-book, which he successfully produced, and for a
few shillings additional he executed a vignette represent-
ing some national emblems. Invested with these attractions, the song-book was soon put in boards, and otherwise
prepared for disposal. I sold the whole either in single
copies at a shilling, or wholesale to other stall-keepers at
a proper reduction, and, after paying all expenses, cleared
about nine pounds by the transaction.

Nine pounds was not a large sum, but it served an important end. I was able to make some additions to my
scanty stock of types, which I procured from an aged
printer with a decaying business. To be prepared for executing posting-bills, I cut a variety of letters in wood with
a chisel and pen-knife. For such bold headings, therefore,
as " Notice," " Found," or " Dog Lost," I was put to no
straits worth mentioning. One of my most successful
speculations was the cutting in wood of the words " To
Let," in letters four inches long, an edition of which I disposed of by the hundred at an enormous profit, to dealers
who sold such things to stick on the fronts of houses to
be let.

Through the agency of book-hawkers who purchased
quantities of my " Burns's Songs," I procured some orders
for printing " Rules " for Friendly and Burial Societies.
These answered me very well. The Rules were executed
in my old brevier, leaded, on the face of half a sheet of
foolscap, and were therefore within the capacity of my
font. A person who was a lessee of several toll-bars in
the neighborhood of the city, found me out as a cheap
printer, and gave me a job in printing toll-tickets, which I

executed to his satisfaction. Another piece of work of a similar character which came in my way was the printing of tickets for pawnbrokers. My principal employer in this line was a lady whose establishment was a second floor in High Street. She was a short, plump, laughing, good-natured woman, turned of fifty years of age. Her family consisted of a niece, who attended to business, and an aged female domestic, who went by the name of " Pawkie Macgouggy." Pawkie, who had been a servant in the family for upwards of twenty years, received me when I called with a package of tickets, and kindly gave me a seat in the kitchen till her mistress could be communicated with.

The lady was so obliging as to show me some politeness, and then, as well as a few years later, I learned a part of her history. She had travelled abroad, and brought with her to Edinburgh a knowledge of Continental cookery. With this useful acquirement, she set up a tavern business in South Bridge Street, and there she laid the foundation of her fortune by a dexterous hit in the culinary art. This consisted in the invention of a savory dish possessing an odor which, it was said, no human being could resist. To this marvelously fascinating dish she gave the name of Golli-Gosperado. The way she attracted customers was ingenious. Her tavern was down a stair, and was lighted by windows to the street, protected by iron gratings, over which the passengers walked. Having prepared her Golli-Gosperado, she put a smoking dish of it underneath the gratings in the pavement. According to her own account, the odor was overpowering. Gentlemen in passing were instantly riveted to the spot. They declared they must have some of that astonishing dish, whatever it was, and at whatever cost, and down-stairs they rushed accordingly. For a time there was quite a furore in the town about the

Golli-Gosperado. The happy inventor retired from the
trade with so much money that she was able to set up as
a pawnbroker. In that profession she was likewise successful, and ultimately retired altogether from business to
a villa in the neighborhood, where she died, being attended in her last moments by the faithful and sorrowing
Pawkie Macgouggy.

My means being somewhat improved, it did not appear
unreasonable that I should enlarge my stock of letter by
ordering a moderate font of long primer adapted for pam-
phlet-work from an aged type-founder, named Matthewson,
who carried on business at St. Leonard's, and with whom
I had become acquainted. In his walks, he occasionally
called to rest in passing, and hence our business dealings.
His cut of letter was not particularly handsome, but in the
decline of life, and in easy circumstances, he did not care
for new fashions.

Disposed to be familiar, Matthewson gave me an outline of his history. He had, he said, been originally a
shepherd boy, but from his earliest years had possessed a
taste for carving letters and figures. One day, while attending his master's sheep, he was accidentally observed
by the minister of the parish to be carving some words on
a block of wood with a pocket-knife. The clergyman was
so pleased with his ingenuity that he interested himself
in his fate, and sent him to Edinburgh to pursue the profession of a printer. Shortly afterwards, he began to
make himself useful by cutting dies for letters of a particular description required by his employer, there being
then no type-founder in the city. While so occupied, he
attracted the notice of Benjamin Franklin on his second
visit to Scotland. This was about 1771. Franklin was
pleased with the skill of the young printer, and offered to
take him to Philadelphia, and there assist him in estab-

lishing a letter-foundry. Matthewson was grateful for the disinterested offer, of which, unfortunately, for family reasons, he could not take advantage. He set up the business of letter-founding in Edinburgh, which he had all to himself until the commencement of establishments with higher claims to taste in execution.

To vary the monotony of my occupation, I had for some time been making efforts at literary composition. It was little I dared to attempt in that way, for anxiety concerning ways and means impelled me to disregard every species of employment that partook of recreation, or which was not immediately advantageous. With a view to publication at the first favorable opportunity, I wrote an account of the Scottish Gypsies, for which I drew on my recollection of that picturesque order of vagrants in the south of Scotland, and also the traditions I had heard regarding them. It was a trifle — nothing worth speaking of; but being now provided with a tolerably good font of long primer, also some new brevier suitable for foot-notes, I thought it might be made available. I accordingly set up the tract as a sixpenny pamphlet; and for this small brochure a coarse copper-plate engraving was furnished by that versatile genius, Peter Fyfe. It represented a savage gypsy-fight at a place called Lowrie's Den, on the top of Soutra Hill. The edition was sold rapidly off, and I cleared a few pounds by the adventure. What was of greater service, I felt encouraged to put my thoughts on paper, and to endeavor to study correctness and fluency of expression. The tract on the Gypsies also procured me the acquaintance of a few persons interested in that wayward class of the community.

My enlarged typographical capabilities led to new aspirations. Robert, who had made corresponding advances in business, but exclusively in connection with booksell-

10

ing, was occupying his leisure hours in literary composition, which came upon him like an inspiration at nineteen
years of age. His tastes and powers in this respect suggested the idea of a small periodical which we might
mutually undertake. He was to be the editor and principal writer. I was to be the printer and publisher, and
also to contribute articles as far as time permitted.

The periodical was duly announced in a limited way,
and commenced. A name was adopted from the optical
toy invented by Sir David Brewster, about which all classes
were for a time nearly crazy. It was called the " Kaleidoscope, or Edinburgh Literary Amusement." In size it was
sixteen pages octavo, — the price threepence, — and it was
to appear once a fortnight. The first number was issued
on Saturday, October 6, 1821. The mechanical execution
of this literary serial sorely tested the powers of my poor
little press, which received sundry claspings of iron to
strengthen it for the unexpected duty. My muscular powers
likewise underwent a trial. I had to print the sheet in
halves, one after the other, and then stitch the two together. I set all the types, and worked off all the copies,
my younger brother, James, a fair-haired lad, rolling on the
ink, and otherwise rendering assistance.

This was the hardest task I had yet undergone ; for,
being pressed by time, there was no opportunity for rest.
Occupied with business, the composing-frame, and the
press, also with some literary composition, I was in har-
ness sixteen hours a day ; took no more than a quarter of
an hour to meals ; and never gave over work till midnight.
Sometimes I had dreadful headaches. Of course, I do not
justify this excessive application. It was clearly wrong. I
was acting in violation of the laws of health. Enthusiasm
alone kept me up ; certainly no material stimulus. My only
excuse for this ardently pursued labor, which must have

been troublesome to quietly disposed neighbors, was what at the same period might have been offered by my brother for his incessant self-sacrificing exertions ; a desire to overcome a condition that provoked the most stinging recollections. I should probably have broken down but for the weekly repose and fresh air of Sunday, when, after attending church, I had an exhilarating ramble on the sands and links.

Robert wrote nearly the whole of the articles in the "Kaleidoscope," verse as well as prose. My contributions consisted of only three or four papers. The general tone of the articles, by whomsoever produced, may be acknowledged to have been unnecessarily caustic and satirical. There was also a certain crudeness of ideas, such as might be expected from young and wholly inexperienced writers. Nevertheless, there was that in the "Kaleidoscope" which was indicative of Robert's future skill as an essayist ; for here might be found some of the fancies which were afterwards developed in his more successful class of articles. In particular, may be mentioned the paper styled the "Thermometer of Misfortune," in which occur the ideas that were in after years expanded into the essay on the luckless class of intemperates popularly known as "Victims."

This little periodical also contained a few articles descriptive of a wayward class of authors in the lower walks of life, written from personal knowledge, and marked by that sympathy for the unfortunate which characterized my brother through life. I feel tempted to give one of these sketches. It refers to Stewart Lewis, a hapless being with whom Robert had become acquainted, when he himself was in straits previous to commencing his small business.

STEWART LEWIS.

"It was towards the end of 1816, when I lived in a cottage on one of the great roads which lead to this metropolis, that I was engaged in a mercantile concern in the city, and travelled thither every morning, and, after the duties of the day were performed, came back in the evening. I was one evening, after my return, entertained by my mother with an account of two extraordinary persons who had called during my absence; and who afterwards proved to be Stewart Lewis and his wife, travelling on an expedition to Haddington, selling a small volume of poems which he had just published.

"The appearance and singular manners of these visitants were described to me in such terms of respect as made me regret my absence when they called; and the volume of poems which they had left increased my desire to see their author: for the acquaintance of a poet, and one who had actually printed his productions, was at that time an object of very great interest, and even curiosity.

"On the very next evening, however, my curiosity was destined to be gratified, for who should drop in upon us but poor Lewis with his wife! They had, to use the wife's expression, 'never been off their feet' since early in the morning, and were very much fatigued accordingly. I was then introduced to the poet, and in the course of five minutes we were engaged in as sincere a friendship as if we had lived together from infancy. Whether it was from the naturally ardent enthusiasm of his temper, or a secret instinctive discovery that I was afterwards to become one of his own brotherhood, I will not, cannot determine. From what I can recollect of his appearance and countenance, he was dressed in a suit of shabby clothes, mostly of a gray color; his person was slender; his face interesting, and bearing peculiar marks of genius and intelligence; his forehead was high, his hair gray and thin, and he had a countenance wrinkled with care and squalid with poverty. He never spoke but under the influence of a sort of furor; and he even did not return thanks for the favor of another cup of tea without an excitation of feeling and expression which had in it something of poetic fervor.

"His wife was a little old woman, with no remains of that beauty which had captivated the high-toned heart of Stewart Lewis thirty years before. He had thus addressed her on the thirtieth anniversary of their marriage : —

> " ' Though roses now have left thy cheek,
> And dimples now in vain I seek ;
> Thy placid brow, so mild and meek,
> Proclaims I still should love thee.

> " ' How changed the scene since that blest day !
> My hair 's now thin and silver gray ;
> Though all that 's mortal soon decay,
> My soul shall live to love thee.'

She spoke in a low, querulous voice, subdued in its tones by a long course of misery. They addressed each other by terms of endearment as strong, and spoke with as great an affection, as they had done on their marriage day. An instance of conjugal attachment has seldom been found like that of Stewart Lewis and his sorrow-broken spouse. He had addressed several poems to her even in her old age, some of which are eminently beautiful, and breathe the spirit of as fond an affection as if they had still been the accents of a first love, unbroken and unproved.

"They were much fatigued when they arrived ; but a refreshment of tea soon revived their spirits ; and though the success of their journey had been very limited, the poor bard was soon elevated to a state of rapturous excitement; while yet in the intervals of his joy, the wife, who had less of a poetic temperament, and whom misfortune had taught the very habit of sorrow, would interfere, with a voice mournfully soothing, and warn him of his inevitable griefs to-morrow.

"After this we had frequent visits of Stewart Lewis ; but as these were generally through the day, when I was engaged in the duties of my profession, I had little opportunity of seeing him. He had left several copies of his poems with us, and I afterwards succeeded in disposing of a few to the most poetical of the neighborhood, which raised a small sum. I then resolved to pay him a visit. My father accompanied me in this adventure, out of curiosity to see his dwelling. After searching all the closes at the west end of the Cowgate for his habitation, we were at length directed to it by an old woman, who appeared like a corpse from the grave, rising out of a low cellar in a very dark close — such a pallid and wrinkled crone as I have seen full oft in my antiquarian researches through the ancient lanes of the town, emerging from her dark dungeon at midday to taste one breath of a somewhat purer atmosphere than that of her own subterranean domicil. With her shriveled arm she pointed up a narrow crazy stair which winded above her head, and told us that the object of our search lived there. We thanked her, and ascended. At the second landing-place we entered a dark, narrow passage from which a number of doors seemed to diverge, the habitations of miserables, and in one of which dwelt Stewart Lewis.

" On entering this wretched abode we found the unfortunate bard, with his son, a lad of seventeen, sitting at a table and employed in stitching up various copies of his poems in blue paper covers. At our entrance he started up with an exclamation of surprise, and welcomed us to his humble shed. I perceived, however, that his countenance presently lost that bold smile of welcome, and his tongue that vehement gush of poetical, enthusiastic language habitual to him in even the lowest occurrences of common life ; while his mind seemed engaged in recollecting whether there was anything in the house with which he might entertain us. I soon eased him of his fear on that account by laying in his hand the small sum which I had collected for his benefit from the sale of his poems. His face immediately assumed its former smile, and, after thanking me, he sent away his son with two thirds of the money to purchase whiskey — an act of improvident extravagance which I could not help condemning with perhaps too great vehemence for a guest. He did not seem offended by my remonstrances. It was obvious, however, that the cause of his miserable and hopeless condition had been disclosed.

" After this interview I never saw Stewart Lewis more. His wife died shortly after, and he came to my father's house in my absence, in a state of distraction for his loss. He waited many hours for my return, but at last went away without seeing me. The depth of his sorrow was intimated to me in a way perhaps more affecting than any personal interview might have been. He left a letter, in which was written, in a hand which I could scarcely decipher, and in characters which strayed over the whole page, —

"'MY DEAR SIR,

I AM MAD.

STEWART LEWIS.'

"The affection which this poor man entertained for the benign being who, for upwards of thirty years, had shared with him a constant train of sorrow and poverty without ever repining, had in it something truly romantic. She was the first and only woman he had ever loved, and he always declared that he could not survive her loss. Their love was mutual, and her devotion to him had been often shown by more substantial proofs than words.

"She had frequently, even when they were in a state of starvation, worked a whole day at some coarse millinery work to earn a sixpence, that she might, with mistaken kindness, supply her husband with spirits. The unfortunate habit of drinking intoxicating liquors, which he had acquired after an early disappointment in life, never afterwards left him; and whether to drown reflections on his own misery and blasted prospects, or to inspire him with the faculty of versification, he found the indulgence of that propensity, as he imagined, necessary to his existence. But never was the brow of this woman clouded with a reproof of the cause of all her sorrows, and a word of remonstrance against his foibles was never heard to escape her lips. He has commemorated his unutterable affection in several beautiful songs. In one, which he calls his 'Address to his Wife,' I find the following pathetic verses : —

"'In youthful life's ecstatic days,
I've rapt'rous kissed thae lips o' thine ;

> And fondly yet, with joy I gaze
> On thee, auld canty wife o' mine.
>
> " ' When fortune's adverse winds did blaw,
> And maist my senses I wad tine,
> Thy smilin' face drove ill awa',
> Thou ever dear auld wife o' mine.
>
> " ' Lang round the ingle's heartsome blaze,
> Thy thrifty hand made a' to shine ;
> Thou'st been my comfort a' my days,
> Thou carefu' auld wife o' mine.
>
> " ' When life must leave our hoary head,
> Our genial souls will still be kin',
> We'll smile and mingle wi' the dead,
> Thou canty auld wife o' mine.'

After the death of his wife he wandered all over Scotland and the northern counties of England, reckless of his fate. He lamented her death in ceaseless complaints, and seemed careless of life. The remainder of the copies of his poems which he had left with us — a considerable number, — were sent to him while he was at Inverness, and he subsisted entirely on what the sale of them provided for upwards of a twelvemonth. When weary of existence, and worn out with fatigue, he died at an obscure village in Dumfriesshire about the end of 1818. He left three daughters, none of whom I ever saw, and one son, who had latterly been the companion of his wanderings, — a youth unfortunately weak in his intellects, and of whose fate I have been able to learn nothing."

My brother's poetical pieces were the best. Some of them were touching and beautiful, particularly the address " To the Evening Star," which has been often reprinted by compilers of volumes of poetry without intimating its origin, which is not surprising, for who knows that the obscure periodical in which it first made its appearance ever existed ? It may be given as a specimen of his powers of versification at nineteen years of age.

TO THE EVENING STAR.

Soft star of eve, whose trembling light
  Gleams through the closing eye of day,
Where clouds of dying purple bright
  Melt in the shades of eve away,
And mock thee with a fitful ray,
  Pure spirit of the twilight hour,
Till forth thou blazest to display
  The splendor of thy native power.

'Twas thus, when earth from chaos sprung,
  The smoke of forming worlds arose,
And, o'er thine infant beauty hung,
  Hid thee awhile in dark repose ;
Till the black veil dissolved away,
  Drunk by the universal air,
And thou, sweet star, with lovely ray,
  Shone out on paradise so fair.

When the first eve the world had known
  Fell blissfully on Eden's bowers,
And earth's first love lay couched upon
. The dew of Eden's fairest flowers ;
Then thy first smile in heaven was seen
  To hail the birth of love divine,
And ever since that smile hath been
  The sainted passion's hallowed shrine :
Can lover yet behold the beam
  Unmoved, unpassioned, unrefined ?
While there thou shin'st the brightest gem,
  To Night's cerulean crown assigned.

Since then how many gentle eyes
  That love and thy pure ray made bright,
Have gazed on thee with blissful sighs, —
  Now veiled in everlasting night !
O, let not love or youth be vain
  Of present bliss, and hope more high ;
The stars — the very clods remain —
  Love, they, and all of theirs must die.

Now throned upon the western wave,
Thou tremblest coyly, star of love !
And dip'st beneath its gleamy heave
Thy silver foot, the bath to prove.
And though no power thy course may stay,
Which nature's changeless laws compel,
To thee a thousand hearts shall say, —
Sweet star of love, farewell, farewell !

The "Kaleidoscope" did not last. It sold pretty well, but only to the extent of paying expenses, yielding no reward whatever for literary effort. Yet it was not an absolutely valueless undertaking. It was a trial of one's wings, and encouraged to higher flights in more favorable times and circumstances. The concluding number appeared on 12th January, 1822.

From about this time, new and enlarged views began to predominate. Early difficulties had been successfully mastered. Three to four years of a funny, scheming, struggling, tolerably hard-working existence, to be remembered like a dream or chapter of a romance, had effected every reasonable anticipation. Robert's originally small stock had increased to be worth about two hundred pounds, and I had made a similar advance. The Walk, as we thought, had fairly served its day. With sentiments somewhat akin to those of Tom Tug, in the "Waterman," when bidding a pathetic farewell to his "trim-built wherry," we were disposed to bid an affecting and grateful adieu to stall and trestles, and bequeath to others the advantages, the drolleries, and classic associations of open-air traffic. Migration was accordingly resolved on, and we had sundry communings as regards where we should respectively attempt to establish ourselves in Edinburgh.

It was now that Robert, as will be afterwards stated in his own words, became known to Sir Walter Scott, by writing for him, and presenting, through Mr. Constable, a transcript of the songs of the " Lady of the Lake," in the small and neat style of calligraphy to which I have made some reference.   Immediately afterwards, in 1822, he removed to India Place ; I removed to Broughton Street in the spring of 1823 ; both places, as we diffidently ventured to hope, being intermediate to something better.

CHAPTER VII

M Y brother's literary efforts had hitherto been on a
limited scale. He had composed some pieces, remarkable, perhaps, for his years and the untoward circumstances in which he was placed ; but, except by a few acquaintances, none augured that he would make any progress
as an author. His first production, not a very high flight,
was entitled " Illustrations of the Author of Waverley."
It consisted of short sketches of several individuals,
chiefly connected with the south of Scotland, popularly
believed to have been the originals of characters in the
earlier fictions of Sir Walter Scott, as, for example, Davie
Gellatley, Dominie Sampson, Meg Merrilies, and Dandie
Dinmont. The south-country people who came about
us — one of them a retired parish minister given to gossip
— formed a convenient source of information on the
subject.

In a book which speculated on the identification of actual scenes, incidents, and characters with what had given
rise to the fictions of the novelist, it would have been
strange if the writer had not sometimes gone a little wide
of the mark. According to the Introduction to the anno-
tated edition of the " Monastery," an erroneous conjecture
had been hazarded respecting Captain Clutterbuck, who,
not a little to the surprise of Sir Walter, was identified
with a friend and neighbor of his own. Apart, however,

from misapprehensions of this kind, the "Illustrations" pointed, in a wonderfully correct manner, at the originals of some of the principal characters in the earlier novels. The work, issued in 1822, formed a small volume, of which I was the printer. It was well received, and was subsequently (1824) republished in better style by an Edinburgh bookseller.

After being settled in India Place, Robert carried out the design of writing the "Traditions of Edinburgh," a work for which he was in a degree prepared by those youthful explorations already adverted to, as well as by his having meditated over the subject. Professedly, the book was to consist of amusing particulars concerning old houses, distinguished characters, and curious incidents, such as could be picked up from individuals then still living. The scheme met with general approval. There were still alive persons who had some remembrance of the Scottish capital in the early part of the reign of George III., when persons of rank were as yet dwellers in the tall tenements and dingy closes of the Old Town. One gentleman in the decline of life remembered as many as fifty titled personages, some of them of historical note, who dwelt in the Canongate (formerly the Court end of the town) as lately as 1769. There were others whose recollections did not extend so far back, but who in youth had been acquainted with interesting public characters who had disappeared. By procuring information from these various individuals regarding a past state of things, traditions were gathered together which in a few years later would have entirely vanished.

The "Traditions," thus happily put in shape while there were still living memories to draw upon, well suited the antiquarian tastes of my brother, and he entered on the work with the keenest possible relish. It was issued in parts, and I was, of course, the printer and publisher, the whole case and press work being as hitherto executed with my own hands. The result was a book in two volumes, with the date 1824. In an introductory notice to a new edition in 1868, the author gives the following account of the manner in which the work was produced and received.

" I am about to do what very few could do without emotion : revise a book which I wrote forty-five years ago. This little work came out in the Augustan days of Edinburgh, when Jeffrey and Scott, Wilson and the Ettrick Shepherd, Dugald Stewart and Alison, were daily giving the productions of their minds to the public, and while yet Archibald Constable acted as the unquestioned emperor of the publishing world. I was then an insignificant person of the age of twenty ; yet, destitute as I was both of means and friends, I formed the hope of writing something which would attract attention. The subject I proposed was one lying readily at hand, — the romantic things connected with Old Edinburgh. If, I calculated, a first *part* or *number* could be issued, materials for others might be expected to come in, for scores of old inhabitants, even up perhaps to the very ' oldest,' would then contribute their reminiscences.

"The plan met with success. Materials almost unbounded came to me, chiefly from aged professional and mercantile gentlemen, who usually, at my first introduction to them, started at my youthful appearance, having formed the notion that none but an old person would have thought of writing such a book. A friend gave me a letter to Mr. Charles Kirkpatrick Sharpe, who, I was told, knew the scandal of the time of Charles II. as well as he did the merest gossip of the day, and had much to say regarding the good society of a hundred years ago.

"Looking back from the year 1868, I feel that C. K. S. has himself become, as it were, a tradition of Edinburgh. His thin, effeminate figure, his voice pitched *in alt.*, his attire, as he took his daily walks on Princes Street, — a long blue frock-coat, black trousers, rather wide below, and sweeping over white stockings and neat shoes ; something like a web of white cambric round his neck, and a brown wig coming down to his eyebrows, — had long established him as what is called a character. He had recently edited a book containing many stories of *diablerie*, and another in which the original narrative of ultra-presbyterian church history had to bear a series of cavalier notes of the most mocking character. He had a quaint, biting wit, which people bore as they would a scratch from a provoked cat. Essentially, he was good-natured, and fond of merriment. He had considerable gifts of drawing, and one caricature portrait by him of Queen Elizabeth dancing, 'high and disposedly,' before the Scotch ambassadors, is the delight of everybody who has seen it. He was intensely aristocratic, and cared nothing for the interests of the great multitude. He complained that one never heard of any gentlefolks committing crimes nowadays, as if that were a disadvantage to them or the public. Any case of a Lady Jane stabbing a perjured lover would have delighted him. While the child of whim, Mr. Sharpe was generally believed to possess respectable talents, by which, with a need for exerting them, he might have achieved distinction. His ballad of the 'Murder of Caerlaverock,' in the 'Minstrelsy,' is a masterly production ; and the concluding verses haunt one like a beautiful strain of music : —

> " ' To sweet Lincluden's haly cells
> Fu' dowie I'll repair ;
> There Peace wi' gentle Patience dwells,
> Nae deadly feuds are there.

" ' In tears I'll wither ilka charm,
    Like draps o' balefu' yew ;
    And wail the beauty that could harm
    A knight sae brave and true.'

" After what I had heard and read of Charles Sharpe,
I called upon him at his mother's house, No. 93 Princes
Street, in a somewhat excited frame of mind. His servant conducted me to the first floor, and showed me into
what is generally called amongst us the back drawing-
room, which I found carpeted with green cloth, and full
of old family portraits, some on the walls, but many more
on the floor. A small room leading off this one behind,
was the place where Mr. Sharpe gave audience. Its
diminutive space was stuffed full of old curiosities, cases
with family bijouterie, etc. One petty object was strongly
indicative of the man, — a calling-card of Lady Charlotte
Campbell, the once adored beauty, stuck into the frame
of a picture. He must have kept it at that time about
thirty years. On appearing, Mr. Sharpe received me very
cordially, telling me he had seen and been pleased with
my first two numbers. Indeed, he and Sir Walter Scott
had talked together of writing a book of the same kind
in company, and calling it ' Reekiana,' which plan, however, being anticipated by me, the only thing that remained for him was to cast any little matters of the kind
he possessed into my care. I expressed myself duly
grateful, and took my leave. The consequence was, the
appearance of notices regarding the eccentric Lady Anne
Dick, the beautiful Susanna, Countess of Eglintoune, the
Lord Justice-clerk Alva, and the Duchess of Queensberry
(the ' Kitty ' of Prior), before the close of my first volume. Mr. Sharpe's contributions were all of them given
in brief notes, and had to be written out on an enlarged

scale, with what I thought a regard to literary effect as far as the telling was concerned.

" By an introduction from Dr. Chalmers, I visited a living lady who might be considered as belonging to the generation at the beginning of the reign of George III. Her husband, Alexander Murray, had, I believe, been Lord North's solicitor-general for Scotland. She herself, born before the Porteous Riot, and well remembering the Forty-five, was now within a very brief space of the age of a hundred. Although she had not married in her earlier years, her children, Mr. Murray of Henderland and others, were all elderly people. I found the venerable lady seated at a window in her drawing-room in George Street, with her daughter, Miss Murray, taking the care of her which her extreme age required, and with some help from this lady, we had a conversation of about an hour. She spoke with due reverence of her mother's brother, the Lord Chief-justice Mansfield ; and when I adverted to the long pamphlet against him written by Mr. Andrew Stuart at the conclusion of the Douglas Cause, she said that to her knowledge, he had never read it, such being his practice in respect of all attacks made upon him, lest they should disturb his equanimity in judgment. As the old lady was on intimate terms with Boswell, and had seen Johnson on his visit to Edinburgh — as she was the sister-in-law of Allan Ramsay the painter, and had lived in the most cultivated society of Scotland all her long life, — there were ample materials for conversation with her ; but her small strength made this shorter and slower than I could have wished. When we came upon the *poet* Ramsay, she seemed to have caught new vigor from the subject ; she spoke with animation of the child-parties she had attended in his house on the Castlehill during a course of ten years before his death, an event

11

which happened in 1757. He was 'charming,' she said ; he entered so heartily into the plays of children. He, in particular, gained their hearts by making houses for their dolls. How pleasant it was to learn that our great pastoral poet was a man who, in his private capacity, loved to sweeten the daily life of his fellow-creatures, and particularly of the young ! At a warning from Miss Murray, I had to tear myself away from this delightful and never-to-be-forgotten interview.

"I had, one or two years before, when not out of my teens, attracted some attention from Sir Walter Scott, by writing for him and presenting (through Mr. Constable) a transcript of the songs of the 'Lady of the Lake,' in a style of peculiar calligraphy, which I practiced for want of any better way of attracting the notice of people superior to myself. When George IV. some months afterwards came to Edinburgh, good Sir Walter remembered me, and procured for me the business of writing the address of the Royal Society of Edinburgh to his Majesty, for which I was handsomely paid. Several other learned bodies followed the example, for Sir Walter Scott was the arbiter of everything during that frantic time, and thus I was substantially benefited by his means.

"According to what Mr. Constable told me, the great man liked me, in part because he understood I was from Tweedside. On seeing the earlier numbers of the 'Traditions,' he expressed astonishment as to 'where the boy got all the information.' But I did not see or hear from him till the first volume had been completed. He then called upon me one day, along with Mr. Lockhart. I was overwhelmed with the honor, for Sir Walter Scott was almost an object of worship to me. I literally could not utter a word. While I stood silent, I heard him tell his companion that Charles Sharpe was a writer in the

'Traditions,' and taking up the volume, he read aloud
what he called one of his *quaint bits.* 'The ninth Earl
of Eglintoune was one of those patriarchal peers who live
to an advanced age; indefatigable in the frequency of
their marriages and the number of their children; who
linger on and on, with an unfailing succession of young
countesses, and die at last leaving a progeny interspersed
throughout the whole of Douglas's " Peerage," two volumes, folio, reëdited by Wood.' And then both gentlemen went on laughing for perhaps two minutes, with
interjections: ' How like Charlie! ' ' What a strange being he is! ' '*Two volumes, folio, reëdited by Wood* — ha,
ha, ha! There you have him past all doubt ; ' and so on.
I was too much abashed to ·tell Sir Walter that it was
only an impudent little bit of writing of my own, part of
the solution into which I had diffused the actual notes of
Sharpe. But, having occasion to write next day to Mr.
Lockhart, I mentioned Sir Walter's mistake ; and he was
soon after good enough to inform me that he had set his
friend right as to the authorship, and they had had a *second*
hearty laugh on the subject.

" A very few days after this visit, Sir Walter sent me,
along with a kind letter, a packet of manuscript, consisting of sixteen folio pages, in his usual close handwriting,
and containing all the reminiscences he could at the time
summon up of old persons and things in Edinburgh.
Such a treasure to me! And such a gift from the greatest literary man of the age to the humblest! Is there a
literary man of the present age who would scribble as
much for any humble aspirant? Nor was this the only
act of liberality of Scott to me. When I was preparing
a subsequent work, 'The Popular Rhymes of Scotland,'
he sent me whole sheets of his recollections, with appropriate explanations. For years thereafter, he allowed me

to join him in his walks home from the Parliament House, in the course of which he freely poured into my greedy ears anything he knew regarding the subjects of my studies. His kindness and good-humor on these occasions were untiring. I have since found, from his journal, that I had met him on certain days when his heart was overladen with woe. Yet his welcome to me was the same. After 1826, however, I saw him much less frequently than before, for I knew he grudged every moment not spent in thinking and working on the fatal tasks he had assigned to himself for the redemption of his debts.

" All through the preparation of this book, I was indebted a good deal to a gentleman who was neither a literary man nor an artist himself, but hovered round the outskirts of both professions, and might be considered as a useful adjunct to both. Every votary of pen or pencil amongst us knew David Bridges at his drapery establishment in the Lawnmarket, and many had been indebted to his obliging disposition. A quick, dark-eyed little man, with lips full of sensibility and a tongue unloving of rest, such a man in a degree as one can suppose Garrick to have been, he held a sort of court every day, where wits and painters jostled with people wanting coats, jerkins, and spotted handkerchiefs. The place was small, and had no saloon behind ; so, whenever David had got some 'bit' to show you, he dragged you down a dark stair to a packing-place, lighted only by a grate from the street, and there, amidst plaster-casts numberless, would fix you with his glittering eye, till he had convinced you of the fine handling, the 'buttery touches' (a great phrase with him), the admirable 'scummling' (another), and so forth. It was in the days prior to the Royal Scottish Academy and its exhibitions ; and it was left in a great measure to David Bridges to bring forward aspirants in art. Did such a person long for notice, he had only to give David one of his best 'bits,' and in a short time he would find himself chattered into fame in that profound, the grate of which I never can pass without recalling something of the buttery touches of those old days. The Blackwood wits, who laughed at everything, fixed upon our friend the title of ' Director-general of the Fine Arts,' which was, however, too much of a truth to be a jest. To this extraordinary being I had been introduced somehow, and, entering heartily into my views, he brought me information, brought me friends, read and criticised my proofs, and would, I dare say, have written the book itself if I had so desired. It is impossible to think of him without a smile, but at the same time a certain melancholy, for his life was one which, I fear, proved a poor one for himself.

"Before the 'Traditions' were finished, I had become favorably acquainted with many gentlemen of letters and others, who were pleased to think that Old Edinburgh had . been chronicled. Wilson gave me a laudatory sentence in the 'Noctes Ambrosianæ.' The Bard of Ettrick, viewing my boyish years, always spoke of and to me as an unaccountable sort of person, but never could be induced to believe otherwise than that I had written all my traditions from my own head. I had also the pleasure of enjoying some intercourse with the venerable Henry Mackenzie, who had been born in 1745, but always seemed to feel as if the ' Man of Feeling' had been written only one instead of sixty years ago, and as if there was nothing particular in antique occurrences. The whole affair was pretty much of a triumph at the time. Now, when I am giving it a final revision, I reflect with touched feelings, that all the brilliant men of the time when it was written are, without an exception, passed away, while, for myself, I am forced to claim the benefit of Horace's humanity : —

" ' Solve senescentem mature sanus equum, ne
Peccet ad extremum ridendus, et ilia ducat.' " [1]

In this recent edition of the "Traditions" are comprehended a variety of particulars gathered since the first
appearance of the work, and calculated to heighten the
legendary picture of Old Edinburgh. A great proportion
of this new matter was drawn from a small work which
my brother wrote under the title of "Reekiana," which
appeared in 1833. The new edition of the "Traditions"
is therefore a considerable improvement on the old. One
does not read without interest an account of interviews
with aged persons, such as Sir William Macleod Banna-
tyne, who recollected the circumstance of "his father
drawing on his boots to go to make interest in London in
behalf of some of the men in trouble for the Forty-five,
particularly his own brother-in-law, the Clanranald of that
day." Perhaps the most interesting of these interviews
was one narrated as follows, with Mrs. Irving, a venerable
lady who possessed by inheritance the patent of Ander-
son's pills, a drug which took its origin from Dr. Ander-
son, a physician of the time of Charles I. : —

"In 1829, Mrs. Irving lived in a neat, self-contained
mansion in Chessels's Court, in the Canongate, along with
her son, General Irving, and some members of his family.
The old lady, then ninety-one, was good enough to invite
me to dinner, where I likewise found two younger sisters
of hers, respectively eighty-nine and ninety. She sat firm
and collected at the head of the table, and carved a leg
of mutton with perfect propriety. She then told me, at
her son's request, that, in the year 1745, when Prince
Charles's army was in possession of the town, she, a child
of four years, walked with her nurse to Holyrood Palace,

[1] Discreetly unharness in good time a horse growing old, lest in
the end he make a miserable break-down.

and seeing a Highland gentleman standing in the doorway, she went up to him to examine his peculiar attire.
She even took the liberty of lifting up his kilt a little way;
whereupon her nurse, fearing some danger, started forward for her protection. But the gentleman only patted
her head, and said something kind to her. I felt it as
very curious to sit as a guest with a person who had mingled in the Forty-five. But my excitement was brought to
a higher pitch, when, on ascending to the drawing-room,
I found the general's daughter, a pretty young woman,
recently married, sitting there, dressed in a suit of clothes
belonging to one of her nonagenarian aunts — a very fine
one of flowered satin, with elegant cap and lappets, and
silk shoes three inches deep in the heel, — the same having been worn just seventy years before at a Hunters'
Ball at Holyrood Palace. The contrast between the former and the present wearer — the old lady shrunk and
taciturn, and her young representative full of life, and
resplendent in joyous beauty — had an effect upon me
which it would be impossible to describe. To this day, I
look upon the Chessels's Court dinner as one of the most
extraordinary events of my life. Mrs. Irving died in
1837, at the age of ninety-nine."

Passing to the next of my brother's productions: In
November, 1824, there was a week of calamitous fires
in Edinburgh, which desolated a portion of the High
Street and Parliament Square. To help the fund raised
on behalf of the sufferers on the occasion, he wrote a popular account of the chief " Fires which have occurred in
Edinburgh since the Beginning of the Eighteenth Century." In the excitement of the moment it had a considerable sale, and was so far useful.

The success of the " Traditions " encouraged the preparation of a companion to that work, applying to the general features of the city, and partly devoted to the service of strangers. It was styled " Walks in Edinburgh," and was issued in 1825. From the pleasing, anecdotic style in which the book was written, it was well received, and added to the literary repute of the writer.

Diligent, painstaking, and with a love of what was old and characteristic, Robert had for some time been collecting a variety of familiar sayings in rhyme, and these appeared early in 1826, under the title of " Popular Rhymes of Scotland." As has been already mentioned, Sir Walter Scott, with his accustomed kindness, forwarded some contributions to the work, which has passed through three editions. As regards the purport of this collection of national rhymes, the following explanation is given in the preface to the third and considerably extended edition : —

" Reared amidst friends to whom 'popular poetry furnished a daily enjoyment, and led by a tendency of my own mind to delight in whatever is quaint, whimsical, and old, I formed the wish, at an early period of life, to complete, as I considered it, the collection of the traditionary verse of Scotland, by gathering together and publishing all that remained of a multitude of rhymes and short snatches of verse applicable to places, families, natural objects, amusements, etc., wherewith, not less than by song and ballad, the cottage fireside was amused in days gone past, while yet printed books were only familiar to comparatively few. This task was executed as well as circumstances would permit, and a portion of the ' Popular Rhymes of Scotland ' was published in 1826. Other objects have since occupied me, generally of a graver kind ; yet amidst them all, I have never lost my wish to complete the publication of these relics of the old *natural literature* of my native country."

Among the persons to whom my brother applied for materials for the work was William Wilson, a young man of about his own age, who had similar poetical and archæological tastes, and for a time edited a literary periodical in Dundee. Between the two there sprung up an extraordinary friendship, which was not weakened by Wilson some years later emigrating to America, and setting up as a bookseller at Poughkeepsie, a pretty town on the Hudson, in the State of New York. The letters which passed between them bring into view a number of particulars concerning my brother's literary aims and efforts. Writing in January, 1824, to Wilson, whom he always addressed as his " dear Willie," he refers gratifyingly to the " Traditions," and the manner in which the book had brought him into notice : " This little work is taking astonishingly, and I am getting a great deal of credit by it. It has also been the means of introducing me to many of the most respectable leading men of the town, and has attracted to me the attention of not a few of the most eminent literary characters. What would you think, for instance, of the venerable author of the " Man of Feeling " calling on me in his carriage to contribute his remarks in manuscript on my work ! The value of the above two great advantages is incalculable to a young tradesman and author like me. It saves me twenty years of mere laborious plodding by the common walk, and gives me at twenty-two all the respectability which I could have expected at forty."

Later in the same year, he incloses a lyrical effusion to Wilson, the inspiring heroine of which can be guessed at from the name of a young lady, who was prevented by her mother from forming an intimacy with one not supposed to be in the category of an "eligible." It is to be regretted that " Leila " was not afterwards particularly fortunate in her marriage.

" Fair Leila's eyes, fair Leila's eyes,
  Oft fill my breast with glad surprise —
  Surprise and love, and hope and pride,
  With many a glowing thought beside.

" The light that lies in Leila's eyes
  No trick of vain allurement tries,
  But sheds a soft and constant beam,
  Like moonlight on the tranquil stream ;
  Yet as the seas from pole to pole
  Move at yon gentle orb's control,
  So tumults in my bosom rise
  Beneath the charm of Leila's eyes.
            Fair Leila's eyes, fair Leila's eyes, etc.

" For Leila's eyes I'd gladly shun
  The flaunting glare of Fortune's sun,
  And to the humble shade betake,
  Which they a brighter heaven could make.
  The wildfire lights I once pursued
  Should ne'er again my steps delude :
  I'd fix my faith, and only prize
  The steadfast light of Leila's eyes.
            Fair Leila's eyes, fair Leila's eyes, etc."

Improving in his prospects, Robert removed with his
bookselling business to Hanover Street, where the conducting of his establishment fell partly on James, who had
been reared as a coadjutor. In 1826, following next after
the " Rhymes," appeared his " Picture of Scotland," a
work in two volumes, the materials for which had been
gathered together by a succession of toilsome peregrinations over a large part of the country, exclusively of previous historical studies. An ardent attachment to Scotland had led him to undertake the work ; for, as he said,
" Instead of the pilgrim's scallop in my hat, I took for
motto the glowing expression of Burns : ' I have no
dearer aim than to make leisurely journeys through Cale-
donia ; to sit on the fields of her battles ; to wander on

the romantic banks of her streams ; and to muse by the stately towers of venerable ruins, once the homesteads of her heroes.' " In the main topographical, the book comprehended an interlarding of native anecdote and humor, along with illustrations of the manners of a past age. "The reclamation of that which is altogether poetry — the wonderful, beautiful past," he adds, was a primary object of the book, being "conscious and certain that, though many of his own generation may not give him credit for so exalted a purpose, the people who shall afterwards inherit this romantic land will appreciate what could not have been preserved but with a view to their gratification."

The " Picture of Scotland " was followed in rapid succession by several works which still further extended Robert's popularity as a writer. The quantity of literary work of one kind or other which he went through during some years at this period was astonishing, more particularly when we know that he continued to give a certain degree of attention daily to business. Indeed, with all his love of letters, he by no means relied on his efforts with the pen. He used to repeat a sage remark of Scott, that literature is a good cane to walk with, but not a staff to lean upon ; an observation too apt to be neglected by young and inexperienced writers.

Archibald Constable, in his attempts to revive a publishing business after the catastrophe of 1825, happily struck out the idea of a series of cheap popular works, by which employment was found for a number of persons with literary tastes and of tried ability. Robert was one of the earliest so pressed into the service of " Constable's Miscellany." In 1828, appeared his "History of the Rebellion of 1745," in two volumes ; at the close of the same year was issued his " History of the Rebellions in

Scotland under the Marquis of Montrose and others from 1638 to 1660," in two volumes ; this was followed, in 1829, by a "History of the Rebellions in Scotland under Viscount Dundee and the Earl of Mar in 1689 and 1715," in one volume ; and finally, in 1830, he contributed the "Life of James I.," in two volumes. Such, however, was not the entire amount of his literary labor. Intermediately, he edited "Scottish Ballads and Songs," in three volumes (1829), and the "Biography of Distinguished Scotsmen," in four volumes. Besides which, he furnished Mr. Lockhart with a variety of valuable notes for his "Life of Robert Burns."

Of all these works, that which attained the greatest and most enduring popularity was the "History of the Rebellion of 1745," the materials for which were gathered from the principal sources of information available in 1827. Several families, whose ancestors had been compromised in the insurrection, obligingly furnished traditional anecdotes for the work, which thereby assumed a character considerably different from one consisting of dry historical annals. While received with general approbation, the "History of the Rebellion," from the *feeling* with which it was written, led to a notion that it was the work of a Jacobite. Such seems to have been the opinion of a writer in the "Quarterly Review," who, in reviewing Lord Mahon's "History of England" (1839), refers to the "many curious details, gleaned with exemplary diligence, and presented in a lively enough style," in the histories of the rebellions of 1715 and 1745, by "Mr. Robert Chambers, a bookseller and antiquary of Edinburgh," adding: "His Jacobitism seems that of a rampant Highlander ; and we doubt not, had he flourished at the proper time, he would have handled his claymore gallantly ; nor are we at all surprised to hear that he enjoys considerable popularity

among certain classes in Scotland ; but we cannot antici-
pate that these historical performances will ever obtain a
place in the English library."

To conclusions as to his supposed Jacobitism, my
brother made some demur. He declared that he "dis-
approved of the insurrection of 1745, and held that it
undoubtedly was a crime to disturb with war, and to some
extent with rapine, a nation enjoying internal peace under
a settled government. But, on the other hand, it was
evident that those who followed Charles Edward acted
according to their lights, with heroic self-devotion, and
were not fairly liable to the vulgar ridicule and vitupera-
tions thrown upon them by those whose duty it was to
resist and punish them. Accordingly, it was just that the
adventures of the persons concerned should be detailed
with impartiality, and their unavoidable misfortunes be
spoken of with humane feeling." Such is the vindicatory
remark he makes in a prefatory note to the seventh edition of the work, issued as lately as 1869 ; and in the
present day, few will be disposed to challenge the accuracy of this view of the matter. Whether this historical
performance has obtained a place in what the reviewer is
pleased to call " the English library," I am not prepared
to say, further than that, without adventitious aid, it has
been very extensively diffused in all parts of Great Britain,
and remains, to appearance, a generally received work on
the subject.

The new edition of the " History " just referred to has
been so greatly extended as to be almost a new work.
The prolific source of the fresh information that was
obtained, was a collection of ten volumes in manuscript,
styled on the title-pages the " Lyon in Mourning," which
had been prepared by the anxious care of the Right Rev.
Bishop Forbes, of the Scottish Episcopal Church, and

who was settled as a minister of that communion in Leith at the middle of the eighteenth century. Laboring under the suspicion that he was a Jacobite dangerous to the reigning dynasty, he was confined in Edinburgh Castle during the rebellion, and only liberated in 1746. By this means he was saved from the disasters of the falling cause, and brought into leisurely communication with a number of the insurgents, who were seized at various times and placed in confinement along with him. After regaining his liberty, Bishop Forbes prosecuted the design of collecting from the mouths and pens of the survivors of the late enterprise such narratives, anecdotes, and memorabilia as they could give from their own knowledge, or as eye-witnesses, respecting this extraordinary historical episode. The whole of the trustworthy information so acquired was written on octavo sheets, which in the end formed volumes ; and nothing can exceed the neatness, distinctness, and accuracy with which the whole task appears to have been performed. In allusion to the woe of Scotland for her exiled race of princes, the ten volumes composing the work were bound in black, and styled the "Lyon in Mourning." The poor bishop died in 1776, leaving the collection to his widow, who, after many years, sold it to Sir Henry Steuart of Allanton, who had been induced to turn his attention to the subject ; and he commenced a work designed to present a historical re-view of the different attempts made to restore the Stewart family to the throne. The work had been carried a certain length, when it was interrupted by ill-health, and permanently laid aside. On a visit to Allanton House in 1832, my brother first heard of the " Lyon," and was so fortunate as to have it assigned to him for literary pur-poses. The result (1834) was the " Jacobite Memoirs of the Rebellion of 1745." But from the wide-spread information contained in the collection, were drawn innumerable particulars of a deeply interesting kind for the revised edition of the " History."

Between 1823 and 1835, Robert amused himself, and gave relief to his feelings, by occasionally writing poetical pieces, which he collected and printed in a volume for private circulation. The following is one of these effusions, purporting to be written July, 1829, in reference to the very amiable young lady, Miss Anne Kirkwood, whom he married in December of that year.[1]

THOU GENTLE AND KIND ONE.

" Thou gentle and kind one,
　　Who com'st o'er my dreams
Like the gales of the west,
　　Or the music of streams ;
O softest and dearest,
　　Can that time e'er be,
When I could be forgetful
　　Or scornful of thee ?

" No ! my soul might be dark,
　　Like a landscape in shade,
And for thee not the half
　　Of its love be displayed,
But one ray of thy kindness
　　Would banish my pain,
And soon kiss every feature
　　To brightness again.

" And if, in contending
　　With men and the world,
My eye might be fierce
　　Or my brow might be curled ;

[1] December 7, 1829. — Robert Chambers married to Anne Kirkwood, only child of the late John Kirkwood, Custom-house, Glasgow. — *Newspaper Notice.*

That brow on thy bosom
   All smoothed would recline,
And that eye melt in kindness,
   When turned upon thine.

" If faithful in sorrow,
    More faithful in joy —
Thou shouldst find that no change
    Could affection destroy ;
All profit, all pleasure
    As nothing would be,
And each triumph despised,
    Unpartaken by thee."

Always ready to lend a helping hand to the promotion of any literary object connected with his native country, my brother, in 1830, contributed historical and descriptive notices to a work styled the "Picture of Stirling." An opportunity was thereby afforded of giving an account of an object formerly of national inportance, known as the " Stirling Jug," — such having been the legal standard for the old Scotch pint (equal to about an English quart), which is referred to, as some may perhaps think, rather too frequently in the verses of Burns and others. As little is popularly known regarding the history of the Stirling Jug, we may copy it for general edification : —

"By an act of the Scottish Parliament, in 1437, various burghs in the Lowlands were appointed to keep the various standard measures for liquid and dry goods, from which all others throughout the country were to be taken. To Edinburgh was appointed the honor of keeping the standard ell ; to Perth the reel ; to Lanark the pound ; to Linlithgow the firlot ; and to Stirling the pint. This was a judicious arrangement, both as it was calculated to prevent any attempt at an extensive or general scheme of fraud, and as the commodities to which the different standards referred were supplied in the greatest abundance by the districts and towns to whose

care they were committed ; Edinburgh being then the principal
market for cloth, Perth for yarn, Lanark for wool, Linlithgow
for grain, and Stirling for distilled and fermented liquors. The
pint measure, popularly called the Stirling Jug, is still kept with
great care in the town where it was first deposited four hundred
years ago. It is made of brass, in the shape of a hollow cone
truncated. . . . . The handle is fixed with two brass nails :
and the whole has an appearance of rudeness, quite proper
to the early age when it was first instituted by the Scottish
Estates as the standard of liquid measure for this ancient bac-
chanalian kingdom. It will be interesting to all votaries of
antiquity to know that this vessel, which may in some measure
be esteemed a national palladium, was rescued, about eighty
years ago, from the fate of being utterly lost, to which all circumstances for some time seemed to destine it. The person
whom we have to thank for this good service was the Reverend
Alexander Bryce, minister of Kirknewton, near Edinburgh, a
man of scientific and literary accomplishment much superior to
what was displayed by the generality of the clergy of his day.
Mr. Bryce (who had taught the mathematical class in the college
of Edinburgh during the winter of 1745–46, instead of the eminent Maclaurin, who was then on his death-bed) happened to
visit Stirling in the year 1750 ; when, recollecting that the
standard pint jug was appointed to remain in that town, he
requested permission from the magistrates to see it. The
magistrates conducted him to their council-house, where a
pewter pint jug was taken down from the roof, whence it was
suspended, and presented to him. After a careful examination,
he was convinced that this could not be the legal standard. He
communicated his opinion to the magistrates ; but they were
equally ignorant of the loss which the town had sustained, and
indisposed to take any trouble for the purpose of retrieving it.
It excited very different feelings in the acute and inquiring
mind of Dr. Bryce ; and resolved, if possible, to recover the
valuable antique, he immediately instituted a search ; which,
though conducted with much patient industry for about a
twelvemonth, proved, to his great regret, unavailing. In 1752,
it occurred to him that the standard jug might have been bor-

12

rowed by some of the coppersmiths or braziers, for the purpose of making legal measures for the citizens, and, by some chance, not returned. Having been informed that a person of this description, named Urquhart, had joined the insurgent forces in 1745 ; that, on his not returning, his furniture and shop utensils had been brought to sale ; and that various articles, which had not been sold, were thrown into a garret as useless, a gleam of hope darted into his mind, and he eagerly went to make the proper investigation. Accordingly, in that obscure garret, buried underneath a mass of lumber, he discovered the precious object of his research.

"Thus was discovered the only standard, by special statute, of all liquid and dry measure in Scotland, after it had been offered for sale at perhaps the cheap and easy price of one penny, rejected as unworthy of that little sum, and subsequently thrown by as altogether useless ; and many years after it had been considered by its constitutional guardians as irretrievably lost. For his 'good services' in recovering the Stirling Jug, Mr. Bryce was presented with the freedom of the city of Edinburgh, January, 1754."

Towards the close of 1831, Robert made what many may think a bold attempt in literature. It was, by a collection of sayings and anecdotes, "to vindicate, for the first time, the pretensions of the Scottish nation to the character of a witty and jocular, as they are already allowed to be a painstaking and enlightened race." The book, styled "Scottish Jests and Anecdotes," certainly contained a prodigious array of good things, collected from all imaginable sources, including personal experience in general society. It being the first attempt of the kind, the editor says he felt as if "entitled to some share of that praise which is so liberally bestowed upon discoverers like Cook and Parry, and might expect to be celebrated in after ages as the first man who extended the Geography of Fun beyond the Tweed." The work was pretty well received, and went through two editions; after which, dropping out of notice, it was left for the Very Rev. Dean Ramsay to take up the subject in that more earnest spirit which has insured a great share of public approbation.

That my brother had any merit in discovering that the Scotch are a " witty " people, will be doubted by those who think them incapable of getting beyond a certain species of dry and caustic humor. One thing certainly remarkable in all works purporting to be collections of Scottish jests and anecdotes, is the abundance of droll sayings and doings of parish ministers, beadles, and old serving-men. As a specimen of what Robert collected of this nature, we may give an anecdote referring to what he calls

THE UNLUCKY PRESENT.

" A Lanarkshire minister (who died within the present century) was one of those unhappy persons, who, to use the words of a well-known Scottish adage, 'can never see green cheese but their een reels.' He was *extremely covetous*, and that not only of nice articles of food, but of many other things which do not generally excite the cupidity of the human heart. Being on a visit, one day, at the house of one of his parishioners, a poor lonely widow, living in a moorland part of the parish, he became fascinated by the charms of a little cast-iron pot, which happened, at the time, to be lying on the hearth, full of potatoes for the poor woman's dinner, and that of her children. He had never, in his life, seen such a nice little pot — it was a perfect conceit of a thing — it was a gem — no pot on earth could match it in symmetry — it was an object altogether perfectly lovely. 'Dear sake ! minister,' said the widow, quite overpowered by the reverend man's commendations of her pot; 'if ye like the pot sae weel as a' that, I beg ye'll let me send it to the manse. It's a kind o' orra' [superfluous] 'pot wi' us; for we've a bigger ane, that we use for ordinar, and that's mair convenient every way for us. Sae ye'll just tak a present o't. I'll send it ower the morn wi' Jamie, when he gangs to the schule.' 'O!' said the minister, 'I can by no means permit you to be at so much trouble. Since you are so good as to give me the pot, I'll just carry it home with me in my hand. I'm so much taken with it, indeed, that I would really prefer carrying it myself.' After much altercation between the minister and the widow on this delicate point of politeness, it was agreed that he should carry home the pot himself.

"Off then he trudged, bearing this curious little culinary article alternately in his hand and under his arm, as seemed most convenient to him. Unfortunately the day was warm, the way long, and the minister fat, so that he became heartily tired of his burden before he got half-way home. In these distressing circumstances it struck him that if instead of carrying the pot awkwardly at one side of his person he were to carry it on his head, the burden would be greatly lightened. Accordingly, doffing his hat, which he resolved to carry home in his hand, and having applied his handkerchief to his brow, he placed the pot; in inverted fashion, upon his head. There was, at first, much relief and much comfort in this new mode of carrying the pot, but mark the result. The unfortunate minister, having taken a by-path to escape observation, found himself, when still a good way from home, under the necessity of leaping over a ditch which intercepted him in passing from one field to another. He jumped, but unfortunately the concussion given to his person in descending caused the helmet to become a hood; the pot slipped down over his face, and resting with the rim upon his neck there stuck fast. What was worst of all the nose, which had permitted the pot to slip down over it, withstood every desperate attempt on the part of its proprietor to make it slip back again; the contracted part, or neck, of the pot being of such a peculiar formation as to cling fast to the base of the nose, although it had found no difficulty in gliding downwardly over it. Was ever minister in a worse plight? What was to be done? The place was lonely; the way difficult and dangerous; human relief was remote, almost beyond reach. It was impossible even to cry for help; or if a cry

could be uttered, it would not travel twelve inches in any direction. To add to the distresses of the case, the unhappy sufferer
soon found great difficulty in breathing. What with the heat
occasioned by the beating of the sun on the metal, and what
with the frequent return of the same heated air to his lungs, he
was in the utmost danger of suffocation. Everything considered, it seemed likely that if he did not chance to be relieved by
some accidental wayfarer there would soon be *death in the pot.*

" The instinctive love of life, however, is omniprevalent.
Pressed by the urgency of his distresses, the poor minister fortunately recollected that there was a smith's shop at the distance of about a mile across the fields, which if he could reach
he might possibly find relief. Deprived of his eyesight, he
acted only as a man of feeling, and went on as cautiously as he
could with his hat in his hand. Half crawling, half sliding,
over ridge and furrow, ditch and hedge, the unhappy minister
travelled with all possible speed, as nearly as he could guess,
in the direction of the place of refuge. I leave it to the reader
to conceive the surprise, the mirth, the infinite amusement of
the blacksmith and all the hangers-on of the *smiddy*, when, at
length, torn and worn, faint and exhausted, blind and breath-
less, the unfortunate man arrived at the place and let them
know (rather by signs than by words) the circumstances of his
case.

" The merriment of the people who assembled soon gave way
to considerations of humanity. Ludicrous as was the minister,
with such an object where his head should have been, and with
the feet of the pot pointing upwards, it was necessary that he
should be speedily restored to his ordinary condition if it were
for no other reason than that he might continue to live. He
was, accordingly, at his own request, led into the smithy, bystanders flocking around to tender him their kindest offices or to
witness the process of release ; and having laid down his head
upon the anvil the smith lost no time in seizing and poising his
goodly forehammer. 'Will I come sair on, minister?' exclaimed the considerate man of iron in at the brink of the pot.
' As sair as ye like,' was the minister's answer ; ' better a chap
i' the chafts than die for want of breath.' Thus permitted, the

man let fall a blow which fortunately broke the pot in pieces
without hurting the head which it inclosed, as the cook-maid
breaks the shell of the lobster without bruising the delicate
food within. A few minutes of the clear air, and a glass of the
guidwife's cordial, restored the unfortunate minister; but assuredly the incident is one which will long live in the memory
of his parishioners."

We have not yet completed the review of literary work
in which Robert was engaged from about 1829 to 1832.
Busied as he was, he undertook the editorship of the " Edinburgh Advertiser," a newspaper of old standing, as well
as an old style of politics, that has been latterly discon-
tinued. This species of employment had the effect of
bringing him in contact with some local public characters,
and of widening his acquaintanceship among the political
party who viewed the proposed changes in the constitution
with distrust. It may be conceived that his connection
with the old " Advertiser " was not uncongenial with the
feelings of Sir Walter Scott. But between the great novelist and my brother personal intercourse had ceased, for
Sir Walter was now an invalid at Abbotsford. Letters,
however, passed between them, as is observable from Robert's private papers, sometimes in reference to literary matters, and on other occasions concerning the introductions
of strangers. A Miss MacLaughlin, with musical acquirements, having visited Edinburgh, besought for herself and
her mother an introduction to Sir Walter, which being
granted, the following letter was shortly afterwards received, dated from Abbotsford, March 7, 1831 : —

"MY DEAR MR. CHAMBERS, — I was quite happy to see
Miss MacLaughlin, who is a fine, enthusiastic girl, and very,
very pretty withal. They — that is, her mother and she —
breakfasted with me, though I had what is unusual at Abbotsford, no female assistance. However, we got on very well,

and I prepared the young lady a set of words to the air of 'Crochallan.' But although Miss M. proposed to leave me a copy of the Celtic harmonies, I suppose the servant put it in her carriage. Purdie is the publisher. Will you get me a copy of the number containing ' Crochallan,' with a prose translation by a competent person, and let me know the expense ? [1]

" I fear I cannot be of use to you in the way you propose, though I sincerely rejoice in your success, and would gladly promote it ; but Dr. Abercrombie threatens me with death if I write so much. I must assist Lockhart a little, for you are aware of our connection, and he has always shown me the duties of a son ; but except that, and my own necessary work at the edition of the Waverley Novels, as they call them, I can hardly pretend to be a contributor, for, after all, that same dying is a ceremony one would put off as long as he could. . . . . I am, dear Mr. Chambers, very faithfully yours,

"WALTER SCOTT."

The next letter received, which has the date Abbotsford, August 2, 1831, bears a melancholy record of Sir Walter's growing bodily weakness : —

" DEAR MR. CHAMBERS, — I received your letter through Mr. Cadell. It is impossible for a gentleman to say no to a request which flatters him more than he deserves. But even although it is said in the newspapers, I actually am far from well. I am keeping my head as cool as I can, and speak with some difficulty ; but I am unwilling to make a piece of work about nothing, and instead of doing so I ought rather to receive the lady as civilly as I can. I am much out, riding, or

---

[1] The origin of the beautiful song of *Chro Challin* takes a conspicuous place in the traditions of the Scottish Gael. Chro Challin is the *Cattle of Colin.* In the song, a maiden, anxious to make out a favorable case for her lover, who is a hunter, describes him as possessing large herds ; but does this in a metaphorical manner, so that, in the long run, it turns out that his cattle are only the deer of the mountains. . . . . Other romantic origins are given to the song and air, which still charm the Highland ear. — R. CHAMBERS, in *Land of Burns.*

rather crawling about my plantations in the morning when the weather will permit ; but a card from Miss Eccles will find me at home, and happy to see her, although the effect is like to be disappointment to the lady. I am your faithful, humble servant.

" I have owed you a letter longer than I intended; but I write with pain, and generally use the hand of a friend. I sign with my initials as enough to represent the poor half of me that is left, but am still much yours, W. S."

This appears to have been the last letter received by my brother from Sir Walter Scott.

CHAPTER VIII

ROBERT'S success with the "Traditions," and my own progress in the new field I had selected, left nothing to regret. The "Dark Ages" had vanished into the dim past. The mediæval period had dawned. There was no longer a fierce skirmishing with difficulties, but there was much less drollery. As men get up in the world they, as a rule, take on the gravity which by immemorial usage pertains to what are called the respectable classes. They are likewise apt to part convoy with a number of individuals who have hitherto kept within hail. The reason is plain. Each, from choice, pursues his own line of navigation. Mankind are roughly divided, in unequal proportions, into two sets — those who consume day by day all they can lay their hands on, thinking no more of what is to be their fate in a year or ten years hence than the lower animals ; others — a much less numerous body — who are always looking ahead and acting with less or more regard to the future. What impressive examples one could produce of these differences of taste! Two young men, of good education, start in life with pretty equal chances of success. One of them rises by gradations to be Lord Chancellor : where do we find the other? Seated with his back to the wall, drawing figures in red and white chalk on a smooth piece of pavement, in the hope of retiring to his evening haunt with the sum of half a crown in six-

pences and half-pence, to be spent probably in the felicity
of a carouse. That, we may presume, is the line of life
he has deliberately preferred. He had worked for beg-
gary, and he has got it. When a man will make no sacrifice of his pleasures, but sets his heart on freshly beginning
the world every day, or every week, it is not difficult to do
so. The facility with which the thing can be done ex-
plains much of what seems to perplex society and drive it
almost to its wit's end.

In the strange complication of human affairs, luck, no
doubt counts for something ; but have we properly considered what is luck ? Surely, the business of life cannot
be said to be conducted on the hap-hazard principles of a
game of roulette ! Is there no prearrangement, no Providential design, leading by a series of circumstances to results which have been hitherto shrouded from our finite
intelligence ? To be lucky, as it is called, one requires to
make some reasonably strenuous exertion — probably to
make some unpleasant sacrifices. Erskine might not,
perhaps, have risen to be Lord Chancellor but for the fortunate sprain which caused him hastily to relinquish an
intended visit, and return home, where he was waited on
by a worthy old maritime gentleman, whose intricate case
he took up, mastered, and carried through triumphantly.
But we must bear in mind that he had by previous and
toilsome exertion, and no little self-sacrifice, prepared himself to benefit by the fortunate accident which brought
him into notice.[1]   It is a pity that one has to make so
many sacrifices of inclinations, to *thole* a good deal, possibly to relinquish some amusements, in order to attain
anything like permanent comfort ; but so it is, and ever
will be. When my brother and I got emancipated from
the Dark Ages, it was our fate to proceed on a course

[1] Campbell's *Lives of the Chancellors.*

wholly different from that which several persons we had known were pleased to pursue. Their policy being to live all for the present, and not for the future, sent us naturally in opposite directions. Apparently wishing to end as they began, they spent daily or weekly all they earned, and were ever at the same point of progress. They doubtless, however, enjoyed themselves to their own satisfaction, and there we must leave them.

Relaxing no effort, five to six years had effected a beneficial change of circumstances. We were both, in a sense, raised to a higher platform, and had, indeed, reached that social status, if not something above it, which had been lost by the family calamity of 1812. It seemed as if the gales of fortune were at length about to blow steadily in our favor, without disturbance from any cross-current. We were not, however, to be let off so easily. Fate had one more trial in reserve.

My father had come to live in Edinburgh. Afflicted with dreary recollections, sometimes half-distracted, and ready to catch at delusive hopes, he plunged into proceedings which I can only refer to with any degree of patience, from the insight which they afforded of new and diverting phases of character. Among his dreams of the past, he raked up the fancy of trying to recover a piece of property which had long ago belonged to the family, but had somehow been suffered to drift, improperly, as was alleged, into other hands. The property in question was a wretched old house, perhaps not worth £200, and the proposal of fighting for it in the Court of Session was repugnant alike to my brother's feelings and my own. Unfortunately, any remonstrances on our part, and also strong objections urged by my mother, were unavailing. The suit was commenced, and its history might almost furnish materials for a tragi-comic drama.

The prime adviser in the case was a person who, from his reputed knowledge of law, was held in high esteem by certain classes of people. He was a neat little man, in drab breeches and white woolen stockings, who labored under the infirmity of a stiff, crooked knee, on which account he walked very oddly, by successive jerks, with the help of a stick. Having been bred in the office of a country solicitor, this erudite person had formed an acquaintance with legal forms and technicalities, and adding to this a theoretic knowledge of Scotch law from Erskine's " Institutes," he was qualified, as many thought, for acting as counsel to those who stood in need of legal advice. With his acquirements, it was perhaps only as an act of considerable condescension that he made his living as a dealer in wines, spirits, and other liquids, in an inferior part of the city. As a friend of the oppressed, the little man had much pleasure in bestowing his knowledge of the law gratis. He took no fees. All he expected from those who favored him with their company in his pleasant back-room was, that they would pay for what liquor they thought fit to call for, and that certainly was not unreasonable.

The fame of this legal oracle travelled beyond the narrow precincts of the locality. His renown as a gossip on legal and other matters attracted the occasional visits of a club of convivialists, who were in the habit of spending an hour or two daily in discussing public affairs over some inspiriting liquid delicacies. These assemblages, wherever they happened to be held, were greatly more amusing than gatherings of this kind usually are, for they were open to all who, with a little time at their disposal, could add to the hilarity of the company. The meetings were sometimes honored with the presence of certain officials from the Excise Office, whose duties, consisting mainly of drawing their salaries and reading the morning's newspaper, admitted of this kind of recreation. Among this set there were two or three who shone as stars of the first magnitude. It is true they related the same jokes perhaps daily for years, but as the sederunt was a variable body, and as it was a standing rule in this club of convivialists to laugh at every whimsicality, no matter how often repeated, the old jokes were always as good as new.

One of these assiduous government officials whose presence was always peculiarly acceptable, was a Mr. Moffat, a genteelish, middle-aged personage, with a red nose, dressed in a white neckcloth and a blue coat with yellow metal buttons, and who was always licking his lips, as if he had just partaken of some delicious repast. He had one story about himself, which he was ordinarily called on to relate : —

" By the by, Mr. Moffat, that was a curious anecdote you told us one day about the Board of Excise ; I am sure the gentlemen present would like to hear it."

" O, by all means ; if I can remember it rightly." Then brightening up, taking a sip at his potation, and licking his lips with more than usual vehemence, he would proceed.

" Well, gentlemen, you must know, I was one day in my room at the office. It was a busy day with me. I had to sign several papers brought to me by Grubb. After that was over, when I was just sitting down to the newspaper, a message was brought, requiring my presence at the Board. I could not imagine why I was sent for. Surely, thinks I, it cannot be on account of going out a few minutes daily for necessary refreshments. However, there was no time to consider. So off I went to the Board-room, trusting to put as good a face on the matter as possible. Well, to be sure, there were the whole of the Com-

missioners — a very full meeting that day — seated around
the table covered with green cloth, each of them with
fresh pens and sheets of paper before him, as if about to
take down a deposition.   I am going to be pulled up,
thinks I.   Things certainly looked very bad.   My feelings
were a little calmed when the chairman — a polite man,
exceedingly so — requested me, in a softened and pleasant tone of voice, to take a chair near him.   Well, gentlemen, I sat down accordingly, making a bow to the Board.
The chairman then addressed me :   ' Mr. Moffat, the Commissioners have had a great difficulty under their consideration.   It is a thing of no small importance, for it concerns the interest of the Department.   Some of the
Commissioners incline to one view of the matter, and
some to another.   In short, not to keep you in suspense,
that which puzzles the Board is the pronunciation of a
word — a very important word ; not, indeed, that I am
puzzled, for my mind is clear upon the subject.   To settle the matter definitely, we appeal to you.   Knowing
your scholarly acquirements, and more particularly your
acquaintance with the drama and the correct elocution of
the stage, we have agreed to abide by your decision.'
Here, of course, I again bowed.   ' Yes,' continued the
chairman, ' we put ourselves into your hands.   To be perfectly fair, I will not utter the word, but write it down,
letter by letter thus : —

R-e-v-e-n-u-e,

and leave you to determine how it should be pronounced.'
I felt honored.   I had for years studied the word.   I had
made up my mind about it.   Bowing once more to the
Board, and turning towards the chairman, I said : ' Sir, I
feel the importance of the occasion.   That word is certainly a very important word.   It is a word in which the

whole nation has a very great interest. Knowing especially its value to the Department, I have for years made
it my study, and will state the opinion at which I have arrived. The common or vulgar pronunciation of the word
is Rev'enue ; but that is decidedly incorrect. The true
pronunciation, which *I* hold by, is that of John Kemble —
namely, Reven'ue — a heavy emphasis to be laid on the
n.' Instantly there was a shout of applause from various
members of the Board, and the chairman, who was vastly
pleased, said to me most emphatically : ' Thank you, Mr.
Moffat ; you and I must eat mutton together ! ' "

Influenced by frequent and animated consultations with
the smart little man with the crooked knee, and convinced
that he had Erskine on his side, my father passed into
the hands of an *habitué* of the back-room, a man of advanced age, who wore a brown duffel great-coat and a
low-crowned hat, whose function consisted in bringing
cases to certain practitioners before the supreme courts.
I saw him once or twice. In character and appearance
he reminded me of the miserable order of professionals
whom I had seen in the Old Tolbooth. His coarse features possessed the singular faculty of appearing to smile
in the lower department, while they were grave and
thoughtful above, the line of division of the two expres-
sions being across from the point of the nose. My father
was introduced by this legal jackal to an operator in
whom he said he had every confidence ; having first assured himself that there were persons behind backs who
would be good for the expenses. At this time there were
practitioners in Edinburgh well qualified in the art of
fleecing. One of them was known in the Parliament
House under the jocose name of Pillage, while another of
the same category was called Plunder. Each had a son
who helped in his father's business, and hence people

pleasantly spoke of Old Pillage and Young Pillage, and Old Plunder and Young Plunder. Both firms were believed to be one concern. They were in some sort a confederacy, which, through the devices of scouts, like the gentleman in the brown duffel great-coat and low-crowned hat, procured the conducting of cases *pro* and *con;* and they would jointly so manage matters through a dragged-out process, for which the forms of court offered opportunities, that the respective litigants did not get a final decision till not another shilling could be wrung from them.

In the present unhappy case the end came with more than usual celerity, for means soon ran dry. My father, as we all foresaw, lost his suit, and my brother and I, as had been safely prognosticated, had to stand in the breach and incur obligations, in order to avert certain unpleasant consequences. It is sickening to think what sufferings are incurred through the follies of litigation. Money that I could ill spare was swept away, and Robert lost a large part of what he had realized by the " Traditions," as much, I think, as about two hundred pounds. The only grudge entertained on the subject was, that the money should have been sacrificed so unworthily. These losses kept us back one or two years.

It was about this time that the family renewed acqaintance with a clerical functionary, who, through his wife, was somehow, in a remote degree, related to us. I recollected seeing him among the habitual visitors of the Tolbooth, where, with the reputation of being a worthy man, who had been unfortunate in life, and always took a lenient view of human infirmities, he was held in general esteem. He held the office of Morning Lecturer in one of the city churches, an antiquated benefice in the gift of the magistrates and council. His duty was to preach early in the Sunday mornings, for which he received some thirty pounds a year. Since 1639, when the office was instituted by the bequest of David Mackall, a pious citizen, the fancy for going to church before breakfast had so greatly fallen off that the congregation consisted usually of only the precentor, and a respectable spinster of middle age, who occupied a floor in the Lawnmarket, and who, of all the inhabitants of Edinburgh, appreciated the Morning Lecturer for his discourses.

To judge from his bulk, gravity of aspect, and tastefully powdered white hair, this amiable divine might have stood high in ecclesiastical matters. Of no point in his personal appearance, however, was he so proud as his nails. These nails of his, as everybody soon learned from his wife, were a singularly precious inheritance. They had come into his family a long time ago through his great-grandmother, an heiress, who had married, her friends thought, beneath her. In some of her descendants, " the nails " cast up, and in others they did not. Our friend was one of the lucky owners ; and with this handsome token of aristocracy, as also a certain solemnity of features, his parents resolved to make him a minister. Not very fortunate in his career, it was well for him that he could derive some consolation from the points of his fingers, seeing that the support of a family and the rent of a dwelling in an upper floor had to be encountered, with no more to depend on in the regular course of things than the small salary assigned to him by the civic corporation. As to that salary, it was the Morning Lecturer's fixed opinion that he was shamefully cheated. He always maintained that the magistrates and council had grossly misappropriated Mackall's bequest, and that, if he had his due, he should, at the very least, have a thousand a year. Before his face, people condoled with him about

13

his misusage ; but, excepting perhaps the aforesaid spinster, no one actually thought him to be underpaid.

So long as the Old Tolbooth lasted, the lecturer possessed a pleasant forenoon resort, where there was always
something doing in the way of general conviviality.
Mingling in the festivities of the West Enders, he was in
reality among friends and customers whom he served in
the clerical line of business. For years, he had managed
to eke out his means of livelihood by baptizing the children of persons who did not claim membership with any
of the ordinary congregations, and who had a special dislike to answering troublesome questions. His flock, in
this respect, were a scattered body all over the Old Town,
but with a certain density about the Fleshmarket Close
and the head of the Canongate.

In undertaking jobs for his employers, this accommodat-
ing divine preferred visiting them at their own homes in
the evening, at which time, under the blaze of candle-
light, and with the mellowing influence of supper, the
heart is more beneficently inclined than during the day. It
being contrary to rule in Scotland to receive fees for religious solemnities, this poor clergyman resorted to a device,
which for a time mitigated the distresses of the household.
The Being who tempers the wind to the shorn lamb, gave
him a child, who was for a time the daily provider of his
family. This child, Bobby, was a boy in petticoats, who
had the misfortune to have a bad squint, but by raising
emotions of compassion, the squint was rather a good
thing than otherwise. As soon as Bobby was able to
toddle about, he invariably accompanied papa on his bap-
tismal excursions. Before setting out, his mother provided him with a small but conspicuous pocket of colored
silk, which she hung outside his dress, ready for receiving
any money-present which might be munificently slipped

into it, in requital of the religious ordinance that was performed.

It was an interesting thing to see the pair, father and child, sally out, after the street-lamps were lit, on a mission to the foot of some long, dingy close, and there to climb up some long, crooked stair, — the father stumping on in his faded tartan cloak, with his cane in one hand, and holding Bobby with the other, — both gleeful of what would possibly be deposited in that pretty little pocket, and of what pleasure there would be in taking it home to mamma. Bobby relished these expeditions into the by-corners of the city, although the long dark stairs were almost too much for his little legs ; and when kept late he was apt to get sleepy. But he was usually treated to something nice by the hostess, and had the satisfaction at departure of finding a crown-piece — occasionally half a guinea, wrapped in a piece of paper — lying at the bottom of his pocket, about which there was not a little sprightly talk on the way home.

I heard the Morning Lecturer speak of a frightful piece of villainy that had been perpetrated on Bobby, amounting, as he thought, to worse than sacrilege. On one occasion, the reward slipped into the child's pocket was a coin wrapped in paper, which, on inspection at a street lamp, proved to be only a farthing, a circumstance which we may take as indicating the class of persons to whom these spiritual services were occasionally rendered. On the whole, the produce of the child's wallet for several years kept the wolf from the door ; and it was a great grief to the family that Bobby at length grew too big for petticoats, and also too big to be taken uninvited to baptisms. What with the removal of that dear old haunt, the Tolbooth, and afterwards Bobby's overgrowth for financial purposes, it was a sad business for our poor friend, whose last days in his upper flat were, as we had occasion to know, not quite so comfortable as befitted one with such a superior quality of nails, or who was so useful a member of the clerical profession.

Now came a domestic affliction. My unfortunate father never got over the loss of his law-suit, and the way he had been led into it by the versatile genius with the crooked knee, and his coadjutor in the duffel great-coat. Under his accumulation of disasters and fresh cankering reminiscences, ascribable in a great degree to his excessive simplicity of character, he died in November, 1824, in the week of those conflagrations of which Robert has given some account.

Shortly after the issue of the " Traditions," it became expedient for me to relinquish printing, and to adhere more exclusively to other branches of business, including some undertakings of a literary nature. The parting with my poor little press, which had latterly been superseded by newer mechanism, was not unaccompanied with that kind of regret with which one bids farewell to an old and cherished companion. It is pleasing, however, to know that it did not suffer destruction, but was purchased by a person in Glasgow, who aspired to begin as a printer in a way similar to myself; and for anything I know to the contrary, this little machine may still be creaking and wheezing on the banks of the Clyde, for, like many who are afflicted with asthma, it possessed a wonderful degree of vitality.

Partly with the design of furnishing a companion to the " Picture of Scotland," I commenced a work, purporting to describe the institutions, secular and religious, peculiar to our northern kingdom, and which I styled the " Book of Scotland." The work required considerable research as well as personal knowledge, and the task

was one for which I avow myself to have been ill qualified. I sold it to a publisher for thirty pounds. It is
now very properly forgotten. Independently of its imperfections, the subjects treated of would now stand in
need of a new elucidation, in consequence of innumerable
recent legislative alterations. Poor as was this production, it procured me the honor of being employed along
with Robert to prepare the " Gazetteer of Scotland " for
a publisher ; the price to be paid for it being a hundred
pounds. It was to be a compilation from all available
and trustworthy sources, along with such original matter
as could reasonably be infused into it. To impart a sufficient degree of freshness, I made several pedestrian
journeys to different parts of the country, gathering here
and there particulars which I thought would be of value.

In these excursions I had necessarily to husband time
and exercise a pretty rigorous economy. Lodging at the
humbler class of inns, my expenses did not exceed a few
shillings a day. My object was to see as many places as
possible, and fix their situation and appearance in my
mind. I took notes only of dates, inscriptions, and other
matters demanding great precision. I now found the value
of cultivating the memory, and of having learned to rely on
recollections of places which I had seen. From practice,
I acquired the art of summoning up the remembrance of
scenes and places which I had visited, and persons I had
seen, even to very minute particulars. Gathering and stor-
ing up observations in this way, I traversed Fife and the
lower parts of Perth and Forfar shires. My longest stretch
in one day was from the neighborhood of Cupar to Edinburgh, by Lochlevin, Kinross, Dumfermline, Inverkeithing,
and Queensferry, a stretch of forty miles, varied by the
passage of the ferry. It was a delightful ramble in a long
day in June, which left the most pleasing recollections,

notwithstanding that I was a little foot-sore on reaching home. By such means as this I was able to impart some originality to the ordinary descriptions in the " Gazetteer."

Although my brother was ostensibly associated with me in this production, his duties were chiefly those of final supervisor of the press. As the work was a thick octavo volume, double columns, in small type, the mere penmanship of it extended to ten thousand pages, many of which I wrote twice or thrice over, to insure accuracy. My share of the price of copyright was seventy pounds. This book was a great literary exercise, and as such, remuneration was of inferior consequence. I wrote the whole of it, as I had previous productions, behind the counter, amidst the involvements and interruptions of ordinary business, by which means I acquired a kind of facility of dropping and resuming a subject at a moment's notice, which proved of considerable value. To finish the work at the appointed time, I was frequently compelled to remain at the desk for two or three hours after closing up for the night. The labor incurred by so much thinking and writing, together with close application otherwise, unameliorated with any sort of recreation, brought on an illness which for some time assumed a threatening appearance. But this was happily got over without any permanently bad effects.

The publication of the "Gazetteer" helped, perhaps, to bring me a little more into notice ; but if local notoriety was desirable, that was incidentally effected by writing a series of letters in an Edinburgh newspaper, concerning that species of civic administration which terminated shortly afterwards in a financial collapse. These letters bore my name, for it has been with me a rule in life never to write an anonymous letter. If ever there was an instance of the value of this species of candor, it was on the present occasion. The letters engaged public attention, and when issued in a collected form in a small pamphlet, the sale was immense. On looking back to this exploit, I feel that the strictures were much too severe, and visited on individuals that which properly belonged to a system.

Though these and some other literary exercises were of no pecuniary advantage adequate to the time and trouble spent upon them, they were immensely serviceable as a training, preparatory to the part which it was my destiny to take in the cheap literature movement of modern times. It is regarding that movement, and the change which it wrought in my brother's as well as in my own course of life, that something is now to be said.

CHAPTER IX

NOT the least curious thing about the rise of cheap literature in the form of detached sheets in our times is, that it is in reality a " Renaissance." Differing only in degree, it is a revival of what had long passed away and been popularly forgotten. Let us look a little into the matter historically, saying a few words in the first place regarding the oldest cheap literature of all, — the Penny Chap Books of our simple-minded forefathers. Like the corresponding Folk Lore of the Germans, the old Chap .Books, consisting of coarsely printed sheets, duodecimo, embellished with equally coarse frontispieces, aimed at no sort of instruction, such as we now understand by the term ; yet they furnished amusement to the humble fireside. They appealed to the popular love of the heroic, the marvelous, the pathetic, and the humorous. Many of them were nothing more than an embodiment of the legends, superstitions, ballads, and songs, which had been kept alive by oral tradition before the invention of printing. Superstitions, as may be supposed, formed the stable material. So numerous were the books for telling fortunes, discovering and averting witchcraft, narrating the appearance of ghosts, prognosticating the weather, interpreting dreams, and explaining lucky and unlucky days, that the extent and depth of public credulity must have been immense.

Objectionable and pitiable in character as were the greater number of Chap Books, miserable as they were in appearance and aim, they are nevertheless to be taken as illustrative of popular intelligence and taste during the lengthened period in which they bore rule; and as such, reflect a certain light on the social progress of Great Britain. It would seem, indeed, that just as a crop of worthless indigenous plants grow up on a meagre uncultivated soil, so do Chap Books spring up in the mental infancy of the common people, and continue till displaced by a literature equally entertaining, but of a standard which corresponds to a state of higher advancement. Another consideration suggests itself. A country may be renowned for its scholarship, its science, its exquisite proficiency in the fine arts, and yet not be beyond its Chap Book era. Such is the case at this moment in Italy, where took place the revival of letters, where universities have longest existed, and where sculpture and painting have for ages been carried to an enviable pitch of excellence. With startling discordance, under the very shadow of the university of Padua, the cathedral of Milan, and the glorious galleries of the Uffizi at Florence, a Chap Book literature is copiously dispersed, as primitive in character and as poor in appearance as anything which satisfied our illiterate peasantry of a past age. The moral that may be drawn from the fact of a country being rich in universities, and at the same time abounding in books for interpreting dreams and expounding lucky numbers in the lottery, will occur to every one.

Pervading town and country as a literature in request among all the humbler classes who could read, English and also Scottish Chap Books were extirpated by no edict, but disappeared slowly through the united effects of education, and a demand for something equally exhilarating and much more conformable to improved manners and feelings. Some circumstances, not to be referred to without regret, conspired to prolong the Chap Book era beyond the time at which it would probably have vanished. Newspapers, which began to assume a determinate form as miscellaneous intelligencers about the period of the Restoration, attained to a considerable standing and popularity shortly after 1695, when they were relieved from the licensing act that had hitherto oppressed them. The press, now in effect free, and the public mind entering, as it were, on the new phase which had been initiated at the Revolution, we are led by innumerable evidences to conclude that a great change was about to ensue in the matter of popular literature.

We see the dawn of this hopeful transition in the reign of Queen Anne, when much was done, and much more was unscrupulously checked. We now look, not without surprise, on penny newspapers and penny literary sheets, but these are no new thing. There were papers of both kinds, or of a mixed nature, equally low-priced, a hundred and fifty years ago. As yet these cheap papers did not attempt to supersede the Chap Book literature, but we cannot doubt that such must soon have been the issue. Let me pause for a moment on this outcrop of improved popular prints at the commencement of the eighteenth century.

The first cheap periodical which contained observations written with literary skill was a paper called the " Review," begun by Daniel Defoe while he was confined in Newgate for publishing his ironical pamphlet, " A Short and Easy Way with the Dissenters." In spite of depressing circumstances, he kept up his " Review " for nine years. Commencing in 1704, it lasted till 1713, and formed the predecessor of, as well as the exemplar for, the " Tatler,"

which was begun in 1709 by Richard Steele, assisted by
his friend Addison. The "Tatler" appeared three times
a week, and was sold for a penny. Soon after its close
in 1711, the same writers commenced the "Spectator,"
also issued at a penny, but appearing daily. Here, then,
to all appearance, was a most auspicious beginning of a
cheap and popular literature, of a quality which leaves us
nothing to regret, but very much to admire. One can
scarcely write with any degree of temper of the overthrow
of so promising a department of literature.

As early as 1701, a bill had been brought into parliament to impose a halfpenny stamp on newspapers ; but
such was the clamor raised by the printers, that the
scheme was dropped. Beat off for a time, the House of
Commons, which had then little sympathy with social
progress, successfully renewed the attack on the press,
and the 12th of August, 1712, saw the newspapers, as
well as the purely literary sheets, issued with a stamp ; a
halfpenny if half a sheet, and a penny if a whole sheet.
At the same time, a tax of a shilling was imposed on
every advertisement. The pretext for these measures was
a wish to stem allegedly impertinent discussions on public
affairs. But the good was swept down as well as the bad.
The "Spectator," which had been the vehicle for the noble writings of Addison, immediately experienced a severe
reverse. The price was doubled, to meet the new expenses, but the expedient failed. Any rise in the charge
for a cheap periodical is generally fatal to its circulation.
After a vain struggle, the "Spectator" expired in 1713.
No man in the present day would dare to vindicate the
policy which thus obstructed the growth of a wholesome
popular literature. That there was as yet neither capital
nor mechanical appliance to facilitate the issue of large
impressions, is admitted. But who can tell what might

have ensued under an unrestricted issue of newspapers, and the cheaper kinds of literary sheets?

It is painful to peruse the history of what followed. Such was the growing demand for newspapers, that there were constant attempts, some of them wonderfully successful, to evade the law. In the reign of George II., unstamped halfpenny and penny sheets were sold to such an extent by hawkers in the streets of London, that an act was passed in 1743 to suppress this contraband traffic, and any newsboy who dared to offer one of these low-priced intelligencers did so at the risk of three months' imprisonment. Additional stamp and other duties, though in various ways repressive, never utterly quenched the chief popular press, and only postponed its final triumph. Embarrassed with fiscal duties, the news and literary sheets which struggled on through the reign of the first three Georges were, along with the magazines and reviews that sprung into popularity, of no small importance in rearing and primarily affording a maintenance to a brilliant series of eighteenth-century writers: Defoe, Steele, Addison, Johnson, Goldsmith, Smollett, and others.

Although books, chiefly reprints, were in time cheapened and greatly popularized by a series of enterprising publishers, beginning with Alexander Donaldson (father of the founder of Donaldson's Hospital, Edinburgh), and although books of all kinds were rendered generally accessible by circulating libraries, the more aspiring of the humbler orders, particularly those at a distance from towns, still experienced great difficulty in procuring works to improve their knowledge or entertain their leisure hours. Perusing the memoirs of Robert Burns, James Ferguson, Thomas Telford, George Stephenson, and others who, by dint of genius and painstaking study, raised themselves from obscurity to distinction, we perceive what were their difficulties in getting hold of books ; such as they did procure being mostly borrowed from kindly disposed neighbors.

Usually, in these untoward circumstances, the mind of the rustic youth took the direction of rhyming in the style of Ramsay and Robert Fergusson. This was specially observable in the case of Telford, who, while still a journeyman mason in his native Eskdale, contributed verses to Ruddiman's "Weekly Magazine," under the unpretending signature of "Eskdale Tam." In one of these compositions, which was addressed to Burns, he sketched his own character, and the efforts he made to improve his stock of knowledge by poring over a borrowed volume with no better light than what was afforded by the cottage fire : —

> " Nor pass the tentie curious lad,
> Who o'er the ingle hangs his head,
> And begs of neighbors books to read ;
> For hence arise
> Thy country's sons, who far are spread,
> Baith bold and wise."

So matters remained ; the protracted French War and its immediate consequences postponing any substantial improvement, at least as regarded the less affluent classes. From 1815 till 1820, while the marvelous fictions of Scott and the poems of Byron were issuing with rapidity from the press, low-priced and scurrilous prints, ministering to the fancies of the seditious and depraved, were also produced in vast numbers. It was an era of transition from war to peace, and as yet society had not composed itself decorously in the new state of things. There was much to rectify, and little patience was exercised in the process ; and, above all, there was little or no harmony among the different classes of the community. So much may be mentioned to extenuate the unscrupulous charac-

ter of the cheap political prints that swept over the country, which time, free discussion, and various meliorations
would have counteracted or extinguished. More abrupt
measures, however, were adopted. Certain statutes killed
off the whole at a blow in 1820.

No cheap unstamped paper could be safely attempted
immediately after this, unless it were purely literary, and
abstained from any comment on public affairs. Of this
class was the obscure periodical attempted by my brother
and myself in 1821. In 1822, a cheap weekly sheet,
styled the " Mirror," was begun in London by John Lim-
bird, but with little pretension to original writing. It was
illustrated with wood-engravings, was generally amusing,
and so far might be defined as a step in the right direction.

From about this time, benevolently disposed and
thoughtful men set about devising methods for improving
the intelligence and professional skill of artisans. The
School of Arts, the earliest of its class, was founded in
Edinburgh in 1821. Two years later, Dr. Birkbeck
founded a Mechanics' Institution in London, and another
in Glasgow. How views of this nature should now have
at length assumed a practical shape would lead to a too
lengthened exposition. Reference may merely be made
to the influence exercised by the writings of Scott, Campbell, Wordsworth, Southey, and Byron during the early
years of the century ; likewise to the efficacy of the newer
class of reviews and magazines, as well as, more lately,
the improved character of the newspaper press. Per-
meating, as it were, down through society, literature, in
various inviting forms, had vivified and brought to the
surface new orders of readers, and, besides, set a fashion
for seeking recreation in books and periodicals, which
was favorable to any cheapening of these engines of instruction and entertainment.

To causes of this nature are we chiefly to impute the Mechanics' Institution movement, and what was coeval with it, the rise of the Society for the Diffusion of Useful Knowledge, which was founded in 1825. Viewed as a distinct and imposing effort to stimulate the popular understanding, this association, with all the mistakes which marked its short career, is never to be spoken of without respect. As is well known, the Society was commenced under the auspices of several noblemen and gentlemen, who have for the greater part left their impress on the age — Lords Auckland and Althorp (afterwards Earl Spencer), Lord John Russell, Lord Brougham, Sir James Mackintosh, Matthew D. Hill, Dr. Maltby, Mr. Hallam, and Captain Basil Hall, to which a long list of names could be added. The object of the Society was to issue a series of cheap treatises on the exact sciences, and on various branches of knowledge. In 1827, the year which saw the first of the Society's works, Archibald Constable, a man of bold conceptions, commenced the issue of his " Miscellany " of volumes of a popular kind ; and others catching the contagion, for a time there was a perfect deluge of works, designed for the instruction and amusement of the multitude, and so moderate in price, that no one could now complain of being unable to fill his shelves at a small outlay. We also ought not to forget the service done to literature by such papers as the " Literary Gazette " and " Athenæum," this last surviving as the representative of its class.

It is interesting to look back on those times, and note the progressive steps towards a thoroughly cheap yet original and wholesome literature. There was merit in the very shortcomings and failures, for, with their temporary or partial success, they showed that the public were not indisposed to support that in which they could have reason to place confidence. Some mistakes had been committed. The prints suppressed in 1820 had dealt principally in invective, of which no good can come. And those which were established afterwards, such as the " Mirror," were purposeless in their aims.

The reign of William IV. was the true era of the revival of cheap periodical literature. The political agitations of 1831, by stirring up the popular feelings, helped materially to stimulate the appetite for what would excite, instruct, and amuse. So far as the humbler orders were concerned, it almost appeared as if the art of printing, through certain mechanical appliances — particularly the paper-making machine and the printing-machine — was only now effectually discovered.

To meet the popular demand, a number of low-priced serials of a worthless or at least ephemeral kind were issued in London in 1831. At the same time, there were several set on foot in Edinburgh. The forerunner and best of these was styled the " Cornucopia," which consisted of four pages, folio, and was sold for three-halfpence. The editor and proprietor of this popular sheet was George Mudie, a clever but erratic being, who, I believe, had been a compositor. As the " Cornucopia " contained a quantity of amusing matter, and in point of size resembled a newspaper, it was deemed a marvel of cheapness ; for at this time the ordinary price of a newspaper was fivepence. Eminently successful as a commercial undertaking, Mr. Mudie's sheet, if properly conducted, could not have failed to be permanently successful.

As a bookseller, I had occasion to deal in these cheap papers. One thing was greatly against them. They were frequently behind time on the day of publication ; and any irregularity in the appearance of periodicals is generally fatal. It was also obvious that they were conducted on no definite plan. They consisted for the most part of disjointed and unauthorized extracts from books, clippings from floating literature, old stories, and stale jocularities. With no purpose but to furnish temporary amusement, they were, as it appeared to me, the perversion of what, if rightly conducted, might become a powerful engine of social improvement. Pondering on this idea, I resolved to take advantage of the evidently growing taste for cheap literature, and lead it, as far as was in my power, in a proper direction.

It is, I think, due to myself and others to offer this explanation. I have never aspired to the reputation of being the originator of low-priced serials ; but only, as far as I can judge, the first to make a determined attempt to im-part such a character to these productions in our own day, as might tend to instruct and elevate independently of mere passing amusement. Professionally, I considered that the attempt was a noble and fair venture, one for which I might not be disqualified by previous literary experiences, hum-ble as these had been. The enterprise promised to be at least in concord with my feelings.

Before taking any active step, I mentioned the matter to Robert. Let us, I said, endeavor to give a reputable lit-erary character to what is at present mostly mean or trivial, and of no permanent value ; but he, thinking only of the not very creditable low-priced papers then current, did not entertain a favorable opinion of my projected undertaking. With all loyalty and affection, however, he promised to give me what literary assistance was in his power, and in this I was not disappointed. Consulting no one else, and in that highly wrought state of mind which overlooks all but the probability of success, I at length, in January 1832, issued the prospectus of " Chambers's Edinburgh Journal," a weekly sheet at three-halfpence. Announcing myself as

14

editor, I stated that " no communications in verse or prose
were wanted." In this, there was an air of self-confidence,
not perhaps to be justified, but, as showing that my periodical was not to be composed of the contributions of
anonymous and irresponsible correspondents, the effect
was on the whole beneficial.

The first number appeared on Saturday, the 4th of February, 1832. It contained an opening address, written in a
fervid state of feeling, as may be judged by the following
passages : —

" The principle by which I have been actuated, is to
take advantage of the universal appetite for instruction
which at present exists ; to supply to that appetite food of
the best kind, in such form and at such price as must suit
the convenience of every man in the British dominions.
Every Saturday, when the poorest laborer in the country
draws his humble earnings, he shall have it in his power
to purchase with an insignificant portion of even that
humble sum, a meal of healthful, useful, and agreeable
mental instruction. Whether I succeed in my wishes, a
brief space of time will determine. I throw myself on the
good sense of my countrymen for support ; all I seek is a
fair field wherein to exercise my industry in their service.
It may perhaps be considered an invidious remark, when
I state as my humble conviction, that the people of Great
Britain and Ireland have never yet been properly cared
for, in the way of presenting knowledge under its most
cheering and captivating aspect, to their immediate observation. The scheme of diffusing knowledge has certainly
been more than once attempted by associations established
under peculiar advantages. Yet, the great end has not
been gained. The dearth of the publications, official in-
flexibility, and above all, the plan of attaching the interests
of political or ecclesiastical parties to the course of instruc-

tion or reading, have separately or conjunctly circumscribed the limits of the operation ; so that the world, on the whole, is but little the wiser with all the attempts which have been made. The strongholds of ignorance, though not unassailed, remain to be carried. Carefully eschewing the errors into which these praiseworthy associations have fallen, I take a course altogether novel. Whatever may be my political principles, neither these nor any other which would be destructive of my present views, shall ever mingle in my observations on the arrangements of civil society." I concluded by notifying the species of subjects which would receive particular attention.

High as were my expectations, the success of the work exceeded them. In a few days there was, for Scotland, the unprecedented sale of fifty thousand copies ; and at the third number, when copies were consigned to an agent in London for dispersal through England, the sale rose to eighty thousand, at which it long remained, with scarcely any advertising to give it publicity. To the best of my recollection, all the other cheap papers issued in Edinburgh immediately disappeared. In London, some also were dropped, but others sprung up in their stead. For a time, indeed, there was not a week which had not a new serial ; but few of these candidates for public approval outlived the second or third number. So many began and never went farther, that a gentleman whom we happened to hear of possessed a large pile of first numbers of periodicals of which a second never appeared.

On the 31st of March, 1832, being about six weeks after the commencement of "Chambers's Journal," appeared the first number of the "Penny Magazine of the Society for the Diffusion of Useful Knowledge." We learn from Mr. Charles Knight, its publisher, that the "Penny Magazine" was suggested to him on a morning

in March, and that the Lord Chancellor (Brougham), who
was waited on, cordially entered into the project, which
was forthwith sanctioned by the Committee of the Society.[1]   The "Penny Magazine," begun under such distinguished auspices, and which, as is understood, had a
very large circulation, terminated unexpectedly in 1845 ;
though not without having exerted, during its comparatively brief career, an influence, along with similar publications, in stimulating the growth of that cheap and
wholesome literature which has latterly assumed such
huge proportions.

Why the "Penny Magazine," with its alleged success
as regards circulation, its large array of artists and writers,
and its body of distinguished patrons, should have perished so prematurely, while there were still considerable
strongholds of ignorance to be attacked, no one has ever
ventured to explain.   A silence equally mysterious hangs
over the close of the Useful Knowledge Society, the proceedings of which were so vigorously heralded and sustained by articles in the "Edinburgh Review," that no one
could say the association failed for want of recommendation from the highest literary quarters.   In the absence of
any explanations on the subject, it may be conjectured that
with all the ability displayed, and the best intentions of

---

[1] *Passages in a Working Life,* vol. ii. p. 180.   This explanation dis-
poses of a strange mistake which a writer has fallen into, doubtless
from erroneous information, regarding *Chambers's Journal.*   He speaks
of my having seen a prospectus of the *Penny Magazine* a long time
before the periodical itself appeared ; that I forwarded to the pro-
moters certain suggestions calculated to improve the chances of its
success ; that no answer being vouchsafed, my self-love was wounded ;
and that I determined to realize my unappreciated ideas myself, in
the form of *Chambers's Journal.*   This is altogether incorrect.   I did
not hear of the *Penny Magazine,* nor could I, till shortly before its
appearance, and after the *Journal* had been some weeks established.

every one concerned, the treatises of the Society were on the whole too technical and abstruse for the mass of operatives ; they made no provision for the culture of the imaginative faculties ; and, in point of fact, were purchased and read chiefly by persons considerably removed from the obligation of toiling with their hands for their daily bread. In a word, they may be supposed to have been distasteful to the popular fancy. If any other reason be wanted, it probably lay in the fact that a society cannot, as a rule, compete with private enterprise.

It is not my duty to sit as critic on aims and efforts not unlike my own. There are different ways of doing things, and it may happen that one is as good as another. All that need be said is, that it has been a matter of congratulation, that "Chambers's Journal" owed nothing, in its inception or at any part of its career, to the special patronage or approval of any sect, party, or individual. In the whole proceedings of my brother and myself, we never courted the countenance or recommendation of any person or persons, or of any body of people, civil or religious ; and after an experience of forty years, circumstances would point to the conclusion that this has not been the worst, besides being the least obsequious, line of policy.

CHAPTER X.

A S in the case of a dissolving view, when, as if by magic, a bleak wintry scene is transformed into a landscape glowing with the warmth and verdant garniture of summer, so by the appearance of the "Journal," and the wide popularity it secured, was there effected an agreeable and wholly unforeseen change on my own condition, and that of others connected with me. The revolution was abrupt, and of a kind not to be treated with indifference. The moderate and not very conspicuous business in which I had been engaged was immediately relinquished, in consequence of the absorbing and prospectively advantageous literary enterprise in which I had embarked ; and removing to a central part of the town, new and enlarged premises were acquired. Until the fourteenth number of the work, Robert was only in the position of contributor. Then abandoning his separate professional relations, he became joint-editor, and was also associated with me in the firm of W. & R. CHAMBERS.

Had " Chambers's Journal " been commenced in London, no mechanical difficulty would have been experienced. The case was very different in Edinburgh, where, at the time, there were obstructions as regards both paper and printing. John Johnstone, a genial old man, husband of the authoress of " Clan Albyn," and other novels, was a printer, and by him the work was for a time executed, as well as it could be in the circumstances. Other printers were afterwards employed, but their hand-presses, even with relays of men toiling night and day, proved altogether inadequate for the large impressions that were required. At length, a set of stereotype plates of each number was sent weekly to London, from which copies were printed for circulation in England ; while from another set impressions were executed in Edinburgh by machines which we procured for the purpose. Steam settled the difficulty. The work was at first a sheet folio, subsequently the size was reduced to a quarto, and at last to an octavo form.

Entering on the comprehensive design of editing, printing, and publishing works of a popularly instructive and entertaining tendency, Robert and I were for a considerable length of time alone, — our immediately younger brother, James, having, to our distress, died in February, 1833, — and such was the degree of mutual confidence between us, that not for the space of twenty-one years was it thought expedient to execute any memorandum of agreement.

Though unusual, the combination of literary labor with the business of printing and publishing, is not without precedent. We may call to mind the examples set by Edward Cave, Samuel Richardson, and Robert Dodsley last century. We might, indeed, point to Sir Walter Scott in our own times ; the only thing to be deplored in the case of that great man being that he kept his connection with the printing establishment of the Ballantynes a profound secret, through an apprehension of losing caste among his law friends, instead of avowedly, like Richardson, becoming the printer, as well as holder of the copyrights, of his own productions.

A happy difference, yet some resemblance, in character,

proved of service in the literary and commercial union of Robert and myself. Mentally, each had a little of the other, but with a wide divergence in matters requisite as a whole. One could not have well done without the other. With mutual help there was mutual strength. All previous hardships and experiences seemed to be but a training in strict adaptation for the course of life opened up to us in 1832. Nothing could have happened better — a circumstance which may perhaps go a little way towards inspiring hopes and consolations among those who may be destined to pass through a similar ordeal.

The permanent hold on the public mind which the " Journal " fortunately obtained, was undoubtedly owing, in a very great degree, to the leading articles, consisting of essays, moral, familiar, and humorous, from the pen of my brother. My own more special duties were confined for the most part to papers having in view some kind of popular instruction, particularly as regards the young, whom it was attempted to stimulate in the way of mental improvement. There likewise fell to my share the general administration of a concern which was ever increasing in dimensions. In conducting the " Journal," the object never lost sight of was not merely to enlighten, by presenting information on matters of interest, and to harmlessly amuse, but to touch the heart, to purify the affections, thus, if possible, imparting to the work a character which would render it universally acceptable to families.

At no time was there any attempt to give pictorial illustrations of objects in natural history, the fine arts, or anything else. Without undervaluing the attractions of woodcut engravings, the aims of the editors were in a different direction. Their desire, it will be perceived, was to cultivate the feelings as much as the understanding. Hence the endeavor to revive, in a style befitting the age, the essay system of last century. In this effort, it may be allowable to say that Robert was eminently successful. His own explanations on the subject, embraced in the preface to a collection of his essays (published in 1847), are worthy of being quoted : —

" It was in middle life that I was induced to become an essayist, for the benefit of a well-known periodical work established by my elder brother. During fifteen years I have labored in this field, alternately gay, grave, sentimental, philosophical, until not much fewer than four hundred separate papers have proceeded from my pen. These papers were written under some difficulties, particularly those of a provincial situation, and a life too studious and recluse to afford much opportunity for the observation of social characteristics. Yet perhaps these restraints have had some good effect on the other hand, in making the treatment of subjects less local and less liable to the accidents of fashion than it might otherwise have been. One ruling aim of the author must be taken into account : it was my design from the first to be the essayist of the middle class, — that in which I was born, and to which I continued to belong. I therefore do not treat their manners and habits as one looking *de haut en bas*, which is the usual style of essayists, but as one looking round among the firesides of my friends. For their use I shape and sharpen my apothegms ; to their comprehension I modify any philosophical disquisitions on which I have entered. Everywhere I have sought less to attain elegance or observe refinement, than to avoid that last of literary sins — dullness. I have endeavored to be brief — direct ; and I know I have been earnest. As to the sentiment and philosophy, I am not aware that any particular remark is called for. The only principles on which I have been guided are, as far as I am aware, these : whatever seems to be just, or true, or useful, or rational, or beautiful, I love and honor ; wherever human woe can be lessened, or happiness increased, I would work to that end ; wherever intelligence and virtue can be promoted, I would promote them. These dispositions will, I trust, be traced in my writings."

The year that saw the beginning of " Chambers's Journal," brought gloom over the literary world. After an unavailing search for health in the south of Europe, Sir Walter Scott returned to Abbotsford in the course of the summer — to die. The scene was gently closed on the 21st September, 1832. The funeral of this illustrious Scotsman was appointed to take place on Wednesday the 26th. Among the very few mourners from Edinburgh who attended, were my brother and myself. We saw the remains of the great man laid with appropriate solemnities in his grave amidst the picturesque ruins of Dryburgh.

Indebted to Sir Walter for so many kindnesses some years previously, and in correspondence with him till the close of 1831, my brother felt that he had lost his most honored friend. Almost immediately he proceeded to write a memoir of the deceased, from such materials as were within reach, as well as from personal recollections. The memoir was issued by us in a popular form, and had an extraordinary sale — as many as eighty thousand copies.[1] It is referred to in the following letter from Allan Cunningham, with whom my brother had opened a correspondence. The letter is for other reasons interesting.

> "27 LOWER BELGRAVE PLACE,
> *27th October*, 1832.

"MY DEAR SIR, — Your letter was a welcome one. It is written with that frank openness of heart which I like, and contains a wish, which was no stranger to my own bosom, that we should be known to each other. You must not suppose that I have been influenced in my wish by the approbation with which I know your works have been received by your country. It is long since I took to judging in all matters for myself, and

---

[1] This memoir has been revised and reissued, *Life of Sir Walter Scott*, by Robert Chambers, LL. D., with *Abbotsford Notanda*, by Robert Carruthers, LL. D. (1871).

the 'Picture of Scotland' and the 'Traditions of Edinburgh,' both of which I bought, induced me to wish Robert Chambers among my friends. There was, perhaps, a touch or so of vanity in this, — your *poetic, ballad-scrap, auld-world, new-world, Scottish* tastes and feelings seemed to go side for side with my own. Be so good, therefore, as send me your promised 'Book of Ballads,' and accept in return, or rather in token of future *regard,* active and not passive, my 'Rustic Maid of Elvar,' who has made her way through reform pamphlets and other rubbish, like a lily rising through the clods of the spring. There's a complimentary simile in favor of myself and my book ! You must not, however, think ill of it because I praise it ; but try and read it, and tell me what you feel about it.

" I have been much pleased with your account of Sir Walter Scott ; it wears such an air of truth, that no one can refuse credence to it, and is full of interesting facts and just observations. I have no intention of expanding, or even of correcting, my own hasty and inaccurate sketch. Mr. Lockhart will soon give a full and correct life of that wonderful man to the world. The weed which I have thrown on his grave — for I cannot call it a flower — may wither as better things must do. Some nine thousand copies were sold ; this we consider high, though nothing comparable, I know, to the immense sale of ' Chambers's Journal.' I am truly glad of your great circulation ; your work is by a thousand degrees the best of all the latter progeny of the press. It is an original work, and while it continues so must keep the lead of the paste and scissors productions. My wife, who has just returned from Scotland, says that your 'Journal' is very popular among her native hills of Galloway. The shepherds, who are scattered there at the rate of one to every four miles square, read it constantly, and they circulate it in this way : the first shepherd who gets it reads it, and at an understood hour places it under a stone on a certain hill-top ; then shepherd the second in his own time finds it, reads it, and carries it to another hill, where it is found like Ossian's chief under its own gray stone by shepherd the third, and so it passes on its way, scattering information over the land.

" My songs, my dear sir, have all the faults you find with

them, and some more. The truth is, I am unacquainted with any other nature save that of the Nith and the Solway, and I must make it do my turn. I am like a bird that gathers materials for its nest round its customary bush, and who sings in his own grove, and never thinks of moving elsewhere. The affectations of London are as nothing to me ; in my ' Lives of the Painters,' I have, however, escaped from my valley, and on other contemplated works I hope to show that though I sing in the charmed circle of Nithsdale, I can make excursions in prose out of it, and write and think like a man of the world and its ways.

　" I remain, my dear sir, with much regard, yours always,

　　　　　　　　　　　　" ALLAN CUNNINGHAM.

" To ROBERT CHAMBERS, Esq."

. It was gratifying for us, as editors of " Chambers's Journal," to receive the approbation and good wishes of so prodigious a popular favorite as " Honest Allan," for, independently of the wide circulation of the work, his good word was an assurance that the principles on which it had been started and inflexibly maintained, were commendable. It will now seem strange to mention, that the success of this unassuming periodical led to a species of persecution. On all hands we were beset with requests to give it the character of a " religious publication." It was in vain for us to state that that was not our *rôle ;* that our work was addressed to persons of all shades of thinking, religious and secular, and that we could not, without violation of our original profession, take a side with any one in particular. We only got abused, and were called names. The era of this species of persecution, for such it was, however grotesque and ridiculous, extended for nearly twenty years after the commencement of the work ; and we had often cause to be amused with the unreasonableness of the demands which were preferred, also to wonder if others in like circumstances were similarly assailed.

On one occasion we were impelled to address our readers, partly in explanation of the reasons for maintaining the principles on which the " Journal " was established. Some passages may be quoted as specifying the literary character of the work : —

" With so many good results before us, it would surely be unwise were we to alter our plans in order to please the fancies of any sect, party, or individual. It is our firm conviction that any attempt to do so would be attended by failure. The many would be lost for the sake of the few who would be gained, and the work would soon dwindle into deserved insignificance. So much we say in all friendliness to those who seem inclined to fasten upon us functions for which we have no vocation. No, no ; we must decline usurping the mission of the politician and the divine ; we must leave the newspaper and the evangelical magazine to follow out their respective aims. To us, be it enough that we hold by the original charter of our constitution. ' Chambers's Journal ' shall never be written for this or that country, nor to meet this or that fashion of opinion, but remain to the end what it has been from the beginning : a Literary Miscellany, aspiring to inculcate the highest order of morals, universal brotherhood, and charity ; to present exalted views of Creative Wisdom and Providential Care ; and to impart correct, or, at all events, earnest and carefully formed, ideas on subjects of economic or general concern ; endeavoring at the same time to raise no false expectations, to outrage no individual opinion, and to keep out of sight everything that would set man kind by the ears."

While resolutely holding to our appointed course, the establishment of rival publications less or more differing from our own in character, some of them religious, or colorably so, was so far from giving us uneasiness, that we ever hailed them as coadjutors, all laboring for the public good in their respective vocations; for it is only by such varied means that every department of the community can be reached. In April, 1834, Leigh Hunt set on foot the " London Journal," which the editor, in his address, spoke of as being "similar in point of size and variety to 'Chambers's Edinburgh Journal,' but with a character a little more southern and literary." Now that Mr. Hunt and my brother have both passed away, it is more than ever pleasing to peruse the correspondence that took place between them on the subject of this new claimant for popular favor. My brother wrote as follows : —

"EDINBURGH, *April* 15, 1834.

"DEAR SIR, — I take leave to address you in this familiar manner for several reasons. The chief is your kind nature as exemplified in your writings, which prove you the friend of all mankind ; the lesser are your allusions, on more occasions than one, to writings of mine when you did not perhaps know the exact name of the author. My purpose is to congratulate you on the first number of your ' Journal,' which I have just seen, and to express my earnest and sincere hope that it will repay your exertions and render the latter part of your life more prosperous than you say the earlier has been. You will per-haps appreciate my good wishes the more that they proceed from an individual who, according to vulgar calculations, might expect to be injured by your success. I assure you, so far from entertaining any grudge towards your work on that score, I am as open to receive pleasurable impressions from it as I have ever been from your previous publications, or as the least literary of your readers can be, and as hopeful that it will suc-ceed and prove a means of comfort to you as the most ancient and familiar of your friends. I know that your work can never do, by a tenth part, so much ill to my brother and myself as it may do good to you ; for every book, however similar to others, finds in a great measure new channels for itself; and still more certain am I that the most jealous and unworthy feelings we could entertain would be ineffectual in protecting us from the consequences of your supplanting our humble sheets in the public favor. My brother and I feel much pleasure in observing that a writer so much our senior, and so much our superior, should have thought our plan to such an extent worthy of his adoption, and hope your doing so will only furnish additional proof of the justice of our calculations. This leads me to remark that, while I acknowledge the truth of your pretensions' to having been the reviver of the periodical literature of a former age, and have looked to your manner of treating light subjects as in part the model of our own, I must take this and every other proper opportunity of asserting my elder brother's merit as the originator of cheap respectable publications of the class to which your 'Journal' is so important an addition. In the starting of 'Chambers's Edinburgh Journal,' in February 1832, he was unquestionably the first to develop this new power of the printing-press ; and considering that we had some little character (at least in Scotland) to lose, and encountered feelings in our literary brethren little less apt, I may say, to deter us from our object than the terrors which assailed Rodolph in the Witch's Glen (a simile more expressive than it is apt), I humbly conceive that when the full utility of my brother's invention shall have been perceived by the world, as I trust it will in time, he will be fully entitled to have his claims allowed without dispute.

" That we have regretted to find ourselves the objects of so many of the meaner order of feelings among our brethren it would be vain to deny. I must say, however, that we would have been ill to satisfy indeed if the admission of our weekly sheet into almost every family of the middle rank, and many of the lower throughout the country, had not more than compensated us for that affliction. Our labors, moreover, are profitable beyond our hopes, beyond our wants, besides yielding to us a ceaseless revenue of pleasure in the sense they convey to us of daily and hourly improving the hearts and understandings of a large portion of our species. That you may aim as heartily at this result, and be as successful in obtaining it, is the wish of, dear sir, your sincere friend and servant,

" ROBERT CHAMBERS.

" To LEIGH HUNT, Esq."

There was a reply, lively and characteristic, a copy of which appeared in the fourth number of the " London Journal," being introduced with some complimentary remarks : —

> "4 UPPER CHEYNE ROW, CHELSEA,
> *April 21, 1834.*

" MY DEAR SIR, — I should have sooner acknowledged the receipt of your kind and flattering letter had I not, in the midst of a great press of business, been answering it in another manner through the medium of the ' London Journal,' in the columns of which I have taken the liberty of putting it. I hope you will excuse this freedom, which I could not have taken with you had I respected you less ; and I trust I have anticipated any delicacies you might have had on the point by stating to the reader that you had ·given me no intimation as to whether I might so use it or not. But setting aside other reasons for this step — injurious, I trust, to neither of us — it appeared to me too good a thing for the public to lose, as an evidence of the new and generous good-will springing up among reflecting people, and specially fit to be manifested by those who make it their business to encourage reflection. It would have been like secreting a sunbeam — a new warmth — a new smile for the world. Nor will you think this image hyperbolical when you consider the effect which such evidence must have upon the world, however your modesty might incline you to depre- cate it personally. Mankind, in ignorance of the sweet and bright drop of benevolence which they all more or less carry in their hearts ready to bathe and overflow it in good time, have been too much in the habit of returning mistrust for mistrust, and doubting every one else because each of themselves was doubted. Hence a world of heart-burnings, grudgings, jeal- ousies, mischiefs, etc., till some even of the kindest people were ashamed to seem kind or to have better opinions· of things than their neighbors. Think what a fine thing it is to help to break up this general ice betwixt men's hearts, and you will no longer have any doubt of the propriety of the step I have taken, even supposing you to have had any before, which I hope not. I forgot to say one thing in my public remarks on your letter, which was to express my hearty agreement with you as to the opinion that publications of this kind do no injury to one another. But this was implied in my address to the public in the first number, and I hope is self-evident. Most unaffectedly do I rejoice at hearing your own words confirm, and in so pleasant and touching a manner, the report of the great success of you and your brother in your speculation. I cannot pretend, after all that I have suffered, not to be glad to include a prospect of my own success in it, however it may fall short of its extent. Any kind of a bit of nest of retreat, with powers to send forth my young comfortably into the world, and to keep up my note of cheerfulness and encouragement to all ears while I have a voice left, is all that I desire for myself, or ever did. But in consequence of what I *have* suffered, and conscientiously suffered too, I claim a right to be believed when I say that I could rejoice in the success of other well-wishers to their species, apart from my own, and have often done so ; and in this spirit, as well as the other, I congratulate you. That you and your brother may live long to see golden harvests of all sorts spring up from the seed you have sown, and to reap in consequence that ' revenue of pleasure ' you speak of, as well as the more ordinary one, is the cordial wish of, dear sir, yours faithfully,

"LEIGH HUNT.

"To ROBERT CHAMBERS, Esq."

No one could more regret than we did that Mr. Hunt's literary venture was not permanently successful. At the sixty-second number, he united with his journal a periodical called the " Printing Machine," at the same time raising the price from three-halfpence to twopence, and altering the day of publication. Changes of this kind are hazardous, if not usually injurious. From whatever cause, the publication, as far as can be remembered, did not reach its hundredth number, although, from the quality of its contents, it merited a much longer existence.

15

CHAPTER XI.

L OOKING back to 1833, memory brings up recollections of Robert living in the bosom of a young family, in a home noted for its genial hospitality, as well as
for certain evening parties, in which were found the most
enjoyable society and music; his wife seated at the harp
or pianoforte, which he accompanied with his flute, — the
old flute which had long ago sounded along the Eddleston Water, and had been preserved through many vicissi-
tudes; the entertainment being sometimes varied by the
tasteful performances of worthy old George Thomson —
Burns' Thomson — on the violin; my mother living with
the junior members of the family in the composure and
comfort which she had so meritoriously earned; and I settled in my newly-married life. Such was the position of
affairs. All the surroundings agreeable.

The sad thing in these recollections is, that so many
who composed our general society, and figured among
the notables of the period, have passed from the stage of
existence. A lady with whom we formed an intimacy,
and who greatly enjoyed these evening parties, was Mrs.
Maclehose, the celebrated "Clarinda" of Robert Burns.
Now a widow in the decline of life, short in stature, and
of a plain appearance, with the habit of taking snuff, which
she had inherited from the fashions of the eighteenth century, one could hardly realize the fact of her being that

charming Clarinda who had taken captive the heart of
" Sylvander," and of whom he frenziedly wrote, on being
obliged to leave her, —

> "She, the fair sun of all her sex,
> Has blest my glorious day;
> And shall a glimmering planet fix
> My worship to its ray ? "

Vastly altered since she was the object of this adoration,
Clarinda still possessed a singular sprightliness in her
conversation, and, what interested us, she was never tired
speaking of Burns, whose unhappy fate she constantly deplored.

Another of our acquaintances, but seen only at times
when he came to town, was James Hogg, the Ettrick
Shepherd. I saw him first at my brother's house in 1831,
and was amused with his blunt simplicity of character and
good-nature. It did not seem as if he had the slightest
veneration for any one more than another whom he addressed, no matter what was their rank or position ; and
I could quite believe that he sometimes took the liberty,
as is alleged of him, of familiarly addressing Sir Walter
Scott as " Watty," and Lady Scott as " Charlotte." The
Shepherd, however, was a genuinely good creature and
agreeable acquaintance. On one occasion, he invited
my brother and myself to what he called " a small evening party," at his inn in the Candlemaker Row, intimating,
in an easy way, that we might bring any of our friends
with us. We went accordingly. Some time afterwards,
when poor Hogg was no more, Robert gave an account,
not in the least exaggerated, of this extraordinary entertainment, which may here be introduced as a specimen
of the lighter class of articles in the early years of the
" Journal."

THE CANDLEMAKER ROW FESTIVAL.

" The late James Hogg was accustomed, in his latter
days, to leave his pastoral solitude in Selkirkshire once or
twice every year, in order to pay a visit to Edinburgh.
He would stay a week or a fortnight in the city, professedly lodging at Watson's Selkirk and Peebles Inn in the
Candlemaker Row, but in reality spending almost the
whole of his time in dining, supping, and breakfasting with
his friends ; for, from his extreme good-nature, and other
agreeable qualities as a companion, not to speak of his
distinction as a lion, his society was much courted.   The
friends whom he visited were of all kinds, from men high
in standing at the bar to poor poets and slender clerks ;
and amongst all the Shepherd was the same plain, good-
humored, unsophisticated man as he had been thirty years
before, when tending his flocks amongst his native hills.
In the morning, perhaps, he would breakfast with his old
friend Sir Walter Scott, at his house in Castle Street,
taking with him some friend upon whom he wished to
confer the advantage of an acquaintance with that great
man.   The forenoon would be spent in calls, and in lounging amongst the back-shops of such booksellers as he
knew.   He would dine with some of the wits of ' Blackwood's Magazine,' whom he would keep in a roar till ten
o'clock ; and then recollecting another engagement, off he
would set to some fifth story in the Old Town, where a
young tradesman of literary tastes had collected six or
eight lads of his own sort, to enjoy the humors of the great
genius of the ' Noctes Ambrosianæ.'   In companies of
this kind he was treated with such homage and kindness,
that he usually got into the highest spirits, sang as many
of his own songs as his companions chose to listen to, and
told such droll stories that the poor fellows were like to

go mad with happiness. After acting as the life and soul
of the fraternity for a few hours, he would proceed to his
inn, where it was odds but he would be entangled in some
further orgies by a few of the inmates of the house.

"The only uneasiness which the poet felt in consequence of his being so much engaged in visiting, was that
it rendered his residence at Watson's little better than a
mere affair of lodging, so that, in his reckoning, the charge
for his bed bore much the same proportion to that for
everything else which the sack bore to the bread in Fal-
staff's celebrated tavern bill. To remedy this, in some
degree, the honest Shepherd was accustomed to signalize
the last night of his abode in the inn by collecting a vast
crowd of his Edinburgh friends, of all ranks and ages and
coats, to form a supper party for the benefit of the house.
In the course of the forenoon, he would make a round of
calls, and mention, in the most incidental possible way,
that two or three of his acquaintances were to meet that
night in the Candlemaker Row at nine, and that the addition of this particular friend whom he was addressing,
together with any of *his* friends he chose to bring along
with him, would by no means be objected to. It may
readily be imagined that, if he gave this hint to some ten
or twelve individuals, the total number of his visitors
would not probably be few. In reality, it used to bring
something like a Highland host upon him. Each of the
men he had spoken to came, like a chief, with a long train
of friends, most of them unknown to the hero of the evening, but all of them eager to spend a night with the Ettrick Shepherd. He himself stood up at the corner of one
of Watson's largest bedrooms to receive the company as
it poured in. Each man as he brought in his train, would
endeavor to introduce each to him separately, but would
be cut short by the lion with his bluff, good-humored dec-·
laration, ' Ou ay, we'll be a' weel acquent by and by.'

"The first two clans would perhaps find chairs, the
next would get the bed to sit upon ; all after that, had to
stand. This room, being speedily filled, those who came
subsequently would be shown into another bedroom.
When it was filled too, another would be thrown open,
and still the cry was, 'They come !' At length, about ten
o'clock, when nearly the whole house seemed 'panged'
with people, as he would have himself expressed it, supper would be announced. Then such a rushing and
thronging through the passages, up-stairs and down-stairs,
such a tramping, such a crushing, and such a laughing
and roaring withal, — for, in the very anticipation of such
a supper, there was more fun than is experienced at
twenty ordinary assemblages of the same kind. All the
warning Mr. Watson had got from Mr. Hogg about this
affair was a hint, in passing out that morning, that *twae-
three* lads had been speaking of supping there that night.
Watson, however, knew of old what was meant by *twae-
three*, and had laid out his largest room with a double
range of tables, sufficient to accommodate some sixty or
seventy people. Certain preliminaries have in the mean
time been settled in the principal bedroom. Mr. Taylor,
commissioner of police for the ward which contains the
Candlemaker Row, is to take the chair, — for a commissioner of police in his own ward is greater than the most
eminent literary or professional person present who has
no office connected with the locality. Mr. Thomson,
bailie of Easter Portsburgh, and Mr. Gray, moderator of
the Society of High Constables, as the next most important local officials present, are to be croupiers. Mr.
Hogg is to support Mr. Taylor on the right, and a young
member of the bar is to support him on the left.

"In then gushes the company, bearing the bard of
Kilmeny along like a leaf on the tide. The great men of

the night take their seats as arranged, while others seat themselves as they can. Ten minutes are spent in pushing and pressing, and there is after all a cluster of Seatless, who look very stupid and nonplused till all is put to rights by the rigging out of a table along the side of the room. At length all is arranged ; and then, what a strangely miscellaneous company is found to have been gathered together ! Meal-dealers are there from the Grassmarket, genteel and slender young men from the Parliament House, printers from the Cowgate, and booksellers from the New Town. Between a couple of young advocates sits a decent grocer from Bristo Street ; and amidst a host of shop-lads from the Luckenbooths, is perched a stiffish young probationer, who scarcely knows whether he should be here or not, and has much dread that the company will sit late. Jolly, honest-like bakers, in pepper-and-salt coats, give great uneasiness to squads of black coats in juxtaposition with them ; and several dainty-looking youths, in white neckcloths and black silk eye-glass ribbons, are evidently much discomposed by a rough tyke of a horse-dealer who has got in amongst them, and keeps calling out all kinds of coarse jokes to a crony about thirteen men off on the same side of the table. Many of Mr. Hogg's Selkirkshire store-farming friends are there, with their well-oxygenated complexions and Dandie-Dinmont-like bulk of figure ; and in addition to all comers, Mr. Watson himself, and nearly the whole of the people residing in his house at the time. If a representative assembly had been made up from all classes of the community, it could not have been more miscellaneous than this company, assembled by a man to whom, in the simplicity of his heart, all company seemed alike acceptable.

" When supper was finished, the chairman proceeded to the performance of his arduous duties. After the approved fashion in municipal convivialities, he gave the King, the Royal Family, the Duke of York and the Army, the Duke of Clarence and the Navy, and all the other *loyal and patriotic toasts*, before he judged it fit to introduce *the toast of the evening.* He then rose and called for a real, a genuine bumper. 'Gentlemen,' said he, 'we are assembled here this evening in honor of one who has distinguished himself in the poetical line ; and it is now my pleasing duty to propose his health. Gentlemen, I could have wished to escape this duty, as I feel myself altogether incapable of doing justice to it ; it is my only support in the trying circumstances in which I have been placed, that little can be required to recommend the toast to you. (Cheers.) Mr. Hogg is an old acquaintance of mine, and I have read his works. He has had the merit of raising himself from a humble station to a high place amongst the literary men of his country. You have all felt his powers as a poet in his " Queen's Wake." When I look around me, gentlemen, at the respectable company here assembled, — when I see so many met to do honor to one who was once but a shepherd on a lonely hill, — I cannot but feel, gentlemen, that much has been done by Mr. Hogg, and that it is something fine to be a poet. (Great applause.) Gentlemen, the name of Hogg has gone over the length and breadth of the land, and wherever it is known, it is held as one of those which do our country honor. It is associated with the names of Burns and Scott, and, like theirs, it will never die. Proud I am to see such a man amongst us, and long may he survive to reap his fame, and to gratify the world with new effusions of his genius ! Gentlemen, the health of Mr. Hogg, with all the honors.' The toast was accordingly drunk with great enthusiasm, amidst which the Shepherd rose to make his usual acknowledgment: 'Gentlemen, I was ever proud to be called a poet, but I never was so proud as I am this nicht,' etc.

"This part of the business over, the chairman and croupiers began to do honor to civic matters. The chairman gave the Magistrates of Edinburgh, to which Mr. Thomson, one of the croupiers, felt himself bound to return thanks. Mr. Thomson then gave the Commissioners of Police, which brought the chairman upon his legs. 'Messrs. Croupiers and Gentlemen,' said he, 'I rise, as a humble member of the body just named, to thank you, in the name of that body, and my own, for this unexpected honor. I believe I may say for this body, that they do the utmost in their power to merit the confidence of their constituents, and that, if they ever fail in anything to give satisfaction, it is not for want of a desire to succeed. But let arithmetic speak for us. You all know that the police affairs of the city were formerly administered at an expense to you of no less than one-and-sixpence a pound on the valued rental. And you all know what a system it was, how negligent, inefficient, and tyrannical. Now, gentlemen, our popularly elected commission has been seven years in existence, during all which time we have watched, and lighted, and cleaned you at thirteenpence halfpenny!' (Great and prolonged cheering.)

"There is now for two hours no more of Hogg. The commissioners, bailies, and moderators, have the ball at their foot, and not another man can get in a word. Every imaginable public body in the city, from the University to the Potterrow Friendly Society, is toasted, most of them with the honors. Then they come to individuals. A croupier proposes the chairman, and the chairman proposes the croupiers. One of the latter gentlemen has a gentleman in his eye, to whom the public has been much indebted, and whose presence is always acceptable, and after a long preamble of panegyric, out comes the name, the honored name of Mr. John Jaap, ex-resident commissioner of police for the next ward. It is all in vain for Mr. Hogg's literary or professional friends to raise their voices amidst such a host of bourgeoisie. The spirit of the Candlemaker Row and Bristo Street rules the hour, and all else must give way, as small minorities ought to do. Amidst the storm of civic toasts, a little thickish man, in a faded velvet waistcoat and strong-ale nose, rises with great solemnity, and, addressing the chair, begs leave to remind the company of a very remarkable omission which has been made. 'Gentlemen,' said he, 'I am sure, when I mention my toast, you will all feel how much we have been to blame in delaying it so long. It is a toast, gentlemen, which calls in a peculiar manner for the sympathies of us all. It is a toast, gentlemen, which I am sure needs no recommendation from me, but which only requires to be mentioned in order to call up all that feeling which such a toast ever ought to call up, a toast, gentlemen, a toast such as seldom occurs. Some perhaps, are not aware of an incident of a very interesting nature which has taken place in the family of one of our worthy croupiers this morning. It has not yet been announced in the papers, but it probably will be so to-morrow. In the mean time I need only say " Mrs. Gray, of a daughter." (Cheering from all parts of the house.) On such an occasion, gentlemen, you will not think me unreasonable if I ask you to get up, and drink, with all the honors, a bumper to Mrs. Gray and her sweet and interesting charge.' (Drunk with wild joy by all present.)

" About two o'clock in the morning, after the second reckoning has been called and paid by general contribution, Mr. Taylor leaves the chair, which is taken by the young advocate. Other citizenly men, including the croupiers, soon after glide off, not liking to stay out late from their families. As the company diminishes in number, it increases in mirth, and at last the extremities of the table are abandoned, and the thinned host gathers in one cluster of intense fun and good-fellowism around the chair. Hogg now shines out for the first time in all his lustre, tells stories, sings, and makes all life and glee. The ' Laird o' Lamington,' the ' Women Folk,' and ' Paddy O'Rafferty,' his three most comic ditties, are given with a force and fire that carries all before it. About this time, however, the reporters withdraw, so that it is not in our power to state any further particulars of the Candlemaker Row Festival.

.   .   .   .

" The Shepherd now reposes beneath the sod of his native Ettrick, all the sorrows and joys of his checkered career hushed with his own breath, and not a stone to point pale Scotia's way, to pour her sorrows o'er her poet's dust. While thus recalling, for the amusement of an idle hour, some of the whimsical scenes in which we have met James Hogg, let it not be supposed that we think of him only with a regard to the homely manners, the social good-nature, and the unimportant foibles, by which he was characterized. The world amidst which he moved was but too apt, especially of late years, to regard him in these lights alone, forgetting that beneath his rustic plaid there beat one of the kindest and most unperverted of hearts, while his bonnet covered the head from which had sprung ' Kilmeny' and ' Donald Macdonald.' Hogg, as an untutored man, was a prodigy, much more so than Burns, who had had comparatively a good education ; and now that he is dead and gone, we look around in vain for a living hand capable of awaking the national lyre. The time will probably come when this inspired rustic will be more justly appreciated."

One thing leads to another. The continued success of the " Journal " brought on, as if by a natural sequence, fresh enterprises, to which, with some assistance, we could give proper attention. In 1833, we projected and issued the work styled " Chambers's Information for the People." It consisted of a series of sheets, on subjects in which distinct information is of importance among the people generally ; such as the more interesting branches of science, physical, mathematical, and moral ; natural history, political history, geography, and literature ; together with papers on fireside amusements and miscellaneous topics considered to be of popular interest. As latterly improved, the work is comprehended in two octavo volumes, illustrated with wood-engravings. First and last, its sale has amounted to upwards of a hundred and seventy thou·sand sets, very nearly two millions of sheets. How far the diffusion of this enormous quantity of popularized knowledge at a small price may have proved beneficial, it is not for us to say. The work was reprinted in the United States, but with what success we never heard. With some changes of subject, a translation appeared in Paris under the title of " Instruction pour le Peuple." There was also a translation of a portion of the work into Welsh by Ebenezer Thomas, or Eben the Bard, a person of no mean celebrity in Wales.

Next, in 1835, was announced and begun a literary undertaking very much more onerous and elaborate. This was " Chambers's Educational Course," consisting of a series of treatises and school-books, constructed according to the most advanced views of education, both as a science and an art. In the series of books which followed was comprehended a section on physical science, the first time, as far as we were aware, of anything of the kind having been attempted in a form addressed to common understandings. Of the series of books my brother wrote several, including " History of the British Empire," and " History of the. English Language and Literature," this being the first time that anything of the kind had been attempted as a class-book.

To acquire some knowledge of the state of education, and the nature of the treatises employed, in the kingdom of the Netherlands, I made a deliberate journey through that country in 1838, visiting the schools in the principal towns, everywhere seeing with much pleasure the satisfactory manner in which the "religious difficulty," as it is called, had been overcome. What fell under notice was described in a "Tour in Holland and the Rhine Countries " (1839), and it vindicated the plan which had been adopted in constructing our " Educational Course " free of matter that could lead to controversy. No more need be said of the "Course" than that it met with a friendly reception at home and in the colonies, and that this acceptability is still increasing.

Writing to his old friend Wilson at Poughkeepsie, in 1835, my brother says : " I am continuing to pursue that course of regular plodding industry which you have witnessed since its commencement. Personally, I have now hardly anything to do with business, but I participate with my elder brother in the great advantage of uniting the duties of a publisher with those of an author. Of the ' Journal,' about sixty thousand are now sold ; and in England the circulation is steadily rising. That work seems now indeed received and sanctioned as a powerful moral engine for the regeneration of the middle and lower orders of society. We have just commenced the publication of a series of educational works, designed to embrace education, — physical, moral, and intellectual, — according to the most advanced views. To all appearance, this will also be a successful undertaking. While my brother has been married two years without any surviving children, I have now no fewer than four. . . . . We all enjoy good health ; and I often think I realize in my domestic circle that happiness which authors have endeavored to represent as visionary. Men, it is allowed, are apt to speak of things as they find them ; and, for my part, I would say that it is possible to lead the life of a literary man without any of those grievances and evil passions which others picture as inseparable from the profession. I envy none, despise none, but, on the contrary, yield due respect to all, whether above or beneath me. I am but little disposed to pine for higher honors than I possess ; they come steadily, and I am content to wait till they come. The result is, that hardly such a thing as an annoyance ever breaks the calm tenor of my life, and that there is not one person with whom I was ever acquainted whom I cannot meet as a friend."

From 1835 to 1837, as is seen by my brother's papers, he was in pretty frequent communication with Hugh Miller on literary subjects. Settled at Cromarty as an assistant in a bank, Miller had some spare time on his hands, which he wished to devote to writing stories and other articles for " Chambers's Journal," the reading of that · periodical having apparently been to him a means of mental stimulus. Limits, unfortunately, do not admit of the insertion of Miller's letters in full. In one, dated 19th March, 1835, he refers to the difficulties he had encountered in acquiring a facility in writing for the press : —

"Oblige me by accepting the accompanying volume. It contains, as you will find, a good many heavy pieces, and abounds in all the faults incident to juvenile productions, and to those of the imperfectly taught ; but you may here and there meet with something to amuse you. I have heard of an im-

mensely rich trader who used to say he had more trouble in
making his first thousand pounds than in making all the rest.
I have experienced something similar to this in my attempts to
acquire the art of the writer ; but I have not yet succeeded in
making my first thousand. My forthcoming volume, which I
trust I shall be able to send you in a few weeks, will, I hope,
better deserve your perusal. And yet I am aware it has its
heavy pieces too, — dangerous-looking sloughs of dissertation
in which I well-nigh lost myself, and in which I had no small
risk of losing my readers. One who sits down to write for the
public at a distance of two hundred miles from the capital has
to labor under sad disadvantages in his attempts to catch the
tone which chances to be popular at the time ; more especially
if, instead of having formed his literary tastes in that tract of
study which all the educated classes have to pass through, he
has had to pick them up by himself in nooks and by-corners
where scarcely any one ever picked them up before. Among
educated men the starting-note, if I may so express myself, is
nearly the same all the world over, and what wonder if the
after-tones should harmonize ; but alas for his share of the
concert who has to strike up on a key of his own. . . . . All
my young friends here, and I have a great many, are highly
delighted with your volume of Ballads."

Some years later, Mr. Miller made distinct overtures to
be a contributor. Under date 14th September, 1837, he
writes : —

" I have been a reader of your ' Journal ' for the last five
years, a pleased and interested reader ; and a few days ago
the thought struck me that, so far at least as one contributor
goes, I might also be a writer for it. . . . . I have been writing a good deal of late, — mostly stories ; but the vehicle in
which I have given them to the public " [a collection of tales]
" does not quite satisfy me. Some of my brother-contributors
are rather more stupid than is agreeable in one's associates ;
and besides there is less pleasure in writing sense in the name
of another than in one's own. Every herring should hang by
its own head. May I ask you, without presuming too far on

your good nature and the kindness you have already shown me, to read one or two of my stories, and say at your convenience whether I might not find some way of disposing of such to better advantage. . . . . I send you also a copy of verses which I addressed about two years ago to a lady, who has since become my wife. I do not know that they have much else besides their sincerity to recommend them, but sincerity they have. It is, I believe, Cowper who tells us that 'the poet's lyre should be the poet's heart.' "

The articles sent were duly acknowledged and inserted. Others followed in 1838, chiefly of familiar papers on geology. It is one of the things to look back upon with gratification, that Hugh Miller had been, not only an early reader of, but a contributor of interesting papers to, "Chambers's Journal."

Shortly after this period, considerable additions were made to our establishment, to meet the requirements of an ever-growing business. It is not the purpose, however, of the present Memoir to diverge into any account of the various enterprises in which we happened to engage. Only two may be mentioned as peculiarly furthering the distribution of a cheap, and, as it was hoped, useful species of publications among the less affluent classes in the community. One of these undertakings was " Chambers's Miscellany of Useful and Entertaining Tracts," a work completed in twenty volumes, adapted for parish, school, regimental, prison, and similar libraries. The circulation was immense ; and to keep the work abreast of the age, it has recently undergone considerable revision.

The other of these enterprises was one which exceeded all former efforts. This was " Chambers's Encyclopædia, a Dictionary of Universal Knowledge for the People," a work begun in 1859, and which continued to be issued till its completion in ten volumes in 1868. Unless with the assistance of a large and varied body of contributors, a book of this comprehensive nature could not have been attempted. This assistance was procured, and what was of greater importance, Dr. Andrew Findlater entered with much spirit into our views, and brought his erudition and habits of assiduous literary labor into exercise as acting editor. For all parties, however, the task was herculean. In commencing the work, my brother and I felt excusable in describing it as our " crowning effort in cheap and instructive literature."

When we entered on the undertaking, it was considerably more than a hundred years since Ephraim Chambers gave to the world his " Cyclopædia, or Universal Dictionary of Knowledge," the prototype, as it proved to be, of a number of similar works in Britain as well as in other countries, which must have contributed in no small measure to increase the sum of general intelligence. In nearly all these works there was a tendency to depart from the plan of their celebrated original, as concerns some of the great departments of science, literature, and history ; these being usually presented, not under a variety of specific heads, as they commonly occur to our minds when information is required, but aggregated in large and formal treatises, such as in themselves form books of considerable bulk. By such a course, it is manifest that the serviceableness of an encyclopædia as a dictionary of reference is greatly impaired, whatever be the advantages which on other points are gained. The Germans, in their " Conversations Lexicon," were the first to bring back the encyclopædia to its original purpose of a dictionary. The " Penny Cyclopædia " was another effort in the same direction, but it was extended to such dimensions as to put it out of the reach of the very classes for whom it was designed. Our object was to give a comprehensive yet handy and cheap Dictionary of Universal Knowledge, no subject being treated at greater length than was absolutely necessary. As now completed, it will be for the world to judge whether the work realizes the object aimed at.

It would have been impossible to give concentrated attention to the various works mentioned, as well as to those of which Robert was exclusively the author or editor, without a proper organization in one large establishment. As regards "Chambers's Journal," we were fortunate in having a succession of able and zealous literary assistants — among others, Mr. T. Smibert (deceased), Mr. W. H. Wills, Mr. Leitch Ritchie (deceased), and Mr. James Payn — to whom be every acknowledgment.

So aided, and with twelve printing machines set to work, there was at length a fair average produce of fifty thousand sheets of one kind or other daily. Under one roof were combined the operations of editors, compositors, stereotypers, wood-engravers, printers, book-binders, and other laborers, all engaged in the preparation and dispersal of books and periodicals. The assemblage of so many individuals in various departments, actuated by a common purpose, suggested the idea of annual entertainments to all in our employment. The first of these entertainments, which had for its express object the promotion of a good feeling between employers and employed, took place in the summer of 1838. The meeting was in the form of a temperance *soirée*, with some slight refreshments and music. It was held in one of the large apartments of our printing-office ; and to grace the assemblage, some persons of local distinction were invited. Among the notabilities who attended on the occasion were Lords Murray and Cunningham ; also Mr. James Simpson, a keen educationist, but best remembered for his amusing account of a visit to the field of Waterloo, shortly after the battle. Usually at these *soirées* there were about two hundred of all classes, and of both sexes, present, all in evening dress, and joyous for the occasion. In the intervals of the instrumental music, addresses were delivered, and songs were sung; on one occasion, as I have pleasure in remembering, George Thomson delighted the company with the song of the " Posie," the warbling of which sent the mind back to 1792, when our national bard was pouring forth his matchless lyrics. The addresses on both sides were of that friendly nature which was calculated to promote a spirit of mutual amity not to be forgotten.

The presence of my mother was a pleasing feature at the earlier of these annual *soirées.* Now at an advanced age, but retaining her buoyancy of feelings, she entered sympathizingly into the spirit of the occasion. Grateful for many unexpected blessings, her existence drew placidly to a close. She died in 1843, having exemplified in her life the brightest virtues that can adorn the matronly character.

CHAPTER XII.

THERE is no pleasing everybody. My brother's connection with "Chambers's Journal" gave no small dissatisfaction to a writer who affected to mourn over his desertion of what at one time promised to confer " distinction in the historical and antiquarian departments of literature." So much (and a good deal more) was querulously said of him in a leading critical organ in 1842. The accomplished reviewer who, in a spirit of patronizing sorrow, fell into this disconsolate frame of mind, had wholly failed to remember that the most precious writings of Steele and Addison made their appearance in penny papers ; that the classic essays of Johnson were issued originally in the same form ; and that the immortal fiction of Defoe first appeared chapter by chapter in the columns of a London newspaper. Forgetting all that, and possessing no sympathy with the cause of popular enlightenment, the lofty-minded reviewer perceived only a lamentable loss of caste for all who attempted to give their ideas to the world at anything under the quality of a handsome twelve-shilling octavo, fit for the " English library."

The critic was a little rash in his speculations. So far from devoting himself exclusively to the cheap periodical which roused so much temper, Robert continued to employ a large portion of his time on separate works, which raised him considerably in the estimation of the literary world. Abstaining from interference in public affairs, for which he never had any aptitude, his life was now, as it had been for many years, that of a literary recluse, who indulges in but a limited amount of recreation. His papers for "Chambers's Journal" occupied him for only one or two days a week. At the very time he was so unceremoniously called in question, he had completed, in conjunction with Professor Wilson, a most elaborate work on the "Land of Burns," which, extending to two highly embellished quarto volumes, is understood to have rewarded the enterprise of the publishers by whom it had been undertaken. The success of his small educational book on English literature led to the conception of a work vastly more comprehensive. He projected a "Cyclopædia of English Literature" that should form a history, critical and biographical, of British authors, from the earliest to the present times, accompanied with a systematized series of extracts — a concentration of the best productions of English intellect, headed by Chaucer, Shakespeare, Milton ; by More, Bacon, Locke; by Hooker, Taylor, Barrow; by Addison, Johnson, Goldsmith ; by Hume, Robertson, Gibbon ; and more lately by Byron and Scott — *set* in a biographical and critical history of the literature itself. This was certainly no mean enterprise. The end which, if possible, was to be attained, was the training of an entire people to venerate the thoughtful and eloquent of the past and present times. "These gifted beings," it was justly observed, "may be said to have endeared our language and institutions — our national character, and the very scenery and artificial objects which mark our soil — to all who are acquainted with, and can appreciate their writings."

It being impossible, with all his self-sacrificing diligence, to execute so onerous a task single-handed, my brother besought and received the aid of his friend Dr. Robert Carruthers of Inverness, who, both by his literary tastes and professional pursuits, was eminently qualified to coöperate in the undertaking. Completed in two volumes octavo, and issued in 1844, the "Cyclopædia of English Literature" had a most successful career, and continues to be popular, not only for private reading, but as a book for the higher class of students.

In 1847 were issued his "Select Writings," in seven volumes, for which several characteristic illustrations were furnished by David Roberts, R. A. A copy having been presented by the author to his friend, D. M. Moir — the "Delta" of "Blackwood," — it was acknowledged as follows : —

"Allow me to congratulate you on the publication of your 'Select Writings,' — a thing which you owe to yourself and your family, and of which both will have reason to be proud. . . . . In these days of flash and fury, when a certain class of writers seem to think that a work is valuable only in as far as it departs from the regions of good taste and common sense, the essays will stand forth as a beacon to the unwary, and as a token that some minds have escaped the infection. Nor can I doubt that they will attain a large degree of popularity which they deserve. In last night glancing through the volumes I have again made myself more intimate with many old acquaintances, highly characteristic of Scotland and the author, and equally creditable to our 'auld respectit mother,' and to her son."

It will probably be allowed that the essays comprehended in three volumes of these "Select Writings," were the greatest of my brother's productions. In them were seen his depth of thought on moral and economic subjects, also his sense of humor, with power of discriminating character. Old readers of "Chambers's Journal" will remember the recurring weekly pleasure of reading these essays :

" General Invitations," " The Pleasures of Unhappiness," " The House of Numbers," " The Unconfined," " Danger of Appearing Ill-used," " The Downdraught," etc. In a preceding chapter, a specimen of the more humorous class of papers is given in " The Candlemaker Row Festival." Perhaps in the whole round of his four to five hundred leading articles, none was more appreciated for the delicacy of its conceptions than one which is now brought back to light.

IDEA OF AN ENGLISH GIRL.

" ' Girl ' is a word of delightful sense. It suggests ideas of lightness, elegance, and grace, joined to simplicity, innocence, and truth, all embodied in that class of human beings which make the nearest approach to the angelic. The very sound of the word is appropriate ; it comes upon the ear and the heart like a flourish of fairy trumpets. The letters which compose it seem to be all dancing as they trip along. There is no slur or drag in this exquisite syllable ; it is a kind of perpetual motion. How far the same ideas may be suggested by the corresponding words in other languages I will not stop to inquire ; it is enough for me that *our* word is suitable to the character of *our* girls, — English girls, I mean, — for the word has nothing to do with Scotland, where ' lassie ' has its own delicious sense and admirable appropriateness. The English ' girl ' is the being whom the word was meant to describe, and no being or thing could have a designation more descriptive.

" Neck of lily, cheeks of rose, and eyes of heaven. Hair of sunny auburn, whose tiny tendrils dance with the slightest motion. A face nearer round than oval, but irradiated by the unsetting sun of a kind nature. A figure meek and graceful, wreathed in innocent muslin, and perpetually un-

dulating and bending into lines of beauty. Such is the
fair Saxon girl of Old England, as she grows in some sheltered nook of the merry land, unsmirched by the smoke
and sophistications of cities, and little knowing of any
other world than the little one which forms her home. It
is the fortune of few eyes to behold this fair girl, for her
parents prefer a life of retirement; but to the few who
have once seen her, she is as the recollection of the Caaba
is to the Mohammedan pilgrim, an idea to be cherished
forever. She chiefly holds intercourse with nature; with
the more beautiful parts of it; for there is a sympathy in
lovely things that makes them love one another. She
dotes upon flowers — fair roses, sisters to herself, and rho-
dodendrons that strive to match her in stature; nor is
there even a little violet in the garden but every day ex-
changes with her kind looks, as if the dewdrop lurking in
it were a mirror to her own smiling loveliness, diminishing
the object, but not leaving a lineament unexpressed. Out
of these troops of floral friends she is ever and anon choosing some one more endeared than the rest, to wear for a
while in her bosom; a preference which might make those
which remained die sooner than that which was cropped.
Her favorite seat is under a laburnum, which seems to be
showering a new birth of beauty upon her head. There
she sits in the quiet of nature, thinking thoughts as beautiful as flowers, with feelings as gentle as the gales which
fan them. She *knows* no evil, and therefore she *does* none.
Untouched by earthly experiences, she is perfectly happy;
and the happy are good.

"Affection remains in her as a treasure, hereafter to be
brought into full use. As yet she only spends a small
share of the interest of her heart's wealth upon the objects
around her; the principal will on some future and timely
day be given to one worthy, I hope, to possess a thing so

valuable. Meanwhile, she loves as a daughter and a sister may do. Every morning and evening she comes to her parents with her pure and unharming kiss ; nor, when some cheerful brother returns from college or from count-ing-house to enliven home for a brief space, is the same salutation wanting to assure him of the continuance of her most sweet regards. Often, too, she is found intertwining her loveliness with that of her sisters — arm clasping waist, and neck crossing neck, and bosom pressed to bosom, till all seems one inextricable knot of beauty. No jealousy, no guile, no envy, no more than what possesses a bunch of lilies growing from the same stem. She has some spare fondness, moreover, for a variety of pets in the lower orders of creation. There are chickens which will leave the rich-est morsels at the sound of her voice, and little dogs which will give up yelping, even at the most provoking antago-nists, if she only desires them. Her chief favorite, however, is a lamb, which follows her wherever she goes, a heaven-sent emblem of herself. To see her fondling this spotless creature on the green, innocence reposing upon innocence, you might suppose the golden age had returned, and that there was to be no more wickedness seen on earth.

"Our 'English girl' may be seen in various places. You meet her on a walk, and are charmed with her fresh complexion and blue modest eyes, as half seen under the averted bonnet. Then there are her neat shoes and white stockings, so pretty as compared with the hard outline of the booted foot, in which the ladies of other countries de-light. There are also her gauzy frock, and its streaming sashes and ribbons, and her hair depending in massy ring-lets adown her lovely neck. The whole figure breathes of the free and pure mind which animates it. At another time she is found in some pretty withdrawing-room, whose casements open upon flowery walks or green verandas.

Her head is now invested only with the grace of nature, — her flowing hair. Her countenance, instead of being flushed, as in the other case, by the open air, beams from the gentle toil of some domestic duty in which she has been assisting her mother.

"Appropriate to her late task, she still wears her neat apron, edged with blue trimming, and from the front of which perk out two smart, provoking-looking pockets, which gush over with all kinds of female paraphernalia, such as scissors, cotton-balls, and knitting-wires. You enter, and, being a friend of the family, she is *so* glad to see you. In five minutes you know all about the accomplishments of her canaries, the late behavior of Bob, the spaniel, an accident which happened that morning to her best frock, and the *annual* which she has received as a present, — 'from a friend,' as the inscription has it, — and here she evidently wishes you rather to look into the inside of the book than dwell on the initial pages. She has also a few of the nothings called 'ladies' work,' light, visionary fabrics of card and wafers, which she has been executing for a charity sale that is soon to take place ; these are all brought out and displayed before you. Then there is her album, with holograph poems, by three authors of reputation, and a thousand contributions, both original and selected, from less distinguished persons, the whole being garnished by her own drawings. All these things you must inspect, for she only shows them in the hope of entertaining you ; and then she turns to music.

"She has had selections from the last opera sent to her, and these she runs over, for your amusement, on the pianoforte ; carefully taking you bound, however, to observe that she has not yet sufficiently practiced them to be quite perfect in their execution. In truth you little need such apologies for her deficiencies. It is not for her external

accomplishments — though these are considerable — that
you value this fair specimen of humanity. You appreciate
her for her beauty, — which nature could never have conferred if it had not been intended as a reverence-com-
pelling merit for her gentle and artless nature, so well
enshrined in that form of native and indefeasible grace,
— and because, by dwelling on the contemplation of such
a being, your estimation of your kind is elevated ; a gratification in itself, and one of the highest order.

"Such is the 'English girl,' as she still exists in many
of the happy homes throughout this pleasant land. She
is one of the creations of nature, which, though decaying
in generations, live nevertheless forever as a race. It
would be as absurd to expect that the next spring should
fail to prank the sod of England with primroses, as to suppose that there will ever be a time with us when the cheeks
of girls shall not bloom, and their hearts cease to be stored
with those blessed influences which tend so much to cheer
the rest of their kind. We may be ruined twice over, —
in the newspapers, — but there will never be a time when
the lover of nature shall want objects to solace himself
withal. For him shall the ground, year after year, be
covered with a new robe of green, the trees redress their
disheveled locks, the flowers once more put on their
bloom ; and for him there shall never be wanting sweet
faces decked with maiden smiles, and painted with peren-
nial roses, to assure him that England is still 'right at the
heart.'"

It might almost be conjectured that my brother's "Idea
of an English Girl" had been partly suggested by the un-
affected manners and happy looks of one or other of
his own daughters. Essentially what is called a "family
man," he experienced immense delight in the society of

his children, who were treated with the utmost tenderness
and consideration. Ultimately, he had eight daughters
and three sons ; the daughters charming girls, most of
them with flaxen ringlets, all with pet names, and so merry
and entertaining, that their presence shed a continual sunshine through the dwelling. Two of the girls, Janet and
Eliza, were twins, and so closely resembled each other,
that you could scarcely have told one from the other, — a
circumstance which was often diverting in its consequences.
Clustered round their mother, Mrs. R. Chambers, a woman
of brilliant musical powers, much vivacity, and of literary
tastes, — the " Mrs. Balderston " of a number of amusing
essays, — the evening musical parties were now more enjoyable than ever ; for by way of variety the girls, in their
childish glee, would sing together some droll and lively
ditty, to the delight of the company.

For some purpose connected with his young family, my
brother removed to St. Andrews ; his residence being a
villa called Abbey Park, prettily situated outside the town.
While here in 1843, he interspersed his usual literary oc-
cupations with writing pieces of verse concerning his children, the daughters, of course, coming in for the largest
share of these rhyming fancies. · To show how a literary
man may gracefully unbend from graver studies to amuse
the innocent beings around him, I copy the following
verses from his note-book, under date 1843 : —

A LAY OF ABBEY PARK.

The King of the Fairies was wanting a wife,
And thought he would try the kingdom of Fife :
So he came to St. Andrews, where soon the gay spark
Found his way through the town to sweet Abbey Park ;
Rung the bell, was shown in, made an elegant bow.
  Mrs. Chambers requested that he'd take a chair ;
He did so, but said that he scarcely knew how
  To begin to inform her about his affair :

The fact was, the Queen of the Fairies was dead,
And he wanted again to be happily wed ;
So, hearing reports of the six Misses C.,
   All booming and handsome (though not much purse),
He thought how exceedingly nice it would be
   If one would take him for better for worse.
His queen, he said, was kept not ill—
   Pin-money handsome, a coach of her own,
A palace built snug in the side of a hill ;
   And further, he said, he could not depone.
Mamma thought the offer a capital chance,
So she called in her troop like an opera dance,
   And told his kingship that he might
   At least of her beauties have a sight ;
Papa, she said, would soon be in
   (For he, good man, had gone to golf),
When they might talk of it chin to chin,
   And so it would either be on or off.
Just then comes in Pa, hears the story, quite grave :
" Well, which would your majesty choose to have ?
Here's Jane, the eldest, we'll begin with her,
Or I never would hear an end of the stir."
" O," says the king, " she's too much grown,
A full head taller than me, you'll own."
" Well, here's our charming maid, Miss Mary,
Who seems already one half a fairy—
The dark gazelle, the Andalusian ! "
" O, such eyes in my kingdom would breed confusion ! "
" Then here's Miss Annie, an honest young woman,
Who is fond of everything that's at all uncommon ;
Although in good sense surpassed by few "—
" O, a blonde in Fairyland won't do."
" Well, here are our twins ; and first Jenny,
A gentle, benevolent sort of a henny,
Who would tend you kindly if you were sick—
Next pranksome Lizz, full of fun and trick."
" O, these are but one, though two appear ;
I couldn't take half a queen, I fear.
I rather would err on the other side,
And have something more than *one* for my bride."
Delighted, cries Pa : " Here's the very thing,

Our Major Amelia, who well can sing,
For she's two pretty misses in one !"
At once, then the king cried : "Done, sir ; done ! "
So Amelia was dressed in a frock of green,
And away she tripped as the Fairy Queen,
And at Abbey Park ne'er again was seen."

In 1840, Robert was elected a member of the Royal
Society of Edinburgh, from which time to 1850 he carried
on an extensive epistolary correspondence with men of
literary and scientific repute ; and at this period he often
visited London, where he mingled in the society of men
of letters. His mind had become occupied with speculative theories which brought him into communication with
Sir Charles Bell, George Combe, his brother Dr. Andrew
Combe, Dr. Neil Arnott, Professor Edward Forbes, Dr.
Samuel Brown, and other thinkers on physiology and mental philosophy. Of Sir Charles Bell, he says in a note,
on hearing of the sudden death of that eminent surgeon
and physiologist (1842) : "Sir Charles was my father at
the Royal Society — a most ingenious, excellent man."
He had likewise, in a more particular manner, acquired a
fancy for geological investigations, which introduced him
to another class of inquirers. Returning to Edinburgh, and
residing at Doune Terrace, his house was open to all
strangers of literary or scientific tastes who were pleased
to visit him ; and he now may be said to have acquired a
wide circle of acquaintances. His *conversaziones* at this
period will still be remembered. Often they had some
specific object, such as showing antiquities of historical
interest, and saying something regarding them for the
amusement of the guests ; or of discussing some curious
point in geology that had lately been exciting remark ; for
example, the traces of glacial action disclosed on the face
of a huge boulder by the cutting of the Queen's Drive

on Arthur's Seat. With such phenomena as this he was familiar, as is seen by his communications to the Royal Society of Edinburgh.

My brother took up geology, not as a plaything, but as a matter to be pursued with his usual quiet earnestness of purpose. He went off from time to time on trips to different parts of England, Scotland, and Ireland; his explorations, however, being confined in a great measure to the sea-coast, the shores of lakes, and banks of rivers, in order to trace the mutations that had in the course of ages taken place on the earth's surface, as regards the relative level of sea and land. The result of these excursions, and of much consideration on the subject, was the work, " Ancient Sea-Margins," published in 1848. The facts detailed were geologically instructive, as well as interesting from another point of view; for the explanations regarding raised beaches at once put to flight the mythic legends concerning the old parallel roads of Glenroy, and similar terrace-like appearances.

While partially occupied by pursuits of this kind, and neither from his habits nor inclinations suited to engage in the turmoil of civic administration, he weakly and unfortunately, at the close of autumn, 1848, permitted himself to be brought forward as a candidate for the office of Lord Provost of Edinburgh, which was about to be vacated. The movement, though well meant, was ill-timed. Sectarianism ran high. Means the most unscrupulous were employed to injure him in general estimation. A city for which he had done something not readily to be forgotten, was invoked to do him dishonor. And, as might have been anticipated from his singularly sensitive nature, he threw up his candidature in disgust, leaving the field open to his more favored adversary. The whole thing was a mistake. Robert ought on no account to have suffered

himself to be brought into a position so alien to his feelings. He might have been well assured that a rumor to
the effect that he was the author of a work which had
caused no little exasperation, "Vestiges of the Natural
. History of Creation," would be used to his disadvantage,
and that anything he might say on the subject would be
unavailing. As if to cover the whole affair with ridicule,
the theories propounded in the work which caused so
much civic commotion, have since been rivaled, if not outdone, in seeming extravagance by Darwin, without incurring any particular animosity. It appears now to be generally recognized that the utmost latitude may be allowed
to scientific research and speculation, without endangering
the foundations of religious belief; so greatly has the
world advanced in liberality of sentiment during the last
quarter of a century.

It is grateful to turn from this brief but unpleasant episode to some notice of an excursion which he made to the
north of Europe. In the summer of 1848, he had visited
Rhineland and Switzerland, with a view to satisfy himself
on the subject of glacial action, the theories regarding
which of Agassiz and Forbes, had lately raised much interest among geologists. As Norway was known to offer
some striking examples of the effects produced by glaciers,
my brother resolved to proceed thither. Quitting Edinburgh in the latter part of June, 1849, he sailed from Hull
to Copenhagen ; thence he went to Göttenburg, from
which he made a deliberate journey through Sweden and
Norway, sometimes going by steam-vessels, sometimes by
carioles, and at other times by boats on the fiords that in-
dent the coast ; but always making explorations on foot
wherever it was expedient to do so. The result of the excursion was given in a series of papers in " Chambers's
Journal," at the close of 1849 and beginning of 1850, under

the title of "Tracings of the North of Europe." Besides any scientific value attaching to these papers, they offered amusing sketches of the social condition of the country as far as Hammerfest, or nearly to the seventy-first degree of north latitude.

The accounts given of the simple politeness and kindly hospitality of the people form the most agreeable part of the narrative. These qualities were well exemplified when boating with some fellow-travellers in the Altenfiord. A few passages may here be presented: —

SCENE IN NORWAY.

"In the afternoon, after rowing upwards of twenty miles, we began to approach Komagfiord, where we designed to spend the night. The washed, shattered coast here presents remarkable disturbances of the slate strata, with curious interjections, veinings, and contortions. Many blocks appear, lying on the slate, of totally different kinds of rock, and therefore presumably brought from a distance. By-and-by terraces begin to appear, with many of these travelled blocks reposing on them. Such stones speak, and the tale which they tell is as truthful, perhaps more truthful, than most of those narrated in black and white.

"At length, at an early hour of the evening, we turned into a comparatively small, but sheltered and almost landlocked recess, where we first see palings along the green hill-sides, indicating pastoral farming, and then a neat house seated a little way back from the shore, with a number of smaller buildings scattered near it, including one which advances as a wharf into the sea. That pretty red and yellow mansion, so *riant* with its clean dimity window curtains, and a little garden in front, is the kiopman's house of Komagfiord. It has a small porch in the centre, with a wooden esplanade and a short flight of steps de-

17

scending on either hand. A good-looking man, in the prime of life, leans over the rail at the wharf, to receive us as we land. We are met by him with a few courteous words in English ; we present our letter of recommendation for Mr. Buch, the kiopman, who presently appears, a bulkier and older man, of remarkably open genial countenance, reminding me much of Cowper's description, though not exactly true so far as dress is concerned, —

> ' An honest man, close-buttoned to the chin,
> Broadcloth without, and a warm heart within.'

He meets us with welcome, and we are speedily conducted, with our baggage, to the house, a few steps from the shore, where we are at once introduced into a clean parlor, adorned with family portraitures and some of the favorite prints of Sweden and Norway, particularly the never-absent royal family. Mr. Buch, however, does not speak any language besides his own. He only looks the welcome he feels. His wife presently appears, a pleasant looking matron ; likewise his daughter and sole child, whom we by-and-by discover to be the wife of the younger man. Two or three little children, too, the offspring of the young couple, make their way into the room to see those extraordinary beings the English strangers. The younger man, Mr. Fantrom, knowing a good deal of English, we speedily, through that channel, become acquainted with the whole of this amiable family, from whom I was eventually to receive a greater amount of kindness than it almost ever was my lot to experience from strangers. We desired, of course, to be considered as travellers taking advantage in all courtesy of the obligation under which the kiopman lies to receive such persons into his house ; but it will be found that we could not induce our kind hosts to regard us in that light. The family seemed to be in very comfortable circumstances, and the union in which the three generations lived together was beautiful to contemplate. I shall not soon, I trust, forget the kiopman's house of Komagfiord.

" After the refreshment of tea — for we had taken a good luncheon at sea — we went out to examine the neighboring grounds, and soon ascertained that a terrace of detrital matter and blocks goes entirely round the little valley, at the height of about sixty-four feet above the sea. Walking along it round the angle which divides the fiord from the open sea in Varg Sund, we find it become a terrace of erosion on the rough coast there, with huge blocks everywhere encumbering its surface — blocks of foreign rock. Mr. Fantrom obligingly went along with us over this ground, and seemed glad when I could employ him in holding the levelling staff for a few minutes. We soon found him a very sensible, well-informed man, though geology and geodesy were new ideas to his mind.

" The latter part of the evening proved extremely beautiful, and we were tempted to take seats on the esplanade in front of the door, to enjoy the cool but still balmy air, a delightful refreshment after the heat of the day. The little fiord lay like glass below our feet, with a merchant sloop moored in the entrance ; the rugged mountains beyond the Sound rose clear into the bright blue sky, where the light was yet scarcely dulled. Mr. Buch sat down with his long pipe, emitting alternate puffs of smoke, and sentences addressed to his son-in-law and grandchildren. The bustle of Mrs. Buch engaged in her household duties made the smallest possible stir within. All besides was as calm as nature before the birth of sound. Having nothing better to do, I proposed at this juncture to bring out my flute, and play a few airs, provided it should be agreeable to all present.

"This being cordially assented to, I proceeded to introduce the music of my native country to these simple-hearted Norwegians. The scenery and time seemed to give magic to what might otherwise perhaps have proved of very little interest ; and finding my audience give unequivocal tokens of being pleased with my performance, I was induced to go on from one tune to another for fully an hour. It was curious to think of my audience hearing for the first time strains which are an inheritance of the heart to every Scottishman from his earliest sense — to myself, for instance, since three years old — and to reflect on some of our national favorites, as the 'Flowers of the Forest,' 'Loch Erroch Side,' and the 'Shepherd's Wife,' now floating over the unwonted ground of a Norwegian fiord. With each air, in general, the idea of some home friend, with whom it is a favorite, was associated. There was scarcely one which did not take my mind back to some scene endeared by domestic affection, or the love which, in common with every Scot, I cherish for the classic haunts of my native land. It was deeply interesting now to summon up all these associations in succession, in the presence of an alien family who could know nothing of them, and to whom it would have been in vain to explain them, but who, from that very incapability of sympathy, made them in the existing circumstances fall only the more touchingly and penetratingly into my own spirit."

On returning from his northern excursion, my brother set to work on a subject for which he had long been accumulating materials — "The Life and Works of Robert Burns." As the brilliant and painful history of Burns had been already written by seven of his countrymen, it might seem unnecessary to resume its consideration. Something, however, was wanting. There still survived persons who were acquainted with the poet, but they were passing away, and now was the time for gathering from them such facts and reminiscences as might serve for a full and authentic biography. Among others whose memory might be reckoned on, was Burns's youngest sister, Mrs. Begg ; and she, on being communicated with, entered cordially into the project. George Thomson was also at hand, and glad to be of any service. As regards the works of the poet, a peculiar arrangement was contemplated. This consisted in presenting the various compositions in strict chronological order, in connection with the narrative, so that they might render up the whole light they were qualified to throw upon the history of the life and mental progress of Burns ; at the same time that a new significance was given to them by their being read in connection with the current of events and emotions which led to their production. Acting on this plan, and after minute personal investigations, the " Life and Works of Robert Burns " was produced in 1850. It was well received, and passed through several editions, to suit different classes of purchasers.

Already, a small pension on the roll of Her Majesty's Charities and Bounties for Scotland had been granted to Mrs. Begg and her two daughters, and some private efforts had been further made in their behalf. My brother set on foot the collection of a fund, which was moderately successful. In writing from Edinburgh, May 4, 1842, to his wife at St. Andrews, he says : " On Monday, the first fruits of my application for Burns's sister appeared in two tributes, one of ten pounds from Mr. Tegg, bookseller ; the other, ten guineas from Mr. Procter, the poet. Isn't that capital ? " To increase these resources, the profits of a cheap edition of the " Life and Works of Burns " were set aside. The sum realized was not great, but it helped. Writing under date May 15, 1856, to James Grant Wilson, son of his friend Wilson of Poughkeepsie, and who had lately been in Scotland, Robert says: "I am glad you saw old Mrs. Begg, but it was a pity to miss the black eyes and intelligent face of her daughter, Isabella, who is a charming creature of her kind and sort, and more a reminiscence of Burns than even her mother. Just about a fortnight ago, W. and R. C. had the pleasure of handing two hundred pounds to the Misses Begg, being the profits of the cheap edition of the "Life and Works of Burns" edited by me, as promised by us at the time of publication. This sum will lie at interest, accumulating till Mrs. Begg and her annuity cease, when, with one hundred and sixty pounds of the fund formerly collected for Mrs. B., it will be sunk in distinct annuities for the daughters. The result, with their several pensions of ten pounds, will place them above all risk of anything like want. They well deserve all that has been done for them by their self-devotion to their mother in less bright days. I have great pleasure in thinking of that happy family on the banks of Doon, and reflecting on the little services I have been able to render them."

In June, 1855, he had an excellent opportunity of visiting the Faröe Islands and Iceland, and this, for geological reasons, he did not neglect. The *Thor*, a Danish screw war-steamer, touched at Leith on its way to Iceland, and at a certain charge six gentlemen were accommodated as passengers. It was a pleasant trip. Reikiavik, the capital of Iceland, was reached in safety; and in a day or two began a journey, in a rude fashion, on the backs of ponies, to the famed Geysers, a distance of seventy miles across a wild country, with no proper places for rest or lodging. Yet, as he describes the ex-

cursion, it was, though rough, a novel, hilarious affair
after all. At Thingvalla, the only accommodation for the
night was to bivouac in the church, and the only means
of lingual communication with the clergyman who acted
as host, was in a corrupt Latin. Robert made his couch
in the pulpit. On the second day the party got to a
farm-house in the vicinity of the Geysers ; and next
morning some of these hot water volcanoes were in ebulli-
tion. The chief curiosity is the Great Geyser, a kind of
well, nine feet in diameter, and eighty-seven feet deep,
from which were seen thrown up violent jets of water to
a height of from seventy to a hundred feet. The heat of
the water is extraordinary. " It has been found that the
water of the Great Geyser at the bottom of the tube has
a temperature higher than that of ordinary boiling water,
and this goes on increasing till an eruption takes place,
immediately before which it has been found as high as
261° Fahrenheit," or 49° above ordinary boiling-point,
a circumstance inferring enormous compression under violent heat, until the water bursts out into the atmosphere.

Returning by the way they had come, the excursionists
were again glad to take up their quarters in the establishment of the parish minister, who, it appeared on a
cross-examination in Latin by my brother, supported a
wife and eight children, performed his parochial duties,
and travelled once a month to a preaching station eighteen miles distant, all for five-and-twenty pounds a year.
" We could not but wonder how so large a family, besides a
horse, could be supported on means so small. In wandering about the place, I lighted upon his little stithy, which
reminds me to tell that in Iceland a priest is always able
to shoe your horse if required." The little book in which
these particulars were given, entitled " Tracings in Iceland and the Faröe Islands," was published in 1856.

A number of years had elapsed since he wrote a "History of Scotland" for a series of books issued by Richard Bentley. The subject was so familiar that he now applied himself with zest to a work entitled the "Domestic Annals of Scotland." It was comprised in three volumes. Two of these were issued in 1859, and a third appeared in 1861. The period over which the annals extended was from the Reformation to the Rebellion of 1745, nearly two hundred of the most interesting years in Scottish history. The work, however, was not a history in the usual sense of the word. It consisted of a chronicle of occurrences of a familiar, sometimes amusing nature, beneath the region of history, but calculated to convey a correct notion of the manners, customs, passions, superstitions, and ignorance of the people; the pestilences, famines, and other extraordinary events which disturbed their tranquillity; the traits of false political economy by which their well-being was checked; and generally those things which enable us to see how our forefathers thought, felt, and suffered, and how, on the whole, ordinary life looked in their days. The materials for this assemblage of facts were searched for in public records, acts of parliament, criminal trials, private diaries, family papers, histories, biographies, journals of transactions, etc.; the whole amounting to nearly a hundred different authorities, while the passages selected were so strung together chronologically as to offer a progressive picture of the times. On this work, so laborious, yet coincident with his feelings, he occupied himself at times during five years without in any respect remitting his writings for "Chambers's Journal."

About this time (1860), he edited and wrote an introductory notice to a volume purporting to be the "Memoirs of a Banking-house," by Sir William Forbes of Pitsligo, Bart., author of the life of the poet Beattie. The banking-house so signalized was that which was set on foot in Edinburgh by John Coutts & Co., who occupied as business premises an upper floor in the Parliament Close. The Coutts family were from Montrose, and began as corn-merchants and negotiators of bills of exchange. One of them, John Coutts, was Lord Provost of Edinburgh in 1742. He had four sons — Patrick, John, James, and Thomas. By these the business was continued, and received as apprentice the youthful Sir William Forbes, in 1754. In the whole round of biography, there is nothing finer by way of example to the young than the life of Sir William Forbes. Born in 1739, heir to a baronetcy, and left fatherless at four years of age, without patrimony, he was, commercially speaking, a self-made man, though, like many youths in similar circumstances, he owed much to the care of an amiable and intelligent mother, who, dwelling in a small house in one of the dingy lanes of Edinburgh, maintained on the most slender means the style and manners of a lady. Her son, Sir William, a boy fourteen years of age, instead of being bred to one of the "learned professions," was put apprentice to Messrs. Coutts ; from an apprentice, he became a junior clerk ; from a clerk, he rose to be a partner ; and finally, when several of the partners died or quitted Edinburgh, the firm was transformed into that of Sir William Forbes & Co., of which he was the leading member. The firm, as is well known, is now merged in the Union Bank of Scotland.

Sir William, as we learn from the memoir, was reared, and acquired strict habits of business, chiefly under the eye of John Coutts ; for Thomas, his brother, the youngest son of the Lord Provost, removed to London. There, founding the banking concern of Coutts & Co., he died in 1822, at about ninety years of age ; his youngest daughter

Sophia, married to Sir Francis Burdett, being mother of the much-esteemed Baroness Burdett Coutts. The memoir, which contains many curious particulars about banking in the olden time, was written by Sir William Forbes with a view to impress his son and successor with the paramount importance of exercising, with diligence in his profession, the highest principles of integrity, for only by such could he expect to sustain the enviable reputation of the house. The universal mourning on the death of Sir William Forbes, in 1806, shortly after he had completed his " Life of Beattie," caused Sir Walter Scott to refer to him in one of the cantos of " Marmion," when addressing the amiable banker's son-in-law, and the poet's friend, Mr. Skene of Rubislaw : —

> " Scarce had the lamented Forbes paid
> The tribute to his minstrel's shade, —
> The tale of friendship scarce was told,
> Ere the narrator's heart was cold.
> Far we may search before we find
> A heart so manly and so kind."

In editing the autobiography of this distinguished banker, my brother enjoyed a pleasure instead of performing a task. The same might be said of a series of detached papers, written at spare intervals, or to deliver as lectures. The subjects of these tracts, ultimately issued in 1861 under the title of " Edinburgh Papers," were various — old domestic architecture, merchants and merchandise in old times, the posture of the scientific world, some notions on geology, and the romantic Scottish ballads. By this last-named paper, the accepted opinions regarding several popular ballads, as given by Percy and Scott, were considerably ruffled. In it he ventured to show that, so far from being ancient, these ballads had been written, in an affectedly old style, not earlier than the beginning of the eighteenth century — the surreptitious manufacture being executed by a woman clever at versification, Lady Wardlaw of Pitreavie. Professor Aytoun, amongst others, was, of course, not well pleased at this unhappy overturn of certain literary traditions, but could not disprove the accuracy of the view that had been adopted. There was at the time considerable discussion on the subject.

My brother and I had talked of visiting the United States and Canada. We had pretty extensive business relations in these countries ; but what chiefly interested us was the social aspect of affairs beyond the Atlantic. I was able to make this desired trip in 1853, the account of which appeared as " Things as they are in America " (1854). Robert's excursion was postponed for a few years longer.

When the old Theatre Royal in Edinburgh was about to be taken down in 1859, in order to make way for the new General Post-office, he, at the request of some amateurs of the drama, wrote a historical sketch of the old building, with its successive managers, and the great theatrical stars who had made their appearance on its stage. The pamphlet was a trifle, but not devoid of some amusing particulars ; for example, the account given of the visit of Mrs. Siddons, in May, 1784, when she performed twelve nights, extending over a period of three weeks, and during which she played her principal characters, including Mrs. Beverly, Jane Shore, Isabella, Lady Randolph, and Euphrasia in the " Grecian Daughter : " —

MRS. SIDDONS.

" The furor created in the town by the performances of this illustrious lady was extraordinary. Prodigious crowds attended hours before the performance for the chance of a place. It came to be necessary to admit them at three, and then peo-

ple began to attend at twelve to get in at three.   The General
Assembly of the Church, in session at the time, found it necessary to arrange their meetings with some reference to the hours
at the theatre, for the younger members had discovered that attendance on Mrs. Siddons's performances was calculated to be
of some advantage to them as a means of improving their elocution. People came from distant places, even from Newcastle,
to witness what all spoke of with wonder. There were one
day applications for 2,557 places, while there were only 630 of
that kind in the house. Porters and servants had to bivouac
for a night in the streets on mats and palliasses, in order that
they might get an early chance of admission to the box office
next day. At the more thrilling parts of the performance the
audience were agitated to a degree unprecedented in this cool
latitude. Many ladies fainted. This was particularly the case
on the evening when 'Isabella, or the Fatal Marriage,' was performed. . The personator of Isabella has to exhibit the distress
of a wife on finding, after a second marriage, that her first and
loved husband, Biron, is still alive. Mrs. Siddons herself was
left at the close in such an exhausted state that some minutes
elapsed before she could be carried off the stage. A young
heiress, Miss Gordon of Gight, in Aberdeenshire, was carried
out of her box in hysterics, screaming loudly the words caught
from the great actress : 'O, my Biron ! my Biron !' A
strange tale was therewith connected. A gentleman, whom
she had not at this time seen or heard of, the Honorable John
Biron, next year met, paid his addresses, and married her. It
was to her a fatal marriage in several respects, although it gave
to the world the poet Lord Byron. Strange to say, a lady lived
till January, 1858, the Dowager Lady G——, who was in the
house that evening, and who never could forget the ominous
sounds of 'O, my Biron !' The writer of this little memoir
has heard the story related by another lady who was also in
the house that night, and who died in 1855. By her performances in Edinburgh on this occasion Mrs. Siddons cleared
nearly £1,000, her benefit alone yielding £350 ; all this being
over and above the profits of a night given to the Charity-
Workhouse. It was remarked that the doctors ought to have

given her a piece of plate, for there prevailed for some time after her visit a disorder called the 'Siddons fever' — a pure consequence, as was believed, of the unusual exposure, excitement, and fatigue to which she had been the means of subjecting a large part of the community."

Robert, accompanied by his wife, effected his long desired visit to America in 1860, everywhere receiving much attention from men of literary and scientific tastes. Unfortunately, his dear old friend and correspondent, Willie Wilson, had died shortly before his arrival in the country. Of his extensive excursion my brother did not give any regular account, but contented himself with writing two or three articles in " Chambers's Journal." One of these, entitled " A City Elevated," was a description of the method of raising houses bodily four to five feet above the level on which they had been built, without the slightest derangement to the walls or contents of the building. This extraordinary method of elevation he saw at Chicago in October, 1860, the object of the process being to raise the rows of dwellings sufficiently high above Lake Michigan to give an outfall to the drainage of the town. The work, he says, was executed by contract, the raising of a huge pile of buildings costing £3,500. This process of house-raising seemed to him a wonderful novelty in engineering. A few passages as to how the thing was done may be quoted : —

A CITY ELEVATED.

" The first step is to scarify away all the ground or fabric of any kind around the base of the building, supplying, however, provisional galleries and gangways for the use of the public during the process of elevation. Then the earth is dug out from under a portion of the foundations and strong beams inserted, supported by rows of jack-screws set together as closely as possible. When this is properly arranged another piece of the foundations is removed in like manner, and so on till beams with jack-screws are under every wall of the mass of building. In the case of the block in question, there were in all six thousand screws employed.

" The next step is to arrange for putting the screws into action. To every ten a man is assigned, furnished with a crow-bar. At the signal of a whistle he turns a screw one fourth round, goes on to another which he turns in like manner, and so on till all are turned. The screw having a thread of three eighths of an inch, the building has thus been raised a fourth part of that space throughout, or exactly 3-32d of an inch. The whistle again sounds : each crowbar is again applied to its series of ten screws, and a similar amount of vertical move-ment for the whole building is accomplished. And this opera-tion is repeated till the whole required elevation is accomplished. When the desired elevation is attained, the beams are one by one replaced with a substructure of masonry, and the pavement is restored on the new level. In this case the elevation of four feet eight inches was accomplished in five days, and it is stated that the cost of new foundations and pavement was from forty to fifty thousand dollars. The block, which was full of inhab-itants, contained much plate-glass, elegantly painted walls, and many delicate things ; but not a pane was broken, a particle of plaster or paint displaced, nor a piece of furniture injured. The writer deems it not superfluous to say, that he saw and partly inspected this mass of building, and certainly found nothing that could have led him to surmise that it had origi-nally rested on a plane nearly five feet below its present level.

" Let us English people ponder on these heroic undertakings of our American cousins. They are well worthy of imitation. It is the misfortune of many of our cities that large portions of them are built on ground so little above the level of an ad-jacent river as to be but imperfectly drainable. Southwark is a notable example, and Belgravia, with finer buildings, is no better off in this important respect. Sanitary considerations point out how desirable in these cases it is that the buildings should be raised a few feet. Chicago, a town of yesterday, scarcely yet to be heard of in geographical gazetteers, has shown that it can be done, and, comparatively speaking, at no great expense."

We now approach the end. On my brother's return from America, there were consultations on the project of a work, likely to be successful, but which could not be executed in Edinburgh. It required the resources of the British Museum. For this purpose it was resolved that he should migrate, with his family, to London, if his stay should be only for a few years. So to London he went, his residence being in one of the pleasant villas at St. John's Wood. The work which had suggested this wrench in accustomed habits was the " Book of Days," a miscellany of popular antiquities in connection with the calendar, including anecdotes, biographies, curiosities of literature, and oddities of human life and character. Formed somewhat on the plan of Hone's "Every Day Book," the work was considerably more elaborate and searching.

It is painful to relate what happened. Some anticipated help having failed, and forced to rely too exclusively on himself, his mental powers underwent a strain they were ill able to bear. The work was finished, but the author was finished also. Not that he died on the spot, but his system was shattered, and he could not in future incur any continuous exertion. To aggravate his disorder, he experienced some sad domestic bereavements. In September, 1863, he lost his wife, and almost immediately thereafter Janet, a favorite twin-daughter of much promise. Like most other works he produced, the " Book of Days " proved a success. But at what a cost ! He was heard to say : " That book was my death-blow," and such it really was.

Returning to Scotland in an enfeebled state of health, my brother took up his residence in St. Andrews, a place to which he had twenty years previously become attached, on account of its agreeable society, its bracing atmosphere, and its extensive links, or downs, noted for the game of golf, a healthful out-door amusement, not demanding too great an amount of physical exertion. There we may leave him for a little space, in the society of his youngest and unmarried daughter, Alice — his windows overlooking the Firth of Tay, and the celebrated Bell-rock Light-house flashing far in the east, like a lustrous gem on the bosom of the German Ocean.

CHAPTER XIII.

THERE is a skeleton in every house! All have some thing or other to trouble them, however well off and at ease they may appear to be. For twenty-one years after the commencement of "Chambers's Journal," and while all seemed to be going on prosperously, my brother and I were plagued with a skeleton, of whom the world had no means of being cognizant. The nature of the skeleton was this. Operating from Edinburgh as a centre, we had necessarily to intrust a large commission business to a bookseller in London, who had us pretty much at his mercy. Things might be going right or wrong with him, for anything we could satisfactorily discover. At first, there was no cause for uneasiness; but in the progress of events, when a small grew into a great concern, we could not divest ourselves of apprehensions of a catastrophe.

Such was our skeleton! Perhaps we were no worse off than our neighbors, but that is always a poor consolation. We might possibly have rid ourselves of the skeleton. That, however, would perhaps only have amounted to a substitution of a new for an old source of distrust. So we were fain to temporize, and to make the best of things as they stood. In a social point of view, we were on excellent terms with the personality of our skeleton, and there was not a little pleasant intercourse among us.

I was often for weeks in London ; and by these visits an acquaintanceship was kept up with various esteemed contributors, among whom we had great pleasure in numbering Mrs. S. C. Hall, who wrote for us some admirable stories of Irish life, and through whom we procured a juvenile story from the venerable Maria Edgeworth.

On one of these occasions of visiting the metropolis, a new and unexpected acquaintance was formed. It was in 1844, when residing in Greek Street, Soho. One day about noon, a carriage drives up to the door — not a vehicle of the light, modern sort, but an old family coach, drawn by a pair of sleek horses. From it descends an aged gentleman, who, from his shovel hat and black gaiters, is seen to be an ecclesiastical dignitary. I overhear, by the voices at the door, that I am asked for. " Who, in all the world, can this be ? " A few minutes solve the question. Heavy footsteps are heard deliberately ascending the antique balustraded stair. My unknown visitor is ushered in — his name announced : " The Rev. Sydney Smith." I hasten to receive so celebrated a personage as is befitting, and express the pleasure I have in the unexpected visit — wondering how he had discovered me.

" I heard at Rogers's you were in town," said he, " and was resolved to call. Let us sit down, and have a talk."

We drew towards the fire, for the day was cold, and he continued : " You are surprised possibly at my visit. There is nothing at all strange about it. The originator of the ' Edinburgh Review ' has come to see the originator of the ' Edinburgh Journal.' "

I felt honored by the remark, and delighted beyond measure with the good-natured and unceremonious observations which my visitor made on a variety of subjects. We talked of Edinburgh, and I asked him where he had lived. He said it was in Buccleuch Place, not far from

Jeffrey, with an outlook behind to the Meadows. "Ah," he remarked, "what charming walks I had about Arthur's Seat, with the clear mountain air blowing in one's face I I often think of that glorious scene." I alluded to the cluster of young men — Jeffrey, Horner, Brougham, himself, and one or two others, who had been concerned in commencing the "Review" in 1802. Of these, he spoke with most affection of Horner, and specified one who, from his vanity and eccentricities, could not be trusted. Great secrecy, he said, had to be employed in conducting the undertaking, and this agrees with what Lord Jeffrey told my brother. My reverend and facetious visitor made some little inquiry about my own early efforts, and he laughed when I reminded him of a saying of his own about studying on a little oatmeal — for that would have applied literally to my brother and to myself. "Ah, *labora, labora,*" he said sententiously, "how that word expresses the character of your country!"

"Well, we do sometimes work pretty hard," I observed : "but for all that, we can relish a pleasantry as much as our neighbors. You must have seen that the Scotch have a considerable fund of humor."

"O, by all means," replied my visitor, "you are an immensely funny people, but you need a little operating upon to let the fun out. I know no instrument so effect· ual for the purpose as the cork-screw!" Mutual laughter, of course.

There was some more chat of this kind, and we parted. This interview led to a few days of agreeable intercourse with Sydney Smith. By invitation, I went next morning to his house in Green Street, Grosvenor Square, to breakfast ; and · the day following, went with him to breakfast with a select party, at the mansion of Samuel Rogers, St. James's, when there ensued a stream of witticisms and repartees for pretty nearly a couple of hours. This was assuredly the most pleasant conversational treat I ever experienced. On quitting London, I bade good-by to Sydney Smith with extreme regret. We never met again. He died in February the following year.

Years pass on; in each, excursions being made with some literary object in view. While residing in London in 1847, I was honored with the acquaintance of Miss Mitford, whom I visited by invitation at her neat little cottage, Three-mile Cross, near Reading; the pleasantest thing about the visit being a walk with the aged lady among the green lanes in the neighborhood — she trotting along with a tall cane, and speaking of rural scenes and circumstances. I see by the lately published life of Boner, that in a letter to him, under date December 16, 1847, she refers to this visit, stating that she was at the time engaged along with Mr. Lovejoy, a bookseller in Reading, in a plan for establishing lending libraries for the poor, in which, she says, I assisted her with information and advice. What I really advised was that, following out a scheme adopted in East Lothian, parishes should join in establishing itinerating libraries, each composed of different books, so that, being shifted from place to place, a degree of novelty might be maintained for mutual advantage.

In 1848, I visited Germany, mainly to look into educational and penal arrangements; and at Berlin, through the polite attention of Professor Zumpt, had the satisfaction of becoming acquainted with the Prussian compulsory system of education, which, in its later developments, has had so startling an effect on the affairs of continental Europe.

I had visited France several times: to see the extinct volcanoes of Auvergne, and the Roman remains of Pro-

vence ; to see the prison discipline at Roquette and
Fontrevault, and the juvenile reformatory at Mettray ; to
see Voisin's method of rousing the dormant intellect
of imbecile children at the Bicêtre, and so on. I again
visited the country in 1849 ; on this occasion remaining
longer than usual in Paris, and seeing more of the social
life of the people. For this, let me acknowledge myself
indebted to the Dowager Countess of Elgin (a Scottish
lady of the Oswalds of Dunnikier), who found me out in
the Boulevard des Italiens, and introduced me along with
my wife to an agreeable literary circle, including M. Lamartine, M. Mohl and Leon Faucher. Lamartine, — tall,
thin, and unimpassioned, — the centre of a group of admirers, listened with cold complacency when I told him
that a translation of his " Voyage en Orient " had been
eminently popular in England. Faucher was greatly more
conversible. He was interested in hearing about our
system of poor-laws, municipal government, and other
topics connected with social economy, on which I did my
best to give him some information.

On one of these evenings, I was introduced to a young
Frenchman, son of a noted revolutionist during the Reign
of Terror, who had afterwards saved his life by hiding
himself, and changing his name, until he could again
appear publicly. He had recently died, and his whole
effects were about to be sold, in order that the produce
might be equally divided among his family. The articles
were said to be curious ; and such I found to be the case,
on going by invitation to see them in an old dignified
mansion, near the Temple — the most curious thing of all
being the identical proclamation which Robespierre had
begun to write at the Hôtel de Ville, when his assailants
burst in upon him, and he was shot through the jaw. He
had got only the length of scrawling the words, " *Courage,*

mes compatriotes," when, being struck, the pen fell from his hand, and big drops of blood were scattered over the paper. Bearing these marks of discoloration, how strange a memorial of the horrors of 1794 !

I was much delighted with the simplicity and inexpensiveness of the evening parties at the house of the countess, which was situated in the neighborhood of the Rue de Bac, and had been a palace of some pretension in the days of the old monarchy. People came to see and converse with each other — not ceremoniously to eat and drink, and go away in a state of discomfort. The few weeks I spent in Paris on this occasion were among the most delightful in my whole existence.

How my brother and I, as fancy directed, should have had leisure to spend months in rambling up and down the world, is worth a little explanation. In one of Robert's essays, he moralizes on the advantage of blending with pursuits that amount of leisure which will enable us to cultivate the higher class of feelings ; for, by neglect on this score, life in the long-run will only be looked back upon as a disappointing dream. On principles of this kind, we endeavored to act, but could have obtained no success in the attempt, by following the too common practice of hurrying into one project after another, irrespective of consequences. At the outset, we laid down three rules, which were inflexibly maintained : Never to take credit, but pay for all the great elements of trade in ready money ; never to give a bill, and never discount one ; and never to undertake any enterprise for which means were not prepared. Obviously, by no other plan of operations could we have been freed from anxiety, and at liberty to make use of the leisure at our disposal.

No anxiety ? — yes, there was some. We had still the skeleton, which had so grown and grown in dimensions as to be at length truly formidable. About 1852, matters became critical. It was as clear as could be, that we were to incur a heavy loss. In nothing in his whole life did my brother manifest more vigor of character than in determining to get rid, at all hazards, of this source of disquietude. He thought of Scott and the Ballantynes, and how, by an extreme and misplaced confidence, arising from kindness of heart, a man may be irretrievably ruined. Without further periphrasis : taking all risks, we withdrew our agency in 1853, and established a branch business in London under charge of our youngest brother, David — the Benjamin of the family — on whose fidelity we could rely.

Now comes a startling and melancholy fact, from which it would not be difficult to draw a moral. The concern that had for twenty-one years possessed our agency, had reaped a profit from it of not much short of forty thousand pounds — a sum equal to about eight times what Gibbon received for his " Decline and Fall of the Roman Empire," and eighty times what poor Robert. Burns ever received for all his world-famed writings ! All was gone, and a vast deal more — vanished into empty space. A fortune such as few are born to had been absolutely thrown away.

The whole of this affair, with some collateral circumstances, reviewed over a course of years, furnished an interesting and not uninstructive commercial study. In London, as any one may observe, there are two prevailing methods of ruination : extravagance in living, and trading beyond means ; substituting sanguine expectations, along with borrowed money, for capital. Such, no doubt, are errors everywhere, but in the metropolis they revel without restraint, almost without rebuke. And from the glimpses obtained, I regret to say, they are not unknown

in certain sections of the publishing profession. In whatever department of trade, so frightful is the hurry, that
means are not suffered to accumulate in order to allow of
ready-money payments. The whole transactions subside
into a system of bills — bills to wholesale stationers, bills
to printers, bills to artists, bills to writers, bills to everybody. In the same wild way, bills that are received are
hurried off for discount. There is great seeming prosperity, but so is there too frequently a great bill-book — dismal record of difficulties and heart-aches. The chief difficulty is how to effect discounts. Hours are perhaps spent
daily in the effort. Commercially, there is a struggle between life and death every four-and-twenty hours. Who
would covet existence on such terms?

The banks, somehow, fail to monopolize the discount
trade. They are rivaled by private capitalists, who, in
ordinary slang, are known as "parties." There is always
a "party" — some mysterious being who lives at Bath, or
Boulogne, or somewhere — to whom, through a "party"
more immediately visible, succor is looked for in emergen-
cies. The "party" dealt with is sometimes a mighty
pleasant and presentable person — jolly, good-natured
countenance; punctilious in dress; abounding in anecdotes about the drama and the "Derby;" well read, and,
avowing a high opinion of Campbell as a poet, can give
with proper effect quotations from the "Pleasures of
Hope." Meeting him at a ceremonious family dinner,
you would never, from his appearance and high-souled
chivalric ideas, take him for a "party," but half the guests
know that he possesses that imposing character in relation
to the unfortunate host, whom he could any day crumple
up at pleasure, and only bides his time to do so. When
Junius made the famous remark, that "party is the mad-
ness of many for the gain of a few," he spoke the truth in
more ways than one.

Usually, in one way or other, the money-lending " party " becomes the final beneficiary. Should the advances be made to some unhappy publishing concern, copyrights are assigned in security, and seldom do they return to their original owner. Valuable literary property, the fruit of ingenuous conception and enterprise, is thus constantly undergoing a process of transfer and confiscation. We may feel shocked with the tyranny of capital, but the blame is due to the extravagant credit system, along with an insane overhaste to be rich ; along, also — for we must not forget that — with an insane extravagance in living, which yields comfort to neither body nor mind ; this, how- ever, is a circumstance so very commonplace as to engage little or no attention.

It will be remembered how James King, our early friend and fellow-laborer in scientific experiments, had emigrated to Australia, in order to follow out an industrial career. From one thing to another, he became proprietor of vine- yards at Irawang, New South Wales, and there devoted himself to the perfection of the wine-manufacture in the colony. In this pursuit he was, by his chemical knowl- edge, perseverance, and enterprise, eminently successful ; but what avails professional eminence with loss of health ? Returning to England, he travelled over the continent, and established a friendship with Baron Liebig, who furnished valuable suggestions as to improving the quality and aroma of his wines. Hints of this kind, however, he did not live to profit by. I found him in London, a wreck — sad con- trast to what he had been when departing, as a high- spirited youth, to push his fortune abroad. A renewal of intercourse was scarcely practicable, for he heard and spoke only with difficulty. He died in London in 1857, leaving a widow and son to conduct his affairs in the colony.

Amidst literary and other avocations, my brother and I never forgot Peebles. We visited the place, — notably so in 1841, to be complimented with the " Freedom of the Burgh," — and tried to keep up an acquaintance with old friends, ever diminishing in number till scarcely one of them was left. Remembering the benefits we had received from Elder's library — long since extinct — in 1859, I gifted to the town a suite of buildings consisting of a library of ten thousand volumes, reading-room, museum, gallery of art, and lecture-hall, with the view of promoting the mental improvement of the humbler classes ; but whether the institution so organized will have any such effect, seems, after an experience of twelve years, exceedingly doubtful. So slight has been the success, that others may well pause before venturing on a similar experiment. Perhaps the only other incident concerning myself worthy of notice, is that of having been elected Lord Provost of Edinburgh in 1865 — an office that was held by me for four years, and regarding which little is left to reflect on with satisfaction, but the circumstance of having projected and obtained an act of parliament for the sanitary improvement of the city.

While giving some attention to " Chambers's Journal," now in its forty-first year, it may be permitted me to mention that latterly I was able to add a few books to the list already mentioned : " The Youth's Companion and Counselor," 1860 ; " Something of Italy," 1862 ; " History of Peeblesshire," 1864 ; " Wintering in Mentone," 1870 ; and " France : its History and Revolutions," 1871.

It is not for me to say a single word regarding the influence which " Chambers's Journal," and other publications, edited by my brother and myself, may have exerted in the cause of popular enlightenment during the past forty years. Of that, the public must be the judge. Much more pleasing is it to think that the mass of cheap and respectably conducted periodical literature, which sprung intermediately into existence under a variety of conditions and auspices, has proved one of the many engines of social improvement in the nineteenth century. Referring to the example of patience which was set by the operatives of Lancashire under the agonizing calamity of famine which unhappily visited them, a minister of the crown did not hesitate to declare " that to the information contained in the excellent cheap papers of this country he attributed much of the calm forbearance with which the distressed had borne their privations." [1] This unexpected acknowledgment receives significance from the fact — which history will scarcely fail to notice — that the state, under successive ministries, so far from facilitating the diffusion of a cheap and wholesome literature, unconsciously did all in its power for its repression, by means of exorbitant excise duties on paper, the removal of which was effected only after a long and costly process of popular agitation. In plain terms, the cheap press, in its early and struggling stages, owes nothing to the state, and, it may be added, little to the learned and affluent. It has grown up by the force of circumstances, not by any special favor. Looked superciliously on throughout, it had its origin in the People, and from the People alone has it received substantial support and encouragement.

[1] Right Hon. Mr. Milner Gibson's speech at Ashton-under-Lyne, January 21, 1863.

CHAPTER XIV.

CHANGE of air and scene is said to work wonders on the overtasked brain. It did so to a certain extent on Robert. The fresh air and tranquillity of St. Andrews, with some moderate exercise at golf, had a beneficial effect on his health. He wished for peace, and here it was, enlivened with converse in the society of old friends. He had built for himself a house, with a spacious saloon-library, entering from which was a small apartment fitted up as a study. Environed by his books, a very choice collection, he was now enjoying a luxurious and " learned leisure." All task-work was at an end. Sometimes he came for a few days to Edinburgh ; and, extending his journey, he occasionally visited Mrs. Priestley in London, or some other of his married daughters. At the new-year, as long as he was able, he made an excursion across the Tay to Fingask Castle, in the Carse of Gowrie, to pass a day or two according to old fashions with his friends, the Thrieplands.

No house, to look at, could be more pleasant than that which he had constructed according to his fancy at St. Andrews. In it he constantly received company, and was always the same kindly and entertaining host. But apart from these receptions, his establishment was cheerless, contrasted with former days, when his home was enlivened by a troop of merry-hearted girls. Possibly it was from a sense of comparative solitude, that he formed a second matrimonial alliance. He married (January, 1867) the widow of Robert Frith, a lady of musical accomplishments, and of that liveliness of disposition which was calculated to soothe his declining years.

In 1868, the University of St. Andrews conferred on him the honorary degree of LL. D. He was after that known as "the Doctor," and the doctor's dinner and evening parties had something in them of the smack of old times. All could see that he was gradually declining in health ; but then he never failed in his accustomed cheerfulness, his love of music, and his anecdotic, though now slowly uttered remarks.

The pen was now taken up only as an amusement ; but such was the pleasure he derived from writing, that he felt as if the abandonment of literary exercise would kill him outright. Little by little, he finished a book that he had long been employed upon. It was the "Life of Smollett," interspersed with characteristic specimens of his writings. This was a slight work, in one volume, but which had the recommendation of adding something to the personal history of Smollett and his family, and presenting a curious fragmentary memoir, written by the novelist's grandfather, Sir James Smollett, a stern old Whig Presbyterian, knighted by William III. This was the last of my brother's printed productions, and with it his literary career closes.

No one can live at St. Andrews without taking keenly to golf. It is the staple out-door recreation of the place. The links over which it is played are peculiarly favorable for the game, because the ground is beset with that amount of difficulties which gives a piquancy to the sport. There are nine holes in the links, as so many goals to be successively reached by the golfer in making his round. These holes formed a theme for a series of half-comic, half-moralizing sonnets, which were intended to be nine in number. My brother, however, completed only the following three : —

THE NINE HOLES OF ST. ANDREWS.

IN A SERIES OF SONNETS.

1. *The Bridge Hole.*

" Sacred to hope and promise is the spot —
    To Philp's and to the Union Parlor near,
    To every golfer, every caddie dear —
Where we strike off — O, ne'er to be forgot,
Although in lands most distant we sojourn.
    But not without its perils is the place ;
    Mark the opposing caddie's sly grimace,
Whispering, ' He's on the road ! ' ' He's in the burn ! '

" So is it often in the grander game
    Of life, when, eager, hoping for the palm,
Breathing of honor, joy, and love, and fame,
    Conscious of nothing like a doubt or qualm,
We start, and cry : ' Salute us, muse of fire ! '
And the first footstep lands us in the mire.

2. *The Cartgate Hole.*

" Fearful to Tyro is thy primal stroke,   .
    O Cartgate, for behold the bunker opes
    Right to the teeing place its yawning chops,
Hope to engulf ere it is well awoke.

That passed, a Scylla in the form of rushes
    Nods to Charybdis which in ruts appears :
    He will be safe who in the middle steers ;
One step aside, the ball destruction brushes.

" Golf symbols thus again our painful life,
    Dangers in front, and pitfalls on each hand :
    But see, one glorious cleek-stroke from the sand

Sends Tyro home, and saves all further strife !
He's in at six — old Sandy views the lad,
With new respect, remarking, ' That's no bad ! '

3. *The Third Hole.*

" No rest in golf — still perils in the path :
    Here, playing a good ball, perhaps it goes
    Gently into the *Principalian Nose*,
Or else *Tam's Coo*, which equally is death.
Perhaps the wind will catch it in mid-air,
    And take it to the *Whins* — ' Look out, look out !
    Tom Morris, be, O be a faithful scout ! '
But Tom, though *links-eyed*, finds 't not anywhere.

" Such thy mishaps, O Merit : feeble balls   .
    Meanwhile roll on, and lie upon the green ;
'Tis well, my friends, if you, when this befalls,
    Can spare yourselves the infamy of spleen.
It only shows the ancient proverb's force,
That you may farther go and fare the worse."

Those who were unacquainted with his private habits of thought may be surprised to know that, chiefly about this time, he wrote a number of prayers, and graces to be said at meals, all breathing the purest religious spirit. He began the " Life and Preachings of Jesus Christ, from the Evangelists." It was a work apparently designed for the edification of youth, and was left unfinished. He likewise began a catechism for the young, which he did not live to complete. The reminiscences of his early life, from which some extracts have been given, were also among his latest compositions. The mass of papers which he accumulated, and left as literary remains, is indescribable in variety. A considerable number of these fragments refer to Scottish Songs and Ballads, for which he entertained a great affection ; and this reminds me, that with some trouble he collected, from the singing of old persons in Liddesdale and elsewhere, the airs of twelve of the Border Ballads, and had them printed for private circulation, in 1844.

One of the more bulky papers which he left is a species of inquiry into the so-called manifestations of spiritualism. Without pronouncing an opinion dogmatically, he considered the subject worthy of patient investigation. "The phenomena of spiritualism," he says, "may be the confused elements of a new chapter of human nature, which will only require some careful investigation to form a respectable addition to our stock of knowledge. Such, I must confess, is the light in which it has presented itself to me, or rather the aspect which it promises to assume." Acknowledging so much, perhaps he thought of a saying he had heard used by Sir Walter Scott, that, "If there be a vulgar credulity, there is also a vulgar incredulity." In his anxiety for fair-play, he perhaps leant to the side of credulity.

Among the papers amassed by my brother, some old and some new, we have the evidence of a mind that for half a century had never been free from some kind of literary assiduity. His casual thoughts, things he heard spoken of, anecdotes, stories, fragments of family history, —all, sooner or later, assumed shape in sentences and paragraphs. He never forgot anything. His memory, from a faculty of concentrativeness, was altogether remarkable. He could tell you any date in history; he remembered all the people of any note he had conversed with, and how they looked, and what they said, if it was at all worth remembering. Every place he had visited was fresh in his recollection.

With a memory so stored, he was always writing down odds and ends, as if assembling materials for books, which years would have been required to work into shape. To give an idea of these memoranda, I select the follow-

ing, some of them being from a small note-book with
dates : —

ANECDOTE OF HUGH CHISHOLM.

" Shortly after writing the ' History of the Rebellion,'
I heard an anecdote of two Jacobites, — one of them,
Colquhoun Grant, who had been at the battle of Preston-
pans, and there having mounted the horse of an English
officer, whom he had brought down with his broadsword,
chased for miles a body of Cope's recreant dragoons ; the
other, Hugh Chisholm, a Highlander, who had been also
out in the '45, and lived in Edinburgh for a considerable
period between 1780 and 1790. Sir Walter Scott saw him
at that time, and says something regarding him in the
' Tales of a Grandfather.' The anecdote is this : —

" ' Hugh Chisholm, who had been associated with the
Prince in his wanderings, was supported latterly by a
pension, which was got up for him by some gentlemen.
Lord Monboddo was much attached to this interesting
old man, and once proposed to introduce him to his table
at dinner, along with some friends of more exalted rank.
On his mentioning the scheme to Mr. Colquhoun Grant,
one of the proposed party, that gentleman started a number of objections, on the score that poor Chisholm would
be embarrassed and uncomfortable in a scene so unusual
to him, while some others would feel offended at having
the company of a man of mean rank forced upon them.
Monboddo heard all Mr. Grant's objections, and then assuming a lofty tone, exclaimed, "Let me remind you, Mr.
Grant, Hugh Chisholm has been in better company than
either yours or mine !" The conscience-struck Jacobite
had not another word to say.

" ' Chisholm was accordingly brought to Monboddo's
table, where he behaved with all the native politeness of a
Highlander, and gave satisfaction to all present. He was

19

very much struck with the appearance of Lord Monboddo's daughter, Miss Burnet, — Burns's Miss Burnet,[1] — who presided over the feast. He seemed, indeed, completely rapt in admiration of this singularly beautiful woman, insomuch that he seldom took his eyes off her the whole night. One of the company had the curiosity to ask what he thought of her, when he burst out with an exclamation in Gaelic, indicative of an uncommon degree of admiration, "She is the most beautiful living creature I ever saw in all my life!"' "

STORY OF A FOUNDLING.

(Feb. 9, 1845.) "Miss Edmondstone, a lady of ninety, relates a curious story of a foundling. About eighty years ago Mr. Gordon of Ardoch, in Aberdeenshire — a tall castle situated upon a rock overlooking the sea — was one stormy night alarmed by the firing of a gun, apparently from a distressed vessel. Collecting his dependents, and furnishing himself with lights and ropes, he hurried down to the beach, amidst the peltings of one of the severest storms he had any recollection of. On arriving there, he and his people could discern no ship ; they saw no light ; they heard no cry. But, searching about, they found an infant lying in a kind of floating crib or cradle, as if it had been brought ashore from a perished vessel by the force of the winds and the waves. The young stranger was removed to the castle, and taken care of; and in the morning there were indubitable signs of a shipwreck on the beach, but no other person seemed to have got ashore.

"Mr. Gordon, unable to trace the history of the infant (it was a female), brought her up with his own daughters, and became as much attached to her as to any of his children. The foundling received, in all respects, the same

[1] *Address to Edinburgh,* and *Elegy on the late Miss Burnet of Monboddo.* She died of consumption, 17th June, 1790.

treatment and the same education as the young ladies with whom she was associated, and in time she grew to woman's estate. About that time a similar storm occurred. Mr. Gordon hurried as usual to the shore ; but this time was so happy as to receive a shipwrecked party, among whom was a gentleman passenger. After a comfortable night spent in the castle, this stranger was next morning surprised by the entrance of the young ladies, upon one of whom he fixed a gaze of the greatest interest.

"'Is this your daughter too?' said he to his kind host. "No," said Mr. Gordon ; 'but she is as dear to me as if she were.' And then he related the story of the former storm, and of the discovery of the infant upon the beach. At the conclusion, the stranger said with much emotion that he had all reason to believe that the young lady was his own niece. He then stated the circumstances of a sister's return from India, corresponding to the time of the shipwreck ; and explained how it might happen that Mr. Gordon's inquiries for the parents of the child had failed. 'She is now,' he said, 'an orphan ; but her father has left her the bulk of his fortune, to be bestowed upon her, if she should ever be found.'

" All these things being fully substantiated by the stranger, it became necessary that the young lady should leave Ardoch, to put herself under the care of a new protector ; but this was a bitter trial, and she could at last be reconciled to quit Ardoch, only on the condition that one of her friends, the daughters of Mr. Gordon, should accompany her. This was consented to, and the whole party soon after left Scotland to proceed to Göttenburg, in Sweden, where her uncle carried on a large mercantile concern.

"There is no further romance in the tale as far as the young lady was concerned ; for fact does not always go as fiction would. But a curious circumstance resulted, nevertheless, from the shipwreck. Miss Gordon was wooed and won at Göttenburg by a young Scottish merchant named Erskine, a son of Erskine of Cambo in Fife, a youth of narrow fortunes, and *seventeen* persons between him and the title and estates of the Earl of Kelly. The seventeen died, and this young man became an earl. More than this, a sister of Miss Gordon was, through the same connection of circumstances, married to a younger brother of the former, who succeeded to this title. Thus, through the accident of the shipwreck, two daughters of an Aberdeenshire laird became Countesses of Kelly. Unfortunately, neither had any children ; so that the title has reverted to the Earl of Mar, the representative of the family of which that of Kelly was a branch." [Since the preceding was written, the earldoms of Mar and Kelly have been disjoined, in consequence of the Earl of Mar and Kelly having died without issue, 1866, when the earldom of Mar passed to heirs-general, and the earldom of Kelly to heirs-male.]

VISIT TO MISS PORTER.

(July 4.) " Accompanied Mrs. Hall to a house in Kensington Square, to be introduced to Miss Porter. Tall, thin old lady, reclining on a sofa. Weakly health. Above seventy. Kindly Scottish manners. We talked of her young days spent in Surgeon's Square, Edinburgh. Her mother occupied part of the long house on the south side of the square, the west half ; Lady Henderson the other. Knew the Kerrs of Chatto as neighbors. Miss Porter, when a little girl, saw one day a thin, elderly gentleman, in a light-colored coat with a plaid, in the square. Went up to him, and said he was like her grandpapa, and for that reason asked him to come in. He followed her into the house, where she introduced him to her mother, as being so like grandpapa. He fell into conversation about the army, led to it by seeing the sword of Miss Porter's father over the fireplace. He said he had also been a soldier ; having fallen in love with his mother's waiting-maid, he had taken to that life in consequence of a quarrel with his friends. He had been at the battle of Culloden, and mention of this seemed greatly to affect him. By-and-by he went away. It should be mentioned that Miss Porter, on taking his hand at first, had observed it to be small, thin, and blue-veined like a lady's. A few days after, a young medical student, visiting Mrs. Porter's, mentioned the curious circumstance that an old gentleman had been run over by a wagon in the streets, had been carried to the infirmary, and was there found to be a female. It was afterwards learned that this singular person was the sister of a clergyman, a person of good connections, who had a slight craze, and believed himself to be Jeanie Cameron, of whom an untrue scandal had been reported. The injured female died in the infirmary.

" Miss Porter's brother, Robert, when a mere child, had been taken to drink tea with some of the rest of the family in a house where they met Flora Macdonald. A picture attracted his attention, and he showed a curiosity to see it nearer. Flora put him upon a chair to see it, told him it was the battle of Preston, and gave him some explanations about it. This, he used to acknowledge afterwards, was his first lesson in historical painting.

" Lady Anne Barnard told Miss Porter that she had written 'Auld Robin Gray,' in order to raise a little money for the succor of an old nurse, having no other means. She had heard from her music-master, that so much as five pounds was sometimes got for a successful song, and she thought she would try. It was successful in the object. Lady Anne wrote much poetry besides, which is preserved by one of her relations." [The Miss Porter above referred to was Jane, authoress of "Thaddeus of Warsaw" and the "Scottish Chiefs." She died 1850.]

PLAYFULNESS OF ANIMALS.

(July 22.) "It is well known that lambs hold regular sports apart from their dams, which only look on at a little distance to watch and perhaps enjoy the happiness of their offspring. Monkeys act in the same manner. Mr. Leigh Hunt, with whom I supped this evening, told me that he had observed a young spider sporting about its parent, running up to and away from it in a playful manner. He has likewise watched a kitten amusing itself by running along past its mother, to whom she always gave a little pat on the cheek as she passed. The older cat endured this tranquilly for awhile; but at length, becoming irritated by it, she took an opportunity to hit her offspring a blow on the side of the head, which sent the little creature spinning to the other side of the room, where she looked extremely puzzled at what had happened. An irritated human being would have acted in precisely the same manner."

ADAPTIVENESS.

(July 27.) "There is a quality of human nature which may be called adaptiveness. Some persons readily adapt themselves to any new society into which they may be thrown; others not. When a man rises in the world, it is often found that his wife does not, cannot rise with him. Sometimes this does not proceed solely from want of the intellect and taste requisite for the purpose, but from a kind of willfulness. Not feeling that new acquaintances attribute any peculiar merit to her, or pay her any particular attention, she affects to hold lightly the marks of approbation bestowed upon her husband, and takes a kind of pleasure in not favoring his advance. In some

cases, the mere sense of awkwardness under the new circumstances may operate to the same effect. Women
ought to consider it as a duty to adapt themselves, as far
as they may, to their changed condition. A regard for
the happiness of the husband and family demands it."

IGNORANCE OF NATURAL HISTORY.

" At the meeting of the British Association at Cambridge (June, 1845), Mr. Goadby, who had his beautiful
anatomical preparations of the lower animals exhibited at
the model-room, was greatly struck by the appearance of
ignorance in the gownsmen, as shown in the remarks
which they made and the questions they asked. One
who had a lady on his arm told his fair companion that
these were *models.* Another similarly attended, apparently
wishing to avoid troublesome questions, said to her very
oracularly, ' O, this is all anatomy.' A third collegian
inquired who made those things. ' The glasses, do you
mean ? ' inquired Mr. Goadby. ' No ; the things in the
glasses.' ' The same that made you,' was the reply. Several men, better informed, spoke of the objects comprehensively as insects, though only a portion of them were
of that class in the animal kingdom. None of these men
had ever heard of such a thing as a mollusk or an echino-
derm. Altogether, Mr. G. thinks he never before showed
his preparations to a more ignorant set of visitors than
the gownsmen of Cambridge.

" As an illustration of the benefit that might be derived
from the introduction of natural history into schools, Mr.
Goadby was once lecturing on his preparations at Chel-
tenham, when he had, amongst his other auditors, Lord
M——, of the Irish peerage. Lord M—— is a middle-
aged man, congenitally lame, insomuch that he is dependent on others for locomotion. Possessing an active mind,

and forbidden to take the amusements of other men of his order, he has given his mind a good deal up to study, but not wholly, for the gaming-table had unfortunately asserted a strong claim over him, and he had thus lost the whole of his patrimonial property, reserving only a diminished income from some estates of his wife.   This clever nobleman, whom everybody loved for his amiable dispositions, seemed exceedingly interested in the lecture, and after it was over, he lingered an hour, inspecting and inquiring into the peculiarities of the animals which formed the subject of it.   At last, he burst out : 'If I had been taught such things in my youth, what it would have been for me !' — implying that the having such an amusement for his leisure would have saved him from those wretched pursuits in which he had sought excitement, and which had proved his ruin."

SHYNESS AND MODESTY.

" Shyness is a curious peculiarity of some men, and the explanation of much that is dubious and obscure in their behavior.   It often happens that a man gets the reputation of being haughty or unsocial, when he is only shy. An unconquerable bashfulness oppresses him.   When such a man is drawn into company, participating in the excitement of the hour, and having got over all the difficulties of the first address, he generally comes out ; often we find him talkative and entertaining, so that strangers go away, saying, 'Well, there is one of the pleasantest men I have met with.'   Strange it is to meet the same man next day, and find him make an effort to avoid you. Lord M——, a person of this kind, always walks along the inner side of the pavement, with eyes bent on the ground, as if anxious to escape observing or being observed.   The J. G. (Boyle), who is associated with him on duty every day for one half the year, has actually known Lord M—— to cross to another side of the road on approaching him, and endeavor to escape his notice by pretending to take an interest in something on the other side of the hedge. Men, on the other hand, who get the reputation of being forward, are often merely men of strong animal spirits, these rendering them frank and bold in society, where, from their comparative rank, they are expected to be quiet and respectful.

" In some cases, shyness may arise from modesty, an unwillingness to intrude. Be this as it may, it is well to bear in mind that the world generally takes men at their own apparent estimate of themselves. Hence modest men never do attain the same consideration which bustling, forward men do. It has not time or patience to inquire rigidly, and it is partly imposed upon and carried away by the man who vigorously claims its regards. The world also never has two leading ideas about any man. There is always a remarkable unity in its conceptions of the characters of individuals. If a historical person has been cruel in a single degree, he is set down as cruel and nothing else, although he may have had many good qualities, all but equally conspicuous. If a literary man is industrious in a remarkable degree, the world speaks of him as only industrious, though he may also be very ingenious."

LACTATION.

" Can lactation have any effect in determining the moral character of infants ? A friend of mine has a son who, on account of the death of his mother immediately after his birth, was given out to be nursed by a woman in humble life. This woman was afterwards found to be very worthless. The boy, who is now in his sixteenth year, has already been a source of great distress to his father, in con-

sequence of strong traits of character destitute of probity.
He cannot be corrected by any kind of discipline out of a
propensity to dissimulation. The strange thing about him
is, that no sooner does he commit some gross offense than
he expresses regret for what he has done, promises never
to do the like again, and then all at once commits some
fresh mischief, to be in turn repented of. As a last resource, he was sent to a school at Brussels ; but he ran
away from it in disgraceful circumstances, came to London, and entered the army as a private soldier. This, as
usual, he said he was sorry for, and wished to be bought
off. His father, however, said he would only do so on his
rising, by good conduct, to be a corporal. So he went
with his regiment to India." [There, as was afterwards
learned, he died.] " My friend, the father of this unhappy
youth, imputes his moral imperfections to lactation. He
was, he thinks, vitiated by the milk of his nurse. And he
says he is warranted in this notion by having heard of
other instances of vitiation of character by similar means.
It is worthy of remark that the boy was with his nurse
only during the time of lactation.

" It does not seem unlikely that a child born of virtuous parents, and partaking of their organization, may
partake of a corrupt element from a milk-nurse. The
constitution of the new being in our species is not completed at birth, as it is in some of the lower animals.
The lactation is a portion of the process of reproduction.
That portion being conducted by a distinct parent of inferior moral character, may be the means of introducing a
depravity where, originally, all was morally fair. In other
words, we might say that at birth a child is not thoroughly quit of its mother. Nature designs the connection
to subsist until the period of milk-nursing is past.

" In the ' Coltness Collections,' is a passage expressing

the sentiments of the wife of Sir James Stewart of Coltness, who was Lord Provost of Edinburgh in 1650. She
strictly declined the offer of her husband to have her
children sent out to hired wet-nurses, saying, 'she should
never think her child wholly her own, when another discharged the most part of a mother's duty, and by wrong
nourishment to her tender babe might induce wrong habits or noxious diseases.' She added : 'I have often seen
children take more a strain of their nurse than their
mother.'"

A TRAIT IN PUBLIC AFFAIRS.

"Adverting to the fact that the Civil War broke out in
Scotland, Lord Clarendon remarks that, previously to
that time, no news journal devoted a regular place to
Scottish intelligence. It is almost the same in the present day. If the London newspapers of a twelvemonth
be carefully examined, the small amount of space devoted
to affairs north of Yorkshire, while so much is given to
matters connected with Ireland, will appear very remarkable. The northern moiety of our island makes no history, as history is ordinarily understood. It is a tax-fer-
tile appanage of the British crown which gives no trouble.
This is a circumstance worthy of note, for it seems to say
that it is possible for a country to exist in a state approaching to perfect quiescence, if exempt from external
sources of annoyance. But it is also worthy of notice,
that a country may hardly ask a paragraph a year from
history, as history is usually written, and yet great things
may be doing in it. There is a progress in the materials
by which a people are supported, and in their ideas, feelings, and manners, which goes on silently from year to
year, exciting no particular attention, and yet is more important to it than victories in stricken fields, or struggles

for the change of dynasties. And it is in this real, but unchronicled history that the northern kingdom is great. On the whole, it is a good sign of the Scotch that they attract so little attention in the London newspapers."

From desultory thoughts on a variety of secular subjects in prose and verse, my brother seems to have latterly turned to those literary exercises of a religious nature already specified. It is impossible to say, definitely, on what he was for the last time occupied. I am inclined, however, from appearances, to think that it was the catechism for the young, which, like some other compositions, was left unfinished. As throwing some light on the views he entertained regarding man's destiny, the following passages, at the point where the manuscript breaks off, may appropriately conclude the present chapter. After a series of questions and answers regarding the Divine Government of the world, he comes to some of the duties imposed on human beings.

" *Q.* Have you any special rules to assign for the guidance of men in this world ?

" *A.* Yes ; some rules may be set down which will form a guidance in the common run of circumstances.

" *Q.* How do you describe them ?

" *A.* They may be wholly described as duties, — that is, observances, and doings which we owe to our fellow-creatures.

" *Q.* Have we not also duties towards ourselves ?

" *A.* Some duties are so called ; but a duty is properly something owed, and in owing, another person is necessarily concerned. It can easily be shown, of all duties said to be owing to ourselves, that they are, more comprehensively, duties owing to society.

" *Q.* Will you first describe that class of duties?

" *A.* A man is required to cultivate a sense of dependence on, and responsibility to, GOD, the author and ruler of his being, the arbiter of his final destiny, because it is good for his spiritual nature to do so, and the better he is in this respect it is the better for society. He ought to study to preserve his self-respect, because without that he can bear little value towards his fellow-creatures. He is called on to cultivate the means of preserving his health, because, in sickness and infirmity, he is an encumbrance instead of a benefit to society. It is incumbent on him to practice diligence in his calling, and prudence in his household, because without these qualities in individuals society would be scarcely able to exist.

" *Q.* Do men not sometimes make mistakes as to what seems their duty?

" *A.* Yes; men sometimes entertain feelings of ambition, under a pretext of duty to themselves, with little or no regard to the good of the community. Such feelings, being only selfish, are detestable. On the other hand, to obtain wealth and power by fair means, and employ them generally towards others, is not merely justifiable, but laudable. The unfailing criterion in all such personal matters is, how do they affect our neighbors? If well, then we are doing right ; if ill, then we are doing wrong. Where we only seek to make ourselves as good, wise, useful, as possible, we are certainly fulfilling the ends of God in society, and may claim approval of God and man.

"*Q.* Please now to describe the duties where a more direct reference is made to others.

"*A.* They are partly negative and partly positive. We are called on to abstain from injuring our neighbor, in his property, his health and life, his feelings, his good name, his rights of all kinds, and rather to promote his good in these respects. One most important duty is to practice upon him no deception by word or deed. Another, is to respect his right of forming his own opinions, without which he is marred in the exercise of that final judgment on right and wrong which has been set forth as the Divine voice speaking within him. We must also respect his right of employing his faculties in the way that seemeth to him best, consistently with the good of his fellow-creatures.

"*Q.* Does this view of duties apply also in the affairs of state?

"*A.* Undoubtedly. In political procedure, truth, rectitude, forbearance, and respect for rights are as much required as in ordinary society. And as no man can neglect or violate the simplest laws which bind him to his neighbor, without creating some degree of suffering, which is liable to react against himself, so it is certain that those in authority cannot use it recklessly or oppressively without producing an unhappiness which will turn round to their own annoyance, injury, or destruction. There is, in short, but one rule of duty in the world, and that is summed in 'Love your Neighbor.' . . . . The errors and delusions of mankind are unfortunately endless; and they are to be deplored, not only as occupying much time and thought uselessly, but as obscuring our ideas as to what is of real importance for the fulfillment of the Divine purposes of our being."

These may be considered to be among the last sentiments written by my brother.

CHAPTER XV.

THE year 1870 opened gloomily in that pleasant-looking house at St. Andrews. After a short illness, and very unexpectedly, my brother's second wife died on the 18th January. Now was he again in a sense desolate. Yet, though afflicted with this fresh calamity, and broken down in health, he did not repine. His bereavements only tended the more to bring out his true character. In him were now seen united the piety of the Christian with the philosophy of an ancient sage. " I know," he said, "that my days are numbered. My time cannot be long. I feel the gradual but sure indication of approaching dissolution. But don't let us be dismal about it ; that would be alike futile and sinful." And so he spoke as one reconciled to his appointed destiny. Setting his affairs in order, he looked calmly on the advances of the destroyer. He had done his work, and we may be permitted to think that he had done it nobly.

Pale and feeble, he crept about, took short drives, and received visitors as usual ; for bodily weakness did not in the least affect his spirits. With one of his married daughters, Mrs. Dowie, who had come to visit him, he walked to the Cathedral Burial-ground, and pointed out the spot where he wished to be interred. It was the interior of the old Church of St. Regulus. " There," said he, " I hope to have the honor of finding a resting-place ; I should certainly be in excellent company, for Mr. Lyon, the historian of St. Andrews, told me there is a surprising number of bishops interred here." The desire to be buried in this place of historical note was what might have been looked for. The Church of St. Regulus is one of the most ancient ecclesiastical structures in Scotland. It dates from the twelfth century, and, as seen by its tall, square tower, is built in the Romanesque style. When the cathedral, a more modern and ornamental structure, was laid in ruin by a mob at the Reformation, this adjacent antique church was so far spared, that till this day it remains all, except the roof, in a state of good preservation. Carefully secured as crown property, it cannot be called a part of the general cemetery; and interment within it requires the sanction of the chief commissioner of Her Majesty's Board of Works.

Being recommended change of scene, my brother accompanied Mrs. Dowie to her home at West Kirby, near Birkenhead; and thereafter, in April, went with her, by way of Gloucester, to Torquay, where for a time he took up his abode. Here he felt a slight improvement of health, and was able, not only to attend and fully enjoy an interesting lecture by Mr. Pengelly on the discoveries in Kent's Cavern, but to visit the cave, and make remarks on the objects of natural history that had recently been brought to light. Before returning home, he once more visited Mrs. Priestley in London, and also his surviving sister, Mrs. Wills, at Sherrards, in Hertfordshire, where he greatly enjoyed the beauty of a quiet rural scene. Brightened up a little by these visits among relatives, he returned to Scotland, in the company of his youngest daughter, who describes the fervency of his emotion in crossing the Border and finding himself again in his native country. He got back to St. Andrews in June.

From this time, he did not leave home, where, to keep him company, he was visited, one after the other, by several of his daughters. I went to see him in August, and found him in a frail condition, though able to converse on literary and other topics. His most conspicuous ailment was want of appetite, along with a deadly paleness of countenance. So greatly was his system disorganized, that, on sitting down to table, he could not eat. Nothing that he was solicited to take did him any good, farther than keeping up the spark of life. Still, in a way, he joked and told stories, felt an interest in the stirring news concerning France, and continued to take delight in music.

Towards the conclusion of autumn, a change for the worse took place, and his mind was visibly weakened. Then came winter in more than ordinary severity, with its deadly effects on the aged and invalid. Shortly after the beginning of 1871, he could no longer sit up, and for his accommodation, his study, adjoining the library, had been for some time fitted up as a bedroom. Here I found him in bed on the 27th January. He said he preferred to be in this apartment, for it was on a level with the sitting-rooms, whence he could hear something of the lively conversation of his daughters, and where they could conveniently see him. A piano was placed in the library for his solacement.

Constantly attended by Dr. Oswald Bell, and by great care in nursing, he got through the winter. His married daughters now left him, not anticipating any immediate change. Day by day, however, he lost strength, and Mrs. Dowie was recalled. On her appearance, he said he was glad that she had come back to see the last of him. On Sunday, 12th March, he was able to listen to, and heartily appreciate his favorite prayers and psalms in the Morning

20

Service, ejaculating from time to time : " How true, how beautiful."

In a note to me, Mrs. Dowie gives a simple and touching account of the closing scene : —

" On Wednesday, the 15th, he described himself as " quite wordless," and just pressing our hands, returned our embraces with fervor. He begged for some music, and was much gratified on my playing to him " Macpherson's Farewell," an air he greatly admired, and which in former years he used to play himself on the piano, with my accompaniment. Next day, he seemed very torpid, and scarcely spoke to us, more than answering questions. Early in the following morning, life was fleeting away. His last faintly uttered words were: ' Quite comfortable — quite happy — nothing more ! ' And so, with us sitting in silent tears beside him, at about five o'clock on Friday morning, the 17th March, he gently breathed his last."

At this mournful juncture, I had gone to London on account of the illness of my youngest brother, David, whose health had for some time been in a critical condition — partly the result of a fall from an omnibus, which left injurious effects on the system ; and partly from distress at the death of his wife. He was now confined to bed, and in so delicate a state that intelligence of the death of Robert brought on a paroxysm, which terminated in his decease on the 21st March. Of the last painful scene I could not be a witness, for I was required at St. Andrews to assist at the funeral of my brother Robert.

This solemnity took place on the 22d ; and to meet the wishes of many who expressed a wish to be present, the arrangements were more of a public character than had at first been intended. Service was performed over the body in the Episcopal chapel, by the incumbent, the Rev. L.

Tuttiett; after which the procession of friends and relatives proceeded to the Church of St. Regulus, in the Cathedral Burying-ground, for interment in which permission had been obligingly granted. On approaching the cemetery, the funeral procession was met by the provost and magistrates of St. Andrews, also by members of the Senatus Academicus, with their official insignia. Surrounded by a large and sympathizing crowd, and with the last offices of the Church, the body of Robert Chambers was lowered into the grave, where it reposes amidst the dust of ecclesiastics whose names are now only known by the records of history.[1]

In his sermon on Sunday, 26th, the Rev. Mr. Tuttiett made some remarks on the deceased. A few passages may be quoted : —

" A little more than a year ago, when first I came to minister in this church, there sat before me one to whom I could not but turn with especial interest at that time. He was, I knew, a man dear to many of his fellow-worshippers, dear to the place in which he lived, dear to his country, and to many far away. He was a man of high endowments, great and varied knowledge, deep philosophy, sound judgment, and refined taste. He was also, what is far better than all this, a man of upright and unostentatiously religious life ; noble and kind in his nature, gentle and modest in his manner, genial and warm in his sympathies, faithful in his friendships, and generous in his dealings. He had come from his recently bereaved home to seek comfort in the common prayers of the Christian Brotherhood with whom he delighted to worship. The text of the sermon he heard on that occasion was taken from St. Paul's address in the synagogue of Antioch : ' David, after he had served his

---

[1] He left the following family : Jane (Mrs. F. Lehmann) ; Robert ; Anne (Mrs. Dowie) ; Eliza (Mrs. Priestley ; Amelia (Mrs. R. Lehmann ; James ; William ; Phœbe (Mrs. Zeigler) ; and Alice. Mary (Mrs. Edwards) predeceased him, leaving three orphan children to his care.

own generation, by the will of God, fell on sleep, and was laid to his fathers.' Those words seem to have struck his mind most forcibly. I shall not forget with what earnestness and solemnity he afterwards commented upon them. They suggested, he thought, 'a sublime ideal of human life, and a comfortable view of decease.' Certainly he seems to have kept such an ideal before him. He 'served his own generation' in the way God marked out for him faithfully and well. Let me only remind you how much he has done, in conjunction with the brother who now survives him, for the dissemination of that pure, wholesome literature which, though not coming under the special denomination of religious, has very greatly served the cause of religion by humanizing and elevating the mind, and thus preparing it for the direct teaching of divine truth. Those who, like myself, have been much interested in the work of popular education in England, must ever honor his name for this service to the generation in which he lived. But my object is not so much to speak his praises as to gather out for myself and for you the instruction of his life and example. He was a great lover of Nature, and a patient, nor by any means an unsuccessful student of her works. And he was ever ready to encourage the investigations of every man whose heart was loyal to truth, even though the investigator might seem, in his better judgment, to be proceeding upon a wrong principle. But certainly, in his coversations with myself, he ever evinced the clearest recognition of a Personal God moving amidst his own creation, and ruling it constantly by his Word. . . . . He seems to have had so great a reverence for the deep things of God, and so humbling a sense of his own inability to grapple with them, that he was ever most unwilling to converse about them. He was, I believe, a sincerely attached member of the Episcopal Church of Scotland. He venerated its old historic associations and traditions. He loved its sound and sober standards of faith and devotion. At the same time he very highly esteemed the ministers of the National Establishment ; he did full justice to the good he knew in other communions ; and he never counted men offenders for difference of opinion. . . . . He seemed to be a man of vigorous, manly intellect, sparing no labor, no self-devotion, in the acquirement of whatever knowledge he thought it good, for himself and for his fellow creatures, to possess ; and at the same time a man of pure, gentle, kind, and unselfish character, whom it was impossible to know and not to love."

Here terminates our Memoir. The principal subject of it had passed away in his sixty-ninth year, a victim, as it appeared to himself and his family, of that species of excessive literary labor which, by overtasking the nervous system, often proves so fatal. Of the esteem generally entertained for him in his private character, I do not propose to dilate. His genial and kindly disposition, to say nothing of his acquirements, gave him many friends. Never had children a more loving father. In public affairs, he was not qualified to take a prominent part. At one time, as has been seen, he edited a newspaper in the old Conservative interest, but his politics were of a mild type ; and latterly he was numbered among the friends of social progress within sound constitutional limits. On few things was he more resolute than in upholding the principles of free trade, the opposition to which, particularly as regards the free importation of corn and other elements of food, he considered to be not only a prodigious economic blunder, but a great national crime. His generosity in extending aid to the needy and deserving was a marked trait in his character. His tastes led him to be elected a Fellow of several learned Societies, and he was a member of the Athenæum Club. Diligent, accurate, and upright, he entertained clear views on all ordinary concerns ; and no one could be more unscrupulous in his denunciation of whatever was narrow, mean, or dishonorable. If, in any of these respects, he sometimes cherished resentments that, founded on misconception and prejudice, had better have been forgotten, it is allowable to think that such fail-

ings might fairly be imputed to an overwrought susceptibility of temperament not common in the ordinary walks
of life.

With regard to my brother's literary character and
works, I shall not, having said so much already, attempt
any elaborate estimate or analysis. His best services
were devoted to his native country, and, with the exception of his illustrious contemporary, Sir Walter Scott, no
other author has done so much to illustrate its social state,
its scenery, romantic historical incidents, and antiquities,
the lives of its eminent men, and the changes in Scottish
society and the condition of the people (especially those
in the capital), during the last two centuries. His first
work, the " Traditions of Edinburgh," evinced this strong
bias and ruling passion of his mind. He was, as has been
stated, assisted by Charles Kirkpatrick Sharpe and Sir
Walter Scott, but the great bulk of the traditions and all
their *setting* were his own. He knew every remarkable
house, its possessors, and their genealogy ; every wynd and
close from the Castle-hill to Holyrood ; and in describing
these, he poured forth a vast amount of curious reading
and information, much of which would have been lost but
for the taste and diligence of so enthusiastic a collector.
Perhaps this work will hereafter be considered the most
unique and valuable of all his labors. His next production, however, has enjoyed a still greater share of popularity.
I allude to the " History of the Rebellion of 1745-46," a
work which was very carefully written ; and the subject
had a wide and deep interest, for the enterprise of Charles
Edward was one of those bold and striking events in which
history assumes the color and fascination of romance. As
latterly extended, by materials gathered from the " Lyon
in Mourning,"[1] the book has taken its place among our

[1] This curious and valuable collection of manuscripts has been be-

standard historical works, as a faithful and animated narrative of one of the most striking and memorable periods
in our national annals.

The other popular histories written between 1827 and
1830 are less original and less valuable than the narrative
of the '45. The "Calendars of State Papers" were not
then published, nor had antiquarian clubs and family re-
positories enriched our stores of historical knowledge with
those minute and graphic details which add life, and
spirit, and individuality to the pages of Macaulay and
Froude. My brother's works are of the nature of memoirs. His object was to present a view or portraiture
of the external circumstances of the period embraced —
a series of military narratives — rather than to attempt
" histories of the legitimate description, which should appeal only to the moral faculties of the select few." He
anticipated Macaulay in desiring to make history interesting to the many, embracing details of the manners, customs, social habits, and daily life of the nation ; and with
all young readers, and generally with the middle and
lower ranks of the Scottish people, he was eminently successful. Of a kindred character with these works was the
" Popular Rhymes of Scotland," an amusing embodiment
of folk-lore and mementoes of childhood descending from
one generation to another in various countries of Europe.

By the establishment of " Chambers's Journal," my
brother was happily led into a new walk of literature.
He came forward as a weekly essayist. During fifteen
years, as he has himself related, he labored in this field,
" alternately gay, grave, sentimental, and philosophical,"
until not much fewer than four hundred separate papers
proceeded from his pen. In these were best seen his im-

queathed to the Faculty of Advocates, Edinburgh, in grateful acknowledgment of the many benefits derived from their extensive library.

aginative faculties. His familiar and humorous sketches
of Scottish life and character are allowed to be true to
nature ; they were certainly drawn from the life, and may
be compared to the descriptions of Henry Mackenzie in
the " Mirror " and " Lounger " as to discrimination and
fidelity of portraiture ; but those of the earliest essayist
are confined to the higher ranks of Scottish society.
Many of my brother's essays are also on literary and antiquarian topics, and will be found not only honorable to
his diligence as a self-directed and self-upheld student, but
replete with correct, humane, and manly feeling. Essays
or short disquisitions on scientific subjects were occasionally inserted in the " Journal," for, as has been shown, my
brother, latterly, devoted much time and study to geology
and other departments of physical science ; the result of
which was the work on " Ancient Sea-margins," and a
variety of papers communicated to the Royal Society of
Edinburgh.

The patient investigation, long journeys, and careful accumulation of facts employed in establishing his geological
theories, indicate the true scientific spirit and enthusiasm,
and there can be little doubt that, had the circumstances
of his early life been more favorable, he would have taken
a high place among the men of science who have illustrated the nineteenth century. Considering that his education, as he frankly avows, never cost his parents so much
as ten pounds, the wonder is that he did so much.

As regards his " Cyclopædia of English Literature," his
" Life and Writings of Burns," his " Domestic Annals of
Scotland," his " Book of Days," and the lesser works he
produced, sufficient has perhaps been said in the course of
this Memoir. On none of his later works did he look back
with so much heartfelt pleasure and satisfaction, and none
deserves greater praise, for its remarkable fidelity, than that

concerning Robert Burns. Here, for the first time, the life of the poet, with all its lights and shades, was correctly delineated. The story of Highland Mary, and the dark days of Dumfries, were placed truly before the world, and allusions in the poems and letters were fully explained. Of all future editions of the Scottish poet, this explanatory and chronological one must form the basis.

Altogether, as nearly as can be reckoned, my brother produced upwards of seventy volumes, exclusively of detached papers which it would be impossible to enumerate. His whole writings had for their aim the good of society, the advancement in some shape or other of the true and beautiful. It will hardly be thought that I exceed the proper bounds of panegyric in stating, that in the long list of literary compositions of ROBERT CHAMBERS, we see the zealous and successful student, the sagacious and benevolent citizen, and the devoted lover of his country.

THE END.

THE

MEMOIR ᴸᵒ ROBERT CHAMBERS,

WITH AUTOBIOGRAPHIC

REMINISCENCES OF WILLIAM CHAMBERS.

One vol. 12mo. $1.50.

This work is destined to become a classic in biographical literature. The London *Athenæum* says: " . . . . Nothing that we know in literature is more instructive than the description of how these brothers managed to build up, step by step, from small beginnings, one of the largest printing and publishing establishments in Scotland. . . . It is replete with happy characterization and anecdote. . . . Mr. Chambers has told the tale of his own and his brother's heart-rending beginnings with such concentrated clearness that here may be learned lessons of self-denial, patience, unflagging perseverance, independence and cheerfulness (the greatest sustainer of 'all), which comprise a whole education, not for the humblest in station, but for the least intellectually gifted."

THE HEART OF ARABIA.

A NEW VOLUME IN THE

ILLUSTRATED LIBRARY OF TRAVEL AND ADVENTURE.

Compiled and arranged by BAYARD TAYLOR.

One vol. 12mo. With 14 full-page illustrations. $1.50.

Mr. Taylor here gathers together all that travellers, ancient and modern, have learned regarding this little-known region. The explorations of Palgrave, Niebuhr, and Burton take up the larger part of the volume, and comprise as thrilling incidents of adventure and daring as the literature of travel anywhere furnishes.

THE

HISTORY OF GREECE.–VOL. III.

By Dr. E. CURTIUS. Completing the Peloponnesian War. With a complete index to the three volumes. Revised, after the latest German edition, by W. A. PACKARD, Professor of Latin in Princeton College. One vol. crown 8vo. Cloth. Per vol., $2.50.

This volume of Dr. Curtius' great work completes the Peloponnesian War, one of the most important periods of the history of Greece. The latest additions and revisions by the author have been incorporated in the text by Prof. Packard, making this edition superior to the English.

ELECTRICITY.

A NEW VOLUME IN THE SECOND SERIES OF THE

ILLUSTRATED LIBRARY OF WONDERS.

By J. BAILE. Revised, with additions, by Dr. J. W. ARMSTRONG, President of the Normal School, Fredonia, N. Y.

One vol. 12mo. 65 illustrations. $1.50.

The Wonders of Electricity and the great result achieved through its agency, are here summed up in a compact form. Dr. Armstrong's version of the work, and the additions which he had made, bring it down to the latest dates, and make the volume a most valuable manual

☞ *These works sent post-paid, upon receipt of the price, by*

SCRIBNER, ARMSTRONG & CO.,

Successors to CHARLES SCRIBNER & Co.,

654 Broadway, New York.

POPULAR AND STANDARD BOOKS

SCRIBNER, ARMSTRONG & CO.

(SUCCESSORS TO CHARLES SCRIBNER & CO.)

No. 654 Broadway, New York,

IN 1871.

BIBLE COMMENTARY (THE). Vol. I. The Pentateuch.
1 Vol. Royal 8vo, with occasional Illustrations,.................................$5.00
CURTIUS, Prof. Dr. ERNST. The History of Greece. Vols I. & II.
Cr. 8vo, per vol..$2.50
DE VERE, Prof. M. SCHELE. Americanisms. 1 vol., cr. 8vo, $3.00
ERCKMANN—CHATRIAN NOVELS (THE). Each 1 vol., 16mo.
With Illustrations..cloth 90c.—paper 50c.
——————— The Blockade of Phalsburg.
——————— The Invasion of France in 1844.
FROUDE, J. A. History of England. *Popular Edition*. In twelve vols.
12mo. The Set...$15.00
——————— Short Studies on Great Subjects. Second Series.
1 vol. cr. 8vo..$2.50
HARLAND (MARION). Common Sense in the Household.
1 vol., 12mo..$1.75
HARRIS (Mrs. S. S.) Richard Vandermarck. 1 vol., 12mo., $1.50
HODGE, Dr. CHARLES. Systematic Theology. Vols. I. and II. 8vo.
per vol...$4.50
ILLUSTRATED LIBRARY OF WONDERS (THE). First Series.
In 20 vols. Each 1 vol. 16mo., per vol. $1.50 With numerous Illustrations.
The Set in a neat case for,..$30.00
——————— Second Series. Each 1 vol, 12mo., with numerous Illustra-
tions, per vol...$1.50
——————— ——————— Mountain Adventures.
——————— ——————— The Wonders of Water.
——————— ——————— The Wonders of Vegetation.
ILLUSTRATED LIBRARY OF TRAVEL, EXPLORATION,
AND ADVENTURE (THE). Edited by Bayard Taylor. Each 1 vol.,
12mo. With numerous Illustrations. Per vol...............................$1.50
——————— Japan (with a Map).
——————— Wild Men and Wild Beasts.
JOWETT, Prof. B. The Dialogues of Plato. In four vols., cr. 8vo., $12.00
LANGE'S COMMENTARY. Edited by Dr. P. Schaff. Each 1 vol. 8vo., $5.00
——————— Jeremiah.
——————— John.
——————— Joshua, Judges, and Ruth.
MACDONALD (GEORGE). Wilfrid Cumbermede. 1 vol..
12mo. With 14 full page Illustrations....................................$1.75
MULLER, Prof. MAX. Chips from a German Workshop.
Vol. III. 1 vol., cr. 8vo...$2.50
——————— Lectures on the Science of Reli-
gion. 1 vol.cr. 8vo..$2.00
PORTER, Pres. NOAH. Elements of Intellectual Philosophy.
1 vol. cr. 8vo...$3.00
——————— Books and Reading. *New Edition*. 1 vol.
cr. 8vo...$2.00
TRENCH, R. C. English Past and Present. *Revised Edition*.
1 vol. 12mo..$1.25
UEBERWEG, (Prof.) History of Philosophy. Vol. I, 8vo.......$3.50
WOOD (Rev. J. G.) Insects at Home. Illustrated. 1 vol. 8vo......$5.00

These books sent post-paid by the publishers on receipt of the price.

POPULAR AND STANDARD BOOKS

PUBLISHED BY

CHARLES SCRIBNER & CO.

No. 654 Broadway, New York,

IN 1870 AND '71.

BOWEN, Prof. FRANCIS, Am. Political Economy. One vol. cr. 8vo....$2.50.

BROWNING, Mrs. E. B. Lady Geraldine's Courtship. Illustrated.....$5.00.

CONYBEARE & HOWSON. St. Paul. *Complete Edition.* One vol. 8vo...$3.00.

DERBY'S HOMER. *New Edition.* Two vols. in one. Crown 8vo, reduced to......$2.50.

FISHER, Rev. GEO. P. Supernatural Origin of Christianity. *New Edition.* One vol. 8vo......$3.00.

FORSYTH, W. Life of M. Tullius Cicero. *New Edition.* Two vols. in one. Crown 8vo. Price reduced to......$2.50.

FROUDE, J. A. History of England. *Library Edition.* In twelve vols. crown 8vo. The set......$36.00

———————— *Popular Edition.* In twelve vols. 12mo. The set.....$15.00.

———————— Short Studies on Great Subjects. *First Series.* A New Edition. One vol. 12mo. Price reduced to......$1.50.

HARLAND, MARION. Common Sense in the Household. One vol. 12mo......$1.75.

HOPKINS, Pres. MARK. The Law of Love and Love as a Law. *New Edition.* One vol. 12mo......$1.75.

HUNT, E. M. Bible Notes for Daily Readers. Two vols. royal 8vo......$7.00.

JERNINGHAM'S (JOHN) JOURNAL. One vol. 16mo......75c.

JERNINGHAM'S (Mrs.) JOURNAL. " " ......"

MOMMSEN, Dr. THEODOR. The History of Rome. In four vols. crown 8vo. The set, $8.00 ; per vol......$2.00.

MULLER, MAX. Chips from a German Workshop. Three vols. cr 8vo. $7.50.

PORTER, Pres. N. The Human Intellect. One vol. 8vo......$5.00.

———————— Books and Reading. One vol. crown 8vo......$2.00.

POUCHET, F. A. The Universe. *A New Edition, with Important Additions and Illustrations.* One vol. royal 8vo......$12.00.

SACRIFICE OF PRAISE (THE.) *New and. Cheaper Edition.* One vol. 12mo......$1.25.

SHEDD'S (Dr. W. G. T.) History of Christian Doctrine. *New Edition.* Two vols. 8vo......$5.00.

———————— Homiletics. *New Edition.* One vol. 8vo......$2.50.

SONGS OF LIFE. Illustrated. One vol. small 4to. ......$5.00.

SONGS OF HOME. Illustrated. One vol. small 4to......$5.00

STANLEY'S JEWISH CHURCH. *New Edition.* Two vols. crown 8vo....$5.00.

———————— Eastern Church. *New Edition.* One vol. crown 8vo......$2.50.

———————— Sinai and Palestine. *New Edition.* One vol. crown 8vo......$2.50.

THOMPSON, J. P. The Theology of Christ. One vol. crown 8vo......$2.00.

TRENCH, R. C. English Past and Present. *New Edition.* One vol. 12mo......$1.25.

WOOD, Rev. J. G. Bible Animals. One vol. 8vo. Illustrated......$5.00.

WOOLSEY, T. D., D.D. Religion of the Present and Future. 1 vol. cr. 8vo. $2.00.

These books sent post-paid by the publishers on receipt of the price.

SYSTEMATIC THEOLOGY.

By CHARLES HODGE, D.D., of Princeton Theological Seminary.

To be completed in three volumes 8vo. Tinted paper. Price per vol., in cloth, $4.50.

In these volumes are comprised the results of the life-long labors and investigations of one of the ablest theologians of the age. The work covers the ground usually occupied by treatises on Systematic Theology, and adopts the commonly received divisions of the subject: Theology (Vol. I.), Anthropology (Vol. II.), Soteriology and Eschatology (Vol. III.).

The various topics ranged under these different divisions are discussed with that close and keen analytical and logical power, combined with that simplicity, lucidity, and strength of style, which have already given Dr. Hodge a world-wide reputation as a controversialist and writer, and as an investigator of the great theological problems of the day.

* *Volumes I. and II. are now ready. Volume III. will be published early in* 1872.

THE SPEAKER'S COMMENTARY.

THE FIRST VOLUME OF

THE BIBLE COMMENTARY.

(Popularly known in England as "The Speaker's Commentary.")

THE PENTATEUCH:

Comprising Genesis, Exodus, Leviticus, Numbers, Deuteronomy.

Edited by Rev. HAROLD E. BROWNE, Author of "*Exposition of the Thirty-nine Articles;*" Rev. F. C. COOK, M.A., Canon of Exeter and General Editor of the "Bible Commentary;" Rev. SAM'L CLARK, M.A., and Rev. T. E. ESPIN, B.D., Warden of Queen's College, Birmingham.

1 vol. royal 8vo, 1,000 pages, with occasional illustrations, handsomely bound in extra brown cloth, with black and gilt lines. Per vol., $5.00.

This great work, which has been prepared by a combination of all the leading divines of the Church of England, had its origin in the widely-felt want of a plain explanatory Commentary on the Holy Scriptures, which should be at once more comprehensive and compact than any previously published. The cordial and enthusiastic reception which has been extended to the work, and the praise bestowed upon the first volume in England—even by those whose connections would lead them to the most severe and indeed hostile criticism— demonstrate the great success which the enterprise has already achieved. From the fulness, fairness, thoroughness, and candor with which all difficult questions are discussed, the Bible Commentary is sure to be satisfactory to the scholar; while the plain, direct, and devout manner in which the meaning of the Sacred Text is explained, thoroughly adapt it for the widest popular use, whether in the closet, in the family, or in the Sunday-school.

N.B.—*A full prospectus of the Bible Commentary sent to any address on application. Each volume of the Bible Commentary will be complete in itself, and may be purchased separately.*

These works sent, post-paid, on receipt of the price, by

CHARLES SCRIBNER & CO., 654 Broadway, N. Y.